Jessie

Rule number one when it comes to relationships: don't. Especially if I work for him.

For the last six years I've had one goal in mind—become a music therapist. I'm almost there.

But as a favor to a friend, I show up to an interview for a nanny position. And fall in love with a four-year-old boy whose words are anything but verbal. The only problem? His dad is Chris Rivera, aka Topher Rivers, the bassist for Just One Yesterday. And it only took one glance to fall for his charm.

Getting involved with a musician? Been there, done that, and shredded the souvenir concert t-shirt.

So why can't I stay away?

Chris

I've made a career out of breaking the rules. Otherwise my band would have never made it out of the garage.

Jessie Bryant is all about rules. As my four-year-old son's nanny, she makes me want to create a few of my own. Rule number one: ignore my attraction to the woman thirteen years my junior. Especially when she works for me. When that proves impossible,

I want to ball her rules up and throw them in the trash. Because every day it gets harder not to imagine what she tastes like... what she feels like... what she would look like in my bed.

I've never been good at following the rules. And her rules are ones I'm going to enjoy breaking.

FALLING FOR THE BEAT

HEART BEATS BOOK 5

BREANNA LYNN

ISBN: 978-1-955359-12-2 (ebook)

ISBN: 978-1-955359-13-9 (paperback)

Cover Design by: Y'all That Graphic

Edited by: Jessica Snyder Edits, Kimberly Hunt with Jessica Snyder Edits, and VB Proofreads

Printed in United States of America

https://breannalynnauthor.com

To Stevie
Thanks for cheerleading, for brainstorming, for funny cat pictures, for being my friend, and for so much more!

MUSIC FROM FALLING FOR THE BEAT

〜

Crimson Skis · Black Veil Brides
When Legends Rise · Godsmack
Real One · Smash Into Pieces
Manipulated · Beth Crowley
Monsters · Shinedown
How to Fly · Fireflight
Free Woman · MARINA
willow · Taylor Swift
Sex on Fire · Kings of Leon
Unbreakable · Kingdom Collapse
Trust Issues · Gina Venier
Hand Me Down · Citizen Soldier
Monsters (feat. Demi Lovato and blackbear) · All Time Low
Surface Pressure · No Resolve
Pull Me From the Edge · Like A Storm
Break Into My Heart · Daughtry
If You Ever Change Your Mind · Calum Scott
Are you · A R I Z O N A
moved (Acoustic) · LACES
Shipwreck · Letdown.
I'm Not - Acoustic · Zero 9:36
Lovers · Anna of the North
Heartfirst · Kelsea Ballerini
A Thousand Years · The Piano Guys
A Thousand Years (feat. Steve Kazee) - Pt 2 · Christina Perri
All Comes Crashing · Metric
Hold On To Me · Lauren Daigle

Lovers Death · Ursine Vulpine, Annaca
Remind Me to Forget · Kygo, Miguel
Bleeding Love · Leona Lewis
Try · P!nk
Cut You Off · Smash Into Pieces
Ghost · Justin Bieber
Fingers Crossed · Lauren Spencer Smith
Easy On Me · No Resolve
Bad Liar - Stripped · Imagine Dragons
Dearly Beloved · Daughtry
A New Horizon · Smash Into Pieces
Bonfire Heart · James Blunt
Only You · Saint Raymond
The Phoenix · Like A Storm
Refuse · Skillet
Take My Breath Away · Boyce Avenue, Megan Davies, Jaclyn Davies

You'll find the link for the playlist in the back of the book.

CHAPTER 1

CHRIS

"God dammit."

The phone ringing for the second time in as many minutes distracts me from the chord progression I'm working through. I need to finish this song since it's been partially done for months. But finishing will have to wait—again. With a sigh, I drop the pick and snag my phone from the table.

"Hello?"

"Chris?" Frank Nguyen has been my attorney since I was old enough to need one. And since he was my parents' attorney first, he's been a fixture in my life for a lot longer than that.

"Frank. How's it going?" I set the guitar aside and lean back against the couch.

"I want to say fine, but I just got the strangest phone call. From an attorney named Nathaniel Ramirez."

Fuck.

I should have known. I massage the bridge of my nose where a headache is now taking root.

"Which band member is being sued for paternity now?"

On the surface, it sounds like a strange question. But with the number of times Milo, Finn, or Noah have been accused of fathering a child, it's one I ask far more than I ever thought I would.

For over twenty years, we had more than our fair share of women claiming that one of us had fathered her child. Miraculously, none of the accusations had ever been legitimate. But our luck wouldn't hold out forever. And as the leader of our band, it's my job to handle this. *They* are my responsibility.

Thank fuck Evan is too quiet to cause this kind of shit. I'd bet money Frank is calling me about Milo, since our drummer has chased more pussy than the rest of us combined.

"Er, it's not that. Not really."

"Not really?" Surging off the couch, I walk the length of my music room without finding the comfort it usually brings me.

"Does the name Melanie Sanders mean anything to you?"

I freeze mid-stride and take a breath. Melanie and I met almost seven years ago at a party here in LA. Her friend had somehow scored invitations. The friend had been swooped up by Finn, and I swooped in on Mel, who leaned against a wall seeming more than a little out of place. She had looked at me with those big hazel eyes like I was some kind of savior.

More like Lucifer.

I wasn't her Mr. Right. But our on-again, off-again fling had lasted two years before she broke it off completely when she wanted the monogamy I couldn't give her. But I wasn't overly heartbroken. With the constant tours, I was rarely in LA, and even when I was, we were in the studio recording the next album. I never expected her to wait around for me.

No way was Frank calling me about a paternity issue there. Melanie had my number. And the last time I slept with her had been almost six years ago.

"Melanie? What about her?"

"She's dead."

What the fuck?

I pull the phone away from my ear, staring at it like it will somehow tell me the truth.

"She was thirty-two." As if her age is some sort of protection.

"Car accident." He clears his throat in the awkward silence. "Nathaniel Ramirez is the probate attorney in charge of Melanie's estate."

I'm still struggling to process that Mel is dead. Probate? Estate?

"What? Why did he reach out to you?"

"Chris, Melanie named you in her will as the father of her four-year-old son, Gage Christopher Rivera. She identified you as his guardian in the event that something should happen to her."

I'm overwhelmed by dizziness and reach blindly for a wall, leaning against it as I take several breaths. That first night, Melanie knew me as Topher Rivers, my stage name. But it didn't take long before I tired of her calling out another man's name in bed. So I confided in her and gave her my real name—Christopher Antonio Rivera.

"Son?" I gasp.

I have a son. A four-year-old. Gage. One corner of my mouth quirks at the unique name that reminds me of Mel. She may have seemed like a conservative, librarian type, but she had a wild streak she showed to very few people.

"I already requested that Nathaniel initiate a paternity test—"

"He's mine." I don't need a fucking test.

Mel wouldn't name me as the father otherwise.

"Chris." The lecture is obvious in Frank's tone.

"Frank. I don't doubt he's mine."

"I know you want to believe that. But it would be better to confirm it."

"I don't need a fucking test." My molars click together. Why isn't he listening to me?

"Think about it from the child's—"

3

"Gage."

Frank sighs. "Gage's perspective. He's already lost his mother. We need to be sure before we upend his life again."

Fuck. I didn't think about that.

"Where is he now?"

I don't care what Frank thinks. If Gage is in foster care, I won't hesitate to go pick him up. No child deserves to lose his mother and his home all in one day.

"Melanie's parents have temporary custody."

I never met her parents. But the stories she told me assure me that my son is okay with them for the time being.

"Find somewhere quick, Frank. I want this test over and done with and the results confirmed."

As soon as we hang up, I send a text to the guys.

> Congratulations, you're all uncles.

🎸 🎸 🎸

Four weeks. A month since Frank called to tell me I have a son. But finally, the results are in, and Gage's grandparents can't postpone anymore. They have—twice. But today is the day.

It's been a long four weeks. Once I told Mamá and Papá that they were grandparents—again—I had to beg them to not immediately rush to the Sanderses and meet their new grandson. Fuck, I still hadn't met him.

"This is bullshit," I mutter quietly, but loud enough for Evan to hear me.

"Don't worry. I'll make everyone clear out once they get here."

He and the rest of the guys showed up this morning, despite knowing that the Sanderses are dropping Gage off any minute now.

"What?"

"The guys. I'll get everyone to clear out when they get here."

Evan glances up at me from the pool lounger he's kicked back on while Milo and Finn take turns cannonballing into my pool. Noah is on another chair, dark glasses concealing most of his face and a silver flask glinting in the sun where it presses against his lips.

"I know. I figured that. I just can't believe it's taken a fucking month."

I gesture to Noah, and Evan fixes his attention on our keyboardist. His shoulders tighten despite the heavy sigh he exhales.

"Shit. I'll take him home with me. Make sure he stays out of trouble."

"We need to record the new album. Cornerstone is already breathing fire since it's taken this long. We can't afford for him to go to rehab."

Again.

I don't say it, but I don't need to.

In the last three years, Noah's had three separate stints in rehab. It's been hell on our schedule, and we've barely kept our touring commitments, forget recording anything new.

My phone chimes with a notification from the guard at the gate.

"They're on their way." My heart gallops in my chest and my palms grow clammy. I'm amazed the phone doesn't slide out of my grip.

"All right, boys, that's the signal. Time to go. Milo, Finn, dry off. No way am I letting you in my car soaking wet."

They grumble but grab towels from the outdoor chest before following a surly Noah and a silent Evan to the front door. I bring up the rear, rolling my eyes at the trail of water they leave behind. The guys are barely in Evan's car when another one pulls up behind them.

I was expecting two adults. Instead, three meet me at the front door while Gage hides behind the woman.

"Mr. Rivera?" The man dressed in a suit steps forward with his hand extended. "I'm the Sanderses' attorney, Stephen Chen."

"Attorney?" I shake his hand distractedly. "Do I need to call Frank?"

"Mr. Nguyen? That won't be necessary. I'm here at the request of my clients to ensure the transfer goes smoothly."

I bite back the attitude I want to sling at his smarmy little speech. My son is watching.

"I don't anticipate any issues."

"It shouldn't have to happen at all." If looks could kill, the one Mrs. Sanders shoots my direction would have me six feet under.

"Excuse me?" I turn my attention from the attorney to her.

"He doesn't even know you. Who do you think you are to take our last piece of Melanie away from us?"

"Is that what you think I'm doing?" Her words are sucker punches to my gut. I didn't choose for Melanie to list me as guardian. But if she hadn't, I would have never known about Gage.

"He loves us. He's used to us." Mr. Sanders takes up where his wife left off.

"Mr. Sanders. Mrs. Sanders. I'm terribly sorry for your loss. But I can't be sorry about meeting my son. I don't want to take him from you. I *want* you to have a relationship with him."

Mr. Sanders opens his mouth to reply, but the attorney cuts him off.

"Tom, Bethany." He shakes his head, and I want to know what the fuck he's thinking.

The two other adults say nothing else. I'm missing something here. What the fuck does it take for their attorney to only say their names to shut them up?

"Gage," the lawyer addresses my son and snaps his fingers. "Come here."

My hands clench into fists at my side.

Stay the fuck away from my son.

6

The little boy steps forward, moving out from behind his grandmother's legs. Light brown hair falls across his forehead, and I can't help but trace the similar fall of my hair. Wide hazel eyes remind me of Mel, and his cheeks still show the baby he used to be—the apples dusted pink while small lips purse together as he studies me.

He lets go of his grandma's hand. She gasps and keeps her arm extended awkwardly in the air, like she's ready to snatch him away from me, even though she has no reason—and no right—to do so.

"Does he know who I am?" He approaches me slowly, and I hold my breath.

"We told him we were bringing him to meet his father." The attorney's voice grates against my ears. I can't wait for him to leave.

Gage now stands directly in front of me, and I lower to my haunches and smile at him.

"Hi, buddy."

"Hi."

"Do you know who I am?"

His little head bobs once. "Daddy."

Tears burn behind my eyes, and I blink several times to clear the sensation.

Fuck.

I'm a goner.

I've fallen in love with a kid I just met. No, not simply any kid. My son.

I don't regret my life as a rock star, but for the first time in thirty-six years, I can see the appeal of being a family man.

"That's right, Gage. I'm your daddy."

At that, he steps forward, and his little arms wrap around my neck. I inhale his strawberry and little boy scent. Mrs. Sanders sniffles, and the attorney clears his throat.

"Tom, Gage's bags?"

Mrs. Sanders follows her husband to the car, but she gets in while he and the attorney grab two suitcases and two boxes—one labeled "Books" and one labeled "Toys"—and set them by the porch.

"That's everything."

Mr. Sanders looks at me and then at Gage before waving half-heartedly and joining his wife in the car. The attorney is the last to get in, and I don't relax until his door closes behind him.

"Daddy?"

My attention shifts from the departing car to the little boy standing next to me.

"Yeah, bud?"

"I have to go potty."

"Okay. Let's go potty."

I got this.

I don't got this.

By the end of the first month, even with the help of Lois, my part-time housekeeper, who increased her hours to help, I'm still floundering. I'm practically catatonic from lack of sleep. Every night this week, Gage has either woken up with nightmares, had an accident, or climbed into bed with me for no reason. I had no idea such a small human could take up so much room on a king-size bed, but inevitably, his little foot digs into my kidney whenever he falls asleep.

"Why don't you find a nanny?" Evan asks. He showed up after Gage was asleep so we could work on song selections for the next album.

"I asked my mom to help me find one. Anytime I try to do it, I'm yanked back into band shit."

Band shit. Noah high as fuck last weekend. Milo and Finn whoring and partying it up all over town.

"Are you still meeting with Jax and Nick?"

The co-owners of Arrhythmic Records reached out to me about a song I wrote that Just One Yesterday wouldn't record—

not our sound. But it's perfect for one of their artists, Dylan Graves, and they want me to work with him on the song.

"Yeah. I managed to eke out some time tomorrow afternoon." Trying to add that to my already chaotic schedule has proved almost impossible. It's the weekend, but neither of them balked when I suggested it.

"What about Gage?"

"Mamá." One word, but it's explanation enough.

"He hasn't said anything in days?"

Over the last month, Gage has become less and less talkative. He's gone from a vibrant little boy to a quiet shell of himself. He hasn't uttered a single word since breakfast two days ago when he asked for waffles like he used to have with Mommy. Only I had no idea what kind of waffles she made for him. Apparently, they were Eggos, like the ones in my freezer. But I didn't know.

I didn't understand.

I'm failing. Otherwise, my son would still be speaking.

"No." Sighing, I flop down on the couch next to Evan and run my hands through my hair.

"What's your mom say?"

"She said I need to take him to a therapist. That it's probably his way of grieving."

"You gonna do it?"

Having known Evan since junior high, I ignore his usual snarky tone.

"I need to find someone first."

"Sounds like a lot of work."

"Yeah." And all I want to do is fucking sleep.

But there's no rest for the weary. Or the wicked. And I definitely fall into both categories.

CHAPTER 2

JESSIE

"*J*essie!" Nick and Meredith's daughter, Everly, spots me first, running full tilt until her little arms wrap around my legs.

"Hey, pretty girl." I smile and run a hand through the riot of curls that bounce in every direction.

My name is echoed by Michaela and West's twins. Dylan and Claire's daughter follows the trio silently until they're all close enough to give me hugs.

I'm the last one here, given all the vehicles in the driveway when I pulled up.

My niece, Ken—Jax and Charlie's daughter—runs by me to circle the swing set with Michaela and West's oldest. And that leaves Teddy, the youngest Bryant child, to play with Mia and Garrett's son, as the two drive construction toys through the sandbox.

All the kids are accounted for, but I don't see my brother, Nick, or Dylan.

Since my brother set this whole thing up, he should at least be here. Garrett and West are having a conversation, and all the

BREANNA LYNN

women—except Meredith—are gathered around Claire, who holds baby Oliver.

It's chaos. But my nerves need the distraction. I have an appointment this afternoon with my professor to discuss my thesis.

"Jessie." My sister-in-law, Charlie, looks up from admiring the baby and wraps me in a hug.

"Hey, everyone." I'm enveloped in hug after hug as I join the other adults.

"I wonder if I can convince West that the odds of having twins again aren't as high as the doctors told him." Michaela sighs.

Obviously, baby fever grabbed hold of her as it usually does after one of the couples here has a new baby.

"You want to hold him, Jessie?" Claire asks and lifts Olly toward me.

"I'm sure I'm last on that list by now."

I love this quirky group of people, chaotic kids and all. I've babysat for all of them more times than I can count. I call them all my nieces and nephews, not just Jax and Charlie's kids. They've been there for me since I moved to LA six years ago to start my undergrad.

"We've held him already." Michaela looks like she's ready for another round.

All the other women nod, and I step closer and take him from Claire. Bright blue eyes lock on mine, and I can't help but smile as I adjust his warm weight in my arms.

"Hi, Olly," I whisper and gently bounce him in my arms. "You're so much bigger than when I saw you last."

"I forgot, you haven't seen him since the hospital," Charlie says.

"No. I was stuck at the library when you guys got together a few weeks ago."

Barbeques and dinners are frequent occurrences around here. As if they don't all see each other enough with work at

12

Arrhythmic and Arabesque. But we're like a little family. Well, little is the wrong word. We're more mob sized these days.

"Where are the guys? Where's Meredith?" My pseudo big sister is missing from the backyard.

"She isn't feeling well, so we forced her to lie down," Charlie answers.

"Isn't that baby ready to come out yet?" I joke.

Meredith is almost nine months pregnant, and I've been anxiously waiting for the call from Nick to watch Everly when he and Meredith head for the hospital.

"Any day now." A soft expression crosses her face but is gone before I can study it further.

I don't get the chance to ask her what the look is about before my big brother's voice carries from the studio across the yard.

"Jessie!" He waves me over to where he and the other guys stand next to—holy shit. He's standing next to Topher Rivers.

The Topher Rivers, bassist for Just One Yesterday. Visceral attraction travels through my body at his lean form encased in threadbare jeans and a dark t-shirt that shows off toned muscles. His eyes are covered by mirrored aviators, but I can imagine the deep, soulful brown. Pictures don't do him justice—he's even better looking in person.

"Looks like you're being paged." Claire stands and takes Olly from me with a grin.

"Yeah. I'll be back. I'm not done holding him."

"Jess!" Jax calls obnoxiously, like the impatient big brother he is.

I meet the guys at the path that joins the studio and the backyard and am enveloped in bear hugs by first my brother, then Nick, and finally Dylan.

"Okay, okay, okay, you guys." I tug my t-shirt down where it's ridden up and mock glare at the three stooges. "Did you need me for something?"

I turn toward Jax, who shakes his head.

"Nope. Just figured you might want to meet Topher here, before he leaves."

He turns those full, pouty lips up in a slight smile, and the heat of his attention creates a flush in my body that radiates from my core.

"Topher Rivers." His deep voice creates a frisson of electricity through my body that arcs further as his hand comes into contact with mine.

"Jessie Bryant." Is that my voice? The breathiness sounds nothing like me.

"Jessie's my baby sister," Jax interrupts, stepping between Topher and me so we have no choice but to let go of each other's hands.

He gives me a look full of a dad-lecture, and I roll my eyes. I'm not six or sixteen anymore. If I'm attracted to Topher, what does it matter?

I can be attracted to him. I can file him away in my rub club for a night with my BOB. Because that's as far as I'll ever go with a rock star again.

"Nice meeting you. Thanks for today, guys, but I need to head out."

Nick nods and claps Topher on the back.

"Thanks for the song. You're sure next week is going to work to record?"

They're working on a song with Topher? Did Just One Yesterday break up? Since the library has been my prison for the last few weeks, it's possible, but I'm sure my roommate Sydney would have told me. I'll ask Jax later.

"Yep. I'll let you know if something comes up." He steps by me to leave, and my body tunes to the scent that surrounds him.

That current—the one that reminds me of static electricity—pulls my body to his like a damn magnet, and I lock my muscles to avoid stepping closer. What the hell is wrong with me?

He's a rock star.

And every one of them outside of my brother and his friends is the same way.

Trouble.

"Goodbye." His voice is so low the words must be for me.

I try to ignore the way the smooth notes wrap around me like silk.

He's near the gate by the time I remember how to work my mouth and brain together.

"What the hell was that?" Jax asks, glaring at me.

Nick and Dylan take off. Cowards.

"What was what?"

"That—"

"Jackson, maybe you should start the grill before the natives grow restless?" Charlie asks, walking up to us and wrapping an arm around my shoulders.

"But—fine. You're right. We're not done with this conversation though." He points in my direction.

"I'm always right. Haven't you learned that by now?" Charlie asks her husband, and I laugh as my brother kisses her cheek and heads for the grill.

Meredith steps out of the house once the food is ready. Grimacing, she rubs at her back.

"No more babies after this," she says.

"You say that now. But we always forget about the aches and pains when baby fever hits," Michaela says, and her words earn her a look from West.

"No more babies." He points a bottle of ketchup at his wife.

"I didn't say anything." But her smile says it all.

"Baby, go sit down. I'll bring you a plate." Nick steps next to Meredith and places a hand on the small of her back. He guides her to a patio chair, and once she's comfortable, he grabs a plate of food and a small bag of nacho cheese Doritos for her.

"You know what would be so good with these?" She looks up at him like he's the only one who can rescue her.

"This?" he asks and pulls a small jar of Nutella from his pocket.

She grabs it from him and pops the top before dipping the first chip in.

No, just no. That combination is...disgusting, but happiness emanates from Meredith as she pops another chip in her mouth.

"Why? Why did you do that? Didn't we talk about this being a no-Nutella event?" Jax sits on Meredith's other side and pulls Charlie down next to him.

"You remember what pregnancy cravings are like." Nick shudders dramatically. "Hard pass on saying no to the woman nurturing our unborn child."

"And keeping Everly in check," Meredith adds.

"And keeping Everly from taking over the world," he agrees.

"I didn't have cravings. Not like Meredith and pickles with Everly and now this." Even Charlie looks a little green face to face with Meredith's latest fixation.

"I don't know, gorgeous. How many packages of Oreos have we gone through over the last few weeks?" Jax asks.

It takes a few moments for what he said to process, but almost in unison, everyone stops eating to stare at Jax and Charlie. She fidgets slightly under the scrutiny and side-eyes her husband.

"You really can't keep a secret, can you?" The question holds no heat. That soft smile from earlier returns, and she leans closer and kisses his cheek.

"Charlie, did he say what I think he just said?" Meredith's attention pings between the couple.

Jax and Charlie continue to stare at each other, ignoring our stunned expressions, until he closes the distance and brushes his lips over hers.

"Charlotte Grace Bryant!" Meredith starts to push out of her chair, but Nick wraps a hand around her wrist to keep her in place. "Answer me, woman."

Leaning against her husband, Charlie turns back to all of us and answers Meredith's question—the one we're all silently asking.

"I am. We're almost ten weeks." She puts a hand to her stomach.

Jax presses his lips against her shoulder while he wraps an arm around her waist and interlaces his fingers with hers.

The noise of congratulations and happy squeals startles Olly, so Claire stands and paces to quiet him.

"Um, Charlie. We're due the same month." Mia says, and for the second time tonight, all sound stops.

"Mi?" Michaela looks like she might faint from excitement. "You're pregnant?"

Mia nods enthusiastically, and a smile stretches across her face.

"Twelve weeks tomorrow." Garrett steps behind his wife and rests his hands on her shoulders.

More happy excitement. More baby discussions. More lovey, couple-y stuff.

Instead of saved by the bell, I'm saved by the chime on my phone.

"I need to get going. Thesis appointment."

♪♪♪♪♪

"Dry?" I ask as I try to comprehend Dr. Habib's opinion of the thesis I've spent over a thousand hours on.

"I didn't say that."

"But it's too informative." Frustration takes the form of tears that burn behind my eyes.

I have a job offer in hand from the clinic I want to work with here in LA. Chords, Crayons, and Counseling may not be the number one creative therapy clinic for children, but after interning there last summer, it's where I want to be.

But the offer is contingent on me obtaining my master's degree this semester.

"I didn't say that either. I merely suggested that your thesis could benefit from some examples. Your research is outstanding, but *you* are missing from your words. A good thesis is not a regurgitation of facts alone. It needs to impart how those facts impact its author."

"I-I don't know how to do that," I admit.

Dr. Habib sighs. "Take some time—"

"But I only have the rest of this semester!"

"Take some time. I want you to incorporate who Jessica Bryant is and how she feels about all this research. When you draft something, send it to me, and I'll read through it. Understood?"

"Yes, sir."

Texas manners win out over the aggravation overwhelming me.

Whatever.

I leave Dr. Habib's office thinking about what he said. Maybe I should call the clinic and warn them now. I won't be successful because I don't have any examples.

What about yourself?

Nope. I shut down the question immediately. I'm not putting what I experienced as a pediatric cancer patient in my thesis. Or what I deal with now that strengthens my connection to music.

"No. Give it some time. Could you include an experience with one of your nieces or nephews?" Sydney asks later that day when I get back to our apartment.

Her red hair is piled in a messy bun on top of her head, and her UCLA t-shirt is sporting a massive coffee stain. I caught her working when I got home, so her thick glasses are perched on top of the messy bun. When she's not at school—she's a grad student like me—Sydney spends her time hacking for a local security company, Sentinel Security. Once she graduates, she'll go to work for them full-time.

But unlike me, her job offer isn't contingent on a master's degree.

"Maybe." But I'm not convinced. I lean my head against our couch, exhausted by the thought of coming up with examples.

"We need another girls' night." She shakes my arm. "We haven't done one in a while."

I smile. "We're both trying to graduate."

"Pfft." She waves away my reminder. "What about Wednesday night? It's ladies' night at Aftershock."

"Syd."

"Come on, Jess. It'll be fun. Drinks. Dancing. Dicks."

I giggle at her description. One of the things I love about Sydney is that her take on relationships is similar to mine—we aren't interested in more than scratching the occasional itch. We may have different reasons—she'd rather spend time with her computer than a boyfriend, and I decided after my one and only attempt at a relationship that I wasn't doing that again—but the endgame is the same.

"I have to work on my thesis."

"You can work on your thesis every other night. And every day. I know how obsessive you are." She lifts an eyebrow.

So what if I want it to be perfect?

"Syd. I'm not in the mood."

"I'm not taking no for an answer."

And she doesn't.

Wednesday night, she and I sit at Aftershock's bar, sipping vodka cranberries as she points out different guys for me to scratch my non-existent itch with. I keep telling her I don't need them since I don't have an itch I can't satisfy by myself. My BOB and I have spent a lot of quality time together lately, the images of Topher Rivers continuing to feed that fire.

"What about him?" Sydney asks, practically yelling over the loud music.

I follow Sydney's discreetly pointed finger and guffaw at a guy who screams spokesperson for spray tans. Vodka cranberry snorts up my nose, and my laughter turns to coughing until I can breathe again.

"Syd, that burned."

"I couldn't help it." She straightens from where she's been doubled over in hysterics. "I was being serious before, and you keep saying no. C'mon, there has to be a guy here you're interested in."

"I already told you, I'm not here to pick up a guy. Just dancing and drinks tonight."

"What about him?" She tries again, pointing to another guy in a different direction.

I sigh but humor her. He's cute. Tall. Dark hair. But he reminds me way too much of my ex to warrant going there.

And not enough like a certain rock star that smells like sex on a stick.

My motto? Instead of *say no to drugs*, it's *say no to rock stars*. It's not happening. Not after Bowie.

Hell, after him? I have no interest in dating anyone, but especially musicians.

"He's cute," I admit.

"Ah-ha! Go ask him to dance. Or hang out."

Hang out is Sydney's code word for no-strings sex.

"Syd."

"For real, Jess. Dust off your vag and get some action."

"Dust off my what?" I wince at my shriek.

"Your lady bits haven't seen any action since before the semester break. Time to get you back in the saddle, babe. Or on that saddle, as the case may be." Her words are accompanied by a lewd wink.

I'm torn between shaking my head in disgust and laughing at her.

"I have a vibrator and an active imagination"—seemingly stuck on the sexy bassist for JOY, but I'm not admitting that—"I don't need a guy. I need to get my thesis written."

"If you're still this hung up on your thesis, you need more of those." She points to my nearly empty drink.

"This is my second."

"Have another. Relax."

Before I can tell her no, the bartender drops off refills.

"Compliments of him." She nods her head to a guy at the end of the bar. He lifts his beer bottle to toast us.

"We should go thank him for the drinks." She turns to me, taking a sip of her lemon drop.

I groan, already seeing where this is headed. Either she's going to try to set me up with our drink buyer or hook up with him herself, making me a third wheel.

"Hey there, ladies."

No chance to back out now since he's moved from where he was to the stool on Sydney's other side.

"Hey, handsome. Thanks for the refills." She practically purrs, and I almost choke on my drink.

"Couldn't let two beautiful women go thirsty, could I? I'm Reed."

"Sydney," she says and leans back to include me in the conversation. "And this is Jessie."

I wave but don't say anything, distracted by the way the hairs on the back of my neck lift and the heat that licks between my shoulder blades. Ignoring their chatter, I spin on my stool, searching for the source.

Colored lights wash the club in different shades of green, pink, red, and blue while the music pulses with the crowd on the dance floor. There's no current of awareness as I scan the tables. Training my focus on the VIP area, I jolt when I make contact with a pair of glittering eyes that stare at me from high above the masses.

Topher Rivers.

Here.

What are the chances? Had I not met him last weekend, would I still react like this?

"Jess," Sydney hisses and breaks the staring contest Topher and I are engaged in.

"Huh?"

"You don't mind, do you?" Her green eyes turn pleading.

"Don't mind what?" What did I miss?

She rolls her eyes. "Reed's in the bathroom. I know I pointed him out to you, but—"

"He's all yours."

She squeals and throws her arms around me.

"Are you okay if we go dance? I don't want to leave you here by yourself…"

My attention strays back up to the balcony just as an arm wraps around Topher from behind. A woman steps into view. Her blond hair, heavy makeup, and too-small clothing speak to her groupie status.

I huff out a breath. Of course that's who he surrounds himself with. Groupies. Women who look like her. Someone willing to party.

Typical rock star.

"It's fine. I'm going home anyway."

"But it's barely ten!"

"I was up early. And after two of those"—I point to my mostly full third vodka cranberry—"I'm tired. I'm going to head home. Don't worry about me. Have fun. Be careful."

"Yes, Mom." She shoots me an impish grin before catching sight of her flavor of the night. "You're sure?"

"Go. Have fun."

"Text me when you get home."

"I will. And if I don't hear from you, I'm going to track your phone," I warn her.

"Why do you think I downloaded that app for you?"

After another quick hug, she follows Reed to the dance floor, quickly disappearing into the crowd. Pulling up Uber, I order a ride and down a glass of water while I wait for the little car icon to move closer to my location.

"Refill?" The bartender asks.

My phone pings that my ride is here, and I shake my head. "I'm good, thanks." I drop a five on the bar and stand. "Have a good night."

The long line of people still waiting to get into the club so late surprises me. Clubs, lines, all of it holds little appeal. I came to hang out with Sydney.

I'm too old for the rest.

You're twenty-three. You should be waiting in this line right now. Ready to party.

But after everything I experienced as a kid, I'm an old soul. Something I've learned to love about myself, even if it doesn't lend to a busier social life. I slide into the back of the car and watch the LA lights blur by until we stop at my building. The apartment I share with Sydney is in a decent neighborhood—Jax made sure there was plenty of security for the two of us before we moved in.

He may be my older brother, but more often than not, he gives off the overprotective dad vibe. As if my thoughts conjure him, my phone vibrates as I unlock the apartment door.

JAX

You awake?

I key in my response as I kick off the high-heeled booties Sydney insisted I wear with my skinny jeans.

Duh.

23

Just got home.

From where???

Aftershock.

I don't like that place.

That's because you're old.

Don't be a brat.

You texted me, remember?

I wanted to see how your dissertation thing went.

I'm amazed that he waited this long to ask. But with his and Charlie's impending arrival, maybe he's distracted.

Why was Topher Rivers at your house?

Nice change of subject there.

What happened with your professor?

I got feedback.

That doesn't sound good.

Not really. But it's a long story, and I don't want to get into it tonight.

Maybe we can grab lunch soon? You and me?

Sounds good. It's been a while.

Now what about Topher?

Are you guys signing Just One Yesterday????

JOY has been with Cornerstone since they started. For them

to change labels after twenty years would be huge news. And a big win for my brother and Nick.

No.

I wait for more from him, but my phone is silent.

Is that all I get?

Yes.

Why?

Because I can't say any more.

Secretive.

Will Topher be at your house again?

Why do you want to know?

You're not interested in him, right?

Because he's too old for you.

No more rock stars. You know that.

Jax knows about almost everything that happened with Bowie. And my vow to never date another musician.

I was just curious.

Because if so, I'll need to avoid his house for a while. It'll be easier to ignore my attraction to the rock star when I can pretend I don't fantasize about him. In reality, it's harder to lie to myself.

CHAPTER 3

JESSIE

I wake to my phone vibrating across my nightstand at ten the next morning.

NICK

Be at this address at noon.

His text is accompanied by an address in the Hollywood Hills. What the hell?

Why?

You have an interview for a nanny job.

What?!

The last time I nannied was two years ago!

Not since I nannied for seven kids for an entire summer, working six days a week and twelve hours a day. All summer long. Maria von Trapp, I wasn't. And that job didn't include the *Sound of Music* happy ending with a sexy widower. Both parents were rarely in the country, let alone around.

I already said you'd be there.

Nick!

I'm going to get Meredith to strangle you.

I wouldn't volunteer you if I didn't think you were perfect.

Perfect for what?

My phone rings in response.

"Perfect for what?" I repeat without bothering with a greeting.

"It's one kid, Jess. He's four."

"A lot of people would be perfect for one kid," I fire back.

"He's not speaking right now." Nick's words give me pause.

"But he was before?"

"That's my understanding, yeah."

An image of myself at five years old comes to mind. Surrounded by doctors using big words and lots of machines. The only other kids I saw were other pediatric cancer patients. I lost my voice in the shuffle, overwhelmed by everything and everyone around me. But I never stopped speaking entirely.

"And the parents think a nanny is a good idea?"

If he's not speaking, I wouldn't recommend adding another adult to the mix.

"Parent. The dad. His mom died in a car accident about two months ago."

My heart breaks for the little boy who lost his mom so suddenly.

"That's horrible. Poor baby."

"So you'll do the interview?"

He knew exactly what he was doing by telling me about the little boy. And other than my thesis, I don't have much going on. My plans involve working on rewrites and watching Netflix with a big jar of jellybeans.

"Why me?"

"I think you could help him."

And with those six words, I'm a goner. Sighing, I toss back my covers.

"Okay, okay. You succeeded in buttering me up. I'll do it."

We hang up, and I get ready, rushing since I need to leave my apartment by eleven to make it there on time. The apartment is quiet, and the text Sydney sent last night was so vague, I don't know whether she's asleep in her room. It's not the first time, and it probably won't be the last.

I opt to drive myself since ordering an Uber would cost me more than I want to shell out. Following the GPS voice, I fight the LA traffic and take several turns until I'm staring at a large gate at the end of a long driveway.

"Looks like I'm not in Kansas anymore."

Instead, I'm a country mouse visiting her city cousin. Growing up, Jax and I were raised in a middle-class neighborhood outside Austin. My parents still live there despite how many times I tell them I'm not moving back home. And since my older brother is a rock star and is best friends with two other rock stars and a movie star, it's hard to be overwhelmed by displays of wealth. But this gate—with a driveway that winds around a corner and no house in sight—this is next level. So is the guard shack at the front of the gate. Who the hell are these people?

"I should have asked more questions," I mutter to myself.

Pulling up to the gate, I fight the nerves that fidget in my belly and glance down at my denim capris. Maybe I should have dressed up... No. If I'm going to be this kid's nanny, then this is how I dress. And if the word *uniform* crosses anyone's lips, I'm out.

"Name, miss?" The guard approaches my open window.

"Jessica Bryant. I'm here to meet—" I stop since I don't have a name. "I'm here for an interview?"

He scans the clipboard in his hands and nods once before he lifts his head. He studies my CR-V like he doesn't see many visitors who drive cars like mine.

He probably doesn't.

"You're clear. One moment."

With no other explanation, he ambles back to his post, and the gate slowly opens.

"Ready or not, here I go." I press on the accelerator slowly, glad for the few extra moments when I turn the corner and still don't see the house.

But the nerves don't settle, even when the home appears around the *next* corner. In fact, they're worse. The house—excuse me, mansion—is a dusty beige color, a stark contrast to the greenery on either side of the large front door.

It doesn't look like a kid lives here.

The front of the house is too meticulous, too quiet to give off the vibe that anyone under the age of eighteen lives here, let alone a four-year-old. It's pretty, but wrong. There should be sidewalk chalk on the driveway, cobblestone or not. The yard should be decorated with a sprinkler, just begging to be used in a water fight, and a bike laying haphazardly across the lawn.

Like there was at your house?

I didn't grow up with most of that either. At least not until the cancer was in remission. Even then, Mama was a little *too* overprotective, worried that I might overexert myself or catch some sort of bug and the cancer would mysteriously come roaring back.

Shaking my head, I dispel the depressing thoughts and park in the circular driveway. I run my clammy hands down my thighs and shoulder my bag after I step out of the car. My reflection in the window appears more confident than I feel. My dark hair is pulled into a high ponytail since I tend to fidget with it when I'm nervous. A white t-shirt is semi-tucked into my capris, and my pink espadrilles add a little height to my five-foot-three self.

"You got this," I tell my reflection. Squaring my shoulders, I move to the front door and ring the bell.

The echo is loud, and I cringe. How big is the house? Big or not, I don't wait long before the door is opened. An older woman with stylishly tousled blond hair and green eyes greets me.

"Jessica?" She studies me carefully, her hand on the door like she's ready to close it quickly.

"Yes. Hi, I'm Jessie." I extend my hand.

"Lois." She shakes my hand before gesturing for me to come in.

The foyer is enormous, with high, vaulted stone that likely contributed to the echoing of the doorbell.

"Mr. Rivera is running late, but Mrs. Rivera is here." She gestures to the sunken living room to the left of the foyer, where another older woman sits on the couch while a little boy plays with two dinosaur toys at the table in front of her.

She notices us and stands gracefully, coming to shake my hand.

"Hello there. You must be Jessica. I'm Dawn, and I apologize. My son is running late. He asked me to keep you company until he could get here."

"Jessie, please. Nice to meet you."

Lois disappears down the hall, and I follow Dawn into the living room.

"This is Gage." She ruffles his hair before sitting back down, and I sit gingerly on the other couch, distracted by her familiarity.

The little boy glances up, his big hazel eyes meeting mine before he shifts his attention back to the dinosaurs in his hands. He moves them back and forth so they look like they're having a conversation, but only he knows what they're saying.

"Can I get you anything to drink while we wait for Christopher?" she asks.

"I'm fine. But thank you."

She opens her mouth to say something else, but is cut off by her ringing cell phone.

"I apologize, but this is my husband. Do you mind if I take this?"

"Not at all."

She stands and moves quickly to the edge of the room to answer her call, and I turn to focus on the little boy. He runs a finger along the back of one of the dinosaurs, turning it over and pressing on each of its feet as he studies it.

"Do you like dinosaurs?" I ask.

He nods without looking at me.

"Those are really nice." I move closer, hovering at the edge of my seat for a moment before I slide to the floor—I'm glad I wore pants and not the skirt I first considered.

His attention ping pongs between me and the two dinosaurs before he extends one to me.

"For me?" I want to be sure I understand what he wants.

He nods again and stretches his hand farther, until the nose of the dinosaur pushes against my fingers. I move slowly until I can grasp the toy.

"Do you mind if I sit next to you?"

He considers my question for a moment before he shakes his head, and with his confirmation, I shift until we're sitting next to each other at the table. He prances his dinosaur close to mine.

"Hello, Mr. Dinosaur, how are you today?" I change my voice to sound gruff and deep, and a small smile curves his lips when he looks at me. "What kind of dinosaur are you? Are you friendly?"

He nods the dinosaur's head.

"What do you want to do today?"

He moves the dinosaur to the edge of the table and tips it so it looks down at the floor. I mimic his movements with mine.

"Is the floor lava?" I ask.

His gaze snaps to mine before he nods again. His face is so stoic I bite back a smile. "This is serious business, isn't it?"

The dinosaur's head bobs again.

"What do you like to eat, Mr. Dinosaur?"

He thinks for a moment and finds a green pattern on the carpet next to us. Smart boy.

"*Ohh.* You're a veggie eater. Like me."

The look on his face tells me what *he* thinks about vegetables, even if his dinosaur eats them.

"Do you like vegetables?" I tease. "Broccoli? Brussel sprouts?"

He shakes his head quickly, and I don't hide my smile this time.

"Can I let you in on a secret?" I drop my voice to a stage whisper.

He nods.

"I don't like vegetables either."

His eyes light up, and a wide smile stretches across his face. We play for a few more minutes until he stops and lays his dinosaur on the table like it's sleeping.

"Is the dinosaur tired?"

He nods and leans his head against my upper arm. His little hand curls around mine, and just like that, I fall in love with the four-year-old who sighs as he tangles his fingers with mine. Relaxing my hand and arm, I let him take the lead. He uses a finger to trace each of mine from my hand to my fingertips before moving along the top and back down again.

There's a sniffle in the room, and I look up to see Dawn watching the two of us as tears track down her cheeks.

"Sorry I'm late. Milo and Finn were late—"

The loud voice comes from a different direction from where Dawn is. But as soon as he turns into the room where Gage and I are, he freezes, and his words stop.

Topher Rivers. Rock star. Bassist for Just One Yesterday. And dad?

33

Holy shit.

"What are you doing here?" He finally regains his words.

"Nick called me and told me I had an interview. But he didn't mention it was with you."

If he had, I would have said no.

Even if I am in love with his son, I avoid rock stars who aren't family. Especially a sexily disheveled ones who make me wonder what the scruff on their jaws would feel like against my skin. Or whose obviously sculpted muscles lead me into a fantasy that doesn't involve clothes.

Get a hold of yourself.

I'm not going to think about the way his hands could master my body like he does his bass. Or remember all the times the image of him in Jax's backyard has accompanied a BOB-inspired orgasm…or six.

Deep brown eyes study me with the same intensity as his son. But with a totally different outcome. Whereas the little boy now has me wrapped around his finger, I want to run away from the lust inspired by his father. A piece of chestnut hair falls across his forehead, and he reaches up, moving it out of his way without taking his eyes off me. It's unnerving…it's crazy…and whatever it is wraps around me so tightly I'm seconds from combusting.

I blink, breaking the spell, and release a breath. I need to stand up, say goodbye to Gage and Dawn, and run out of here as fast as possible. I don't need the complications of what I'm feeling to last longer than the few minutes spent in Topher's presence.

"Christopher, hijo, you know Jessie?"

His gaze flicks to his mom. Who I now realize is *the* Dawn Rivera, one of the founding members of Beyond California. The other founding member is Topher's dad, Tony.

"We met at Jax's house last weekend."

"Ah." She nods. "Perhaps you and Jessie would like to discuss the position now that you're home? I'll stay here with Gage."

"Jessie, would you like to speak outside?"

I try—and fail miserably—to ignore the way his lips wrap around my name.

It's a name. My name. One I've heard all my life. But the way he says it sends electricity zipping through my body. I can't tell whether I hate him more for being a musician or for inspiring the ridiculous amount of lust that burns through my body. Either way, it's time to go.

"I'm sorry. I should probably get going." I unfurl from the floor with Gage still clutching my hand.

This is going to be harder than I thought.

"Gage, nieto, let's go find a cookie in the kitchen." Dawn moves closer, and Gage lets go of my hand to rush to his grand-ma's side. "Come with Abuelita."

"This isn't going to work," I blurt out once we're alone.

"Nick told me he had a great candidate for a nanny. He must have meant you. Please. Five minutes?"

He looks so…so…normal in this moment. In a faded gray t-shirt and threadbare jeans, I can almost forget he's a rock star.

"I…" I need to stay strong.

"Please. I need help. For Gage."

With a sigh, I nod and follow him out to the back, where a turquoise pool sparkles in the early afternoon sun. He gestures to one pool lounger and takes the one opposite.

"I didn't realize you were a nanny." He clasps his hands, his elbows resting on his legs. The move limits my personal space, but I don't mind. Why don't I?

I shrug. "It's been several years since I nannied. I'm not sure why Nick recommended me."

Except I still babysit for everyone.

"What do you do now?"

"I'm a grad student at UCLA. Music therapy, specializing in pediatrics."

"That's a thing? Music therapy?"

I bristle at his questions.

"Yes, that's 'a thing.' It's one of the more difficult programs associated with therapy."

He raises his hands in surrender.

"I'm sorry. I didn't mean to offend you. I've just never heard of it before now."

"Listen, Topher, I don't think—"

"Chris."

"What?"

He fixes his attention on me, and I fight the shiver of goosebumps wanting to explode at the emotion in his deep brown depths.

"Topher is my stage name. Chris. I'm Chris." He reaches out a hand, and I move mine slowly, reluctant to place it in his after what happened last time. For good reason.

That same electric spark is there, more intense than before. This is a bad idea.

"Chris."

Chris Rivera, eldest son of Dawn and Tony Rivera. He wanted to make it on his own talent instead of his parents' reputation and adopted Topher Rivers as his stage name before making it big. But even now, after two decades of success, the press refers to him as Topher Rivers. Hell, even Jax introduced him as Topher.

But saying his real name?

It adds a layer of intimacy I don't expect. A layer I can't want.

"Why don't you think this is going to work?"

"It would be temporary. I have a job offer for after I graduate—"

"When is that?"

"Once my thesis is approved." *If* I ever get it approved.

"Nick said you could help. I think I agree. Gage likes you."

"I like him too. That's not the problem."

"What is the problem? Other than being temporary. Because it's more than that."

"I-I don't associate with rock stars."

"You associate with your brother. And his artists."

Touché.

"They're different. They're family."

"I'm different."

"I saw you last night. You're no different from any other rock star I've met."

His eyes widen and he leans back. "What do you mean?"

"All about the party. About the groupies." I shrug and stand, shouldering my bag again.

When he stands as well, he brings our chests close enough that they brush with his breath.

"I *am* different. I was only at Aftershock for a label appearance. They required it as part of a new artist's release."

"And the groupie?" The words are out of my mouth before I can bite them back.

He smirks, and I want to slap it off his face.

"She wanted something I couldn't give her. I politely declined her...advances...and came home. Alone."

Why does that fact spark a surge of relief?

"I..."

For my sanity's sake, I need to decline. Despite what he says.

"Please. I'm desperate." He lifts his hands to cup my upper arms, and my nerves riot at the calloused glide of his fingertips against my skin. "Would you at least think about it?"

No, I can't. No, thank you. No.

One word. Two letters. It's easy to say.

But I nod instead.

"Okay. I'll think about it."

CHAPTER 4

JESSIE

"Syd!" I shout as I slam the door and drop my keys and bags onto the table. "I need to talk to you!"

Belatedly, I remember she may not be here, but I guess I'll find out.

If she's not here, who will you talk about this with?

Shut up!

I stride into the kitchen and open and close cabinet doors randomly without seeing the contents—my mind is too preoccupied by the events of the morning.

Gage.

Dawn.

And Topher Fucking Rivers.

He's sex on a stick—he's been that way since I first started listening to Just One Yesterday's music. He isn't the only one. Every member of the band has all been smacked with the good-looking stick. Which was great when the knowledge was superficial. But rock stars are for looking at or listening to, not for getting involved with.

I avoid that scene at all costs. And since Jax and JOY don't run in the same circles, it's been easy. My brother is more pop, and while they edge that line sometimes, they're more rock.

Dylan is more rock, but he's still signed to Arrhythmic.

Sydney's door rattles, squeaking on the hinges as it opens.

"You want coffee?" I want coffee. Even if I already had one on my way to the interview.

Do you really need another, considering how hyperactive you are right now?

"Yes, please." The voice is too deep to be Sydney's.

Spinning around, I find the guy from the club last night leaning against the doorjamb. His hair sticks out in every direction, and his shirt is barely buttoned as he shoots me a lopsided grin. It might have been charming. It might have even been flirting.

If he hadn't spent last night with my best friend.

"She isn't asking you," Sydney says as she brushes past him into the kitchen. "You were leaving."

"You wouldn't send me out into the world without at least a little caffeine for my efforts, would you?"

I catch Sydney's smirk and lean against the counter, ready to be entertained as she rounds on the poor, unsuspecting flavor of the night and ousts yet another guy from our apartment. This isn't the first time one has assumed he could stay.

"Your 'efforts,' as you call them, were mediocre at best. But, since I managed to get off, I'll give you a gold star for that."

His flirty look fades, but Sydney isn't finished.

"If you want, I can give you a few pointers."

"Pointers?" All the color leeches from his face.

"Well, constructive criticism."

"Umm…" He straightens from his cocky pose in the doorway, his eyes darting around in search of the nearest exit.

"For starters—"

"No!" His voice is loud as he interrupts her. "I mean, no, I'm good. I, uh, I guess I should leave."

He's not the fastest runner we've had, but he isn't among the slowest bunch either. The door closes, and Sydney and I both double over with laughter.

"You're so bad." I gasp between giggles.

She straightens and wipes her streaming eyes. "What? Because I'm honest? I got him to leave, didn't I?"

"I think he left a vapor trail."

"Eh. He wasn't so bad. Not the worst. But I thought he'd be a little better in bed since he was a decent dancer."

"I don't understand your logic." I hold up a hand when she opens her mouth to respond. "And I don't want to know."

"Did you mention coffee?" She changes the subject, padding to the coffee maker.

"I did. I need to tell you about my morning."

Glancing over her shoulder, she lifts her eyebrows. "*Your* morning, huh?"

"Not like that, perv. I had an interview."

"Interview? Hold that thought. I need to pee."

She disappears back down the hall, and I have both cups of coffee ready by the time she's back.

"Here." I hand her one, and we settle into our spots in the living room.

"An interview for what? I thought you already accepted that job offer from Chords, Crayons, and Counseling." She takes a sip of her coffee and sighs happily.

"I still need to have my thesis approved to graduate."

"Easy peasy." She shrugs. To her, it would be that simple.

"No. Not so easy. I have no idea how to make the changes Dr. Habib wants."

"You're overthinking it, Jess. It'll all work itself out. In the meantime, what was this interview you went to today?"

"I talked to Nick this morning. Someone he knew was looking for a nanny—"

"No way! Tell me you're not seriously considering it after your summer from hell."

I take a drink from my cup to give me time to think. But I still don't have the answer. "It's one kid—he's four. And seriously one of the cutest kids I've ever seen. He's got these big hazel eyes that make you want to melt."

"I can see where this is going." Her wry tone is noticeable despite her muttered words.

"He...he doesn't speak." My heart shatters at everything Gage has gone through at such a young age. I was at least older than he was when I was first diagnosed with cancer, and I would consider my childhood before that pretty idyllic.

"Why not?"

"His mom died in a car accident recently. And he didn't meet his dad until after that."

"How awful." She sets her empty cup on the table. "And let me guess, you accepted the job?"

"No." I huff at her automatic assumption. "I said I would think about it."

"What's there to think about, Jess? Outside of your last *Nanny 911* experience, you loved doing it."

"There's more." I fidget with the throw pillow in my lap.

"Duh. Otherwise we wouldn't be having this conversation. Spill it."

"So Gage—that's the little boy's name—his dad is famous. Well, both his dad and his grandma are."

"So is your brother," she deadpans.

The first time I took Sydney to a family barbecue, she'd been tongue tied by the number of famous people in Jax and Charlie's backyard. It was the one and only time I've seen her speechless.

"His grandma is Dawn Rivera. *The* Dawn Rivera of Beyond California."

"Really? I love them."

Dawn and her husband, Tony, had a love story like Romeo

and Juliet's, with a happier ending. Children of rival families from Napa Valley, they fell in love, despite their families' objections. With nowhere else to go, they came to LA, busking on the street until someone from Weeping Willow Records walked by. The rest is history.

"Yep." I wait to see if she'll connect the dots.

"Wait. That would mean his dad is..." Her eyes widen with sudden realization.

"Topher Rivers. A.k.a. Christopher Rivera."

"Holy shit. Is he as hot in person as he is in pictures?"

I didn't tell Sydney about seeing him at Jax's house before—it had been unimportant at the time, a one-off. But now? The visceral attraction that hit my body like a tsunami the few times I saw him was enough to deal with. The heat in his gaze as my eyes had connected with his had made that seem like nothing.

"Better." My voice is breathless with the desire that courses through me at merely the memory.

"Damn. And you're only *thinking* about taking the job? My question would be how soon can I start?" She waggles her eyebrows.

I groan.

"How can I take the job? Yes, I'm attracted to him, but you know how I feel about rock stars. And how will all that work since I'll be there to take care of Gage?"

"You can't help Gage and be attracted to his dad? Attraction doesn't mean anything if you don't act on it. I think my boss is hot. Doesn't mean I'm going to do anything about it." Sydney's boss, Sawyer, is hot—all broody looks and muscles for days. He's also Michaela's brother, although they don't look or act anything alike.

"I'm not saying that."

Her brow wrinkles in confusion. "I'm not sure what you're saying, then."

I want to help her understand, but I'm not sure either. And that's my problem.

From one thing I don't know to another. Even after talking to Sydney, I'm still not sure which way to go. I want to help Gage. But I also don't want to be attracted to his dad. Frustrated with that never-ending loop of what the hell I should do, I leave Sydney to her computer and head to the library to work on my thesis.

♪♪ ♪♪ ♪♪

I spend hours going through my notes. I read and reread my research until it all blurs together. I work through examples from an internship and a personal example that doesn't make me want to throw up. But my brain has decided to take a vacation. Every time I write more than three words, I end up scratching them out. When my phone buzzes across the table, I snatch it up like it's salvation from the apocalypse.

NICK

How'd it go today?

That's how you want to start this conversation?

A little heads-up on who the job was for would have been nice.

I'd say I'm sorry, but that would be a lie.

Thanks for your honesty, you jerk.

Would you have gone if you knew you were meeting with Topher?

You mean Chris?

Fine. Would you have gone if you knew you were meeting Chris?

Would I? I snort a laugh, grimacing when it echoes around me a little too loudly. Fortunately, the library is deserted.

The answer is no. If I had known up-front I was interviewing to nanny for a rock star, I'd have told Nick to find someone else. Musicians are all a bunch of manipulative, cocky assholes—my brother and my friends excluded. And I'm no naïve eighteen-year-old who'll get caught up in the "romance" of an artist's "soul," only to find out it's nothing but a bunch of pretty lies.

Been there. Got that concert t-shirt and shredded the damn thing before lighting it on fire.

> I wouldn't have told you about it if I didn't think you could help.

> Have you met Gage?

> Not yet. But we thought he might want a play date with Everly.

I laugh at the image that comes to mind. Quiet, serious Gage with exuberant, extroverted Everly.

> LOL

> So should we set up that play date with you?

> Not sure yet.

> What does that mean?

> Didn't he offer you the job?

> He did.

> So?

> So I told him I need to think about it

> What's there to think about?

45

Sydney had asked the same question. Only she was focused on how attractive Chris was, and something tells me that's not Nick's motivation.

> He's a musician.

> And you know the only ones I associate with are tied to your label.

He's not Bowie.

Seeing his name on the screen is enough to spark my temper. Is it possible to be enraged and humiliated all at once? Because if so, that's what Bowie did to me. And I wouldn't forget that lesson anytime soon.

> You don't know that.

I get a feeling.

Give him a chance.

> I'm still thinking about it.

Can you help Gage?

I read through Nick's most recent text several times. His change of subject is abrupt, but that's just who Nick is.

> I think so.

It can't be easy. I try to picture Everly in that scenario, and it scares the shit out of me.

> Having your world turned upside down sucks.

Agreed.

And Nick speaks from personal experience. He lost his first fiancée, Emily, to a car crash when they were only eighteen.

What's holding you back?

Besides the whole "working for a musician"
thing?

Isn't that enough?

You tell me, Jess.

Fuck. Doubts are creeping in. Should I really judge the son based on the sins of the father?

When did you become such a philosopher?

Something in your old age? *laughing emoji*

Didn't think I was.

What? A philosopher or old?

Both.

I'm just asking questions.

Your questions are hard.

Never said they weren't.

Let me know what you figure out.

And stop by and see us one night. We'll grab
pizza.

Only if you can convince me that your wife isn't
doing something gross to the pizza.

No promises can be made.

That's what I thought.

I put my phone down and grip my pen again. Instead, I stare at the mostly blank page while the phantom weight of Gage's head leans against my arm.

If I were the kind of person who believed in signs, I'd think the universe was trying to tell me something. But I don't. Not anymore. That's what I tell myself when my phone pings with another text as I'm lying in bed that night.

UNKNOWN
Hello.

I hesitate with my fingers over the keyboard, but before I can ask who's texting, another message appears.

I hope you don't mind that I got your number from Nick.

It's Chris.

Nick gave Chris my phone number?
Wouldn't that be normal since he's considering hiring you to nanny?

CHRIS
I do have the right number, yes?

Jessie?

His texts unlock my fingers.

Yeah.

You have the right number.

Sorry, I should have given it to you earlier.

That's okay.

Don't worry about it.

For a half second, warmth floods me. But then I remember who I'm texting and why. Only the warmth doesn't disappear completely, even if it does fade.

Any chance you have an answer for me?

It's been less than twelve hours.

I don't have any details on the job, either. Other than it would be watching Gage.

What about schedule, other duties, all of that?

Sorry, I guess we didn't really talk about that.

If I'm honest, the way Gage connected to you, I'm willing to give you anything you want.

I roll my eyes, because his offer is exactly what a spoiled, out-of-touch rock star would say.

That's not realistic.

Between the two of us, you're the expert. I've never needed a nanny before.

Just because I nannied before doesn't make me an expert.

Start with schedule. What should I expect?

My last job had been six days a week, at least twelve hours a day. I'm not willing to do that again.

It depends.

On what?

Are you looking for a live-in nanny or someone who commutes?

You probably know I don't have a regular job with set hours.

So live-in?

Yeah.

Live with Chris? No. Not with him. With Gage.

A nanny isn't a replacement parent.

I don't want you to be.

I haven't said I'm accepting the job.

Ouch. Sorry. No, you didn't. I want to be my son's father.

Nope, not my heart melting into a puddle.

You probably have a lot of weekend stuff?

Not so much right now.

Appearances and stuff.

I've been doing a lot of work from the house since we're working on the next album.

So, schedule-wise, would it make more sense for me to take weekends off unless you have something you need to do?

I thought you didn't know if you were accepting the job yet...

Shit.

I don't. This was hypothetical. But the schedule can work for anyone you hire.

Yeah.

Yeah?

I think that schedule makes sense.

But what about through the week? Sometimes meetings or sessions run late.

> That's the bonus of having a live-in nanny. While a commuter would expect to leave at a certain time, a live-in can be more flexible.

Definitely the live-in option then.

> Do you have other duties in mind besides Gage? Cleaning, laundry, cooking?

Not really. Lois—you met her the other day—is my part-time housekeeper. I want to let her drop her hours back down since she's been working more full-time since I got Gage.

> So light cleaning and cooking?

Probably.

> You really have no idea about any of this stuff, do you?

Should I be offended?

> No. I wasn't being snarky.

> It's…cute.

Cute?

That he had no idea what to look for doesn't make me resent him the way I expected it to. His complete lack of knowledge makes him more real, endearing him to me in a way I can't afford.

> Don't let it go to your head, rock star.

Not at all. I'm just hoping that means you're going to take the job.

Am I?

Sydney was right, even if I won't admit that to her. From the moment Gage looked at me with those big hazel eyes, it was inevitable.

> Yes.

Yes?

> I'll take the job.

> When would you like me to start?

Any chance you can move in over the weekend?
Start Monday?

> I could move in on Monday. I have plans this weekend.

I don't. I'm delaying the inevitable, but I need the time to gear myself up to work for a rock star.

Oh, yeah, sure. Absolutely.

Monday.

What time should Gage and I expect you?

> Does 3 work? I don't want to interrupt any plans you have.

The guys will be over for a band meeting at 5.

Is that okay?

> It's your house. You don't need to ask if it's okay.

Only now I need to plan on being overwhelmed by an entire band of sexy musicians instead of one.

I can see if we can meet at Evan's.

The four of them are...chaos.

> Up to you. I'll get settled and keep an eye on
> Gage for your meeting.

Okay.

I appreciate this, Jessie.

I'll see you Monday?

> Yeah. See you Monday.

Putting my phone down, I try to calm the nerves that swirl in my stomach, but it's more than simply nerves. It's an unwelcome attraction. To another musician.

I can and I will ignore my attraction to Chris.

I'll be there to help Gage.

Focus on him.

Easy peasy.

Right?

CHAPTER 5

CHRIS

"*W*hat's with the look?" Evan says, stepping back into the music room where I was texting Jessie.

"What look?"

"The goofy smile."

"I don't have a goofy smile," I deny.

I probably do.

Something about Jessie has drawn me in since I first saw her. I pushed it down when I met her at Jax's house. Especially after he introduced her as his sister. Seeing her in the club had been a pleasant surprise, but before I could extricate myself from the appearance to go down to talk to her, she was gone.

Again, for the best.

But today? She was the best part of a morning that was otherwise a clusterfuck.

Any morning that starts at four thirty is. I don't begrudge Gage for wanting breakfast, but I needed sleep. Instead, I guzzled coffee like it was the only thing between me and a padded room —it probably is at this point

Nick's text that he had a candidate for me to interview as Gage's nanny was a pleasant surprise. When he told me he'd set up the interview for noon, I figured that was plenty of time since I had to head to the studio first.

Instead, Milo and Finn had shown up nearly an hour late, and Noah had shown up right after that, drunk and stoned out of his mind. I knew we wouldn't get anything productive done, but I couldn't leave before calming Marcus, our label rep, down from a nearly apoplectic state. After two years of no new albums, Cornerstone was pissed and ready to retire us to rock and roll history. I couldn't let that happen. I barely got Marcus calmed down before spending twenty minutes talking Evan off his ledge.

The writing was on the wall. We knew Noah would end up in rehab sooner or later. The way things were going, that day was close.

"Who were you texting?" Evan asks, settling onto the couch next to mine.

For once, I don't tell my best friend the entire truth.

"The nanny. She starts Monday." I blow out a breath as relief and anxiety mix in my stomach.

Relief that I found someone who can hopefully help Gage. Anxiety because I can't help wondering how the fuck I'm going to ignore the pull she has over me.

"What?"

"What?" I ask, confused.

"You sighed."

"Jesus Christ. I didn't. Aren't we supposed to be looking at songs?"

"You did. What's the problem with the nanny? If you don't like her, you can find another one."

"No!" I sit up, immediately rejecting the idea of not having Jessie.

Evan stares at me like I'm crazy.

"Want to clue me in, man?"

"She's…young," I admit. Barely old enough to drink based on her status as a student.

"So? Isn't that a good thing?"

"Shouldn't nannies be more like Mary Poppins? Or Mrs. Doubtfire?"

Evan smirks. "You're attracted to her."

"Fuck no I'm not."

"Liar, liar." His sing-song voice sends me back a few decades, reminding me of the ten-year-old boy who razzed me back then.

I groan and drag a hand through my hair.

"So what if I am? Nothing can happen. She's young enough to be my daughter."

His scoff is loud in the otherwise quiet house.

"She's not that young, is she?"

I shrug. "College."

Too young to even fantasize about any more than I already have.

"So what?"

"So I'm thirty-fucking-six."

"Gee, thanks, Grandpa. I'm three months older than you."

I flip him the bird and give him the second reason. The one even more damning.

"Gage needs her. Fuck, I need her help. I need help finding some sort of balance between the band and raising a kid. I don't know how my parents raised four of us."

He falls silent and shuffles through various songs spread on the table in front of us.

"Speaking of, what are we going to do about Noah? He's getting worse." His voice is hushed, resigned.

"I know."

I pick up my guitar, moving my fingers to avoid the crushing thought that our friend—our brother—is fading.

"I tried to give him a ride home earlier, but by the time I got done talking to Marcus, he was gone," he says, catching me up on what happened after I left the studio today.

"He needs to go to rehab again." I try to ignore the guilt and disappointment that swirls in my stomach.

"It hasn't fucking worked the last three times. You think the fourth time's the charm?"

I rest my hand against the strings, silencing the music.

"I don't know. He's been our friend since high school." It's the same reason I told myself the last two times.

"He's changed, bro. He's not the same Noah."

The Noah who helped found Just One Yesterday was full of optimism, a creative genius who helped write or solo drafted most of our songs. He didn't try pot on his own. Or coke. Partying our way through tours was how we did things. Until it got old. I didn't like waking up and not recalling the night before, relying on the paparazzi's version of events because I was too drunk or too high to remember.

Evan and I stopped about the same time. And Milo and Finn stopped the hard shit shortly after that. But without us, Noah spiraled. Three years ago, he stopped writing. He stopped trying to hide his addiction. It was only then that we realized how bad the problem was. And I found him his first rehab facility. He lasted two weeks before he left. Before I found him facedown on a mirror.

And it's getting worse with every failed attempt at rehab.

"So you're saying we just give up on him?"

Can I do that?

He sighs. "I don't want to. But he's not going to get help until he hits rock bottom. Not for good."

"It feels like we're kicking him when he's down."

"He needs to choose. Either the band or the drugs. Which does he want more?"

I'm afraid of what Noah's answer will be right now. And having to follow through with the choice he makes. He, Evan, Milo, and Finn are as much my brothers as Miles and Levi.

"Do you really want to ask him to choose?"

"I don't think we have a choice. He's not giving us any other option."

"Let's keep an eye on him. If it gets worse, then we'll talk about it. It has to be a decision the entire band makes together."

He nods. "Agreed."

What will Milo and Finn say? What about Cornerstone? We came to them as a fully formed band and fought like hell to stay that way. What will they—

A noise at the door catches my attention. Gage stands in the doorway wearing the Power Ranger pajamas he picked out tonight.

"Hey, buddy, what are you doing up?"

He rubs his eyes before padding across the room. His hand finds mine, and his hazel eyes are tired but full of the words he won't say.

I lift him, and his nose finds the space between my neck and shoulder as he lays his head down. If someone had told me a year ago that my favorite feeling would be the warm weight of my son in my arms, I would have scoffed. But right now, I can't think of a better place to be.

"I should get going. It's late." Evan stands and stretches.

I glance at my phone. How is it already after midnight?

"Guest rooms are made up if you want to crash here."

He looks like he might refuse before his shoulders drop.

"Yeah, sure."

He follows me out of the music room and flips off the lights behind us. My arms and my heart are full, but heavy too. I say good night to Evan at the first guest room before heading farther down the hall to Gage's room. I thought he was asleep in my arms, but his hands tighten around my neck when I try to cross the threshold.

"You don't want your room?" I rub his back soothingly.

He shakes his head without lifting it, his soft hair tickling along my jaw.

"Okay, my bed it is."

Another night of lackluster sleep. But if I need to choose, I choose him.

Remember that when it comes to Jessie.

Hands off.

Is it possible for time to both speed up and drag on? Monday took forever to get here, but I'm still not ready for Jessie's presence. To fight my attraction to her since it refuses to let up, despite my best efforts to ignore it.

I'm guzzling water after cardio and weights when the doorbell rings. Gage's head shoots up, his eyes finding me across the room.

"Are you expecting someone?" I tease. I'd kill for a smile from him, but he shakes his head without changing his facial expression. "Should we go see who it is?"

Like he does everything else, he stands silently and waits for me at the door, following behind me like my little shadow. A glance at my phone shows me it's barely two o'clock. Maybe Jessie is early? My heart picks up speed, and I can't blame my workout for the faster tempo.

Not for you. She's here for Gage.

I force my attraction back into the box it escaped from. The only way this is going to work is if I ignore the way my hands itch to delve into her dark hair and find out if it's as silky as it looks. To ignore the questions about how she tastes.

I have to.

Otherwise I'm going to lose what little sanity I have left.

"You're ear—" I break off as Evan, Noah, Milo, and Finn all push into the house. "What are you guys doing here? I thought we were meeting at Ev's at five."

"We need to talk." Evan's jaw is clenched so hard it looks like it could shatter at any moment.

Which is why, almost an hour later, when the doorbell rings, I'm not mentally prepared.

2:45.

Fuck.

Now what?

The doorbell rings again, and Evan eyes me.

"You going to answer that?" he asks.

"I don't have much choice, do I?"

Leaving the boys to their own devices, I walk toward the door, not surprised to find Gage behind me.

"Hi. Sorry I'm a few minutes early." Backlit by the sun streaming under the covered entrance, she looks like an angel.

Angel in the light.

My fingers twitch with the urge to write, and I wonder if I can grab a few minutes while it's this strong.

Gage squeaks with excitement and launches himself around me and at her in the span it takes to blink. Jessie only has a second to drop the duffel bag she's holding to catch him.

"Hey, buddy. Happy to see me?" She laughs at Gage's emphatic nod, the sound weaving its way into my subconscious.

"Hi."

It's the only word I can muster right now. My brain is too busy absorbing details like the way the fine hairs escaping her ponytail frame her face. The faded UCLA t-shirt with the neck stretched out shows off a smooth expanse of shoulder. Long legs that go on and on from under her frayed cut-offs to a pair of sneakers.

Gage wiggles in her arms, and she sets him down with another laugh, then bends to pick up the bag she dropped. The shirt gapes, and I force myself not to look. Barely. But her movements unlock my brain enough to shake the cobwebs away.

"Sorry, come in. Here, let me help with that."

I reach for her bag, and she pulls away. Message received. Hands off.

"I got it," she says quickly and gives me a wide berth when she steps through the door.

"Is that all you brought?"

A backpack, the large duffel bag, and a smaller shoulder bag.

"There are a few boxes in my car. I'll grab them later. What are you guys up to?"

A shout echoes from the kitchen.

I wince. "Sorry, the guys showed up here instead of meeting at Evan's."

She looks between the kitchen and me. "Oh."

I'm not sure what her ambiguous answer means, but I don't have the time to unpack it the way I want.

"Gage is watching a movie—" I gesture to the family room, and she peers around the corner.

"Oh! *101 Dalmatians*. I love this movie!" She drops her bags by the stairs and beelines for the couch next to Gage.

He leans against her, and I'm all but forgotten where I stand in the entryway as they lose themselves in the movie. Okay then. Leaving the two of them, I head back into the kitchen where Evan is wrestling a pan of frozen food from Finn.

"Who was that?" Finn grunts, struggling with the pan.

"Gage's new nanny."

Surprised, he lets go, and Evan spins to put it back in the freezer.

"Does she look more like Mrs. Doubtfire or that lady from the TV show?" Milo asks.

"Nei—guys, can we maybe take this show on the road? To Evan's? You know, later?"

I need to get these guys out of here before they catch sight of Jessie. Evan is aware of my attraction to her, but he's the only one.

He shrugs. "We can, but what's left to talk about that we didn't hash out earlier? We have a plan."

I glance at Noah, who seems relaxed for the first time in months.

Any plans we were going to make for the band will have to wait until we figure out help for him.

"You're sure?"

He nods.

"Okay, guys. Let's get out of Chris's hair."

"But, but enchiladas." Finn gestures to the freezer.

"I'll buy you some fucking enchiladas." Evan grunts out.

Finn's face brightens, and he all but shoves Noah and Milo in front of him while they head for the door. But Milo freezes as he crosses the threshold of the kitchen.

"Fuck me." He breathes out, and I crane my neck to see what caused his reaction.

Jessie is leaning over her bags, searching through her backpack. Her ass fills out the faded cut-offs like they were painted on. A rush of desire pools in my groin, and I barely bite back the groan that wants to echo Milo's sentiment.

Fuck me is right. Preferably in that position right there.

"Hello there, gorgeous." Milo interrupts the inappropriate path my mind had started to wander. He saunters toward Jessie and, while I can't see it, I can picture the lecherous grin on his face. I've seen it a thousand times before. It's his panty-melting grin, the one that always works to get any woman who catches his eye.

But not this woman.

She's mine.

No. She's Gage's nanny.

She jumps and spins around to face Milo head on.

"Hi."

"Who might you be?" he asks, even though he knows who she is.

63

I want to break the finger he uses to graze along the exposed skin of her shoulder.

She steps back from his touch, and I want to pump my fist in the air like it's some sort of victory.

"I'm Jessie, Gage's new nanny."

Before Milo can respond, I stalk toward him and push him to the door.

"Say goodbye, Milo," I grunt.

"See you later, Jessie."

The asshole blows her a kiss on his way out the door. The rest of the guys follow us outside, and I make sure the door is closed before I level a stare at each of them.

"Hands off the nanny," I growl.

"I don't need my hands." Milo waggles his brows.

I step forward until I'm toe-to-toe with him.

"I'm serious, Milo. Hands off the nanny, or I'll fucking level you. She's here for Gage."

Sure. I'll pretend that's why I'm this territorial over her. It's the only *logical* reason anyway.

"But—"

I cut him off with another growl.

"Okay, okay, fine. Hands off," he mutters.

When I only stare at him, he continues.

"Everything off."

"That goes for all of you." My verbal warning to Finn and Noah is accompanied by a glare. I don't need to worry about Evan.

One by one, they all nod. Even Evan.

"Can we maybe go into the studio tomorrow?" Noah asks. He looks more alive than he has in months. "I, uh, need to stay busy."

"Yeah, I'll check with Marcus. We'll plan on meeting at the studio at eleven," I tell him, happy to finally see a light at the end of the tunnel.

"Hasta."

"Later."

"Ev, are you still buying enchiladas?"

One by one, they get in cars, except for Finn, who balances on his bike. But helmet donned, he trails the others.

The sun is shining. Noah is getting help. Jessie is here for Gage.

Suddenly, things are a whole lot brighter than they were this morning.

CHAPTER 6

CHRIS

"Sorry about them," I say, walking back through the door. "And as for Milo, I would love to say that he knows better, but he's just an idiot."

A fleeting smile comes and goes, and I suck in a breath. I want to see that look on her face again. For longer.

"Don't worry about it."

"We were supposed to meet at five, but..." How the fuck do I explain the need for us to meet earlier? The tension between Evan and Noah because of Noah's behavior...

"But?"

I fidget under her stare, the way I would when Mamá would give me her patented I-know-what-you-did-so-you-better-confess look. "We needed to meet earlier."

"Oh."

For the first time since meeting her, the silence between us isn't charged...it's awkward.

"Should Gage and I give you the grand tour?" I change the subject, hoping to overcome the awkwardness.

"Um, sure."

"Gage, let's show Jessie her room and stuff, okay?"

He nods and scampers off the couch to meet us by the stairs. His hand immediately finds Jessie's. The sharp prick of betrayal stings, but then again, I don't blame him. If I had the option to hold Jessie's hand, I would.

"Are you going to show me?" she asks him with a smile. "Let me grab my bag."

"I'll get them." I reach down and shoulder both the bigger bags and motion toward the stairs. "After you."

Bad idea. I should have gone first.

Instead, I have an up close and personal view of her ass in those skintight cut-offs. The sway of her hips calls to my hands, begging me to cage them.

Get a grip.

I clear my throat and follow the two of them up the stairs and down the hall to Gage's room.

"Ah, the most important room in the house first, I see." I chuckle and step into the room, still holding both of Jessie's bags.

"It's a very nice room," she says, moving to the full bookcase with every type of children's book next to an oversized chair. "Do you like to read, Gage?"

She pulls a book off the shelf and holds it out for Gage to see.

"*I Love You, Stinky Face*?" What the hell kind of book is that?

"One of my favorites," she says.

"I'll, uh, I'll take your word for it. I've read a few of those to him before bed."

"Only a few?"

I nod. "He usually falls asleep downstairs, and I carry him up."

Her expression tells me I said something wrong, but she quickly smooths it.

"Gage?"

He looks up at her from playing with two dinosaurs.

"How about I put my bag away and you pick out a book for bedtime?"

He grips one dinosaur and makes his way to the bookcase.

Pulling out books one at a time, he stacks them in a sizable pile before we've even left the room.

"C'mon." I nod toward the door and cross the hall to one of the guest rooms.

Shades of beige and sea green blend in neutral tones in this room. A tall dresser holds a TV on one wall, while the king-size bed sits across from the large picture window that overlooks the pool.

"I hope you don't mind that I put you across from Gage."

"Why would I mind? I'm here for him. I like being across the hall from him in case he needs anything."

I set her bags on the bed and ignore the urge to pull her down to the soft surface next to them.

Quit being a fucking creeper.

I clear my throat and will my dick to calm down as I turn from the lusty images plaguing me.

"My room is next to Gage's, and there are two other guest bedrooms up here."

"Okay."

"There's also a music room and a home gym."

"Music room?" Her face brightens.

Pride fills my chest at her reaction. I did that.

"I'll show you." I step closer and try to ignore the sweet scent that surrounds her, but my traitorous nose breathes deeply.

She smells like cookies. Chocolate chip cookies.

Rolling my eyes at my own weak reaction, I leave her room and turn in the other direction. We pass the gym, where the lights still blaze from my workout this afternoon. My towel and water bottle sit where I left them next to the weight bench.

"Wow." She stops outside the gym.

"Feel free to use this whenever."

"You're sure?" Her attention flicks between the gym and me.

"Of course. Here. The music room is next door."

We leave the gym and step through the next doorway into my

favorite room in the house. Four guitars rest on stands, and amps are scattered around the room. A high-tech keyboard sits waiting, practically unused since I bought it with the hope that it would help Noah write. Spoiler alert—it didn't.

"What's that?" She points to the corner of the room where a sheet covers another unused piece of equipment—a baby grand.

I pull back the sheet, and the glossy black surface reflects the lights in the room.

"This is—this is—" Joy is written clearly on her face as she struggles to find words.

"Paradise?" I offer.

She nods and makes a happy hum.

"Do you play?" Stupid question, given her reaction. But I want to keep that wondrous expression lighting up her eyes.

The look I give Jessie is meant to be fleeting. Instead, my eyes lock with hers, and I can't look away. My breathing speeds up and my heart races. I'm high on the smell of vanilla that surrounds her.

She parts her lips on an intake of breath, my attention zeroing in on the blush-colored flesh. What does she taste like? The need to find out claws at my gut, but I push it back down.

"Ten years of piano. Jax is the guitarist in the family."

"If you're half as good on the piano as your brother is with his guitar, you're very talented."

"I get by. Nothing like him. But enough to help me with my job."

She moves toward the keyboard and presses the power button, lights flashing on with an electric hum. I sit on the couch and lean forward with my arms resting on my knees, unable to pull my attention away from the look of pure delight on her face. She slides her fingers over the keys, pulling a song from the notes. Little feet race toward us, joining the melody, before Gage dashes through the doorway, stopping next to Jessie.

"Did you find a book?" she asks, not missing a note.

He nods proudly.

"Awesome. So we'll have something to read tonight."

His attention locks on her fingers until he lifts his hands to rest them lightly on top of hers. He's never done that before. But while I can play the piano, I prefer bass or guitar.

"Did his—" She stops and nods her head toward Gage. "Did she play the piano?"

My cheeks heat in embarrassment as I squeeze the back of my neck. "I, um, I'm not sure. We never talked about it."

We didn't talk much at all.

"I think she must have." She continues playing, Gage's fingers still set on top of hers.

"He looks so happy." How did I not know this?

"Has he shown any interest in this room?"

I shrug. "He's in here a lot when I am. And he'll stare at the piano…"

Now it makes sense.

"I wonder if she did this with him."

"Me too. I never thought about it before." Why the fuck hadn't I?

Gage is my son. My responsibility. If I don't figure this out, I'm letting him down.

"I want to try a few things with Gage. Are we okay to use this room too?"

"Of course. Anything you want."

Anything to help my son.

"Awesome. Gage, would you want to spend some time in here with me tomorrow?"

The smile on his face is pure happiness.

Could this be the key to unlocking his voice?

🎸 🎸 🎸

Three and a half songs. That's how many I've written since

Gage went to sleep an hour ago. And that was after I gave him a bath, helped him brush his teeth, and read three stories. But at this point, the notes are blurring, and my bed is calling me.

"Oof." Standing, I stretch, trying to work out the kink in my lower back, but grimace when it only tightens.

Time for some ibuprofen then. Twenty years ago, I could sit over songs all day and not feel it. I've only been sitting for an hour, but I'm not sixteen anymore, and my body doesn't let me forget it.

I check on Gage, barely visible under a mountain of stuffed animals in the shadows from his nightlight. Satisfied that he's sleeping peacefully, I turn back out of the room and head for the stairs to grab a glass of water and ibuprofen. I ignore the shaft of light under Jessie's door. Because that way lies madness.

My self-congratulations on avoiding the insanity of thinking of Jessie disappears when I step into the kitchen and find her staring out the window into the darkness. The only lights shine from below the surface of the pool.

Her ponytail is gone, her long dark hair fanning down her back and begging to be wrapped in my hands. Which is fucking inconvenient. Wanting her with an intensity I don't remember having with anyone else doesn't mean it's going to happen. It can't.

Too much is at stake.

She's too young.

Off limits.

"Hi." I shake my head to clear my thoughts and force my feet to move to the cupboard where the ibuprofen sits.

She spins to face me, her fingers wrapped around the handle of a mug.

"Hi." The heat of her gaze warms the spot between my shoulder blades as I shake a few pills into my hand. "Everything okay?"

"My back. Don't get old. It fucking sucks." I try to joke, but it's another reminder.

I'm thirteen fucking years older than her.

"People tell me I'm an old soul," she admits.

I study her for several moments before I nod. "I can see that."

Still doesn't make my attraction to her convenient.

Fuck. I should turn around and go to bed. I'm too tired after the day—make that several years. The enjoyment of being a rock star has morphed to a fear of fame killing one of my best friends.

"You've got the weight of the world on your shoulders, don't you?"

"Sorry?"

My attention drops to where she's got her lip captured between her teeth, like she wished she hadn't said anything. She lifts the drink to her mouth without answering.

"What did you say?" I ask again.

"Forget it."

"Please?"

She blows out a breath and takes another drink from her mug.

"Your sigh"—she says again. I wasn't even aware I *had* sighed —"just sounds like you have a lot on your mind."

I shrug. It's always been this way. Me shouldering the responsibility of the band. And now Gage has been added to the mix.

"You could say that."

"My mom always says there are two things that can help during times like these—hot chocolate and a listening ear." The corner of her lips kicks up.

I want to know about the memory that created that smile. "Does it work?"

"Eh. Fifty-fifty."

"Is that what you're drinking? Hot chocolate?"

She nods. "It's been a busy couple of days. And while my

73

thesis needs more work, my brain is too tired. So I'm going to try to relax and let this"—she lifts her cup—"do its magic."

I could use a little magic in my life.

"Where'd you find the mix?" I didn't know I had any. Must be something Lois bought for Gage.

"Mix?" She wrinkles her nose. "No, no, no. No mix. Only homemade. On the stove."

"Homemade? I don't think I've had anything but hot cocoa powder since I was eight years old."

"It's the only way to drink it." She grabs another mug and fills it, pouring steaming cocoa from a pan on the stove before handing it to me. "Here."

The first sip is rich chocolate with hints of vanilla, or maybe it's her scent that wraps around me to ease some of the tension from my shoulders.

"I should probably go check on Gage." She puts her cup on the counter.

"I checked on him. He's passed out. I don't think he's slept that soundly since he got here."

"A normal routine often helps. Kids want boundaries."

"So do band members," I mutter into my cup, thinking about Noah. He couldn't set the boundaries for himself. Instead, he's relying on me to set them for him.

"What?"

"Sorry, guess I'm feeling a little more ragged than I thought."

"You've had Gage about a month?" She leans against the counter and studies me.

"Yeah."

"It must be a pretty big adjustment to go from no responsibilities to this."

I bristle at her words. "I had responsibilities before."

"But not another person relying on you to take care of him." She shrugs like she understands my life. It's not the first assumption she's made, and I don't like it.

"The band relies on me. Especially Noah. It's my responsibility to help him."

"Help him with what?" she asks.

I don't respond. I can't talk to her about this.

She clears her throat. "It's getting bad again, isn't it?"

"I thought you said you weren't a fan." I try to joke, but my tone comes off more accusatory.

Had she said that? I don't know if she's ever heard anything we've done. She's so young.

"Whatever. Even if I didn't like your music, there are always stories about him. About the drugs."

Fuck.

"I hate those stories. They make him out to be nothing more than a nasty drug addict. Do you know he single-handedly wrote most of the songs from *On Our Own*?"

He'd been the creative force that catapulted us from garage band to more. The first single on that album, "Lost Joys," was the song that sealed the deal for us.

"I know better than to believe everything I read in those stories. Jax has had his share of bad press."

I forget that she's Jax Bryant's sister. That she understands more about this lifestyle than I give her credit for.

"He's drowning." I lean against the counter and drain the rest of the cup. If only the answer for how to help him was waiting for me at the bottom. "He's my brother, you know? Maybe not by blood, but we've put twenty years of sweat and soul into this band."

Her eyes fill with sympathy. "Is he going to get help?"

"Fuck, I hope so. That's why everyone was here when you showed up. Finn, Milo, and Noah were at Club Panic last night. After we had all promised to not go there again."

The club's name brings a bitter taste to my mouth.

"Club Panic? Isn't that the place where…"

The stories she's probably seen or heard about us at the club through the years fill the silence.

"Yeah. Where Noah was photographed doing lines."

"And Milo got caught—"

"Fucking some wannabe pop princess in one of the booths? Two for two."

"Oh." So much judgment exists in those two letters.

"It wasn't always a bad place, but it changed. And I thought everyone was on the same page when we said we wouldn't go there again."

"Except for—"

"Last night. But maybe it's a good thing they ended up there. For the first time in a long time, I saw the real Noah today. And he says he wants help."

"So rehab? Again?"

I nod. "Only he says he wants to try something closer. Not something where he has to stay."

She sinks her teeth into her lip again, her face twisting in an unreadable way.

"What? What's with the face?"

"Nothing."

"It's not nothing. Not with a face like that. You don't seem like you're too shy to share your thoughts."

"Do you know the odds of overcoming addiction if you don't change anything else around you?"

I shake my head.

"It doesn't work. If he needs help, he needs to get serious help."

"Don't you think I realize that?" I cross my arms over my chest.

"Does he?" Her voice is soft. "I'm sorry. It's none of my business."

"No, I'm sorry. I shouldn't have snapped like that. I just...I don't want to bury my brother, and I'm terrified I'm going to have to do that."

I close my eyes against the sharp slice of pain that cuts through my chest at the thought. A gentle hand rests against my arm, and my eyes fly open to find her right in front of me.

"Tell him that."

The warmth of her palm against my skin is a comfort I didn't realize I needed. I want to pull her into my arms and capture her light, her softness, one kiss at a time. To see if it's as hot as I imagine. If it will burn us both into nothing, or if we'll create a phoenix in the embers. I use my other hand to cup her elbow, and it isn't until she clears her throat and pulls away that I re-engage the logical portion of my brain.

"I'm going to head to bed." Her words build all sorts of images that don't make it easier to fight her pull. Her, in my bed, her dark hair spread over the pillows, her fair skin a stark contrast.

But she's not mine. If she's the light, I'm the darkness. And she doesn't need to be corrupted by a devil like me.

CHAPTER 7

JESSIE

*B*y the end of the second week, I have a solid routine set up for both Gage and me. I wake up early, hit the gym for a quick workout, and am showered and dressed before Gage wakes up. Once he's up, we eat breakfast. Then he gets dressed, and we head to the music room if Chris isn't in there. But he's given up using the room so that Gage and I can, choosing instead to work at the studio or Evan's house.

Probably a good thing. Not one of those band members could be classified as anything except smoking hot, and I don't need the distraction. But I didn't experience tingles with any of them.

Except Chris.

Day after day, I ignore those tingles and remind myself of why I'm here.

Gage.

"I've tried all sorts of music," I tell Syd over the phone, happy that she's come up for air and can have conversations that don't revolve around nano bytes or html or whatever it is she does.

"Is he a JOY fan?" she jokes

I roll my eyes with a huff. "He likes all of it. But if he knows any of them, he's not letting on. Usually, he just rests his hands on mine while I play the keyboard and sing."

He is making progress, though. His smiles are quicker and brighter these days.

"Aww."

"And did I tell you about the baby grand in the music room?" I've thought about playing it, but I like the flexibility the keyboard provides.

"Only one or two million times."

"I really want to try it."

"So why don't you?"

"I don't know. I don't have the time." It's an excuse, but a plausible one.

"I call bullshit. You do to have time. Right now, for example."

"It's eleven o'clock at night," I remind her. Given Sydney's job, this wouldn't be the last time she lost track of whether it was day or night.

"So?"

"Syd."

"What's the real reason?"

"I don't know."

"Uh-huh."

"I don't!" I argue.

"It has nothing to do with you being too comfortable if you decide to play the masterpiece?"

"I–" She's right.

So long as I leave it hidden under the sheet, it's another boundary, one I need.

"I don't want to talk about it," I say.

"Your secret is safe with me, babe. How's the whole living with a rock star thing going?"

"I'm not living with a rock star. I'm a nanny for Gage."

"Potato, potahto."

I ignore her retort. "This is the easiest job ever, Syd. He's such a sweet kid. Even when I had to reintroduce a bedtime routine after a month without one."

The first few nights had been the hardest. Bath, story, and lying down with mountains of stuffed animals didn't stop him from getting up several times before he finally fell asleep. Now, he knows exactly what to do. He's tackling this new life head on. And I wish I had even a little of the resilience he possesses.

"And you're telling me the only thing you do after he falls asleep is work on your thesis?"

"Yes. Except for tonight because you called."

"I miss you."

"We can still hang out. I get days off, you know."

The yawn on her end of the phone has me doing the same.

"Sawyer needs me on one more job, and then I'm asking for a vacation."

"You deserve it."

"Okay, lady, I'm going to try to grab a couple of hours. Talk soon? Let's plan a night out."

"'Kay. Night."

We hang up, and my stomach growls as I stand from my spot on the floor.

Dinner was earlier than normal today since we were both starving after spending all afternoon in the pool. Little man swims like a fish, and we played and splashed until we were both wrinkled and exhausted.

Food first. Then bed.

The house is quiet when I step out of my room. Chris left for studio time with the band and then texted around six to tell me not to expect him for dinner. Probably a good thing since Gage and I had eaten two hours earlier.

Chris was still gone when Gage went to bed. And for the first time in almost a week and a half, bedtime was a bit of a challenge. I'll mention it to Chris—Gage needs the stability of his one parent right now. Meaning Chris needs to be present at bedtime. I won't always be here to keep them on track.

All the lights are off on the main level when I make my way downstairs, except for the light above the stove I left on earlier. I open the first cupboard, looking for cereal, and movement catches my attention from my periphery. Heart racing, I'm poised to scream when Chris steps out of the shadows, arms lifted.

"Sorry, only me."

"Holy shit, you scared the crap out of me." I lift a hand to my heart and hope the pressure will slow it back down.

Being startled isn't the only reason it's racing right now, though. He's wearing athletic shorts and a muscle tank—an unusual look for a rock star. But not one I'm mad about. The dim lighting in the kitchen gives me cover while I ogle the definition of his arms.

And suddenly I remember that I'm only in a sleep tank and shorts with no bra.

"What are you doing here?" I ask.

"I live here." His smirk is all bad-boy rocker.

How many women fall at his feet from that look alone?

Shaking my head, I attempt to dispel the question, but it lingers a little too long. "I meant in the dark kitchen at almost midnight."

"It is?" He cranes his neck to the clock on the stove.

11:15.

Not close to midnight, but close enough.

"I didn't realize it was so late."

"You forgot bedtime." I grab the box of cereal out of the open cabinet and a bowl from another. "Gage missed you."

"Fuck." He tugs a hand through his hair. "We were on a roll. By the time we stopped, it was ten."

The nonchalance in his voice pisses me off. He has a kid now. One who needs him.

"What?" he asks, studying me.

"I didn't say anything." The cereal tings into the bowl in the silence between us.

"No, but you have a look."

"What look?" I ask, attention fixed on my cereal bowl.

"You seem—" he searches for the right word. "Disappointed."

I'm not good at filters. Or biting my tongue.

"You need to be here for bedtime. It's important."

"I was busy."

The heat of my temper builds. How dare he brush this off? I take several deep breaths, inhaling the spicy scent of his cologne mixed with something more.

"You smell like a dispensary."

He sniffs his clothes. "I don't smell anything."

I stalk past him for the milk, giving myself a moment, and wait until I'm done pouring it over my cereal to say anything else.

"Gage needs his dad." I slam the carton down on the counter harder than I intend.

"He has me." He furrows his brow, a questioning look in his eyes. He's confused, and why wouldn't he be, considering he's only been a parent for two months?

"He needs you *here*. He needs you at bedtime and playtime. At homework time. And every time in between."

"I-I can't…"

"You have to. If you want him to work through everything that's happened, you need to be here to help him."

"He has you."

I nod. "Yes, he does. But he needs you too. I'm not going to be around forever. Once I graduate…"

The thought of leaving Gage creates a well of sadness deep inside me. In only two weeks, he's woven his way into my heart.

"I know. Your job." His words leave him on a sigh.

"You knew about it before I started," I remind him and take my midnight snack to the table.

He doesn't say anything as he fills his own bowl and joins me.

"I didn't take you for a Cocoa Puffs person." I lift my full spoon to my lips and crunch through the cereal, letting the chocolate flavor burst on my tongue.

"I'm not sure if I should take that as a compliment or not." He studies me warily.

I shrug. "I'm not sure. It's more a statement about the fact that I don't know much about you."

His smirk does funny things to my stomach. And the Cocoa Puffs somersault.

"I find that hard to believe."

"No, really. Sure, some things I know because of what the press has said, but who are you when you're not *Topher Rivers*, bassist and front man for Just One Yesterday?"

He's quiet for a moment.

"I don't know if anyone's ever asked me that."

I snort. "Yeah, I'm unique that way." Self-deprecation colors my tone.

"You are." Even in the darkness, he pins me with so much intensity, my palm goes clammy around the spoon. "How's your paper coming?"

"Paper? You mean my thesis?"

He nods.

"It's going. I wanted to ask you if you would mind if I used Gage as an example."

"Gage?"

"Not by name, of course. But a little bit of a case study."

His face twists. "I'm, uh, I'm not sure. Can I think about it?"

Disappointment pricks, as irrational as it is. Of course he would need to think about it.

"Sure."

Please let him say yes.

"Can I ask you a question?" He takes another bite, but his attention stays locked on me.

"I guess…"

"Why music therapy?"

"That's a long story."

"I'm okay with that." His smile barely curves his lips, but his unwavering focus creates a warmth in my stomach that moves through my extremities.

"People—adults, kids, whoever—need an outlet. Kids especially, because by the time we reach adulthood, we've learned skills for coping with the things that happen to us. But kids don't have that. If they're scared or upset or angry, they don't always have the ability to work through those feelings."

My words come out in a rush, fueled by lingering emotions from a childhood that *should* have been idyllic. Fueled by every memory of sitting in a hospital bed or chemo chair to wait for treatments that made me sicker before they helped me get better.

His hand stops midair, hovering between his bowl and his mouth.

"You sound like you speak from experience."

"You could say that."

"What would you say?" He turns the question around on me.

I fidget under his steady gaze. "I am. I do. I struggled with so much of what was going on around me. I didn't want to tell my mom and dad everything because they were already dealing with so much. And it was my fault."

"Your fault?" He narrows his eyes.

"I was diagnosed with acute lymphoblastic leukemia when I was five. Cancer."

The color drains from his face. Even in the darkness of the kitchen, it's clear.

"Cancer?"

I nod. "Yep."

"You were five?"

"A little older than Gage." I swallow around the lump of emotion in my throat. "For a year, my parents shuttled me from doctor to doctor. I was poked and prodded before being filled with medicine that made me sick and made my hair fall out. But I was brave on the outside because my parents needed me to be."

"They told you that?" Disgust colors his tone.

"No. I think it would hurt them if they knew how I felt back then. That I still remember." Which is why I will never tell them. Or Jax. "It was what I told myself. Be brave so Mama doesn't cry. Don't tell anyone you're scared. They're scared too, and they don't know how to respond. So I held it all in."

"Jesus, Jess." He reaches across the table and covers my hand with his.

"But when Jax was around, he'd play his guitar or sing to me. Did you know he's ten years older than I am?"

Chris shakes his head.

"He...saved me. The music soothed me, helped me handle all those emotions. Even if it was only for little snatches of time."

He rubs a calloused thumb across my knuckles, and I attempt to ignore the goosebumps that shiver down my spine.

"You want to be that person for other kids. Like Gage." His words are quiet but spot on.

"Exactly." My voice cracks over the word.

Tears line my lashes and overflow. He drags his other hand softly against my cheek to capture the errant moisture, but he doesn't move his hand back right away.

"You're amazing," he whispers, awestruck.

"I'm not. I'm just me."

"You're a cancer survivor who wants to help kids. How is that not amazing?"

I shrug. "Other people do the same thing every day. I'm not the first cancer survivor to want to do something with my life to help others."

"Jess."

Huh?"

"Take the compliment. Say thank you."

I inhale deeply and release it. "Thank you."

He quirks a half smile, drawing my attention to his mouth. It's not fair for his lips to look so soft, so inviting.

No. Not inviting. Stop it.

"Was that so hard?"

"Yes."

He laughs, leaning until his forehead meets mine. Did I lean closer too?

"Maybe I should compliment you more often so you get used to accepting them."

Awkwardness fills me at the idea.

"Umm...let's not."

"Hmm...maybe I can help you like you're helping Gage."

"I love working with him. I don't need anything in return."

He ignores me and stands, pulling me down the hallway with him until we're in the dark bathroom.

I groan and squeeze my eyes shut as the bright lights flash on.

"Open your eyes." His demand is a whisper behind me while his hands settle on my shoulders.

I blink several times until the image in the mirror comes into focus. His hands are dark against my pale skin. My nipples press against the cotton of my tank, and I fight the urge to fold my arms over my chest to hide the evidence of my braless state.

When I lift my gaze, his eyes are trained on my chest while his tongue slicks over his lips.

"Now what?" My voice is husky with need.

He clears his throat, his eyes lifting to meet mine in the mirror.

"Some affirmations."

I roll my eyes. "I'm not some new-age obsessed person. This is dumb."

"Have you ever tried it?" he asks, arching one perfect eyebrow.

"Have you?" I counter.

"Yes." His answer surprises me.

"Well, I haven't."

"So how do you know it's dumb?" He leans forward, and his breath rustles my hair.

I can't control or hide the shiver that works its way through my body at how close he is.

"I'm going to let you in on a secret."

"A secret?"

"Mmm. I've used this practice for years. First, I focused on wanting the band to be successful, then building on that fame. Now I tell my reflection how much I want to be a good dad."

"You are a good dad." I spin around to face him. I want him to see my sincerity.

He grips my shoulders tighter. "You're beautiful."

"No, I'm—"

"Really bad at accepting compliments," he interrupts and turns me back to my reflection. "Repeat after me."

The protest dies on my lips at the serious expression on his face. "O-okay."

He doesn't say anything but takes a few deep breaths as he keeps us both pointing at the mirror. My breathing slows to match his, and his hands relax on my shoulders, even though the charge in the air around us only grows.

"I am beautiful."

"I am...this is weird. Why am I saying this to myself?"

"Trust me. I am beautiful."

Trust is so easy to talk about and such a hard concept to master. I roll my eyes but repeat after him.

"I am beautiful."

His lips quirk in an encouraging smile that inspires a little grin from me as well.

"I have an amazing heart."

"I...have...an amazing heart." I stumble over the words but manage to get them out on the first try, and he rewards me with a bigger smile than the last.

"I am enough."

The words lock in my throat. I swallow and spin away from a reflection that reveals too much.

"I am enough," he repeats as he catches my attention, locking his gaze with mine.

I shake my head and close my eyes. I've never felt like enough. More often than not, I've felt like a burden to my family or someone to be used by my ex.

"Jess. Look at me."

"I can't." My words are barely a whisper.

"You can." Amusement is clear in his tone. "Open your eyes."

He doesn't say anything else, but he kneads my shoulders, those big hands warm and strong and gentle, until finally, slowly, I open my eyes, his face all I see.

"Good job. Now repeat after me. I am enough."

"I…" My attention shifts from his lips to his eyes. The determined furrow of his brow tells me I'm not going to get out of repeating this one.

"Keep going."

"Am."

"You are what?"

I lick my lips, and the second I do, his pupils dilate. I squeeze my thighs together as my body responds to his nearness, to his reactions.

"E-e-enough."

"All together." He lowers his voice and moves closer. "I am enough."

I look down, but he uses a thumb under my chin to tilt my head up so I'm forced to look into his hypnotic eyes.

"I am enough." The words a breath as they escape my lips.

"Jess." My name from his mouth is a vibration against my lips.

"Hmm?" My eyelids grow heavy, fluttering shut with the need to close the distance and cover his lips with mine.

"I want to…I want…to say good night."

He pulls his hands from my shoulders as he retreats, and the cool air that rushes into the empty space has my eyes shooting open.

Oh my god, here I was thinking he wanted me. That he felt this intense connection between us too. Embarrassment crawls through my body, and I hug my arms to my chest to hide just how much I wanted *him* to kiss me.

I'm an idiot.

"Oh, um, good night."

I don't wait for a response. I dart through the doorway and up the stairs, not slowing until I lean against the back of my bedroom door.

"What in the hell was that?"

If I use my racing heart and damp panties as an answer, that was a lot of trouble.

I need to stay away from late-night conversations and bathroom affirmations.

CHAPTER 8

CHRIS

I drag several lungfuls of air into my body, fighting the urge to follow Jessie and finish what I started.

I was supposed to work with the guys on the new album, be done by dinnertime, and maybe watch a movie with Jessie and Gage. Jessie installed something called Disney+ on my TV, and she and Gage were slowly making their way through movies I vaguely recalled from my childhood. The few times I joined them, I spent more time watching Gage snuggle against Jessie than I did following along with what was happening on-screen.

But tonight I came home tired and hungry, looking for a quick bite before bed so I could catch up on some much-needed R&R. I'd barely walked through the door from the garage when Jessie had walked through the opposite door, completely unaware of my presence.

Meanwhile, I was so aware of hers that I couldn't smell her perfume without my dick reacting. I stayed quiet, staring. At the way her shorts barely covered her ass. At the sway of her breasts under the thin cotton of her tank top. I was mesmerized, but it was like I didn't exist to her.

Even when I was right in front of her, she focused on Gage.

How much she concentrated on my son, how much love she showed him, was the biggest turn on of all. Thank fuck I remembered that before I fucked it all up by kissing her.

It would have been too easy to close those last few inches. To claim her lips the way my body begged me to.

"Off limits," I tell my reflection before flipping off the light.

I climb the stairs slowly, feeling every minute of my thirty-six years. Twenty years ago, a session like today's wouldn't have left me exhausted. It was amazing—it had been years since we played like that. Things were turning around for us. We'd spent the last few years fending off unwanted attention from Cornerstone. Unreasonable demands for more music, followed by threats of rock and roll obscurity if we didn't produce. It was a fucking nightmare. But tonight, the music felt different. It felt like it used to.

I poke my head into Gage's room, just making out his small form huddled under his blankets next to a pile of stuffed animals while a white noise machine plays. I wouldn't have thought about something like that. But Jessie did. She had said it might help him stay in bed.

And she was right.

She always is. Which is why guilt still gnaws at me after her lecture about missing bedtime tonight.

Never again.

Not wanting to wake my sleeping son, I tiptoe out of his room. And I definitely don't search for a sliver of light under Jessie's door. It's how I've played the last two weeks—deny, deny, deny.

"Fuck." I'm not sure whether to be disappointed or relieved that her light is off.

Relieved.

I don't need to fight for control over my body.

With a sigh, I head into my bedroom and close the door.

You smell like a dispensary.

92

I lift my t-shirt to my nose, the faint traces of pot finally registering. Shit. I didn't smoke, but Milo and Finn lit up inside the control room, and I didn't bother telling them to leave. Shrugging out of my shirt, I tug it off and toss it toward the hamper on my way to the bathroom.

The lights are too bright when I flip them on, and I blink as I kick off my shoes and shorts. Finding the right setting on the shower, I let the water warm up. Without the confines of my clothes, my cock juts forward, hard and demanding, pissed that I denied his demand to lay claim to Jessie earlier.

Maybe you need to get laid.

I snort. "Fuck that."

My voice echoes in the quiet bathroom. The last consistent fuck buddy I had was Melanie. And I don't want to hook up with a random woman. Not with Jessie here.

Fuck.

We're nothing to each other. Boss and employee only. I need to think in terms of Gage. He should be the reason I don't hook up with a random stranger.

When steam billows from inside the shower, I step under the spray, hissing as the hot water hits my skin. With another adjustment of the knobs, the hot needles soothe to a warm massage. Grabbing my shampoo, I lather and rinse. Images flash behind my eyes of Jessie and I looking at our reflection downstairs. The bright lights had showcased her tits, and my hands still tingled with the need to slide down her shoulders and cup the globes in my palms, to find the hardened tips with my fingers.

"Oh, fuck. Think about something else. *Anything* else."

I drag the loofah down my chest and stomach, sucking in a breath when the rough material brushes against my sensitive dick. Despite my wishes, it shows no signs of deflating anytime soon.

"Screw this." I drop the loofah and fist my cock, sliding the soap bubbles back and forth as I twist at the end of my stroke.

Another image takes shape. One that continues to torture me.

I came home earlier that day and followed the sounds of Jessie's laughter and splashing to the pool. Gage didn't have any floaties on, and it took several painful moments for my heart to restart—he can swim as well as I can.

Jessie's squeal as Gage soaked her with a massive wave had pulled my attention to her, and I couldn't look away as she climbed out of the pool. The bikini was royal purple, the halter-style string top barely covering her breasts as water had run in waves down her toned stomach to be soaked up by the scrap of purple fabric tied at her hips. Lust had me choking on my own breath, and I couldn't get to my room fast enough to rub one out.

Just like I'm doing now.

"Fuck. Get a grip, you fucking pervert." I grit my teeth and drop my dick.

It protests the interruption, and I bite back a shout as I flip the water to cold.

"Stop fucking thinking of your son's nanny while you jack off. Imagining it won't lessen your attraction to her. It hasn't worked yet. When you were eighteen, she was five."

Battling cancer. Fuck. Fuck. Fuck. Thoroughly disgusted with myself, I crank off the water.

My phone rings on the bathroom counter when I step out and wrap a towel around my waist.

Evan.

"Hey, Ev."

Maybe I should talk to him about what the fuck I should do. Or get off the phone and go the fuck to sleep.

"Chris." The panic in his voice has adrenaline coursing through my blood. "We need you."

"What is it? What's wrong?" I left the guys less than two hours ago.

My heart jackhammers against my chest.

"Noah—" It's all he says before he takes a deep breath.

Oh fuck.

"What happened?" I drop the towel and rush for my dresser, tossing on boxers and a pair of jeans. I've got my phone propped between my ear and my shoulder while I heave deep breaths in and out, waiting for the inevitable.

"He—he—he OD'd."

No.

No, no, no, no, no. Not possible. He was getting back to his old self again. No.

Tears distort my vision and burn in my nose as I draw in another breath.

Noah, the goofy sixteen-year-old who wore graphic tees with classical composers on them. The one who wrote "Lost Joys" after his high school girlfriend dumped him the night before junior prom. It was the song that got us noticed, our first number one.

I practically collapse on my bed as overwhelming sadness swamps me. Nostalgia, regret, guilt—all those emotions form a ball of grief so heavy it practically suffocates me.

"Is he...?" I can't bring myself to say the word. I can't even think it.

"The ambulance is taking him to Bayview General."

The relief is so crippling I burst into tears.

"What happened? No. Strike that. I'm on my way. Are you guys okay?"

"Finn and Milo called me. They're freaking out. I'm picking them up now." Something in his voice pebbles goosebumps along my skin.

"Picking them up from where?" I want to be wrong. Please God, let me be wrong.

"Club Panic."

Fuck.

"I'll see you guys at the hospital."

🎸 🎸 🎸

By the time I told Jessie I had an emergency and needed to leave, Evan had texted an update. The guys were at the hospital, along with Noah's mom.

"Ev."

He looks up from talking to Mrs. Kelley.

"Chris."

I've got him wrapped in a hug the second he's on his feet.

Milo and Finn are huddled in the chairs along the wall and grip coffee cups like their hold on the Styrofoam is the only thing keeping Noah alive.

Mrs. Kelley looks at me with red-rimmed eyes. The gray in her hair is more pronounced, and the wrinkles around her eyes are deeper than when I saw her last.

I have no idea what happened with Mr. Kelley—he was long gone before we even met Noah. But Mrs. Kelley was one of the moms who always watched out for us. She hounded us about studying and doing homework and taking showers. All the things teenage boys try to avoid.

"Mrs. Kelley."

"Chris." She stands and closes the distance between us, pulling me into a familiar embrace that smells like fresh banana bread. It makes the lump in my throat bigger.

"Ms. Kelley?"

A doctor stands in the doorway, scanning the few of us in the room. She tenses, and I keep my hands on her arms, lending her a strength I don't have but have no choice but to provide.

"Yes?" The tremor in her voice makes my swallow painful.

I wish we were anywhere but here.

"Ma'am, would you come with me?"

Her knees buckle, and I hold her up, wrapping an arm around her waist.

"Doctor…" I start, no idea who I'm even talking to. He's in scrubs, but I don't know if that means anything.

"Vasquez."

"Dr. Vasquez, can you tell us what's going on?"

He looks at Mrs. Kelley, who nods and sinks back into her chair.

With a sigh, he shoves the glasses up his nose.

"Mr. Kelley was brought in unconscious, experiencing respiratory distress and a low heart rate. He was unresponsive when paramedics arrived at the scene and only regained consciousness after being treated with Narcan while en route to the hospital."

"What does that mean?" Evan asks.

"We're still waiting on test results, but I believe Mr. Kelley suffered an opioid overdose—"

"He doesn't take opioids." Milo steps forward. "Just cocaine."

The doctor grimaces at Milo's overshare and clears his throat.

"Be that as it may, Mr. Kelley didn't present with any symptoms of a cocaine overdose, although we've ordered a full drug panel so we can have a clear picture of what we're looking at. Does Mr. Kelley have issues with substance abuse?"

I nod. "He's been to treatment facilities multiple times, but as soon as he's out, he finds drugs again."

"Is he going to be okay?" Finn asks, his expression full of guilt.

What the hell happened tonight?

"We've stabilized him. He's awake but disoriented."

"Can we see him?" I ask.

"At this time, only family is allowed."

We're his brothers, asshole.

But not in the way that matters to him.

"Why don't you go see him and let him know we're here?" I say to Mrs. Kelley.

She glances at me, relief evident in the way her shoulders have loosened. "I will."

She follows the doctor behind the door, and I turn to the

three other men, whose faces probably mirror my own—they all wear expressions of relief mixed with concern. I nod my head toward the back corner of the room.

"Do you two want to tell us what the fuck happened?" I ask once we have what little privacy the corner offers.

"We told Evan already." Milo crosses his arms.

"What's the real story?" Because whatever bullshit they fed Evan isn't the truth. And we all know it.

"We did."

"God dammit, Milo. One of our best friends is laying in a fucking hospital bed. He could be dead. Tell us what the fuck happened." Evan advances on Milo, pinning him in the corner, and I glance around, hoping we haven't attracted any unwanted attention.

So far, we've kept this out of the news, but our luck won't last forever.

"Fine." Finn steps between Milo and Evan. "We'll tell you."

"Finn—"

Finn glares at Milo. "They need to fucking know."

"Start talking." I lock eyes with Milo and then Finn, already tired of their bullshit.

"We were fucking stoked after tonight's session. It felt like old times. We were jazzed, so we decided to grab a beer or something."

"Or something." Evan rolls his eyes at Finn's naïve optimism.

"Taking an addict to a club is a bad idea." I shouldn't need to tell them that, but maybe Evan and I have shielded them from Noah's problems too much.

"How the fuck did you end up at Club Panic?" Evan's attention bounces between Milo and Finn.

"Especially after we promised we weren't going there *again*," I add.

"We checked out a few other clubs first"—of course they fucking did—"but they didn't have the vibe we were looking for."

"What 'vibe' were you looking for?" I glance around again after the question explodes at a louder volume than I planned.

"Don't you remember the music at Panic? The way we could enjoy a beer without being mobbed?"

The urge to smack the shit out of Milo has me curling my fingers into a fist.

"That was years ago. What I remember is you getting caught with your pants down in one of the booths. Finn almost getting shot. Noah facedown on a goddamned mirror. You fucking know that club has changed, and not for the better. Is that where Noah got the drugs?"

Finn shrugs. "He said he was going to the bathroom."

"And you two geniuses let him go...alone." Evan snaps. He's pissed, rightfully so, and these two need to check their IQs.

"He wasn't gone that long. Five minutes, maybe?" Milo looks at Finn, who nods.

"But he seemed off. Zoned out. He couldn't focus on the conversation anymore."

"Then what happened?" I ask.

"One second he was joking around with us, and then he stopped and stared at me and...and..." Finn shudders at the memory.

"He passed out and hit his head on the table. We called 911 and then Evan when you didn't answer your phone," Milo tells me. They must have tried calling when I was in the shower.

"Press?" I ask.

"No, they were too busy with a pop princess who was flashing her goodies on the dance floor...again." Milo grins lasciviously.

But now is not the time to relive his exploits at the club.

"I don't want to know." Fuck. I'm more exhausted than I've felt in a long time.

"Me neither." Evan looks just as wiped as I feel.

"Anybody want a fresh coffee?" I ask.

We sit with our coffees, watching the minutes pass by on an

old clock on the dingy white wall. I doze a little in the chair, waking fully when a warm hand lands on my shoulder.

"Chris."

When I open my eyes, Mrs. Kelley is leaning over me.

"Mrs. Kelley, fu—I'm sorry. I fell asleep. How's Noah?"

"He's sleeping now. They're keeping him down here until they assign him a room."

Milo and Finn are passed out along the wall, while Evan watches the two of us silently.

"Is he okay?"

What else can I say tonight?

"We didn't really talk about it."

"We can talk tomorrow." I try to reassure her. It's been a rough night. No need to go down this path until the morning.

"He wants to try treatment again." She says the words quietly, like if she speaks any louder, she'll jinx them.

"I hope he does."

And fuck, but I want it to work this time. I don't want to bury one of my best friends.

"You should all head home. Get some real sleep."

"Do you need a ride home?" I ask.

She shakes her head. "I'm staying here with Noah tonight."

"You're sure?" I ask, but I know the answer.

"I'm sure."

"Do you want some company?" I'm beat, but if she needs me, I'll stay.

"No, we're okay, I think. I'm going to try to sleep while Noah does."

"Okay, if you're sure. We'll be here first thing in the morning. Will you call us if anything changes?"

"Of course." Her smile is sad but resigned. "Good night, boys." She waves to the other guys, who are now all awake and listening.

Boys. Like we're still sixteen years old, crashing on Noah's floor. A small smile curves my lips at those bittersweet memories.

"'Night, Mrs. Kelley."

My goodbye is echoed by the rest of the band. She leaves first, stepping back through the door she exited through earlier, and the guys and I make our way to the exit.

The flash of lights is blinding in the darkness, and the sound of voices shouting over one another drowns out everything else.

"Topher, Topher, is Noah Kelley dead?"

"Did he overdose?"

"Is he seeking treatment?"

"What about the rest of the band?"

The questions swim in my head. I want to toss all these vultures aside. Fucking leeches.

"No comment," I growl and move swiftly to my car.

It's the only option I have.

CHAPTER 9

JESSIE

*S*unlight wakes me up, reflecting off the pool like a spotlight centered on my face.

"Ugh."

I slam the pillow over my face, not ready to wake up after a disastrous night of sleep. I alternated between embarrassment at almost kissing my boss and concern about how he'd looked like a ghost when he left the house last night.

Opening my door to him after nearly kissing him in the bathroom was not on the list of things I'd hoped to do last night. I was ready to sleep away the whole disaster and refortify against sexy musicians with affirmations. To forget the curve of his lips so close to mine, the intensity of his eyes as they bolstered me, even as they broke down every wall I'd erected—ever.

That type of connection hit all the right buttons. It was as arousing as it was confusing. First, Chris was my boss. And even if it was temporary, I loved working with Gage. Second, despite being a mostly good dad, Chris was also a rock star.

I'd already learned that lesson

The air under the pillow is growing humid, so I lift it off my face, letting the coolness wake me a little more. When my alarm went off early this morning, I turned it off and rolled over, not ready to face the day.

Don't want to now, either.

But if I don't get up, I won't have time to work out before Gage wakes up.

Groaning, I swing my legs to the side of the bed and dig my toes into the soft carpet. My body is stiff from lack of sleep, so I'll focus more on stretching today than anything too vigorous.

"Right. Like anything I ever do can be considered *vigorous.*"

My idea of crazy is a forty-five-minute ride on the exercise bike in Chris's home gym. It has a built-in screen, and I can choose different terrain images so I can pretend I'm biking through a forest or along a beach somewhere. It's relaxing, even if it's exercise.

I pad to the dresser and grab workout clothes, changing out of my pajamas quickly. I don't bother with shoes since I'm only going to stretch.

I open my door to a silent house. When I peek in on Gage, he's still fast asleep. Is Chris home? Asleep? His bedroom door is firmly shut. Come to think of it, I've never seen it open.

Is he one of those guys with mirrors above his bed? Porn left out in the open? I'm not opposed to people making choices for themselves—hell, my vibrator collection would probably raise some eyebrows—but there must be some reason he keeps it closed.

Snap out of it.

I'm standing in the hallway, partially turned in the direction of my boss's bedroom door, when I *should* be focused on getting my workout in. Pivoting, I head for the workout room, turning into the doorway on autopilot.

Oh.

My.

God.

All the moisture in my mouth evaporates, and all my blood

travels south, pulsing in my core, my panties dampening at the fantasy come to life in front of me. Chris faces away. He's at a machine I've never used before—it's tall with two arms facing outward while a bar stretches across the top. I was curious but never knew its purpose. Until now.

Fueling every fantasy ever. That's what it's for.

Chris is using the bar at the top, the muscles in his shoulders and back rippling and flexing, mesmerizing me. Each movement is easy to see since he isn't wearing a shirt.

Why isn't he wearing a shirt?

If he was, I wouldn't be standing here in a puddle of drool. The way his arms flex as he lowers himself, the way the muscles in his back tighten as he lifts himself up to the bar makes my mouth water.

Twin dimples line his spine above the band of his shorts, and the urge to reach out and trace those small indents is so powerful I have to close my eyes and take a breath to dispel the heat filling my body.

I stand, hypnotized by the lift and dip of his body, until he finally drops to the ground and turns in my direction, startling when he sees me.

"Fuck."

If his back was hypnotizing, I don't have words for the front view. My attention is focused on the defined muscles of his chest. They're covered in ink, and a nipple ring catches the light pouring in from the window.

He rips out one of his ear buds.

"Sorry, didn't mean to surprise you." I can't pull my eyes away from the ring of silver on his chest.

Did the piercing hurt? Is it cool to the touch or warmed by the heat of his body? He rests his hands along his hips, pulling my attention downward to the low-slung shorts that reveal an Adonis belt.

My brain short circuits at the sight. The man is 1,000 percent sexy, toned muscles. A combination of discipline and artistry, by the ink that colors his skin.

"Don't you usually work out earlier?" His tone is clipped.

Is he pissed that I'm here?

"Usually. I didn't sleep well last night though. What time did you get back?"

Did he sleep at all? When I can finally yank my attention away from the masterpiece that is his body, dark circles mar his eyes and exhaustion lines his face.

"I don't have to explain my comings and goings in my own house. I don't answer to you."

Excuse him?

The words are slung at me like weapons. He's never spoken to me this way. I take a deep breath, studying the weary look in his eyes. I'll blame the exhaustion and hold my temper in check.

"I didn't mean it like that. You look tired."

"I didn't sleep."

"Maybe you should get some sleep?" A nap would do wonders for his grouchy-ass attitude.

"I can't."

"Why not?"

"I need to leave again soon." He doesn't offer any other explanation.

"But Gage—"

"I don't have time for this."

Those six words sever the thread I was using to hold back my anger.

"Do you *ever* have time for your son? Or will he be raised by nannies? Am I the first of many to make sure he eats meals and brushes his teeth, does his homework, and goes to bed on time?"

"I—"

I'm not done. Not by a long shot now that he's pushed all my buttons.

"I told you last night that your son needs you in his life. You need to prioritize him over all the other bullshit you *think* is more important. He needs you. Not me. Not someone else. You."

I spin, intent on stalking back out of the room—workout be damned. He grabs my wrist and turns me around to face him again. With a tug, he pulls me to crash against his chest, my hands smoothing along the warm skin. I struggle to hang on to my anger as desire overrides every other emotion.

"I-I'm sorry." The hard planes of his face soften. "I'm tired."

"That's no excuse to speak to me the way you did." I grind the words through clenched teeth.

"You're right." The breath he lets out coasts over my neck and collarbone.

Don't shiver. Don't you dare shiver.

His words should calm my temper, but it still bubbles along, ready to snap at the least provocation. His arms circle my waist, holding me to him, and I keep myself stiff, too irritated to melt against him the way I could have five minutes earlier.

"Jess?"

His thumbs find the sliver of skin between my tank and yoga pants. I want to lean into the contact so desperately. How can someone piss me off one minute and then entice me to rub against him like a cat in the next? The last time that happened was with Bowie. Another moody musician who could crank on the charm as easily as he could spew vitriol. I'm not interested in that roller coaster ride again.

Rock stars are bad news.

I push away from him, and he drops his arms, the separation providing the sanity I need.

"I'm gonna go." I thumb over my shoulder.

"Did you want to work out?"

I ignore the husky tone of his voice and shake my head. I need distance more than I want to work out.

"I'll grab one later." I retreat, relieved when he doesn't close the distance between us.

"Jess."

The look on his face tells me more than his words how sorry he is for how he responded to my concerns. He could be making it all up. His apology could be genuine. But I'm swimming in the confusion of lust, frustration, anger, and exhaustion. I can't deal with this too.

"See you later."

I don't turn around. When I step into the hallway, Gage stands a few feet away, rubbing sleep from his eyes while his hair stands in every direction.

"Morning, buddy." My smile is shaky at best, and I shove all my feelings down so I can focus on Gage.

My job.

He runs in my direction and wraps his arms around my legs in a hug I didn't realize I needed.

"Are you hungry?" I ask and squat to his level.

He nods, and his tummy growls. The grin on his face is all boy.

"I guess so. What should we have for breakfast today? Cereal?"

He shakes his head and steps back.

"Can you tell me what you want?" My question is soft, my tone nonchalant despite the weighty question.

He doesn't need the added pressure to talk, but it doesn't hurt to remind him that he can. He tilts his head and studies me in a way that strongly resembles his dad.

"Gage?"

He opens his mouth, and my heart pounds as I wait to hear his voice for the first time.

Come on. You can do it, bud.

"Good morning, little man." Chris steps into the hallway, and my shoulders tense. Gage's mouth snaps shut, and he waves at his dad.

Damn it.

So close.

"What's for breakfast today?" Chris asks.

The heat of him wraps around me from behind, and I fight the urge to either step away or toward it.

No reaction is neutral. And that's what I need to be—indifferent. I'm his employee. I'm not his friend. Gage races to his room and comes back clutching a piece of paper that he hands to Chris.

"Pancakes?" Chris chokes the word out. Is there a story about pancakes?

Maybe I should ask.

Gage nods, and his eyes shine with hope.

"Gage—" Chris struggles to find words that, based on his body language, are going to disappoint the little boy, who gazes up at him adoringly.

"You want pancakes?" I don't care if I'm *only* an employee.

Both Rivera men need me to put my own emotions aside.

Gage looks at me and nods excitedly.

"Then let's go make some pancakes." I hold out my hand, and he leaps for it, wiggling like a puppy with a new toy.

Chris's eyes meet mine, and the gratitude in them adds another layer of confusion to the box of emotions I have under lock and key.

"Are you joining us?" I clear the tickle in my throat that makes my voice raspy.

"I-I can't. I'm supposed to meet the guys this morning."

Right. He doesn't know how to choose his son over the band he's been in for twenty years.

"You'll be home on time tonight, right? I have plans."

"With who?"

Words push at my lips. Ones that sound an awful lot like the ones he used on me earlier. Instead, I ignore his question.

"I'll need to leave here by six. We're going to grab dinner and then head for a club."

He blanches at the word. What's that all about?

"Not Club Panic, right?"

"God no." Club Panic is not my scene. Sydney took me there once, not long after we both turned twenty-one, and Jax practically had a coronary when he found out.

I haven't been back, but it has nothing to do with Jax's reaction. He has no right to control me, and neither does Chris. "Not tonight anyway. We usually hit up Aftershock."

Recognition lights his eyes. I remember the way our eyes connected in the dark club. Apparently, he does too.

"See you tonight." I walk toward the stairs with Gage hot on my heels while Chris stares after us.

"Jess, I—"

The rest fades as I move quickly down the stairs. I said all I need to say.

♪♪♪♪♪♪

The universe is a pain in my ass.

Turns out, Syd had a date tonight, so I decide to hang out at my apartment in a pair of pajamas I left there and binge-watch *Bridgerton.*

Give me Anthony Bridgerton over a rock star any day.

The fourth episode of season two ends, and I glance at my phone. I should probably head back. Clicking off the TV, I stretch my legs and touch my toes to the arm of the couch. I should have brought my laptop. Then I could have been more productive and worked on my thesis.

You wouldn't take your laptop to a club.

And that's where Chris thinks I am. Which means I need to change out of my comfy flannel pants and back into the black skinny jeans I left in. Black jeans, black tank that rests above my belly button, and a black leather jacket. Apparently I was in a dark mood when I got dressed tonight. The red heels on my feet and the matching red stain on my lips are the only color I need.

> Hey, boo, wanted to let you know I was here for
> a bit and am heading back to Chris's.

She's on a date, so the three dancing dots that appear right away surprise me.

SYDNEY

> Give me a little advance notice next time and I'll
> cancel my plans. I'd rather hang out with you
> anyway.

I snort a laugh. Sydney and plans are polar opposites.

> I'm sure you're having a good time. Just be safe.

Okay, Mom.

> Text me tomorrow.

K.

I pocket my phone and lock up, anxious to head back to the house, even if it is long past Gage's bedtime. Weird how my apartment has been my actual home for six years, but now it's missing something that I can't put a name to. It's a restlessness that doesn't ebb until I let myself into Chris's house forty-five minutes later.

The house is dark except for the flicker of the television in the family room. I stop in the doorway, and my heart melts into a puddle at my feet. The menu screen plays repeatedly, but Gage and Chris are asleep on the couch. Gage is sprawled lengthwise, arms over his head in abandon as his little chest moves with even breaths. Next to him, Chris is reclined, his feet on the table and his head leaned back against the couch. His hand jerks slightly on the arm of the couch, and his eyes open to find mine in the semi-darkness. .

"Hi." The rasp of his voice is quiet, husky with sleep.

111

His gaze is soft, dark in the dim light, but my core still recognizes the intensity that exists between us.

"Hi. You guys have fun?"

He gives me a half smile in response, and a part of me wishes I had stayed home with them. He stretches his arms above his head, and a line of toned stomach appears between his shirt and jeans.

"We did. I showed Gage my favorite movie from when I was a kid."

"Oh yeah?" I look at the screen again. "*Oliver & Company*?"

"You have something against Oliver?" he teases.

I giggle. "No."

"Didn't think so. Gage didn't even make it through half the movie before he conked out."

"What about you?"

"About the same."

He stands with a groan and leans over to pick up Gage.

"Do you want any help?" I ask.

"Can you grab the lights down here and his blankets upstairs?"

"Sure." Grabbing the remote, I power off the TV, taking several moments to adjust to the lack of light. "Ready?"

"Yep." Chris shifts Gage slightly in his arms, and the little boy snuffles in his sleep.

We freeze, waiting for him to settle again. I can't keep my eyes off the two of them, and the heat of Chris's return stare is enough to spark fireworks in my blood. He nods toward the stairs, and I lead the way, adjusting lights and pulling back the blankets so Chris can lay Gage down.

"Good night, buddy." I pull off his shoes and brush a kiss along his temple while Chris pulls up the blankets.

It isn't until we tiptoe out of the room that I speak again.

"Good night, Chris."

"Jessie. Hold on a second."

I stop, barely daring to breathe in the darkness. Because with that breath comes the smell of his cologne, and with that comes… dangerous thoughts that I have no business thinking.

"Hmm?"

"Did you have a good time tonight?"

"Yeah. I did."

He doesn't say anything else, and the silence grows awkward.

"Well, if that's it—"

"It's not. I, uh, I wanted to apologize for earlier."

"You already did," I remind him.

"Well, I'm doing it again, then. You didn't deserve that."

"Oh." What else does he want me to say? "Thank you."

He sighs. "I'll let you get some sleep."

A heaviness surrounds him like a second shirt.

"If you ever need someone to talk to, I'm here. Maybe I can help." I blurt the words out before I can give them a second thought.

What happened to just an employee?

He opens his mouth. He's going to tell me no thanks, or that everything is fine.

"Noah OD'd last night."

I don't know what I was expecting, but certainly not his anguish-filled admission.

"Is he…okay?"

He jerks his head in a nod. "I guess."

"You guess?" Has he not checked in on his friend? Is he that self-important?

What an ass—

"I went to the hospital earlier. The guys and I waited all day."

Well, now I feel like a jerk for my terrible thoughts.

"What happened?"

My heart drops into my stomach, his sadness reaching out and gripping me as sure as if it was his hand against my skin.

"He wouldn't see us. We kept asking, thinking maybe he

113

would update his visitor list. But each time, the answer was the same."

"He what? Why?"

Frustration mixes with the sadness, and moisture adds a shimmer to his eyes.

"Chris."

I don't hesitate. I don't stop for one second before I wrap my arms around him.

"I'm so sorry," I whisper.

He pulls me close, his arms around my waist, his fingers grazing the strip of skin below my shirt.

When his breath ruffles the hair on my neck, I shiver, but not from cold.

"He's—he's one of my best friends." The anguish in his voice has my arms tightening around him.

"It's going to be okay."

I don't know if that's true. But he needs someone to be strong for him right now. He pulls back until he can meet my eyes, and I suck in a breath at the sadness that radiates from him.

"You don't know that."

"And you don't know that it won't be."

He smiles at my response. "You like to argue with me."

I return his smile. "No, I don't."

He lifts his hand, his finger sliding along a strand of hair at my jawline before tracing the skin there. His smile fades, and electricity crackles around us.

"Jess."

When he says my name in that tone, I'm powerless. I don't want to fight this constant hum of attraction.

"Hmm?"

"Tell me no." He closes the distance, rubbing his nose along my jaw and nuzzling my ear. I lean my head back, his breath across my neck building a tension in my thighs. I squeeze them to help curb the ache.

"No?"

"I want to kiss you." His lips brush my neck as he murmurs against my skin.

"Mmm."

I don't push him away. Just the opposite. I dig my nails into his biceps to pull him closer.

"I shouldn't," he groans, but his hands fasten to my hips, aligning our lower bodies. I can't stop the mewl when the evidence of his attraction presses between us.

"What if…" I break off with a moan when he trails hot, open-mouthed kisses along my jaw.

"What if what?" He growls against my skin.

"What if I don't want to say no?"

The question is barely past my lips when his mouth claims mine. The kiss holds every heated promise made since the day I first met him. His lips are soft, but still master mine with expert precision. He licks along the seam of my lips but doesn't request entry—he demands it. I give in and open my mouth, my knees buckling as his tongue tangles with mine.

He shifts his hands to my ass, squeezing me through the denim, and the heat of his touch singes me through the thick fabric. I press against him, flattening my breasts against his chest as my entire body comes alive. It's as if I've been asleep all my life, waiting for him. And suddenly I'm awake and desperately need his touch. Everywhere. Right the fuck now.

He advances, moving us until my back hits the wall, his body trapping mine against the hard surface while his erection digs into my stomach. I've never experienced something like this all-consuming fire that creates a need to beg for more. He cups my jaw, his thumbs tracing circles along the line. The small movement makes me feel cherished. And makes the heat between us burn a thousand times hotter. I lift my leg to wrap around his, whimpering as the movement opens me further to him.

When he finally breaks the kiss, he leans his forehead against mine, our breaths mingling as we both struggle for air.

"Jess." His whisper has butterflies swirling in my stomach.

"Yes?"

I lick my lips, savoring his unique taste.

More.

I need more.

"Daddy!"

The small voice startles both of us, and we break apart. Chris rushes back into the room, where Gage is in the throes of a nightmare that has him crying out for his dad in his sleep.

"Shh, Gage, Daddy's here." Chris rubs Gage's small back, his words calming the little boy as much as the physical touch. "It's okay, buddy, I'm here. I'm right here."

Reality and realization slam into me at the same time. Gage spoke. His first words since before I met him. And it has nothing to do with any of my tactics. It's another reminder. I'm a temporary fixture.

Thank God the universe stopped something with Chris before it could go further. Because I wouldn't have. This is my sign. The most important person in this house isn't me. It isn't Chris.

It's Gage. And what matters most is his relationship with Chris.

I need to fucking remember that and keep my hands, lips, and body away from Chris Rivera.

CHAPTER 10

CHRIS

"*T*opher, are you paying attention?"

I blink and bring the room back into focus. "What?"

Marcus is so red in the face he looks like his head is going to explode any second. To be fair, it has nothing to do with me or my lack of attention—he's been this shade since Evan, Milo, Finn, and I walked into the conference room at Cornerstone Records.

Marcus wasn't our original label rep at Cornerstone, but he has been with us for the last eight years.

"Maybe if you actually pay attention to the conversation instead of living in your fantasy world, we can discuss the catastrophic mess you landed yourselves in this time."

Scoffing, I can't help but roll my eyes at his overly dramatic reaction. And I wasn't living in some fantasy world. I was reliving the other night. Gage had spoken again. Sure, it was in his sleep, but the sound of my name from his lips had calmed a little of the anxiety that had been building since he stopped speaking. He hasn't said anything since, but he seems…lighter somehow than before.

All thanks to Jessie.

Reliving the other night also includes remembering that kiss. The temptation had gotten to be more than I could fight. The skintight black jeans, the strip of silky-smooth skin that had called to me like a siren's song. One moment, she was telling me it would all be okay, and the next, it had felt like it really was. The way she tasted—like chocolate and mint—and the sounds she made as my hands mapped curves I couldn't help but imagine were never too far from my memory.

In my defense, I had asked her to tell me no when I couldn't fight my desire anymore. When I didn't want to step back. But that was the last thing I'd wanted. What I *had* wanted—what I had gotten—was someone who was right there with me in the moment. Someone who was consumed. Just like I was. I was half a breath away from dragging her into my room, from taking things further, when Gage had called out.

Thank fucking Christ.

I can't keep her out of my thoughts, even if my brain has no trouble reminding me she's thirteen fucking years my junior. When I kissed a girl for the first time at a birthday party in seventh grade? She wasn't even born yet.

She's my employee. Gage needs her. And acting on the thoughts that consume me can only lead to disaster.

"Topher, fucking pay attention!"

Shit.

Even Evan is looking at me with a what-the-fuck expression. Spittle forms in the corners of Marcus's mouth, and his hair is standing on end. Milo and Finn are staring at me like I'm having a stroke.

I never zone out in meetings with the label. It's one of the reasons I'm the front man for the band as the bass player. That and Evan's near-crippling anxiety. Hell, for the first three years we toured, he was notorious for puking before every show. It was a no-brainer for me to step up. Being the child of celebrities meant that I had spent my life in the public eye. It's second nature.

Marcus keeps his glare on me as he speaks. "Now, for the fourth time. Noah has landed himself and the rest of you in a mountain of shit this time. We're ready to pull the plug on this new record and the upcoming tour."

"What? That's fucking ridiculous. We've been with Cornerstone longer than any other band in the history of the label." And it's in our fucking contract that *we*—Just One Yesterday—have final say on all this shit. Another benefit to having famous parents? We don't sign anything until they've reviewed it.

"How is this any different from when Noah went to rehab before?" Milo asks. His feet are kicked up on the table, and if he leans any farther back, he's going to be on his ass.

"This." Marcus tosses a large stack of tabloids on the center of the table. "This is what makes it worse."

Craning my neck, I can make out the semi-dark interior of Club Panic. Noah is at a table, while Finn and Milo are nowhere in sight. The guy Noah is with is in the middle of an exchange with him—a wad of cash for a visible prescription bottle. The inset image is of Noah on the ground, pale despite the bloody gash on his forehead.

"Fuck."

Couldn't have said it any better myself, Ev.

I shoot a glare at Finn and Milo. "I thought there weren't any pictures." I should fucking know better.

Noah overdosed a few days ago. I was on pins and needles at first, waiting for the story to drop. When it wasn't front-page tabloid news yesterday, I assumed we were in the clear. Wrong again.

Fucking figures it took a few days for someone to sell the pictures.

"My secretary hasn't been off the phone for longer than five

119

minutes all day. Everybody and their goddamn brother is calling to ask for a comment."

"What does the label want us to say?" Better to cut to the chase than to continue to stare at the images of Noah lying on the ground.

Marcus sighs. "You'll tell them that Just One Yesterday severed ties with Noah Kelley—"

"Like hell we will." My chair skids behind me when I surge up.

"Topher—"

"No. We didn't sever anything with Noah. The label can go fuck itself if they want us to use that bullshit line." Even if he is still blocking us from his room.

"Noah is a founding member of this band." Evan stands as well, glaring at Marcus while a muscle ticks in his jaw.

"The label feels it's best for the four of you to continue forward without Noah. Otherwise we're going to reevaluate how much support you have."

"Not happening," I grind out and motion for Finn and Milo to stand. "Just One Yesterday will remain intact as-is. Noah is a part of the band. End of discussion."

"I-I'll need to discuss that with leadership."

"You do that. And while you're at it, take a look at our contract." Ice fills my veins as I stare at yet another person who is after the money we can make them but couldn't give a shit about keeping us together.

Marcus doesn't care about Noah. Neither does Cornerstone. That's fucking obvious.

"We're done here." I nod toward the door, and the other guys filter out one by one until only Marcus and I are left.

"Topher."

Fuck, I'm beginning to hate the sound of that name. But no one at the label calls me Chris. To them, I am Topher.

"What?" My hand is on the edge of the open door. I'm so close to freedom in some ways and in others, never further away.

"You used to have a better handle on this band. Where the fuck is your head lately? Is it the kid?"

Oh, I don't fucking think so.

"*My son* is not up for discussion." The knuckles on my free hand crack as my fingers fist.

"Not like that. But management might be more willing to accept Noah's continued presence with the band if you can keep everyone out of the spotlight for now."

Because that's my job. It's what I signed up for.

"I'll take care of it."

"I mean it. Nothing. No pictures, no rumors, nothing that even has the perception of bad press. You four need to be the poster boys for good behavior. No mistakes. No bad decisions."

Bad decisions like kissing a woman thirteen years younger who tastes like my favorite cookie and happens to be my son's nanny. Message received.

"I said I fucking got it, Marcus."

Because I always do.

Groaning, I sink into the warm water of the hot tub, ready to forget this day ever happened. It had not gotten better after leaving Cornerstone. We all drove to the hospital to see if Noah had added us to his visitor list. One by one, everyone had left until only I remained. We all texted Noah, but he ignored every message.

By the time I walked through the door, it was well past Gage's bedtime. Again. Jessie had come down the stairs, disappointment clear on her face. But instead of lecturing me, she walked by me like I didn't exist.

"Fuck." I lift my head, talking to the starless sky. On nights like this, I cursed the light pollution in LA.

My hot tub will have to help me forget today. From my

vantage point, I can see the bright lights from Jessie's room, but I don't see her. Maybe she's working on her thesis. It's probably a good thing she's holed up in her room since today has been one clusterfuck after another.

I need to forget about that kiss. It's clear she did. With a sigh, I close my eyes and let the jets work their magic.

"Oh."

Blinking one eye open, I find Jessie standing close to the hot tub, a towel gripped in one hand. Maybe I should be glad she isn't in the royal purple bikini from the other day, but the teal one is just as lethal. It hugs her the way I wish I could.

My dick springs to attention at the image she makes standing in front of me. Good thing I'm hidden under the bubbles created by the hot tub jets since I'm a puberty-stricken teenager again—I have zero control over my body's response to her. All her dark hair is piled on top of her head, exposing her slender neck. A pulse fluttering wildly at the base of her neck draws and holds my attention. What does that vibration taste like?

"Hi." I sit up slightly and grab for my water bottle on the concrete next to me.

"Sorry, I didn't know you were out here." I love the way she fidgets with her towel but doesn't try to hide her body. Her confidence is sexy as fuck.

"Rough day. Do you want to join me?"

This has bad decision written all over it. But we'll just be two adults in a hot tub. Nothing more.

Yeah, right.

"Oh, um, no, it's okay. I'll give you some privacy." She turns, but I don't want her to go.

"No. Wait." I sit up farther and shiver as the cool air brushes across my shoulders. "You don't need to leave on my account. Please stay. I want to apologize for missing bedtime. It won't happen again."

Her doubts are written all over her face. She doesn't believe me.

"Promise?"

"I promise. What brings you out here?"

I don't think she's ever used the hot tub, at least not when I'm around, so something must have brought her down here tonight.

"You'll think it's stupid."

"I doubt that."

She hesitates and sinks her teeth into her bottom lip, nibbling slightly on the plump flesh before she finally releases it.

"I-I fell asleep at my desk working on my thesis. When I woke up, I had an awful crick here." She lifts a hand to the back of her neck and winces as she tries to massage the area.

Do not offer to rub her neck. Don't do it. Bad idea.

I manage to avoid the offer, even if it does sit on the tip of my tongue.

"I can't laugh at that. I think that's all this thing is used for anymore. To ease aches and pains—man-made and natural. Sometimes it's like my body has forgotten something it's done for the last thirty-six years."

"What's that?" She drifts closer with a smile hovering on her lips.

"How to sleep in a position that doesn't cause me to wake up sore."

Her light giggle is exactly the balm I need right now.

"I don't have that problem," she teases.

"Yet. You don't have that problem yet. Just wait. One day you'll be old like me, and you'll know exactly what I'm talking about."

"You're not that old."

"Gee, thanks." My voice drips with sarcasm. Nothing like being taken down a peg by being called *not that old*.

She lowers herself to the concrete between me and the door. Even if I try to ignore that she's closer to me. To the hot tub.

"Now if you had said thirty-seven..." Her grin is infectious, and I splash water at her. "Hey!"

Her squeal has happiness bubbling inside me. For the first time in weeks, the weight on my chest lifts.

"Well, I'm glad we've established that I'm 'not that old.'"

You're too old for her, Grandpa.

She unfolds impossibly long legs and stands fluidly—a movement I am both jealous of and confounded by. How can someone who is as petite as she is have legs that long?

"Glad I could be of assistance. I'm going to—"

"Don't go," I practically beg. "For the last few minutes, you've helped me forget my shitty-ass day."

"Glad I could help."

"How about you distract me from my worries, and I help you with yours?"

"What makes you think I'm worried about something?"

I shrug. "A hunch. You spend a lot of time on your thesis."

"Because it needs to be accepted."

"What happens if it's not?"

"I lose my job offer."

The sadness in her expression tugs on my heartstrings. As much as I love having her here with Gage, I want to remove that worry from her eyes.

"I'm a good listener. Maybe I can help?" I gesture to the water.

"I don't want to intrude."

"After a day like today, it's not an intrusion. I would really appreciate the company."

"O-okay."

She moves closer again, and my attention zeroes in on the sway of her hips as she walks. It's not intentional, but it is another tick in the sexy column for her. Hopefully she'll stay on her side of the hot tub.

Would you push her away if she didn't?

The towel she's holding flutters to the concrete, and she

gingerly makes her way in, hissing when the hot water reaches her thighs.

"It's better when you sit down." My assurance is more for my peace of mind than hers. Maybe if she hides her luscious body in the water, I'll stand a chance in hell at controlling mine.

She sinks down on the side opposite me and wriggles slightly before a sigh escapes her lips.

"Better?" I ask.

"Much."

"Now tell me about this thesis."

She does. After working on it for the last six months and receiving some pretty rough feedback from her mentor, she's struggling to apply his recommendations to improve it.

"It's hard though. I don't have enough examples."

"Would it help if you included Gage?"

She studies me for several moments before she finally nods. "Yeah."

"And you'll keep him anonymous?"

"Of course. I'm not even using my name when it's a personal example."

My stomach twists at the reminder of what she's gone through.

"Would you let me read those parts that pertain to him before you submit it?"

"You'll let me include him?" Hope lights her eyes.

"I trust you. So, yeah. You can include him."

She squeals, rushing across the small space to wrap her arms around me. "Thank you!"

I relish the slide of her skin against mine for a heartbeat before she stiffens and quickly retreats to her side of the tub.

"What do you think you'll include?" I ask, trying to forget the weight of her breasts against my arm.

"I want to add in how I'm working with him. And hopefully that it will be successful."

"You don't think it has been?"

She grimaces. "In some ways I do. In other ways, I don't know. He still isn't speaking. And before you say anything, yes, I realize I shouldn't expect miracles, but I wonder if I shouldn't be trying other things too."

"He said 'daddy' the other night," I remind her.

Her smile is sadder and more disappointed than anything else. "But he has so much more to say."

Fuck. She's one of the most amazing women I've ever met.

"He does. When he first got here, he was a little chatterbox. Talked constantly. Until all the words simply stopped."

"Maybe what I'm doing isn't enough."

"And maybe what you're doing is magic. You're healing him, even if it doesn't seem like it to you. He's more...relaxed...since you've been here. I wish you could use your magic on Noah."

"How is he?" The lights of the hot tub shine in her dark eyes, making them look like stars. Exactly what I was missing earlier when I searched the sky.

"No one knows. His mom hasn't reached out to any of us, and he's not letting us see him at the hospital. We go and wait for hours. I was there nearly the whole day, and even though I know he's there, he doesn't respond. It's radio silence. Almost like that overdose killed him."

"Chris." She scoots closer to me, her hand finding mine in the water to squeeze. "I'm sorry."

"There are pictures." The words rip from me at the memory of those images spread across the front page of the trashy magazines.

"Pictures?"

"Of that night. He looked like he was dead. A small part of me wonders if that's what he was trying to do. But then I wonder why when we'd had such a good day. He told us he wanted to get clean. It felt like we were becoming us again."

"And you want to ask him?"

Her hand is still wrapped around mine, and I flip my wrist to interlace my fingers with hers. She doesn't pull away, and I can pretend I didn't do what I just did, my bad decision hidden by the bubbling water around us.

"Maybe? I want him to get better. If that means not talking about it, I won't."

"But is that healthy for you or for him if he has no idea what you think? How you feel?"

"I'll do what's best for him. It's what I always do. For all of them."

"They're lucky to have you."

The bubbles stop, and she gently tugs her hand away to slide back to her original place on the other side of the tub.

"Do you ever wonder what your life would be like if you had made different choices?" I ask.

She studies me in silence for several breaths. "Not really. I think everything that happens in my life leads me where I'm supposed to be."

Hers is a philosophical answer. Mine is anything but.

"I keep thinking about the kiss—our kiss—from the other night."

Her breath catches at my admission.

"Chris…"

"I go back and forth on whether it should have happened. What would be different if I hadn't kissed you that night. If you had told me no when I asked."

"Just because we did it once doesn't mean anything. It happened. But it can't happen again." Her body contradicts those words—her chest rising and falling rapidly in the still water.

"Agreed. But I'm not going to lie, Jessie. You're a very attractive woman. And even though I keep reminding myself you weren't even alive when I had my first kiss, it's not helping."

"How old were you?"

"Twelve. Evan and I went to our first co-ed birthday party.

We were playing spin the bottle, and when I spun, the bottle landed on Heather Daniels. Every guy in our class thought she was cute. And I was the lucky one to kiss her."

"What happened after that?" I love the soft smile that curves her lips.

"We went to school the following Monday and pretended like nothing happened. Until we were juniors in high school ,and she came up to me to tell me she'd had a huge crush on me for forever and asked me out."

"Aww."

"Her timing was pretty coincidental though. The guys and I were getting more and more attention on the local scene. I knew that was why she approached me. So I told her no."

Her smile fades.

"You made a smart decision. I wish I could say the same."

"Your first kiss tried to take advantage of your fame?" I tease, but she doesn't smile at my joke.

"Not quite. My first boyfriend. Bowie."

"What the hell kind of hipster name is Bowie?"

She snorts. "Not his real one. But I didn't know better at the time. It was his stage name. He was in a band and trying to get discovered. He thought people would associate him with David Bowie and that it would help elevate him."

"Oh Jesus Christ." I roll my eyes at the stupidity. Here I was separating myself from my parents' famous names and he was trying to invoke one.

"I was so stupid." She groans and drops her face to her hands.

"First boyfriend, right? You must have been young."

"Still not an excuse to be naïve."

"What happened?"

"We dated for six months. After two weeks, I gave him my virginity. I wanted him to like me, and he was pressuring me for more."

My vision goes red, and I want to go find the fucker and punch him out.

"You didn't need to do anything you weren't comfortable with. Not to get him to like you." The words are hard to force out through my clenched teeth.

"I know that *now*. But I was in a different headspace back then. I've learned a lot through the years."

"You make it sound like you're the old one."

"Maybe not in terms of actual years. But I feel old."

"Because of what you went through as a kid?" I ask.

"Partially, yeah."

"So what happened to Bowie?" I sneer his name.

"From the time he found out Jax was my brother, he asked me to bring him to family events. To invite Jax when he had a show. He wanted my brother to sign him."

"Did he?"

"Hell no. I was really pissed at him when he didn't, but Bowie had zero talent. He only pretended he did."

"He couldn't have been very happy about that," I guess.

Her eyes cloud over—a mix of hurt and anger.

"Nope. I kept promising I would work on Jax. Make him change his mind. One night, I had a late study session, so I couldn't make the show he had. When I got there, I walked backstage to apologize and found him leaning against the wall with another woman on her knees in front of him. Right there where everyone could see."

"Fucking dick."

She huffs a humorless laugh. "I figured that out finally. After he said some not nice things, I left. And I made a promise to myself that I would never get involved with a rock star again. Been there, done that, and even got the commemorative t-shirt to prove it."

"Not all rock stars are like him." The only ones I've met like that are posers, pretenders who think they should be a star and never make it.

"I know. My brother and his friends all adore their wives. But it doesn't change anything for me."

"No more rock stars." Why does that rule make me want to break it? To convince her to give me a chance. Show her I'm not like the douche she dated.

"Nope."

"Was he a rock star though? Or just a wannabe?"

"No one has ever asked me that question before."

"Maybe they should have."

Our eyes meet and hold, the silence stretching between us.

"Something to think about," she whispers. All the emotion disappears from her face, hidden again in the invisible place she keeps it. "This conversation turned depressing."

"It did, huh?"

"You know what's even better for heavy topics than a hot tub?"

"Do I want to know the answer?" I ask, even though I do really want to learn what put the playful smile on her face.

"Hot chocolate."

Her answer surprises a laugh from me.

"You and your hot chocolate. I thought maybe you were going to say alcohol."

"Nope. Although I can't say I don't add alcohol to my hot chocolate now and then."

"It probably makes that little packet of powder taste better."

She wrinkles her nose, affronted by my suggestion.

"That's not hot chocolate. It's sadness in a cup. Now that you've had the real stuff, you have to agree."

"Maybe I need another taste test."

"There're even extras. It's a whole different world when done right." She stands, and water sluices down her curves, dripping from her fingers when she holds out a hand to me. "Want to see?"

"Show me."

I stand, my nipples puckering in the cool air and causing a tug on my nipple ring. Dropping my hand in hers, I let her lead me out of the hot tub to our towels. Does it mean anything that neither of us lets go of the other as we work together to wrap the cotton around us?

"I'm about to change your whole world," she promises as we cross the threshold to the house.

Little does she know, she already has.

CHAPTER 11

JESSIE

The kitchen is dark and quiet when we step through the door. Cool air permeates my towel and damp bikini top, and my nipples pucker against the fabric. Adjusting the terry cloth for better coverage, I opt to leave the bright overhead lights off and only use the light from above the stove to grab my ingredients.

"I'm still not sure how hot chocolate can change my life." The heat of him radiates next to me. The air conditioning doesn't seem to affect him the same way as it does me—he's already discarded his towel.

All the better to study his tattoos more closely.

Yeah, because you can do that without light.

"Wait and see. Although if you want to watch, then you'll know how to make this for Gage."

My swallow is painful at the realization that when Gage is upset, I won't always be here. This will fall on Chris.

"Teach me, oh great master chocolatier." He teases away the prick of sadness.

"Mistress chocolatier." My tongue stumbles over the word mistress.

"Mistress." He bows. "I am your pupil."

Heat crackles between us at the playful banter with an undertone we could take in a totally different direction.

But you're not going to.

Stepping around him, I grab the ingredients from the spice cabinet.

He takes them from me one by one. "Unsweetened cocoa powder? Won't this make it bitter?"

"Just wait." I continue to hand him ingredients.

"Sugar. Semi-sweet chocolate. Salt? In hot chocolate?"

"Keep going," I tell him, biting back a smile at the way he wrinkles his nose. He looks so much like Gage, but all grown up.

"Vanilla extract. Marshmallows."

"Now. The wet ingredients." I move to the refrigerator, and my nipples pucker as cool air escapes the open door.

Please don't let this towel fail me now.

Maybe I should suggest we change into dry clothes. But I don't.

"Here."

"Milk. Half and half. Like for coffee?"

"Yeah, but you can use it in this too. And you can add espresso powder to your hot chocolate if you want. I don't have any here though. And I wouldn't give any to Gage."

He grimaces. "No, I don't think the four-year-old needs espresso. Got it. Chocolate syrup. Caramel syrup." He puts the last of the ingredients on the counter. "Is that it?"

"Yep. Now we cook."

Chris's kitchen is a dream. A massive six-burner stove has all the bells and whistles someone could ever want. And while Lois keeps us stocked with dinners I can reheat, I couldn't help but make a run to the grocery store for ingredients for hot chocolate.

Grabbing a saucepan and whisk, I move everything close to the stove and start. Dry ingredients are measured and placed in the pan before I add the milk and vanilla.

"You don't need these?" he asks as I turn on the burner and stir. He's holding the bag of marshmallows and both syrups for me to see.

I shake my head. "Those are toppings. You can also use graham crackers if you want s'mores hot chocolate. But Gage and I did that last week, and we finished off the crackers."

"Does he like your hot chocolate?"

I smile, remembering the chocolate mustache that surrounded his mouth.

"I think so."

We're silent as I stir the ingredients and let everything blend, soothed by the swirls as they morph to full color.

"You okay?" he asks, interrupting my thoughts.

"Huh?"

"Your towel. You keep tugging at it."

"Oh." The knot keeps slipping down my chest until I tug it up again.

"Did you want a dry one?"

The towel itself is now more wet than I am. "I'm okay."

With a deep breath, I unknot the fabric and toss it toward the chair at the island. The goosebumps on my arms fade, and I shift my weight from foot to foot, impatient for the hot drink to warm me up.

"Is it done yet? My way only takes two minutes in the microwave."

"Almost and faster aren't always better."

"In more ways than one," he mutters.

My heart races at his innuendo.

"What?"

"What what?"

"What did you say?" I ask.

"Nothing. Just ready for a second taste of this life-altering experience."

I can't be one hundred percent sure what he said, but I don't think I misheard him. Choosing not to debate with him, I turn off the burner.

"Can you grab me two mugs?"

He does, his body coming perilously close to the back of mine as he sets them on the counter next to me. I pour the contents of the pan into our mugs, filling them about halfway, then add half and half to cool them before pointing to the toppings.

"Your choice."

One marshmallow goes in his mouth while several others go in his cocoa before being topped with the chocolate and caramel sauce.

"I think you use more of that than Gage did." I laugh at the mountain of marshmallows and the sauce that drips down his cup.

"I have an awful sweet tooth. Always have. My mom used to make two birthday cakes—one for me and one for everyone else."

I laugh and add a few marshmallows and chocolate syrup to my drink.

"Ready?" I hold out my cup, and he touches his against mine.

"Ready."

We pull apart, and he lifts the mug to his mouth. I mimic his motion and take a sip. Chocolate and vanilla flood my tongue, and I moan at the warmth that heats me from the inside out. Chris's Adams apple continues to bob as he finishes his hot chocolate in one go.

"Oh my god." I've never seen someone drink it the way he does—like a shot.

His mug is completely empty when he sets it back on the counter.

"That was delicious." He drags his tongue along his lower lip, completely missing the light sheen of chocolate above his upper one.

"You missed some." I step forward and lift my thumb to wipe it away before I realize what I'm doing.

My retreat is awkward, and I bump back against the counter. "Sorry."

His tongue follows the same path as my fingers, and I struggle to look away from his mouth. It reminds me of our kiss. Of something I need to forget.

But right now, I can't remember why.

"You don't need to apologize." His voice drops to a murmur, the raspy sound creating an ache in my core.

Or maybe it's the look in his eyes as he stares at me. Like I'm his favorite dessert.

And he's starving.

"Chris."

"Hmm?" His eyes don't waver from mine as he closes the distance between us. The desire, the fantasies that exist in his gaze—I suck in a breath, unable to calm my racing heart.

His large hand surrounds mine where I've got it wrapped around my cup, the calluses on his fingertips sliding along my fingers until he can take the mug from me and set it on the counter.

"What are you doing?"

"Something I shouldn't." He grips my bare hips and reels me in, slowly bringing my lower half into alignment with his.

With a gasp, I press myself against his erection.

"Why?"

His hands glide back to squeeze my ass. There's no distance between us, not that I want there to be.

"Why?" he echoes against my skin as his lips blaze a trail from the edge of my shoulder to my neck.

"Yes." I lean my head to the side to grant him full access to the sensitive spots.

"Because I can't seem to resist you."

He boosts me to the counter, and I squeal at the feel of the cold granite beneath me before wrapping my legs around his hips.

"Tell me I'm not alone." His words are whispered against my ear, and I shiver at the light breath.

"You're not." I rest my hands on his biceps and dig my nails into the muscles there.

"Tell me what you want." He presses a kiss below my ear while his fingers play with the string of my bikini bottoms.

"I want you to kiss me."

I shift my hands to the back of his head, threading my fingers through his hair, and pull him to my mouth. He angles himself until his lips are poised to devour mine. I open my mouth, my tongue finding his to tease. He tastes like chocolate and caramel, and suddenly, I understand why he put so much effort into his drink—because I want more. Tightening my legs, I use my feet to bring him closer. The friction of his erection against my center separated by two thin pieces of material is as much a frustration as it is a turn on.

My top loosens, cool air rushing against damp skin when his fingers tug the knot free and follow the strings down to the cups. Pushing the fabric down, he covers my breasts with his warm hands, weighing them in his palms as he drags his calloused fingers over the nipples. He circles the beaded tips until I'm ready to beg for more—if only I could. But his mouth still holds mine hostage, and I don't think he's letting go anytime soon.

My pussy spasms with a sharp pinch of my nipples, and I mewl, finally breaking the kiss, my head catching against the cabinet behind me. His eyes are pitch dark when I blink mine open, but they're so full of fire I'm surprised I'm not a pile of ash right now.

My top is hanging by the thin string around my back, the cups upside down while the halter string tickles my thighs. Reaching back, I grip the final knot and tug. He pulls back a fraction, his face a mix of lust and hunger so powerful that it radiates from my core to my fingertips.

"W-why are you looking at me like that?" My voice is breathy, and my breasts ache for more of his touch.

"Like what?"

"Like I'm dessert."

A lascivious grin curves his mouth. What did I get myself into?

He snakes his arm out beyond us, and when he pulls it back, excitement pools in my belly.

"Chocolate syrup?"

"I told you I have a sweet tooth."

The click of the cap goes almost unnoticed, drowned out by the sound of my breathing and the pounding of my heart.

"Close your eyes," he demands. His grin has me fidgeting against the counter.

I flutter them shut. And the longer I wait, the more shallow my breathing becomes. He's still here, my legs encircling his waist, but the waiting is torture. A cool trickle slides down my neck, followed by the warm drag of his tongue.

"Mmm." The vibration against my throat has every nerve ending ready for what comes next.

Or where.

One shoulder, then the other. My fingers are next, and once those are clean, he places them on his chest, and I play with the cool metal of his nipple ring. His hips pulse against me, so I do it again and am rewarded by a drizzle along my collarbone, followed by the heat of his mouth.

"Please."

"Patience. Didn't you say that faster isn't always better? You have a little here." He laps right above my breast.

Calloused fingers surround my nipple again, tugging and plucking at the tip until I'm ready to come on the spot.

"Chris." I whimper, and my toes curl, a powerful orgasm building in my core.

His fingers still play with one nipple while thick syrup drips around the other. The weird sensation is quickly forgotten as his mouth covers me, his tongue lapping at the chocolate until I don't doubt he's gotten it all. But he doesn't stop licking and sucking before nibbling gently. The impending orgasm tightens my legs, the flashes of light behind my eyelids growing brighter the closer it comes.

"Mmm." He pops his mouth off my breast, and his lips find mine. His tongue is sweet from the chocolate, but different—a spicy undertone I only associate with him.

"You taste good," he murmurs against my lips.

"The chocolate."

"It's you," he argues. "But there's more for me to sample, one more taste I'm dying to try."

He unknots the bikini strings on either hip, and it sinks in. What he's talking about. I move to close my legs on instinct, but I'm stopped by his hips between them.

"Lift up."

My body obeys without my permission so he can yank my bottoms out of the way.

"Chris." My voice shakes, and he stops the glide of his fingers along my legs.

"Jessie."

"I-I'm not sure—"

"What did it feel like a few minutes ago?"

Pleasure. All pleasure.

"So fucking good." I groan and open my eyes in time to witness his mouth curve into a smile.

"Trust me that this will feel as good. Better." He holds my attention as he waits for my agreement.

I could tell him no, and he'd stop without question.

But I want this.

I nod. "Okay."

"Good girl." His mouth consumes mine again, capturing my breath, and I moan as his hands continue to roam up my legs, feathering along the insides of my knees and down to my ankles before they work their way back up. Each hand grips one of my calves, and he lifts until my feet are braced on the counter.

The feeling of exposure wars with the lust and excitement that continues to burn.

He adjusts me slightly until I'm balanced on the edge of the counter and presses my knees apart until I'm open to his exploration.

"Fuck." The word rips from him as he drops to his haunches, his thumb rotating in the line between my pussy and my thigh. The way he's staring at me while he touches me ratchets the touch up to the next level.

Fire licks along every nerve in the path of his gaze, the anticipation building as he continues to hold himself still.

"Please." I don't know what I'm asking for. Maybe for the torture of the stretched moment between us to end. I'm like a rubber band at its breaking point, ready to snap. All because of his hands.

My word breaks the standoff. He lifts an arm and points to the two bottles that are easily within my reach.

"Hand those to me." His voice is all gravel, one thumb still tracing the line that drives me to the brink of sanity.

"W-which one?" I bite my lip to keep from crying out, to hold myself back from flying apart when he's barely touched me.

"Both."

I stretch, his thumb shifting with my movement to trace along the edge of my clit. I want to stay right here.

I want more.

"Now," he says.

My body is completely tuned to his voice, his to command.

I hand him first one bottle and then the other, my fingers brushing along his. The brief contact is the most innocent touch of all, but it brings a depth I can't explain to the moment. He surges up, surprising me so that I teeter on the counter and my fingers grip his biceps for purchase.

"I almost forgot."

The way he studies me in silence is unnerving. What is he thinking? One arm flexes beneath my fingers as he reaches for the bag of marshmallows lying forgotten on the counter.

"W-w-what are those for?"

The smirk on his face is so hot it nearly singes me.

"One for you." He hands me a large marshmallow. "When I tell you to, you're going to put that in your mouth."

"Okay?" Why am I putting this in my mouth?

"Before it's fully dissolved—dissolved, not bitten—I'll have you screaming my name."

Oh.

My.

God.

Everything from my core to my breasts flushes with heat. I'm not a virgin—not by a long shot—but all of this, everything we're doing, is full of an intensity I've never experienced before.

"Understood?" His eyes are molten as he waits for my response.

"O-okay."

Taking the bag of marshmallows with him, he kneels again.

What are those for?

That question scatters at the click of the syrup cap opening again. I stiffen in anticipation, and he rubs a hand along my calf.

"Relax."

I take a deep breath and slowly release it, relaxing the tight muscles as best as I can. And wait. Unsure whether to close my eyes, I fixate on the shift of his muscles when he lifts the first bottle, but my eyes slide shut at the sensation of liquid traveling down my thigh to pool at my center. I had gotten used to the slide of syrup followed by the heat of his mouth, but he changes the pattern.

The same sensation as before overwhelms my body, and I fidget against his hand and the counter. But it's more. Another cap clicking open, and the slide of another line of syrup from the other side.

"Now."

With that cue, I place the marshmallow between my lips.

"Watch."

He holds my legs open with his forearms while he holds another marshmallow between his thumb and forefinger. His focus is on my pussy as he passes the white puff through the pool of sauce between my legs before popping it between his lips, sauce-covered side against his tongue.

"Mmm." The marshmallow disappears little by little into his mouth.

The smile he wears is full of satisfaction as he stares at his handiwork. Opening his lips slightly, he shows me the marshmallow at the end of his tongue while he places one hand on either thigh, keeping me in place.

One heartbeat and then the scrape of his jaw along my thigh. His tongue works down one crease, lapping at the flavor there, and I jump at the pressure against my clit as he presses the marshmallow to it before licking it into oblivion. Only then does he lick the sauce trail from back to front. Over and over again, he works around the spot that aches the most before he finally teases my clit with circles of his tongue alternated with staccato taps.

Lights flicker behind my eyes, and my moan is muffled by the marshmallow. I swallow, trying not to choke on the sugar as it continues to melt at a quick pace. Can he deliver on his promise? Will I scream his name before it completely melts on my tongue?

His mouth leaves my clit, and I whimper as his thumb replaces it, keeping a steady pressure as he continues to clean up the syrup. But even once he's done, he doesn't remove his finger, but presses it forward, filling me while his tongue takes its previous pattern again. The marshmallow is almost fully dissolved, but he's a man possessed, using two fingers to curl inside, to find a spot that locks my body even as he continues to play my clit as masterfully as he does his bass.

"Oh my god." I release my death grip on the counter to fist his hair, pulling him closer.

His response is to suck my clit between his lips, his cheeks hollowing out with the pressure he uses like a honed weapon against me. His hand holding my thigh back shifts, pressing against my lower stomach as his fingers flutter inside me.

"*Chris!*" I scream his name as the orgasm swamps me all at once, catapulting me into the place where all I know is centered on the person kneeling in front of me. He doesn't let up, doesn't slow down, but continues working me until one orgasm blends into a second and my fingers clench in his hair.

He unfurls from his position, slamming his lips against mine as he lifts me from the counter. The rest of the marshmallow is gone by the time he lifts his head to drag his tongue along my jaw to my ear.

"I win," he growls.

"I'm pretty sure I did," I say dazedly.

"I'm just getting started."

CHAPTER 12

CHRIS

I groan at the heat of Jessie's pussy against my naked stomach. My dick feels like it's being strangled as it presses against the mesh netting of my swim trunks. I need to be inside this woman right the fuck now. Her breast drags across my nipple ring, and I grit my teeth at the flood of pleasure.

This moment is even hotter than I imagined.

What are you waiting for?

She opens her eyes, and her gaze meets mine. Her lips are plump, swollen from my kisses, and I want to dive in for more.

"What?" Pink colors her cheeks, and she ducks her head.

"Don't get shy now," I growl and capture her lips again. Shifting one hand down, I rub along her folds, not letting her moan leave the fusion of our mouths.

I savor it the way I intend to do with the rest of her body. And for that, I need a bed. I ignore the mess in the kitchen, my plans for her are my only focus as I take the stairs as fast as I can.

The way she rubs against me has both of us panting by the time I reach the top, but not from exertion. I press her against the wall, cradling her face in my hands as I claim her mouth. Her tongue tangles with mine. Her teeth nip at my lip and tug slightly.

The sting has my dick practically tearing through my shorts.

Now, now, now, now, now.

It's the only word my body recognizes, but I move slowly down the hall on a stealth mission to not wake up my sleeping child. I bypass Jessie's room and open my door, closing it behind us as I lean against it.

I kiss and nip down the column of her throat until I can sink my teeth into the tendon between her neck and shoulder. I relish her broken cry and the way she tilts her head and invites me to do it again. Repeating the caress, I move blindly from the door to the bed.

I lower her feet to the floor and hiss at the continued friction against my dick. She reaches for the waistband of my shorts, tugging at the drawstring with those delicate fingers until they loosen. The way the damp fabric sticks to my hips offers little relief. Her teeth capture her lower lip while she works the clingy fabric down over my hips.

"Wait." I bracket her wrists to stop her movement. "Are you sure?"

I need her to be sure. And if she's not, I'll walk away and forget this happened.

The fuck you will.

Her on the counter in front of me would serve as my only fantasy for the foreseeable future.

She nods. "I'm sure."

I need to take back control if I want a chance in hell of not coming in my shorts.

"On the bed."

I nod toward the head of the bed and watch her crawl on hands and knees, her hips swaying and her ass on display.

Fuck.

Only once she reaches the pillows and turns around do I

allow myself to pull my board shorts down my hips, grateful when my dick doesn't catch on anything. Once my shorts hit the floor, I kick them out of the way before moving to the side of the bed.

"Is that..." She reaches out to brush along the barbell at the end of my dick but drops her hand quickly.

"A PA, yeah." I wrap my hand around my shaft and tug in a downward stroke, groaning as my fingers rub along the piercing.

But I don't close my eyes—I want to see her reaction. And I'm not disappointed. Her irises glitter as she watches me, lips parted as her chest heaves.

"It's...I haven't..." Her flustered words are as much a turn on as her body.

Because it means that this—whatever it is between us—is *something* to her.

Sitting on the bed, I turn toward her so she can still see the piercing.

"I got it when I was twenty." And fuck, had it hurt like a bitch and taken for-fucking-ever to heal.

But the first time I had sex after?

Worth it.

My nipple had come later, and while I occasionally think about taking that one out, this one isn't going anywhere. Even masturbating is better with it.

"Did it hurt?" She lowers her head for a better look.

I can't keep the image of her sucking me off in this position out of my head.

"It did. Like a goddamn bitch. But it doesn't anymore." I reach out, palm up. "You can touch it if you want. I won't bite. Much."

She smiles at my teasing and puts her hand in mine. I pull her closer, wrapping her hand around my dick, her fingers brushing against the piercing underneath.

"Oh fuck." I groan, my head falling back at the sensation of her innocent touch.

147

"I'm sorry." Concern lines her face, and she pulls her hand away.

"Why are you sorry?" I don't let her retreat, tugging her hand back into place despite her slight resistance.

"I hurt you."

Shifting closer, I brush a kiss along her lips.

"You didn't hurt me. The opposite. It feels fucking amazing."

"You're sure?"

She lets me wrap her hand around my dick again, and this time we're both ready for the slight press of her fingers against the piercing. I bite back another moan, bracing myself for the gentle exploration of her fingers as they move up and down.

Pre-cum leaks around the piercing at the end while my dick begs me to keep this party moving, to bury myself in her pretty pussy. She moves closer and shifts to her knees, fidgeting back and forth on her legs.

"Are you trying to get yourself off while you touch me?"

"What? No." Her eyes fly to mine and contradict her words. Busted.

With a few quick moves, I have her on her back while I lie cradled between her thighs, my dick brushing her folds.

"How many orgasms did you have downstairs?"

"Two."

"And you're ready for a third so soon?" I tease.

"I didn't realize what I was doing until you told me."

Looking into her eyes, I find truth in her statement. She had no clue that she was so turned on she was trying to get herself off. Because she was touching me. I close the distance, slanting my lips against hers until she opens on a gasp.

She tastes like chocolate. Like temptation. And I'm not nearly through with her.

She lifts her hips as the kiss continues she wants more. So do I. Breaking the kiss, I drag my lips along her jaw, slithering down her body until I'm eye level with her breasts.

"You have amazing tits."

I pull one into my mouth, swirling my tongue around her nipple before I close my teeth lightly along the puckered tip.

"Chris." Her fingers find my hair on a breathy sigh.

"You want more?"

"Mmm."

"Tell me." I bite down a little harder, and her hips surge up, blocked by my chest.

"Yes. I want more. I want you."

I'm a half second away from moving farther down her body so I can make her come again with my mouth, but my dick is wresting control, snapping through the leash I'm controlling it with. Instead, I move up. I open the drawer on my nightstand and pull out a bottle of lube and a condom.

"Jess."

Her eyes flutter open, the pleasure clearly visible in the black depths where her pupils eclipse the normally dark brown color. I hold up the foil packet.

"Not only does my piercing feel good for me, but for you too. But you won't get the same sensation if I wear this. I will if you want me to. But I had a checkup from my doctor right after Gage came to live with me. Whether I wear this is absolutely 100 percent your choice."

"I…" Her eyes dart to the condom, and I lift the package to my mouth, ready to tear it open. She grabs my wrist and stills my movement. "Wait."

"Wait?"

"Don't."

"No?"

She shakes her head. "I'm on birth control. To regulate my periods."

An expression flits over her face, one I can't name, before it's gone again. But I'm not focused on that so much as what she said.

"So that means—"

"We won't be needing this." She grabs the packet from my hand and tosses it behind me. "Now, where were we?"

I grin at her attitude. She makes me smile while burning me alive. It's another first.

"Right about here." I kneel between her thighs, the bottle of lube in my hand.

I squirt a liberal amount in my palm and run my hand up and down my dick. Every time I get to the head, I nearly buckle at both the sensation of my hand and the sight of her under me. She's not one to simply watch, though, and lifts her hands to her breasts, running her palms over the distended tips at first before pinching and twisting them with her fingers.

Her moan as she rubs her hips back and forth on the bed makes me impossibly harder.

"You're so fucking sexy." I knock her hands out of the way and replace them with mine. They glide along her breasts, but given the lube, don't give her what she wants.

"Chris." My name is a whimper.

"Hmm?"

"Please." Her hips bump against my chest again, and I don't bother to fight my grin.

"Please what? This?" I pinch her nipple between two fingers and tug.

I'm rewarded with a mewl.

She places her hands on my chest, her fingers blindly fluttering over my inked skin before finding the metal of my piercing. Lightning bolts of pleasure connect from where she plays with the ring to my ready cock, waiting at her entrance.

I start with shallow thrusts, barely in and out, pushing deeper with every pulse of my hips. Her breathing turns ragged, and she lifts her chin to expose her throat in silent invitation. My lips and tongue work along the column while her breasts crush against my chest, rubbing against me with every shift of my hips.

"Stop teasing me." Her words come between breaths, and her hands find my ass, pushing on my next thrust and driving me deeper. She cries out, her legs locking around my hips and keeping me in place. Her walls spasm around my dick, and my groan echoes hers.

Flexing deeper, I grind my pelvic bone against her clit, fighting the orgasm that hovers at the edges. I grit my teeth as the telltale tingles settle in my spine.

"Is this what you wanted?"

"God, yes."

Her pussy tightens further, and black dots swim in my vision. When I open my eyes, her grin is all mischief.

"You did that on purpose." I narrow my eyes at her while she tries to morph her expression to one of innocence.

"No."

"Here I was thinking you were an angel, but you're a troublemaker."

"Am I?"

"You know what happens to troublemakers?" An idea takes shape, and a wolfish grin stretches across my face.

"Hopefully another orgasm."

Her comment surprises me, and I bark out a laugh. "Greedy and sassy, huh?"

She shrugs unapologetically.

"Maybe I should do something about that," I say and pull out completely, despite her cry of protest.

She tries to follow me, but I shift back until I kneel between her spread legs. Her nipples are tight and beg for more of my attention while her pussy glistens with a combination of the lube and her arousal.

"Chris." This time my name is a whine while my fingers trace lightly from the arch of her foot to her knee, dragging goosebumps in their wake.

"Yes?" I keep my head down to hide my smile.

Shifting her legs, I move them together so I'm no longer between them.

"Please."

"Another please, hmm? What for, I wonder?" Teasing her is almost as hot as what we did in the kitchen. But even I'm close to the end of my limit.

"Fuck me."

I dart a look to her face as the dirty word registers. With those two words, any thoughts I had of teasing her further disintegrate.

"Fuck you?" I growl.

"Yes."

"On your knees."

She scrambles into position on her forearms and knees, and I kneel behind her. Adjusting her position slightly with my legs, I use my hands to run along her sides, cupping her breasts as I trace my tongue and lips along her spine.

"Is that what you want? For me to fuck you?" I bite her earlobe and am rewarded by her shiver. "Are you ready for me?"

I move one hand to cup her pussy, my fingers sliding through the slick folds until I find her clit. I circle the hard bundle of nerves until she moans and presses herself down against my hand.

"Chris."

Fuck, her whimper has primal need eradicating all rational thought.

"No more teasing, Jessie. But once I stop teasing, I'm not going to stop fucking you until you've had at least two more orgasms."

"Now," she demands, her hips bumping back, seeking my cock.

I graze her shoulder with another kiss as I line up with her entrance.

Pushing in just enough so she feels me, I find her clit with my fingers again. Rubbing circles, I use my thumb to apply steady pressure. She falls forward, and I follow her, keeping the pattern going and staying exactly where I am. Her walls are tightening more and more around me. She's close. Muffled words moaned into the mattress beg me to keep going.

As if I could stop now.

I thrust deep at the same time I pinch her clit between my thumb and forefinger and tug. She shatters around me, screaming my name into the soft cotton of the sheets, her hips moving wildly.

Fuck, I love the way my name sounds on her lips like this. So overtaken with pleasure, it's more a moan than anything else. All she knows is me. What I'm doing to her body in this exact moment.

Pistoning my hips, I drive and retreat, my dick brushing against the spot that immediately builds her pleasure again.

"Oh my god, oh my god, oh my god. Please."

I move my hands to her breasts and pull her up, locking an arm around her waist to keep her upright while I continue to thrust. This angle is even deeper. I tweak both her nipples with sharp pinches before finding her clit again. I rub faster, increasing the speed of my finger until she's writhing against me, right on the edge of coming but with nowhere to go to escape the intense pleasure that buffets her body.

"*Chris.*" Her pussy is so goddamn tight, I'm barely hanging on.

Letting her go quickly, I pull out and push her ass up to find her clit with my tongue. I drag it in the same pattern while my name is mixed with sounds and pants as she rides the edge between pleasure and too much. Placing my thumb against the puckered hole of her ass, I press gently and tap her clit with my tongue.

She wails my name, her arms barely holding her up. The orgasm is still spasming through her pussy when I slide my dick back into her, her tight walls making it difficult to do anything more than pulse little by little until my hips bump against her ass.

"I-I-I can't." Her words are a combination of pants and whimpers.

"Oh yes you fucking can. And you will."

Shallow thrusts force my piercing to tap against her g-spot repeatedly until she screams into the pillow as another orgasm overwhelms her body. I unleash my own, letting it shoot from my spine to my extremities, traveling in a massive electric arc to my balls.

"*Fuck.*"

Her pussy continues to milk my orgasm from me, my muscles locking as I release myself with a groan. Intense pleasure strips me of all sensation other than the feel of the woman writhing under me. When I finally come back down, we're both on our sides on my bed and she's cradled in my arms. My semi-hard cock is still inside her. I brush a kiss against her shoulder at the same time my hand finds her breast.

"Mmm." She arches her back and presses her breast more fully into my hand.

"Sexy," I murmur against her skin and bite back a groan as she nestles her hips against my groin.

"I should go." Her voice is slurred. From pleasure or exhaustion? Both?

"No, you shouldn't." I tighten my hand on her breast.

She looks over her shoulder at me, her hair in disarray and her eyes languid and sated. The image burns itself into my brain. I'll never forget how she looks right now.

"But Gage—"

I silence her with a kiss.

"I locked the door."

"What if he needs us?"

Us. I like the sound of that way too much.

"We'll hear him."

"I shouldn't stay." She tries to pull away, and I tighten my hold on her.

"If you think I'm letting you out of my bed after tonight, you're mistaken."

"Chris."

"Jessie."

Her sigh speaks volumes.

"You're my boss."

"Do you regret what just happened?" Ice fills my veins at the thought.

"What? No. But it's complicated. Let's not make it more so."

I roll us so that I'm on my back and she's on top of me facing the ceiling. Her breath catches. She doesn't want to leave. I cup her breast and toy with her nipple with one hand while the other delves between her thighs.

"Let me convince you," I growl against her shoulder.

CHAPTER 13

JESSIE

I wake up to a warm pressure around my waist and breath blowing evenly against my hair.

It tickles.

Lifting my head, I try to find a clock to tell me what time it is, but peachy light is only starting to color the horizon. It was late when Chris and I finally showered and went to bed, and later still when he woke me up with kisses along my shoulder and his hand buried between my legs.

My body heats remembering the sensation.

"You're up early." His voice is still full of sleep, and he tightens his arm and tugs me closer to his body.

"I could say the same about you." I try to ignore the insistent way his hard cock pushes against my ass.

Warm lips trail across the back of my neck, and he shifts his arm, his hand resting on my breast. It's a casual touch, but I can't help but arch my back and press myself more fully into his hand with a quiet moan. He chuckles quietly, his mouth teasing the sensitive skin behind my ear.

"How did you sleep?" He inserts a thigh between mine while his hand shifts to twist the puckered tip of my nipple.

"Mmm." I rub against him, desire already overwhelming me. "Not enough."

"Maybe we should go back to sleep then." His suggestion is contradicted by the movement of his hand from my breast to my pussy. "Fuck, you're so wet."

I scissor my legs to give him more access, whimpering as he presses a finger in and out slowly while his thumb rotates against my clit.

"Maybe—oh god, Chris—maybe we're still asleep," I murmur, crying out as he pinches my clit between his thumb and finger roughly.

"What does that tell you?" He growls as his teeth sink into my shoulder.

"Not a dream," I pant. A second finger joins the first, and I reach up and back, digging my fingers into his thick hair.

His movements are slow, unhurried, as he shifts us until I'm on my back. His fingers continue working my pussy while he dips his head, capturing one of my nipples in his mouth and sucking lightly.

"Harder," I moan as the pressure on my breast increases. His tongue spars with the tip as my nerves all focus on the pleasure centered where his fingers continue to move.

Reaching, I wrap my hand around his cock, my thumb finding the piercing. I swipe over it once and then again. His moan vibrates around my breast, and his fingers increase their speed. My orgasm is building, washing like ocean waves along my toes, building higher and higher with every thrust of his fingers.

"Come for me, Jessie." His words are growled against my breast before he switches sides. Cool air tightens my nipple further, and I try to shift, to move, but his hand between my legs holds me prisoner and limits my movements to riding his fingers the way I want to ride his dick.

"I'm close." I whimper, the familiar sensation now building in my thighs.

His suction on my breast increases, his hollow cheeks intensifying the ache in my core.

"*Chris.*" His name breaks on a breath, pleading with him to take me further.

Fireworks explode behind my eyes while my pussy clenches around his fingers at the same time my body reaches for the thumb he presses against my clit. Every ounce of my focus is on the bundle of nerves, and I'm practically crying, the strength of my orgasm building rather than breaking.

Bright light overwhelms the fireworks, and I teeter between flying and falling. Sharp teeth sink into my nipple, and I shatter into a million pieces of the peachy sunlight that washes through the room, swamped by wave after wave of pleasure pulsing through me. His fingers only slow as the orgasm ebbs, and he releases my breast with a pop.

The smirk on his face is all confident male, and I yank him up to my lips, pushing my tongue into his mouth to tangle with his. The intense experience of that last orgasm has left me frantic for him. The need to be closer, to show him the emotions he released through my body is intense and obliterates everything else. With all the power I can muster, I flip us both so that I straddle him.

His eyes widen in surprise. "Sexy as fuck." He bites his lip, and I wholeheartedly agree.

He's sexier than sin. Dark hair falls back against the pillow, his brown eyes lit with a fire that I've come to realize is one he shares with me. My hands travel the planes of his chest, tracing the ink I want to ask him about. Later.

Flicking his nipple ring with my fingers makes him hiss. I trace his jaw with hot, open-mouthed kisses back to his ear until I retrace the line and move down his body. I nip at the pulse that pounds in his throat.

By the time I wrap my hand around his cock, my lips surround the metal on his chest, sparring with the piercing while his hands sink into my hair, holding me still.

"Jess." His groan echoes in the room, and arousal coats my thighs.

I play with the ring for several moments, laving the hard nipple with my tongue and tugging the warm metal with my teeth and lips. His hips press upward, driving his cock into my hand. With that reminder of my mission, I slide farther down his body. My tongue dips into his navel, and his fingers tighten in my hair. The slight tug pulls my gaze to his.

"Are you sure?"

"Yes."

His eyes glaze slightly as his lids lower, but he doesn't let go of my hair. The tension is another erotic sensation as I move farther down. The veins of his cock are pronounced, straining against the skin, and I lick my way up the largest one to the head of his cock before surrounding him with my mouth.

"Oh fuck." His stomach muscles flex under my hand, his dick jumping as I tongue the piercing.

It's cool, but not metallic. Taking more into my mouth, I run my tongue underneath until I find the piercing there and give it a little swirl.

"Jessie, fuck. I'm going to come."

He wasn't kidding when he told me this heightened his pleasure. He grows thicker in my mouth, and I push further down, swallowing around my gag reflex until I can't take him any deeper. I hum around his cock, and his hips thrust until he bumps the back of my throat.

"Fuck. That's it, angel. Your mouth feels so fucking good. The only thing better is that sweet little cunt of yours. I want to come in that talented little mouth, but I want your pussy even more." His words rip from him, and he pops me off his dick, tossing me onto my knees and slamming into me with one thrust.

"Ahh." I cry out as the piercing taps against the same spot it did last night. My pussy tightens in a rush as my orgasm goes from zero to sixty.

"Fuck. You're already close. Aren't you?" He groans against my shoulder, his lips pressing there as air saws in and out of his nose. "How close are you, angel?"

"I'm almost there."

His speed increases, and I moan into the mattress.

"Touch yourself. Play with that pretty pussy while I fill it with my cum."

I don't hesitate, my index finger gliding along the smoothness of his dick before I find my clit. I circle it with quick motions, my toes curling into the mattress. He cups my breast with one hand, pinching and twisting the nipple until my muffled screams morph into his name. Only after he roars his own release do we collapse against the bed.

"Fuck." His words whisper against my shoulder as we both draw air back into our lungs.

"Uh-huh."

"Jess, I—this has never happened to me before."

Opening my eyes, I search his face. "What?"

"I can't fucking get enough of you. Even now, I want you again."

He cups my face with one hand, rubbing a thumb across my cheek.

"It's because we shouldn't be doing this. It's the rebel in you."

"Who says we shouldn't?"

"Everybody. I'm your son's nanny. How cliché is that?"

"You're more than that."

"You said it yourself. The age difference—"

He silences that excuse with his mouth and doesn't break the kiss until we're both breathing heavily.

"I don't give a fuck about the age difference."

"You did last night."

"I felt like I should care about it. But I can't. I don't. We're both consenting adults. Who gives a shit what anyone else thinks?"

What would everyone think? The tabloids weren't kind to Jax when he started dating Charlie. Insta-love followed by his bone-headed idiocy followed by a baby? It had taken the press months to calm down about those two.

"I—"

"Do you want to be with me?"

"Chris, I'm not looking for a relationship. I'm not ready for that." If I'll ever be.

"Do you want to be with me?"

"It's not that simple."

"It really is. I want to be with you. I just want you. For as long as I can. Do you want me?"

Even before we slept together, there was a connection between us. An attraction that I couldn't ignore, no matter how hard I tried. But now that we've taken this next step? Now that I know what it feels like for him to play my body like a master? There's no alternative.

"Yes."

His bright smile lights up the room.

"Good. Now that it's settled, maybe we should get some more sleep."

I start to shift off the bed, but he latches on to my arm.

"Where the fuck do you think you're going?"

"To my room. To sleep."

"We had this conversation last night." He reels me into the crook of his arm so my head rests on his chest. "You're not going anywhere."

"Chris. It can't be as easy as that. Gage—"

"What about him?"

"This is only going to confuse him."

"I'm not going to hide what we're doing like some dark secret."

His words send a thrill through my body.

"He's gone through a lot…"

162

"And having him find out while we try and hide it from him is going to be worse." He sounds so sure.

"It's that easy?" I draw a pattern against his chest.

"Yes. You're mine, Jessie. And I'm going to make a couple things clear. I don't fucking share, and I'll be damned if I'm going to hide."

Because nothing hidden is ever good. My stomach tightens at the reminder.

"In fact, why don't we plan a day together? The three of us? No label, no phone calls, no nothing. You, me, and him. We'll hang out by the pool, eat pizza, and watch movies."

"I like that idea." It's a way for us to figure out this new dynamic together.

"Good." He drops his lips to my hair and tightens his arms around me. "Now let's get some sleep before we need to go wrangle a four-year-old in the pool."

He traces a pattern on my shoulder with his fingers, and his heart thumps rhythmically against my ear. I blink several times before I finally give up and keep my eyes closed, the effort too great to open them again.

When I pry my eyes open next, I panic, remembering the mess we left in the kitchen last night. Hoping that Gage is still asleep, I creep out of Chris's room after finding a t-shirt on the floor and tiptoe to my room to grab a pair of sleep shorts. I start to take off my pilfered shirt, but as I lift the fabric to my nose, all I smell is Chris.

I don't want to take off the shirt. I like his smell. I like the way he touches me—like he can't help himself, but he thinks I'm fragile. And the way he kisses me as if he's dying to taste me. Let's face it, I like everything about him.

He's a rock star.

But it's no longer the only thing I think of when he crosses my mind—which is more and more often. He's different. He reminds me of my brother's friends and how they are with their wives and children. I told him I wasn't looking for a relationship. And I'm not. But it doesn't mean that those slivers of attraction don't have the chance of turning into something else. Something...different.

"Oh my god, quit daydreaming and get to work." I shake my head and rush down the stairs.

I flush with embarrassment when I step into the kitchen. The bottles of syrup are tipped over on the floor, the bag of marshmallows kicked by the refrigerator. The saucepan is still on the stove—thank God I turned the burner off before Chris kissed me last night. The coffee cups and all the ingredients are still on the counter, some of them unusable after sitting out all night. My bikini top hangs from a drawer handle, and I find the bottoms lying in the middle of the floor next to my towel, while Chris's towel is still slung over the chair he tossed it on after we came in.

The only problem with cleaning up after what we shared last night? The memories that flood me with each step of the clean-up process. Grabbing the towels and my bikini, I bundle everything together and toss them toward the laundry room before I tackle the marshmallows that are now rock hard and the syrup bottles that ooze liquid as I replace the caps. I swipe my finger across the residual syrup and lick it off, my core throbbing at the flavor. And I didn't even try this on Chris. Only his tongue.

Maybe you should taste it on him.

The throb turns to an ache when I clean the counters and find a small dot of caramel sauce mixed with chocolate syrup. My breathing grows shallow at the memory of the way he'd pulled me to the edge of the counter to clean every drop of syrup from my body and how he'd given me two of the best orgasms of my life.

Face it. All the orgasms he's given you are fighting for the top spot.

Strong arms wrap around my waist as he nuzzles against my ear.

"There you are."

164

"Morning." I lean into his caress.

"I woke up and you were gone. I had plans for you." He wears an adorable pout.

I pop up on my tiptoes and brush his full lips with a chaste kiss. "I remembered all this and thought I should clean it before Gage gets up."

"I'll help." Before he pulls away, his fingers fist in the cotton of his shirt, holding me to him.

"I like you in my shirt."

"It was the only thing I could find to leave your room in."

But that doesn't explain why I'm still in it. The truth is, I like being in his shirt too.

"No complaints from me," he growls before his lips find the sensitive spot behind my earlobe.

I'd rather he keep doing what he's doing, but we need to clean up our mess. Breaking apart, we finish cleaning, and not a moment too soon. The dishwasher barely hums to life when I turn to find Gage in the doorway.

"Good morning, buddy."

"Gage! Come see Daddy." Chris kneels, and the little boy races into his arms.

Clean up, aisle four. I think my ovaries just melted. Or maybe that's my heart in a puddle on the floor.

"Are you hungry? Breakfast?" I ask, trying and failing to not fall in love with the way Gage cuddles into Chris's embrace.

He lifts his head and looks at me for several moments.

"Pancakes."

Tears spring to my eyes at the word. When Chris's gaze meets mine, his are equally shiny. We usually have pancakes. But to ask, he'll point to a picture on the fridge I put there for him or pull leftovers out from breakfast the day before.

"You want pancakes?" My voice wobbles, and Gage squirms in his father's arms.

"Pancakes," he repeats.

165

Wiping my hands under my eyes to capture stray moisture, I smile at the little guy who moves to grab the ingredients he can reach since he's become my official helper.

"We can do pancakes, bud. Let's show Daddy how we make them."

By the time we're finished, there's flour on the kitchen floor and more pancake batter dots the counter than made it into the pan, but I consider it a success. Gage and Chris add large amounts of syrup to their plates, but Gage ends up wearing the majority of his by the end of his first pancake.

At one point, Chris drags a finger through the syrup, looking at me with enough heat to cook the pancakes, and licks his finger clean. I fidget in my chair and take a sip of my juice to cool down in the now stifling kitchen.

"How about after pancakes we hit up the pool?" Chris asks Gage, who nods excitedly.

It's why we leave the dishes stacked in the sink and head upstairs to change. I check on Gage and help him straighten his little trunks with cartoon sharks on them. I barely finish before he tugs me down the stairs, and I'm grateful that Chris said he would grab towels.

"Sunscreen," I tell Gage.

He dutifully stops by the back door so I can spray and rub both of us down, although it takes longer since Gage wriggles like a greased pig in my grip. The day is warm already, the sunlight glinting off the pool when we step outside, and I'm glad I grabbed my dark glasses. Chris sits on a lounge chair, navy blue swim trunks slung low on his hips while mirrored aviators hide his eyes from me. But even though I can't see them, the heat of his gaze is tangible enough on my breasts. The heat there lasts for several moments before it travels down.

Gage releases my hand to run and cannonball into the pool with a small splash. Chris stands, momentarily concerned, but smiles when Gage pops out of the water with a giggle.

"He can swim really well." I step next to Chris, enjoying the heat of his body as much as the warmth of the sun.

"I thought so the other day, but he wasn't under water. No floaties?"

"He's not a fan." As I had learned the first time I tried to put them on him.

"I can see why. Who wants those when you're part dolphin?"

I smile and wave to Gage, who waves back.

"Want to get wet?" Chris's voice is a low growl in my ear. The question is rhetorical, given the current state of my bikini bottoms.

"I'm assuming you mean the pool," I tease, yelping slightly when his hand connects with my ass in a playful slap before dragging quickly over the center of my bottoms, his movements hidden by my body.

"Sure, the pool. But I'd like to discuss the other meaning later."

I squeeze my thighs together at the promise in his voice.

"I'm going to hold you to that."

"Please do. How many colors do you have that swimsuit in?" His question catches me off guard.

Swimsuit shopping is a pain in the ass. Nothing fits me right, so the last time I went with Meredith, I found a style that did and bought one in every color they had.

"Four. Purple, teal, white, and black."

Since the purple one is dirty and the teal one is still damp, I opted for the black. The white tends to turn transparent if I'm in the water too long.

"Do they make other colors?"

"I'm not sure. Why?"

"You should find out. If so, I want you to buy every one."

I laugh at the comment but trail off when he doesn't join in.

"You're serious?"

"Fuck yes." He steps behind me, his hands cupping my ass

167

where his son can't see. My breath catches, and my nipples pebble visibly in my top. "Every color."

"I could always go without."

His hands tighten against my cheeks, his thumbs dipping below the hem and grazing down as far as they can go.

"Be careful what you tease me with, angel."

His voice is a breath of air against my ear, and I shiver.

"Who said I was teasing?" My chest heaves with how needy he makes me.

"Jess." The way he groans my name reminds me of the sound of it on his lips when he comes.

Fuck. This is way too hot to be thinking about in front of a four-year-old.

"To be continued," I say, spinning around and palming him through his trunks. "For now, let's go. We promised Gage a pool day."

"Oh, I always keep my promises."

If my bottoms weren't damp before, they are now. He saunters toward the pool after dropping that line and dives in with a little splash, then pops up next to Gage.

"Jessie, are you coming?"

Not yet. But it sounds like I will be later.

CHAPTER 14

CHRIS

*I*f I were measuring life by the time spent with Jessie and Gage these last few weeks, it would be almost perfect.

And since there's no word from Noah, and Cornerstone backed down, the only time I'm not spending with them is when I leave to hang out with the guys at Evan's. After the comments Milo made to Jessie the day she moved in, I have zero interest in him flirting with her again. I'm afraid if he does, I'll do something stupid like knock him out.

Evan comes over some nights, and we work in the music room once Gage is asleep while Jessie works on her thesis. My family has been asking me to come to dinner, but I keep finding reasons to stay home with my son and the woman I can't seem to get enough of.

It's been two weeks since that night in the kitchen. Two weeks since my first taste, and my addiction to her has only grown stronger. But it's more than her body. It's the way she is with Gage as she works with him in the music room every day. Her infectious excitement that her thesis is getting better. The feel of her cuddled in my arms when I wake up each morning.

Despite her initial excuses about why we shouldn't, I convinced her every night for a week that we could share a bed by showing her the perks of staying. After the first week, she needed no convincing, but it didn't mean we were slowing down anytime soon.

This is only supposed to be fun.

It is fun. But it's also turning into something I'm not sure what to do with.

And Gage. She's healing him a day at a time. Pancakes and piano—a magical combination that seems to be unlocking Gage's voice. He's not as verbal as when he first got here, but little by little, his words are returning.

Gage runs in as I walk through the door from Evan's, and he wraps his wet arms around my jeans.

"Daddy!"

"Hiya, bud. Swimming?" I can only assume they were in the pool based on the amount of water dripping from his swim trunks.

"Gage, wait—oh, I didn't know you were home." Jessie's eyes roam my body much the same way that mine do hers.

"Just got back." I close the distance between us, brushing a kiss against her lips and lingering for a second taste, with Gage still wrapped around my legs.

I refuse to keep what we're doing a secret. She tried to convince me to not be as open, to not show her affection in front of Gage to avoid confusing him. Fuck that. He'd be more confused if I was awkwardly tense around her.

"Daddy." Gage tugs on my damp jeans and draws my attention back down to where he bounces around my legs.

"What's up, buddy?"

"Jessie's making mac and cheese." He pumps his little fist in the air, and I meet Jessie's eyes with a smile.

"Mac and cheese, huh? Like Daddy makes?"

Admittedly, my culinary prowess may be limited to mac and

cheese from a blue box.

Gage makes a face. "No."

"Homemade," Jessie says with a laugh.

I bite back a groan at the word. Since Jessie moved in a month ago, Lois has been cooking less and less. Instead, Jessie cooks one mouth-watering thing after another.

"Looks like I'll be working out tonight while you work on your thesis." I rub a hand over my flat stomach, and she rolls her eyes. "Can't miss out on homemade mac and cheese."

"You want to get Gage cleaned up and I'll start dinner?" Since she's in shorts and a tank, it doesn't look like she was in the water, although I spy the tie of her white bikini under her shirt.

"You sure you don't need a shower?" I lower my voice so only she can hear. Our showers typically last until at least one of us comes, and I wouldn't mind a shower right now.

"If I shower, we'll never eat."

"Oh, I'll eat all right." I wink at her.

"Go take care of your son." She waves her hands at us, but there's laughter in her voice.

"Sure. Come on, buddy, let's go."

Gage hops toward the stairs and then up each step until we reach his bathroom. His swim trunks are kicked off with a wet flop to the floor, and he waits until the tub is finished filling to sink into the mountain of bubbles. I've never met a kid that likes water the way he does. Letting him play for a few minutes, I hang up his shorts and convince him to let me wash his hair before we drain the water. His giggle when I rub the towel across his short hair is one of my favorite sounds.

Fuck, I missed it. He lets me wrap the towel around his waist and leads the way to his bedroom.

"Jammies?" I ask. Safe choice since we don't have plans to go anywhere tonight.

He nods.

"Which ones? *Paw Patrol* or Spiderman?" Six months ago, if

171

someone had told me I'd know what the hell *Paw Patrol* was, I'd have laughed. But now I've watched an episode or twelve of the talking dogs with Gage, who absolutely loves them.

"*Paw Patrol.*"

He wriggles into the pajamas and follows me to my room so I can change out of my more than damp jeans.

"That's Jessie's." He points to a bottle of lotion on my dresser.

Over the last two weeks, more and more of her things have migrated from her room to mine.

"It is." I tense and wait for more questions, like why it's in here, but Gage simply shrugs and makes faces at himself in the full-length mirror next to the dresser.

"Should we go see if dinner's ready?"

"Mac and cheese," he chants, bouncing in place. I lift him up on a bounce, laughing at his squeal as I fly him airplane style back down the stairs.

"Jessie, I'm a plane!" He holds his arms and legs out, mimicking a plane, even though he looks more like a starfish.

"You are! Are you ready for some jet fuel, Mr. Plane?" She holds out a plate of macaroni and cheese with a side of broccoli, and Gage crows his response and demands to be put down.

He's not out of my arms for a second before he's climbing into his seat and shoving pasta into his face.

"Slow down, bud." I chuckle at his exuberance, and he looks up with a cheese mustache ringing the top of his mouth.

"Here." Jessie hands me a plate of the same and holds one for herself while we settle next to Gage.

"Jessie." He looks up from his plate. "Ketchup?"

"Ketchup, what?" she asks.

"Pleeease."

She grabs the bottle from the table and squirts some on his remaining pasta before moving to her plate.

"What are you doing?" I wrinkle my nose as she circles the bottle over her pasta.

"What?"

"Ketchup?" I shudder and enjoy a non-ruined bite of cheese and pasta.

"You didn't seem concerned when Gage wanted some."

"He's a kid."

"So?"

"So, why ketchup?" Why would anyone in their right mind ruin mac and cheese with it?

"Have you ever had it?"

"No, because it's—" I stop talking when she side-eyes Gage.

"If you've never tried it, how do you know?"

"It's yummy." Gage finishes his pasta and moves on to the one vegetable he doesn't fight us about eating—broccoli.

"I like macaroni and cheese by itself. This is delicious." Lifting another forkful to my mouth, I let the flavors melt on my tongue. I have no idea what she put in this, but it's heaven in pasta form.

Heaven and a massive workout in my future.

She blushes and ducks her head, still struggling to take a compliment. Maybe it's time to work on more affirmations.

"It's only pasta and cheese." She tries to shrug off my words.

"And ketchup." I can't help but tease her.

"Try it." She holds out her fork, a small bite covered in ketchup.

"Umm…" How do I politely say no while my son watches me?

"Just a small bite."

She's used those words before. On my four-year-old son. I sigh, ready to agree and create my own forkful to wash down the ketchup covered mess.

"I dare you." Her teeth sink into her lower lip, her eyes filled with the promise of a reward for trying it.

Leaning closer, I slide my mouth onto her fork, then pull back slowly and lick my lips.

"What do you think?"

I chew, not completely revolted, but not as excited about it as the two of them.

"It's okay."

"You're crazy." She grabs another bite and pops it into her mouth with a moan that leaves my dick twitching in my shorts.

Crazy for you.

My eyes widen at the errant self-admission. Maybe I need to slow down. We're nowhere near ready to talk about something serious.

This is casual.

Only casual doesn't share a bed every night for two weeks, does it? Casual means I don't think of her all the damn time. That I don't want her—her body, her mind, and her heart constantly.

But despite it being fast, none of that is true. And once released, my feelings aren't backing down.

So what?

I take a drink of water and mull over the reality of my emotions while Jessie teases Gage until he giggles. It's not love. Not yet. But it's rapidly approaching that point. She looks up, a small smile on her face and love for my son evident in her eyes. I've been so busy being happy, being with both of them, that I didn't realize exactly what our routine had become—a family.

Gage is finally asleep after requesting not one, but three stories before bed. He's enamored with the book Jessie pulled out that first day and said was her favorite—*I Love You, Stinky Face*. The other two stories were books he brought with him. Did his grandparents give them to him? Or did Melanie? I'm afraid to ask. To make his voice fade again.

I asked Mamá what stories I liked at his age, and she gave me a few titles that I'm waiting to be delivered. I'm excited to share some of my favorites with my son. To see if he likes them as much as the books Jessie reads him.

Cardio is already done, and I'm in the middle of my second set of chest presses when Jessie runs in, her excited bouncing reminding me of Gage.

"Guess what!" She launches herself at me, and I rack the weight before I settle my hands on her hips after she straddles me.

"What?"

"I finished!" The hug she gives me is pure exuberance.

"Finished? Your thesis?"

"Yep. I just emailed my final draft to Dr. Habib for any last comments."

"That's wonderful, angel. Congratulations." I pull her mouth down to meet mine, brushing my lips against hers.

It's meant to be quick, a congratulatory kiss. But like any time I touch her, all my intentions burn under the heat that exists between us. Threading my fingers through her hair, I deepen the kiss and moan when she grinds against my growing erection. She runs her hands across my chest, her fingertips skimming the piercing. My hips thrust upward at the sensation, and she moans into my mouth, her tongue tangling with mine while she repeats the caress.

"Oh fuck." I trail kisses along her jaw and grip her hips to stop her from rubbing back and forth. My thin shorts do nothing to hide how much I want her.

"Why do you—oh—" She cries out as I cup her breasts through her sleep shirt. "Why do you work out without a shirt?"

I whip hers over her head and groan at the picture she makes right now. Her hair is wild around her, her nipples pointing in my direction and begging for my touch. Who am I to deny the request? I dip my head, capturing a beaded tip in my mouth while I roll the other between my fingers.

175

"Chris." She drops her head back, pushing her breasts closer to me.

"I don't wear a shirt when I work out—" I nip at her breast before plucking the other one—"because I want to drive you as crazy as you drive me."

She lifts my head up, her lips fusing to mine again in a powerful kiss. If that isn't enough to tell me, her words seal the deal.

"I need you."

The tone of her voice, her words, the way she looks right now —a lethal combination, and my dick twitches in my shorts.

"I'm right here." I try to tease, but the words come out on a growl, my need reaching its breaking point.

"No. Inside me. Right now."

She tugs at my shorts, and I shift my hips to help her. We've almost succeeded when my phone rings from my pocket.

"I need to check that." I groan against her ear.

With an apologetic kiss against her pouty lips, I pull my phone out.

Evan.

"Hey, Ev."

Jessie continues to grind against me, lifting her hands to play with her nipples as she teases me.

I fight to keep my eyes from rolling back in my head after one particular move leaves me ready to come in my shorts. Gripping her hip with my free hand, I trace the line where her thigh meets her body with my thumb. Hopefully I can get Evan off the phone quickly so I can focus on getting my girl off next.

My girl. It sounds right. Like I've waited all my life for Jessie to walk into it.

"Did you see the text from Noah?" he asks, interrupting my epiphany about the woman in my lap.

"Umm…"

Fuck. Did I? I only heard Evan's phone call because of the

length of the ring tone. Placing Evan on speaker, I click out of the call and into my texts. A group text sits unread from Noah to Evan, Finn, Milo, and me.

NOAH

I need to talk to you guys.

It was sent an hour ago, and no one's responded yet.

"Have Milo and Finn seen it?" I ask and hold my phone up for Jessie to see. Her eyes widen, and she puts her hands on my shoulders, rubbing lightly.

"Yeah, but they're waiting for you to answer."

I blow out a breath. Chris, the responsible one. Father Chris, the dad of Just One Yesterday. When am I simply Chris, Gage's dad? Or Chris the man?

"We've been waiting for him to reach out. To open the door, literally and figuratively, and tell us what the fuck is going on," I say.

We've been waiting for him for two weeks. But now that he's finally contacted us, I'm not sure how to feel about it. Relieved? Tired? Worried? All the above? I don't fucking know.

"Do you think he's finally getting help again?" Evan asks.

"Fuck if I know, man. I hope so. We're not us without him."

"Are you going to respond?"

"Yeah. Give me a minute. You guys good with whatever we schedule?"

He snorts. "What else do we have going on right now?"

Good point since we can't record without him.

"Okay. I'll see what I can do."

We hang up, and I stare at the message on my screen while Jessie continues to work my shoulders. The heat of a few minutes ago is gone, and instead, her presence is comforting. I may be out of strength, but she's here lending me hers with every move of her hands against my tense muscles.

"Are you going to respond?" she asks softly.

"Yeah. I need to. But…"

"But what?"

"I'm scared."

Looking up from my phone, I meet her gaze, opening myself up in a way I never have before.

"It's a lot." She understands what I'm feeling.

Fear of the unknown. We haven't talked to Noah in weeks. We know he was discharged from the hospital, but otherwise, we've been in the dark.

Fuck.

She leans her forehead against mine, and our breaths mingle together.

"What can I do?"

"You're doing it. You're here. With me." I draw her into my arms, holding on tightly as our heartbeats sync.

With a sigh, I pull back enough to key in my response.

> Hey, brother, glad to hear from you.
>
> When and where?

I hold my phone, waiting for the three dots to appear. Will he respond? Or was the first text a fluke?

"Patience," Jessie whispers and runs her hands up and down my arms in a soothing motion while I stare at my screen.

Please, Noah, respond.

Finally, the three dots pop up next to his icon—an image of him from our first tour, grinning like a loon from the top of the Space Needle in Seattle. It had been on his bucket list since he was in elementary school. For him, that picture was achieving something he never thought possible. We celebrated by getting so wasted we had no idea where we were the next morning when we woke up. Turns out we got from Seattle to San Francisco with no idea how.

My phone chimes with a text. Surprised by the sound, I bobble the device and nearly drop it.

NOAH

Can you guys meet me at my mom's?

Tomorrow at noon?

We'll be there.

The others give their confirmation shortly after mine.

MILO

Party at Noah's. J/K *wink emoji*

EVAN

Don't be a douche, Milo.

FINN

I'll be there.

EVAN

Me too.

Sighing, I silence my phone. The other guys will probably be blowing up my phone now. I set it down, seeking out Jessie's hands and lacing my fingers with hers.

"Tomorrow at noon."

"It's going to be fine." She squeezes my hand, silently giving me comfort.

"I hope so."

Fuck, do I hope so. I miss my family. I miss the way things used to be for the five of us. We were on top of the world. Until Noah fell.

"Me too."

She frees her hands and lifts them to the back of my head, scratching her nails lightly against my scalp.

"What can I do?" she asks.

My grip on her waist tightens, and I bring my lips close to hers.

"Be with me."

"I'm here."

A lifetime has passed since I said those words to her. But in reality, it's been less than twenty minutes.

"Hold on." She locks her legs around my hips as I stand, heading for our bedroom. I need to lose myself, to find myself, in her. To be with her. "I need to be inside you. Right now."

She claims my mouth as I cross the threshold to our room. Thoughts of Noah, of the meeting tomorrow, fade. My only focus is Jessie. The two of us tangled together until we collapse, falling asleep with me still inside her.

CHAPTER 15

JESSIE

MEREDITH

Play date with the littles today?

We want to meet Gage.

I blow out a breath and look over at Gage, who is devouring a bowl of Cocoa Puffs at the table. I didn't have the heart to wake Chris after he spent most of the night tossing and turning.

Who is we?

Me, Charlie, and Claire.

Mia had an audition, and Michaela is recording with the guys.

Am I in for an inquisition?

You missed the last three barbecues.

I did. But I had no idea how to introduce Chris to the group now that he and I are...doing whatever it is we're doing. And I know better than to try to pass him off as only a friend. So I claimed to have plans during two of the get-togethers and completely ignored the third until later, claiming I had only seen it after.

> I had plans.

Who are you talking to?

My house. 11.

> I didn't say yes.

As if I would give you another option.

I snort. That's true. If I don't show up at eleven, I can expect her, Charlie, and Claire on my doorstep less than thirty minutes later.

> Don't send out the cavalry. We'll be there.

"Gage?"

He lowers his bowl from where he's been slurping his remaining milk.

"Yeah?"

"You want to go play with some other kids today? They're all close to your age."

"Swimming?" His eyebrows raise up, and I laugh at his expression.

"No. Sorry. My friends don't have a pool," I say, and his expression morphs from excitement to crestfallen. "But there is a huge playset."

Never send my brother and Nick to buy anything. They came back with twelve boxes and two sets of instructions, then spent an entire weekend in Nick's backyard coming up with creative ways to cuss out the wood and screws that didn't want to follow the instructions. But at the end of the weekend, one-year-old Everly had a playset she still hasn't grown into two years later.

His face brightens again, and he puts his bowl down completely.

"I'm done. Let's go!" He jumps up from his chair, still dressed in his Power Ranger pajamas.

I giggle. "Slow down, buddy. We have time. Let's clean up your breakfast first, okay?"

"'Kay." Grabbing his bowl, he brings it to the sink, and I rinse it out for him before he grabs my hand. "Let's go, Jessie!"

"In our pajamas?" I tease.

"Oh." He looks down. "No."

"How about we get dressed?"

"Yeah!" The word is a shout over his shoulder as he races for the stairs. "I can do it!"

"Okay." I call back. "Let me know if you need help."

With the few extra minutes, I pour a cup of coffee for Chris and head upstairs. Poking my head in Gage's room, I find him putting his dinosaurs and several books into a backpack, but he's still dressed in his pajamas.

"What are you doing, bud?"

"I wanna take my dinosaurs."

"What about the books?"

He shrugs. "Maybe the other kids will want to read them too."

My hearts swells with love for this sweet little boy.

Clearing the emotion from my throat takes several breaths.

"That's sweet, Gage. I think they'll love that. Once you have that all packed up, don't forget to get dressed, okay?"

"I picked my clothes out already." He waves toward his dresser. Clothes spill out from every drawer, but at least there's a pair of shorts, underwear, and a t-shirt on the top.

I roll my eyes with a smile. I can always help him put everything else away later.

"Good job, buddy. I'm going to take this to Daddy and get dressed. Let me know if you need help."

"I can do it. I'm a big boy."

My breath catches, because even in the last month he's become more and more independent. Pretty soon he won't be a little boy anymore.

Sniffling with the realization, I head down the hall to Chris's bedroom. Well, I guess it's our bedroom now. I haven't spent a night apart from Chris in two weeks. Even though we agreed it's casual between us, it's becoming more. And I'm finding I don't want it to only be a fling.

I pulled the curtains earlier, so only soft light filters into the room when I step inside. He's asleep on his stomach, facing away from me while his back moves rhythmically with his breath. Setting the mug down on his nightstand, I sit on the edge of the bed, rubbing a hand over the smooth expanse of his back.

"Good morning," I murmur and press a kiss against his shoulder. "I brought you coffee."

"Mmm."

He stretches before shifting his head in my direction and blinking his eyes open.

"Hi." His voice is raspy with sleep, and dark circles ring his eyes.

"How are you?" It's obvious. The anxiety wraps around him like the blankets on the bed.

He shifts to his side and tugs me down next to him to wrap his arms around me.

"I don't know if I've ever been this scared." His lips brush my hair with his admission.

I rub my hands along his arms. "It's going to be okay."

"God, I fucking hope so." He tightens his hold and finds my neck with his lips. "Is Gage awake?"

"He is." A smile twitches my lips. "He's getting ready for a play date."

"A play date?"

"Mm-hmm. Meredith texted and invited us over for a play date with the other kids this morning."

"That sounds like fun."

"For him maybe. I think Meredith, Charlie, and Claire plan to grill me about missing the last few barbecues."

He nuzzles my neck, and I sigh and lean back against him.

"I told you to go."

"I didn't want to go without you." My words break off on a moan as his hand comes up to tweak my nipple.

"We'd have gone with you." He sinks his teeth into my earlobe and presses his hips against my backside.

"They would have given us the third degree."

He tugs up my sleep tank, his warm palm now free to drag along the sensitive nipple without a barrier.

"Bring it on." Warm kisses press along my neck and shoulder.

"Jessie, I'm ready!"

I yank my sleep tank into place just as the door slams open.

"You're not dressed," he complains, his bottom lip stuck in a pout.

I bite back a smile. "I'm sorry, buddy. Should I get dressed now?"

"No." Chris's voice is low enough behind me that it doesn't carry outside the two of us.

I bring my elbow back and am met with rock-hard abs.

"Shh," I hiss.

"Yes! I'm ready." He rolls his eyes and props his hand on his hips. I lose the battle and giggle at his expression, but when I do, it grows more serious.

"Okay, okay, buddy. Why don't you go play in your room and I'll be ready in a few minutes?"

"Promise?"

"I promise." I drag a finger over my heart, and Chris groans quietly behind me.

Gage leaves, not bothering to close the door.

"Time to get up." I laugh when Chris's arms tighten around me again. "I promised your son."

With a sigh, he finally lets me wiggle up. "What are you going to promise me?"

I glance over my shoulder at him, and my core pulses at the heat in his eyes.

"I'll make it up to you later."

"Is that a promise?"

Goosebumps shiver down my spine at the way his lips wrap around the word. Leaning down, I find his mouth with mine before I straighten again quickly.

"I promise."

♪♪♪♪♪

"There she is!" Meredith waves excitedly from a lounge chair on the patio.

"You said eleven, right?" Did I get the time wrong?

Charlie and Claire are sitting next to Meredith, while Ken, Mason, and Millie run across the bridge on the playset. Looking around, I find Teddy and Everly in the sandbox.

"Are we late?" I ask, stumbling forward as Gage ducks behind my legs.

"We were a few minutes early," Claire says from where she's nursing Olly on the patio.

"And I'm on baby watch. I brought the kids over right after Nick left." This from Charlie.

Meredith huffs. "I've had a baby before. I know when to call Nick or my mom. Plus, I still have a week."

Charlie shushes her. "It's because we love you. We're your family."

Because that's what this group is. Not merely friends.

Family.

"Is that Gage?" Claire nods at the little boy who peeks out from behind my legs.

Smiling, I nod and hold a hand behind me. He grabs hold of it and steps next to me.

"This is Gage. Gage, this is Meredith, Charlie, and Claire."

He waves at the women who all smile at him.

"Is that Rubble on your shirt?" Charlie asks, pointing to the little bulldog wearing a yellow hat.

He nods, but then shifts his attention to Claire.

"Baby."

"This is Olly. Would you like to come say hello?" Claire asks.

He looks at me.

"It's okay. Why don't you go see him, and then I'll take you to the other kids?"

They beat me to it though. Gage has barely moved when Ken leads the charge, the other kids following behind her.

"Aunt Jessie!" she squeals and throws herself at me in a hug.

"Hey, Ken. Hey, guys. Look how big you are." They all preen at my compliment.

"Who's that?" Mason points at Gage, whose attention dances between the faces of the mini mob of kids.

"This is Gage."

Everly is closest to Gage, and she wraps her smaller arms around him in a hug.

"Hi, Gage. I'm Everly. You like *Paw Patrol*?"

Everly is exactly like her mom—a mini chatterbox whose exuberant energy will wear out most kids, let alone the adults.

The little guy nods.

"Me too. I like Skye. She's pink! I have her over there—" She waves toward the playset. "Wanna come see?"

Another glance at me.

"Go have fun. I'll be right here."

And with that, all the kids except baby Olly tear off toward the swing set.

"Okay, now that the minions are out of earshot." Meredith turns her attention to me, and I squirm under her intense gaze. "Where the hell have you been, Jess?"

"What do you mean?" Heat is already burning up my chest and settling in my cheeks. "I haven't been anywhere."

"Exactly. It's been two weeks since any of us saw you." Meredith arches an eyebrow and studies me shrewdly.

"I've been working." My voice cracks under her scrutiny, and I clear my throat.

"You've had jobs before," Charlie says, jumping into the interrogation. "But still made it to every event."

"I—"

I'm running through excuses in my brain, discarding all of them, since not one can explain my absence at one event, let alone the three I missed.

"Granted, if I were living with a sexy rock star, I wouldn't leave either." Claire smiles. "Oh wait, I am. And even I'm making it to our dinners."

Groaning, I drop my face into my hands.

"You guys."

"Better us than the boys. We figured you were more apt to spill it if your brother wasn't within earshot."

"There's nothing to spill." The lie doesn't taste right in my mouth.

This time, three sets of eyes focus on me and hold.

"Fine. Yes. Okay, yes. There is something going on." I finally break.

Meredith pumps a fist in the air. "I knew it! Tell us everything."

I don't tell them everything. Some things—the night in the kitchen and Chris's piercing—are too private to share.

"You like him." Charlie's astuteness is one of the things I love about her. Unlike Meredith, she isn't loud about recognizing something.

"Of course I do. I wouldn't sleep with him if I didn't."

"No, I mean you *like him* like him."

"Neither of us is looking for anything."

That's what we said.

Because it's the truth.

I don't get involved with rock stars.

What do you call sharing a bed with one for two weeks?

Oh god. I'm in a relationship with a rock star.

"Jessie, you okay?"

I blink and bring the three women back into focus.

"What?" I ask Claire.

"You look a little pale."

"You didn't realize, did you? How much you care about him?" Charlie asks quietly.

"No. I—he's thirteen years older than me."

"Who cares?" Meredith asks with a snort. "Nick is older than I am. West is older than Michaela."

"Thirteen years?"

"Well, no."

"How did this happen?" I look to the three older women for advice. "I swore after Bowie that I would never date another rock star."

"Is Chris anything like Bowie?" Claire has a point.

"I thought he was. At first."

"And now?"

"He keeps showing me he's not. I mean, he's not perfect—"

"Show me any man who is," Meredith interrupts with a laugh. "None of our husbands are."

"What do I do? This is supposed to be casual."

"Are you sure he still wants it to be casual? Maybe you guys should talk about it."

"I can't do that," I tell Charlie. "I was the one who told him I wasn't interested in anything more."

"But it *is* more."

I open my mouth—to contest, to tell them not to tell my brother anything, but I'm interrupted by Everly.

"Mom! Can Gage come to my birthday party?"

"Oh, lord," Meredith says to us with an eye roll. "Her birthday isn't for another six months."

Where will I be in six months? Not with Gage. My new job should start by then. But it doesn't mean that Gage couldn't still come to the birthday party.

"Babe," Meredith calls to her mini-me. "Your birthday isn't for six months."

"So?" Her daughter shrugs like it's no big deal.

When is Gage's birthday? Will I be around to watch him turn five? I send a quick text to Chris.

> When is Gage's birthday?

His birthday?

> Yeah. I just realized I didn't know it.

May 7th

I nearly drop my phone.

> May 7th? Like next Saturday?

Fuck. How did I forget his birthday was coming up?

Parent of the year.

> Don't be so hard on yourself.
>
> You've had a lot going on.
>
> Don't worry. I'll take care of it.

Thank you, angel.

Leaving for Evan's now.

We're going to ride together.

Be safe. Text me if you need me.

I always need you.

Holy shit. Maybe Charlie is right. Maybe his feelings for me are changing exactly like mine are. And now I have a birthday party to plan in less than a week.

"That is the sappiest smile I've ever seen," Nick says to me, walking up behind Meredith and dropping a kiss on the top of her curls while his hand rests on her distended stomach. "What's with the smile, Jess?"

"Yeah, what's with the smile?" Jax comes out of the house, followed by Dylan and Michaela.

"I thought you were recording all day." Charlie stands, only for Jax to scoop her up into his arms. "Put me down, you goof."

"That's the first thing you're going to say to me, gorgeous? You didn't miss me?" He sticks his lower lip out in a pout, and she laughs before covering his mouth with hers.

"Get a room," I tease.

"You're just jealous," Jax says once he comes up for air.

"I don't think Jessie needs to be jealous," Meredith teases.

I shoot her a look. I don't know who has the bigger mouth—my brother, who can't keep a secret, or Meredith, who has no idea what secrets are.

"Why?" Jax's attention swings from Meredith to me.

"Ignore her. Pregnancy brain."

"Yes, ignore me," Meredith nods, realizing her mistake.

Jax shrugs, and I release the breath I was holding.

"I'm glad everyone is here...well, except Mia, but I'll text her later. I just found out Gage's fifth birthday is next weekend. Would you guys want to come over for a pool party?"

Agreements echo in surround sound, so I fire off a text to both Mia and Dawn to tell them about the party too. Dawn says she'll check with Chris's brothers and sister, and I'll have Chris talk to the guys since I'm sure they'll want to come too.

Looks like my tribe is getting bigger.

CHAPTER 16

CHRIS

*M*y stomach roils the closer we get to the house that used to be a second home. The Kelley residence is small, but it was central to all of us, so it only made sense for the band to practice here. So many good memories live here. Hours spent in the basement with pizza and other junk food while we practiced nonstop. Breakthroughs and celebrations and even arguments.

Milo and Finn sit in the back seat without saying a word. It's unusual for them and adds to the stress cramping my stomach. Evan offered to drive, but now I almost wish I had. I sit in the passenger seat, overwhelmed by the silence, the anxiety about seeing Noah for the first time in several weeks bubbling over. I open my mouth, ready to tell Evan to turn around.

But I can't. With a sigh, I close my mouth again.

"What?" Evan asks with a glance in my direction.

I fidget and reach forward to turn on the radio. It's quiet, but the background noise soothes some of the anxiety that threatens to swallow me whole.

"I—what are you thinking about right now?"

Is he as nervous as I am?

"Remember that time Noah's mom caught us with those girls in the basement?" He grins at the memory.

I chuckle. "To be fair, it started as a practice."

"Until your girlfriend showed up." Finn joins the conversation and leans forward.

"With all her friends," Milo says, still leaning back against the seat.

"Not my girlfriend. Even if she wanted to be."

"What was her name again? Amanda?" Finn turns to Milo.

"Ashley," I correct.

She'd tried to persuade me to call her my girlfriend for most of our senior year. When I told her I couldn't hang out, she showed up to our practice with four of her girlfriends. Noah's mom came home to a basement full of teenagers making out and a case of beer on the stairs courtesy of Ashley's older sister.

"I thought she was going to send us all to military school," Evan says.

There's a chorus of "same" and "me too."

"Did anyone ever find out what she said to the girls?" I ask the guys.

"It couldn't have been any worse than what she said to us." I can almost feel Milo's eyes roll from the front seat.

We got a forty-five-minute lecture on trust, followed by another ten minutes on underage drinking. She rounded out the night with a thirty-minute lecture on safe sex. Every part of her cautionary advice had gone out the window as soon as we signed our deal with Cornerstone.

"She was only gone a few minutes when she walked them upstairs."

"Finn's right," I say. "We definitely got the worst lecture that night."

Evan slows the car, turning onto Noah's street, and stops a few houses away.

"What's the matter?" I ask, looking out the windshield and then the passenger side window, but coming up with nothing.

"The last time we were here was the night we signed our contract."

Fuck.

That memory hits me like a freight train. Signing with Cornerstone, high on life, planning for big dreams and a bigger future. We sat in the basement all night, staring at a copy of our signed contract while we toasted each other with sodas.

"I'd forgotten," I whisper around the emotion clogging my throat.

"Are you ready?" Evan looks at me first before turning to the back seat.

We all nod. Ready or not. We're here.

The neighborhood sounds the same as it did almost twenty years ago. Nostalgia mixes with anxiety, and I'm not sure if I should be happy, sad, or somewhere in between. Mrs. Kelley looks older than she did at the hospital when she opens the door. No doubt the last two weeks have aged her another twenty years.

"Boys." A small smile curves her lips, and her shoulders slump.

With relief or resignation?

"Mrs. Kelley." We say it in unison while she ushers us inside and into the living room where Noah and a woman wait.

Noah sits on the couch with his hands clasped in front of him, wearing a baggy flannel over an equally baggy concert t-shirt from a show we saw in high school. With a start, I realize that these *are* his clothes from high school. I couldn't see what the drugs were doing to him. Until now. The look he gives us when we walk into the room is filled with guilt, and the anxiety solidifies in my stomach, a giant rock I can't loosen no matter how much I try to breathe it free.

"Noah." I step closer to him, and relief pushes away the anxiety when he stands and returns my embrace.

"Chris."

Evan, Milo, and Finn follow me until we all stand around awkwardly, no idea what comes next. The woman on the couch nods at Noah, and he clears his throat.

"Thanks for coming, guys."

I nod, but it seems like Noah has more to say.

"I-I wanted to say—fuck, this is hard—I wanted to say how sorry I am." He looks at the woman, and she smiles encouragingly at him.

Who is she?

"I'm sorry for what I put you guys through the last few years. And for what you had to deal with when I overdosed."

His voice cracks with emotion, and goosebumps travel along my arms.

"I, um, I have a problem. Which you know."

"We want to help," I say, and Evan nods his agreement. That's what we were trying to do when he landed himself in the hospital.

"You can't." His words are so quiet I have to strain to hear them, despite the silence in the room.

"What?"

He clears his throat. "You can't."

"What do you mean we can't? We've helped before." Evan paces the length of the room and back.

"It wasn't working. I mean, it did for a little while, but, you guys, each time I left rehab, I wanted to use again. Fuck, I wanted to use in rehab."

"Isn't that what most addicts want to do?" Milo looks as confused as I feel.

"No...yes? I don't know." Noah runs a shaky hand through his hair.

"So what are you saying, Noah? Why haven't we heard from you in two weeks? Fuck, you wouldn't even let us in to see you at the hospital."

There are tears in his eyes when his gaze meets mine. "I was ashamed."

"You have nothing to be ashamed about," I argue.

"Denise, can you…?" Noah looks at the woman—Denise—who nods.

"Of course. Gentlemen—"

"Who the fuck do you think you are?" Finn surges from his spot on the couch. "This is bullshit. I'm leaving."

"Finn." Evan wraps his hand around Finn's bicep. "We need to listen."

"Please let me explain." Denise holds up her hands, and finally Finn shrugs out of Evan's grasp and leans against the wall. "My name is Denise Valdez. I'm a counselor at Phoenix Lane."

"What is Phoenix Lane?" I automatically step into my role as the leader of the group.

"It's a rehabilitation center about an hour and a half northeast of Phoenix."

I look at Noah. "You're going to try rehab again?"

He nods.

"Our program is different from the ones Noah has experienced before," Denise says.

"Different how?"

"Where most programs are between thirty and sixty days, we operate several levels of programs. Noah will enter the intensive level before eventually transitioning to one of the cottages on our property."

"Cottages?" I ask.

She nods. "Think of them like halfway houses. But in residence."

"How long does all that take?" I ask.

What impact will this have on our recording and touring schedule? Can I convince Cornerstone to be more patient?

"The intensive program is typically twelve weeks. However,

we don't like to assign arbitrary timelines. How long Noah spends in that program will depend on him."

"And the cottage transition?"

She shrugs. "We've had some residents stay there six months, and others have remained in residence for two years."

Two motherfucking years? I can't convince Cornerstone to be *that* patient.

I spin to look at Noah. "Are you prepared for that, Noah? Two years?"

"I-I-I don't know."

"What does that mean?" I ask.

But a part of me doesn't need him to answer. And I don't want him to choose us over getting clean. But fuck.

"Chris." The anguish in Noah's voice rips at my gut.

"Noah."

"I, god, I don't want to say this. But I don't have a choice."

My swallow sticks painfully in my throat.

"Don't want to say what?" Evan asks quietly.

He knows. We all do. But Noah makes it real.

"I'm—I'm leaving the band."

"Just until you're better, right?" Milo asks.

Poor, naïve Milo.

"Permanently."

Stepping into my house two hours later, I could rival an octogenarian in mobility. I lean against the door and scrub a hand down my face as I try to muster the energy to keep moving. To keep going.

After Noah's bombshell, I managed to put my own thoughts and feelings aside to calm Milo, but Finn was another story. He left Noah's and grabbed a car back to his place. Evan said he'd check on him later, but the rest of us stayed and spent some time with Noah, who is leaving this afternoon for Cave Creek, Arizona. Noah had joked it would be hard to find trouble in the desert. I'm not so sure about that, but, fuck, do I hope it works for him.

Maybe leaving the band isn't permanent.

Two years is a long fucking time.

"Daddy!" Gage's little voice echoes through the house as he rushes down the stairs and throws himself at my legs.

"Hi, buddy." I pick him up despite his squirming and hug him close to me to soak in a little of his innocence after my day from hell.

"Hey, you're home." Jessie's smile reminds me of a painting I saw once. A beautiful angel surrounded by light.

Her descent is slower than Gage's, and I meet her at the last step, reaching for her to join our family hug before capturing her lips.

"Everything okay?" Concern furrows her brows as she pulls back and searches my face.

I want to break down and tell her everything. To hold her. To have her tell me everything is going to be okay.

"I—" The words lock in my throat, and all I can do is shake my head.

Her lips graze my chin, and the gesture breaks through the numbness surrounding me.

"Later?" she asks.

I shake my head again, and my lips find hers in another quick kiss for strength.

"Noah's leaving the band."

"What?"

"Permanently."

"Chris." She loops her arms around my neck and fits her body against mine.

"Please tell me your day was better than mine. Distract me," I murmur against her hair.

"Gage is having a birthday party here next Saturday."

The band may be falling apart, but I still have my son.

And Jessie.

For as long as she'll let me keep her.

I don't leave the house all week—I talk to Evan on the phone, but otherwise, the week is dedicated to the two best parts of my life—Gage and Jessie.

"Daddy!" Gage bounces into our bedroom as the sun peeks over the horizon. "It's my birthday!"

"It is? Are you sure?"

He nods.

"And how old are you now? Twenty-one yet?"

He giggles and holds up one hand with all five fingers spread. "This many. When are my friends coming?"

"At eleven," Jessie says, sitting up in bed behind me.

"How long is that?"

"You have about seven hours until then, buddy." Amusement is clear in Jessie's voice.

"I'm going to go play." He dashes back out of the room, leaving the two of us alone again.

"Think he'll take a nap before then?" I turn and yank Jessie back down to the pillows.

"Doubtful."

But when I check on him a little while later, he's passed out under his bed, a dinosaur in each hand. I snap a pic with my phone and show it to Jessie when I meet her downstairs in the kitchen.

"Poor tired baby," she coos.

"I'll wake him in a bit and get him dressed. Who's coming today?"

"Your mom and dad are coming. Miles and Levi?"

"My brothers."

"They're coming with their families. Your mom said your

sister would come if she could get off work. My brother is coming with his family. Nick and Meredith. Dylan and Claire. Mia and Garrett. Michaela and West. Sydney. And a whole bunch of kids."

I suck in a breath at the mile-long list. "The guys said they'll be here too."

"Wow, okay, I have work to do." She spins and opens the refrigerator, pulling out ingredients and setting them on the counter.

I step behind her, bumping my front to her back as my lips drop to her neck. "Need any help?"

"I do," she says, turning to give me a look. "But actual help and not what you're suggesting."

"What am I suggesting?" I waggle my eyebrows.

She laughs. "Ever made potato salad?"

By ten thirty, Jessie has made pasta salad, pulled hamburgers and hot dogs out of the fridge for the grill, and sliced at least a dozen tomatoes and onions. Gage's birthday cake, featuring the *Paw Patrol* characters, is sitting on the counter next to a big number five, ready for the big moment. Two cans of sunscreen and a bottle of lotion sit next to the door, ready to be slathered on kids and adults, and Jessie had me stack a mountain of towels by the pool.

Gage is in brand new swim trunks for the occasion, already sunscreened up and bouncing up and down the stairs waiting on his friends, who arrive en masse.

"Hijito, feliz cumpleaños!" Papá lifts Gage, tossing him in the air until his giggles are breathless.

Mamá, along with Miles's and Levi's wives, heads in to check with Jessie to see if she needs help, and the men wrangle children outside as the doorbell rings again. It's almost nonstop for the next thirty minutes, until finally everyone is here, and the sound of children shrieking and splashing is joined by adults as we talk and laugh in small groups.

Jessie steps into the backyard, and I wrap her in my arms.

"This is amazing, Jess."

"Think he likes it?"

I search the kids for Gage, who is doing cannonballs, to Mason's delight.

"I think he loves it." I nuzzle her jaw, my lips coasting up to her ear.

"What the fuck are you doing with my sister, Topher?" Jax stomps toward us, his face twisted as he glares at me, then Jessie.

"Chris. In real life, I'm just Chris."

Charlie joins us as well, but Jessie steps between her brother and me first.

"Knock it off, Jax."

"He was kissing you." Jax comes up short, and Charlie steps in front of him.

"And I was okay with that," she counters. "I was actually enjoying myself until you charged over here like an angry bull."

My lips twitch with a smile at the sight of petite Jessie lecturing her older and much taller brother.

"Jackson. This is not the time or place to discuss this. This is Gage's birthday party." Charlie stares her husband down until his shoulders relax.

"But—"

"But nothing. Now go play with Teddy. He wanted to go swimming. I'm not feeling well." She lays a hand on her stomach, and I remember that Jessie said she was pregnant again.

Jax's eyes widen. "Gorgeous, come on. Sit down, and I'll bring you some water."

They move back toward the chairs, and Charlie looks over her shoulder, sending us a wink that sends Jessie into a fit of giggles.

"I love her so much," she manages through her laughter.

"I love that sound." I fold her back into my arms.

The rest of the party passes uneventfully, despite the death glares Jax shoots my way. We're almost done with cleanup when Meredith gasps.

"Babe?" Nick stills and studies his wife.

We all do, since she's three days overdue.

"My water broke."

Everyone moves at once in this strange sort of organized chaos. My mom and dad offer to stay with all the kids, and I join the large group of adults rushing to cars to follow Nick and Meredith to the hospital.

I'm not sure how I feel about hospitals after Noah's stay, but I push those sensations down and sit in the waiting room. Based on the number of kids at the party today, they must all be used to this. When another woman rushes in with Everly in tow, Jax and Charlie stand.

"Val." Charlie hugs the woman who looks excited and nervous at the same time.

"Val is Meredith's mom," Jessie whispers to me.

"Any news?" the older woman asks.

Jax shakes his head. "Nothing yet."

They sit back down, and Everly moves to the kids' area, pulling out a picture book and turning the pages. She hasn't even finished before Nick pushes a bassinet containing a small, pink-wrapped bundle into the room.

"Everly."

She glances up from the book at the sound of her dad's voice. Her eyes grow round, and her smile stretches across her face.

"Come meet your sister, baby." He lifts the baby from her bassinet and sits down next to Meredith's mom, who's smiling and wiping at her eyes.

Everly moves closer and climbs into the chair on Nick's other side.

"Sister?" Her word is slurred by the finger in her mouth.

"That's right. This is Lainey. Your baby sister."

"Lainey," Everly repeats.

Nick nods and lifts his gaze to Meredith's mom.

"Lainey Nicole Rhodes."

"And Meredith?" she asks.

"Fine. Better than fine. Amazing, considering how fast Lainey here wanted to join the party." Nick's smile is so full of love it's both hard to see and hard to turn away from. "She was resting when we left a few minutes ago, but we need to head back."

Meredith's mom leans over and brushes a kiss against the blanket before placing another on Nick's cheek.

"For Meredith."

Nick leaves again, and each of the couples in the room sits together, talking quietly among themselves. Maybe reminiscing about their baby's introduction to the world? A part of me is jealous at the sight.

"I never got this with Gage," I murmur to Jessie, who seems lost in thought.

She jumps when I rub my hand down her back, confirming my suspicion.

"What? Sorry?"

"This whole hospital waiting room experience. As many times as the guys have been sued for paternity, you might think I'm an old pro at this. But Gage is it. And I missed out on the first four years of his life. I don't know if any of this"—I gesture around us—"is real or not."

"It's been pretty consistent since I moved out here."

"I never asked you. Where are you from?"

"Texas. I grew up outside of Austin."

"And this is home now?"

"It is. This is my family. Mama and Daddy have started to talk about moving out here. Now that Charlie's pregnant again, it'll probably be sooner rather than later."

"Four kids, huh?"

"Yep."

"What about you, Jess?"

The color leeches from her face.

"What about me?"

"You're young, so I'm sure kids are a long way off, but have you thought about it? You're a natural. I assume you want to be a mother someday."

I can already picture her as a mother to our child. Holding our baby. The image is real enough that I suck in a breath, my heart pounding in my chest.

I want that.

Dude, slow down.

"I, um, I need to use the restroom."

She stands and leaves the room so quickly I don't have the chance to snag her wrist before she's gone. Trying to ignore Jax's glare—again—I follow her, waiting outside the women's restroom until she comes out.

When she emerges, she jumps at the sight of me, her hand flying up to cover her heart. "Holy—you scared me."

"Sorry."

Stepping forward, I bring my hands to her biceps and rub slightly. I love the way she relaxes against me, her head leaning forward against my chest and her breath blowing through my t-shirt on a sigh.

"Did I upset you?" I murmur against her hair.

"No. It's fine."

But the tension creeping back into her shoulders tells a different story. Using my thumb and finger, I lift her head until she's looking at me.

"I believe that's the first time you've lied to me, Jessie."

She sinks her teeth into her lower lip as she looks everywhere but at me. I hold my ground until finally her gaze stops on mine.

"What did I say to upset you?"

Tears line her lower lashes, and her brown eyes sparkle like diamonds. My thumbs catch two drops as they run over and onto her cheeks.

I rack my brain. What did I say that would cause this? "Jess?"

She pulls away from my hold and puts her hand in mine, leading me into another hallway. After one more turn, we step out into a small, enclosed garden area. I start to ask how she knows this hospital so well, but then I remember all the kids.

Finding a bench, she sits and tugs me with her while my heart pounds like a horse running the Kentucky Derby. Heartbreak is so clear on her face. I want to fix it. To tell her to forget whatever it was I said.

More tears run down her cheeks when she closes her eyes and takes a deep breath. After a moment, she clears her throat and focuses on me.

"I can't have children."

CHAPTER 17

JESSIE

"*What* do you mean you can't have kids?"

I can't blame him for being momentarily dumbstruck, given the massive bomb I dropped on him. I swallow and swipe my hands under my eyes to clear the tears, even though more quickly replace those I wipe away.

"I told you I'm a cancer survivor."

"Yeah. You had it when you were a kid."

I nod. "One of the side effects of the treatment is that I'll never have children of my own. I'll never be a-a mom." My voice warbles over the word.

"Angel." He pulls me into his arms, and some of the tension eases from my body. "Giving birth is not the only way to become a mom."

"But—" I lean back to argue my point, but he stops me with a kiss.

He slants his mouth and runs his tongue along the seam of my lips until I open. He tastes like the salt from my tears. I shift on the bench to deepen the kiss—I don't want him to taste like my sadness, but I need him. I need his reassurance. He grips my hips and lifts me to straddle him. Anyone could walk by the picture window that highlights the garden or walk through here, but I've lost the ability to care.

I thread my fingers through his hair until my nails scrape against his scalp. His lips leave mine, trailing along my jaw while his hands move my hips back and forth to grind me against him.

Fuck, I want him inside me. But he slows the movement of his hands until my hips stop completely and his breath blows against my neck, sending goosebumps to form along my spine.

"Wow." I lick my lips, capturing the remnants of him left behind.

"I want you." He groans and shifts me back. His erection strains against the denim, giving truth to his words.

"But what I told you—"

"Changes nothing," he interrupts. His eyes lock on mine, and the seriousness there sends heat to lick through my body. "I don't care one way or the other, Jess."

"You don't?"

"Zero fucks." He leans forward and nips at my lips.

I smile at his playful caress. "I didn't expect that response."

I've only told one other person. No one in my family—blood or otherwise—knows. My parents knew the treatment could impact my ability to have kids, but according to the specialist I saw when I moved to LA, it's more than a possibility—it's my reality.

But Chris is right. More than anything, I want to be a mom. But it isn't in the cards for me. And I'm still trying to accept that.

"What response did you get the last time?" he asks.

"It doesn't matter." And I don't want to remember.

"No, angel, it matters. I want to know who made you question how I would respond."

"Chris." I release his name on a sigh.

"Jessie. You can tell me anything. Nothing you say is going to change how I feel about you."

I play with the edges of his hair at my fingertips and study his face.

"Do you mean that?"

"Fuck yes, I mean it. Tell me."

His fingers flex against my hips. It's not painful, but possessive, and the heat of his hands brands me, leaving what feels like permanent marks.

"My ex." It takes several moments to say those two small words.

"Bowie? You told him?" A muscle ticks in his jaw.

I nod. "When I first told him, he said he was fine with it. We were young—fuck, I was nineteen, and he had just turned twenty-one. We weren't thinking about starting a family or anything. But after I saw the specialist, I was really upset. I couldn't stop crying."

As if to prove my point, two more tears roll down my cheeks.

Chris wipes them away gently. "What happened after that?"

"Nothing, really. I was still trying to persuade Jax to sign him. I begged. I offered a lifetime of free babysitting. I even tried to guilt him into it."

The acid of that decision still eats at me. How I told Jax that it was his fault Mama and Daddy treated me like spun glass. Because of all the news stories about him. I told him that I felt more like an observer in my life than a participant.

I'll never forget the look of hurt on his face, the pain in his eyes as he'd asked me if I really felt that way. The hollow tone when he told me that nothing I said was going to change his mind about a singer who was better suited to karaoke bars than a stage.

After breaking up with Bowie, it had taken me a month to work up my nerve to go back to Jax's house. To admit that he'd been right about my now ex-boyfriend. But Bowie'd had to destroy me for me to see it.

"None of that worked," Chris guesses.

I nod once. "Right. Jax had to tell me flat out he would never sign Bowie, but even then, I didn't want to admit it. I kept telling him I could change my brother's mind."

"Until you walked in on him with another woman."

"Yep."

"Fuck, Jess, I'm sorry. That guy was a world class asshole."

"He's so much worse than that. Hell, even Charlie has called him some pretty colorful names."

He smiles and rubs his thumbs softly along my jaw.

"Sounds like everyone knows he was to blame. Not you."

"I know that. Now. But it didn't change the pain he caused when he told me I wasn't a real woman."

His hands still on my face, anger blazing to life in his eyes.

"He said what now?"

I open my mouth to respond, but he shakes his head.

"Never mind. Don't repeat it. I want to track him down and beat the shit out of him."

"He's not worth it." This time I cup his jaw in my hands and cover his lips with mine.

"But you are. I need you to hear me. To recognize that you are worth it."

"I—"

He cuts off my platitude with a kiss that leaves me breathless and back in his lap by the time he lifts his head.

"Does anyone else know about all this? Jax? Charlie?"

"Sydney does. I told Charlie and Jax about the breakup and the other woman. They don't know about…"

"So whatever happened to the douche canoe?"

"Why do you ask?"

I'm not sure if I should tell him since he already threatened to go find him.

"Curiosity." The tone of his voice says it's anything but.

"You have to promise not to go find him."

"I'm not—" The way his eyes flit back and forth is proof he's already looking for loopholes.

"Promise."

"I like your bossy side." He squeezes my ass.

"No distractions." He knows how to push all my buttons with his talented fingers. I squirm and bite back a moan at the feel of him against the center seam of my shorts. "Promise."

He sighs. "Fine. I promise. Happy?"

I nod and tease his lips with quick kisses. "Ecstatic."

"So...?" The word is practically a growl.

"Last I heard, he was working at a chain sporting goods store in the Valley."

He barks out a laugh. "Sounds like karma moved swiftly there."

"I guess. Honestly, it's been four years. I don't think about it a lot."

"Doesn't mean it doesn't still hurt you, Jess. Things change us, alter us. For good and bad."

The look on his face reminds me of the one he wore the day he got back from Noah's. I lace my fingers with his and squeeze.

"I couldn't have made it through the last few weeks without you. I can't stop thinking about how much I need you." The fire in his eyes creates an ache in my core.

"You have me."

"Jessie, I—"

A knock on the window scares the shit out of us, and we jump before I scramble out of Chris's lap. Amusement lights Charlie's eyes as she motions for us to join her.

"Good thing I told Jackson I'd come find you," she says when we join her. "He'd have a stroke if he caught the two of you in there like that."

"We weren't doing anything." I sound like a defensive teenager caught making out with her boyfriend.

"You don't have to explain it to me." She winks. "Sister code."

"Sister code?" Chris asks, his attention bouncing between Charlie and me. "Is that a thing?"

"Is bro code?" she counters.

He holds his hands up in surrender. "Forget I asked."

"What's going on?" I ask.

"We're all packing up. We figured we probably need to rescue your parents," she tells Chris.

"I'm sure Mamá is in heaven."

"I'm ready to go home," I whisper to him. "I have a promise to keep."

His nostrils flare, and his hand finds the small of my back. "Then let's go home."

♪♫♪♫♪♫

By the time we get home, all the kids have been picked up, and Gage is passed out on the couch, overwhelmed by excitement from the day.

"Thank you for keeping all the kids," I tell Dawn as I walk her and Tony to the door. Chris is cradling Gage and taking him upstairs to bed.

"So much fun. Pequeños ángeles," Dawn says, and Tony gives her a look.

"No more bebés." He shakes his finger at his wife.

"No. But more grandchildren. I would love that." Her eyes glimmer. "Jessie, the party was wonderful. Thank you for letting us be a part of it."

"Of course, you're family."

She and Tony hug me before they leave, and I lock up after them. I walk up the stairs slowly, stopping in the doorway to watch Chris lay Gage softly in his bed and press a kiss against his temple. This man continues to show me how different he is. With Gage and with me.

He could have run when I told him my secret. But he didn't.

He stayed. And he began to heal a part of me I didn't think could be healed—the jagged edges of pain smoothing over bit by bit.

I had always said no more rock stars. But Chris was right. Bowie wasn't a rock star. He was an insecure, immature wannabe. Chris is the real deal. And somewhere along the way, he's stolen my heart.

My breath catches in my lungs.

I'm in love with Chris Rivera.

The realization overwhelms me and immediately grows stronger now that I've put words to it. I need to go. To get this riot of emotions out.

I run for the music room and bypass the keyboard, heading straight for the instrument unplayed since I arrived. I tug off the sheet and expose the sleek black finish. The cover slides back smoothly, the keys gleaming in the small light I flipped on as I rushed in here.

Depressing several of the keys, I double check the tune and sit down. My fingers fly as the notes from Christina Perri's "A Thousand Years" circle around me, becoming richer when the sound of a guitar joins in at the right spot.

Startled, I glance up and find Chris moving closer until he stands next to me. We continue to play, neither of us breaking eye contact until the final notes of the song fade.

One breath. Then a second.

"I—"

"I—"

We speak at the same time.

Chris smiles and gestures for me to continue.

"You first." The words I need to say push insistently at my lips.

"I turned around and you were gone. I knew you could play, but nothing like that."

My cheeks heat as I duck my head. "I hope you don't mind. It doesn't look like anyone plays it much."

"Only sometimes. If No—" He breaks off on a painful swal-

213

low. "Only if we think it might give us the sound we're looking for on a track."

"Oh."

"I don't mind." He sets the guitar down and closes the distance. "Play it whenever you want."

"You knew the song I was playing."

He nods. "Yeah."

Straddling the piano bench, his gaze stays fastened to mine. "Jessie, I—"

I twist and mimic his pose.

"I love you." The words rush out of me. They demand to be spoken, refusing to be held back at the intensity in his eyes, at the moment his music and mine fused as surely as our souls have.

It's only after I say the words out loud that anxiety creeps in, edging closer to panic the longer they echo between us without a response.

This is awkward.

Until it's not.

He surges forward, and his hands immediately glide through my hair to move my mouth where he wants it, his tongue finding mine.

I moan as one of his hands lowers to my hip, squeezing and pulling me closer to him on the piano bench.

"Fuck, I love you so fucking much." He growls the words as his lips trail down my neck.

Elation fizzes through my blood, heating my body for him. Always him.

He loves me.

My fingers tease along his chest, finding his piercing through his shirt and dragging my fingertips over it until his head falls back with a groan.

"Fuck." The tendons in his neck strain and draw my attention. When I nip at one of them, he opens his eyes. The glittering obsidian forms an invisible connection to my aching core.

"I need you." Frustrated by the lack of movement the bench offers, I fidget along the wood and dig my nails into his biceps. "Now. I can't wait."

He responds by tugging my shirt off before he moves to his. Once they're off, he tosses both toward the door. Lifting his hands, he traces his index fingers along the lacy edge of my bra before flicking the front clasp open. My breasts spill out into his waiting palms, and I cry out as he teases the tips.

"Please," I beg, grinding against the bench to ease the ache that throbs in my core.

"Tell me again." His demand is accompanied by a rough twist of his fingers on my nipple.

I moan as lights explode behind my eyes.

"I love you. I love you so much. Please. I need you. Make love to me, Chris."

With a growl, he stands, holding me with steady hands that grip my thighs. He lays me down on top of the piano, the surface smooth and cold against my back, a stark contrast to the heat of him as he presses me against the wood.

"I love you." His voice is rough in my ear, soothed by his tongue as he swirls it inside.

My hips lift against his while he works open the button of my shorts with the same ease he did my bra.

"I need you." He pushes them down, taking my panties too, and drops them to the floor.

He runs a finger through my folds, and I mewl at the quick contact.

"Wait." I lift my hips, searching for his finger again.

"Patience."

"I don't have any." I'm rewarded with another brief press of his finger against my clit before it's gone again.

I can't hold back the whimper at the loss.

He chuckles and drags hot, open-mouthed kisses along my collarbone and down my cleavage before lavishing attention on either breast. He circles one stiff peak with his tongue while his fingers toy with the other one.

"Chris." Every sensation of his tongue and lips against my skin is building me higher and higher. I lift my hips again, desperate for friction but not finding any along the smooth surface of the piano at my back.

"Hold on to me." He waits until my hands are secure in his hair before shifting down my stomach.

He separates my legs, resting my feet on the edge of the piano. "Fuck."

The word barely reaches my ears before he dives to drag his tongue from back to front. My fingers tighten in his hair, and my toes curl around the edge of the piano as sensation overwhelms me.

"Chris," I call between panting breaths, moaning as he taps my clit before swirling his tongue around it.

He presses one finger inside and curls it upward, rubbing my g-spot as he sucks my clit into his mouth. I scream his name as the lights behind my eyes pulse faster, and the orgasm rushes at me from all sides.

"Come for me, angel." He growls against the sensitive skin of my inner thigh before nipping at the tendon there. I jolt, unable to stop the orgasm now if I tried.

It buffets me from every direction all at once and drives me so far into the stratosphere that the lights behind my eyes become stars in the dark sky. The only thing I know is the man between my legs as he works me through my orgasm until I collapse bonelessly against the wood.

"You're mine, Jessie." He pulls me from the piano and spins until my back is against the wall. "Mine."

His teeth find the spot between my neck and shoulder, and the sharp sting of his bite is immediately soothed by his tongue.

"Oh god." I lean my head back against the wall as a second orgasm builds.

"I love you." The words are growled against me as he fills me with one snap of his hips.

He masters my body and commands my heart with those three words.

"Ahh—I love you. Oh my god. Please."

This angle is deeper, more intense. More everything. His piercing rubs against my cervix before he shifts his hips and moves the piercing to my g-spot. I bite my lip, trying to hold back my wail as the orgasm sets me on a razor's edge. One breath, and I'm going to topple over.

"Tell me, angel." He grinds his pelvic bone against my clit, and the orgasm edges even closer.

"I-I love you."

"You're mine."

"I'm yours."

"And you own me. Heart and soul. Fuck." His hips pulse shallowly. "Are you close, angel?"

I nod frantically, trying my best to hold on.

"Come with me then. Right now." His hips piston against mine, driving me higher and higher until all that remains is bright white light that surrounds me—surrounds us—as I clutch at his shoulders and he roars his own release.

By the time he slides my legs down his body, they're no stronger than Jell-O, and I lean against the wall for support.

His smile when our eyes meet is enough to make me fall in love with him all over again.

"I love you." He nuzzles his nose along mine, his lips teasing playfully with the words.

"Mmm. I love you too." I rub my hands along the back of his head and scratch my nails lightly against his scalp.

His dick pulses against my thigh, and I gasp.

"Fuck." He groans, pressing himself against my stomach.

"Chris." His name is a whimper as the heat builds again in response to his nearness.

Before I can say anything else, he swoops me into his arms bridal style.

"I love you." He captures my lips again and moves blindly from the music room to his room.

The door snicks shut behind us, and we fall to the bed, desperate for each other. Words of endearment are interspersed with moans.

I and love and you are the clearest words of all.

CHAPTER 18

CHRIS

*J*essie shifts in her sleep, and I pull her naked form against mine.

"Good morning, love." I coast my lips along her shoulder.

"Mmm." She stretches, and I bite back a groan when she presses her ass against my dick. "Morning."

"Is that all you have to say to me?" I nip at her earlobe.

She squeals, then spins and claims my lips with hers. It's the same way we fell asleep last night—so lost in each other that we couldn't keep our hands—or our lips—to ourselves.

"I love you," she murmurs, finally breaking the kiss.

"That's better."

She laughs, and I snuggle her closer, enjoying the quiet moment. What I did to get so lucky, I don't know, but I'll take it. Her breathing is slow, but the tension in her body tells me she's still awake.

"You should get some more sleep."

She pushes a leg between mine. "I'm not tired."

"Should we make breakfast? Maybe make some pancakes?" I walk my fingers down her stomach and wait until her thighs part

219

to continue my journey. Her breath breaks as I find the bundle of nerves I was searching for.

"N-n-no." She grips my wrist, but she doesn't pull me away.

I stop my movements.

"No?"

"To breakfast."

I chuckle and continue my slow exploration, cataloging every broken breath and moan that accompanies the shift of my fingers. When my phone rings, I groan.

"You should answer that. It's early," she pants.

I want nothing more than to ignore the ringtone and continue, but a moment after the ringing stops, it starts back up again.

"Fuck." I disentangle my fingers from their treasure, nearly forgetting about the phone with her whimper. But it stops ringing only to start for a third time. With a sigh, I turn and grab my phone off the nightstand.

Double fuck.

Frank Nguyen.

"Hello?"

"Chris?"

"Yeah, Frank." I yawn and stretch, my attention captured by Jessie's naked body as she pads to the bathroom. "I'd ask who is being sued for paternity now, but the guys have been pretty quiet lately."

Thank fucking Christ.

He chuckles but without joy. Ice skates down my spine, and I sit up against the headboard.

"What's going on, Frank?"

"I know it's early, but I wanted to call you right away."

I grind my teeth. He needs to get to the fucking point.

"About what?" I grit out.

"Stephen Chen contacted me."

"Gage's grandparents' attorney?"

"Yeah." He doesn't elaborate.

"Okay...?"

"Tom and Bethany have petitioned the court for full custody of Gage."

"*What?*"

Jessie pokes her head around the corner, her brows furrowed. The second she sees me, she rushes back to the bed, wrapped in a towel.

Fuck. I can't breathe. My son. They're trying to take my son away from me.

"Chris? Are you there? Chris?"

I clear my throat, unable to dislodge the panic that rests on my vocal cords. "I-I'm here."

"Stephen emailed me a copy of the petition. I'm going to review it thoroughly, and then I want to meet with you. I want Gage to see a psychologist—"

"He doesn't need to see a goddamn shrink."

Jessie flinches, and I wince. She may not be a psychologist, but her job is similar. I rub a hand along her thigh in apology.

"The court is going to want to determine whether Gage is in a stable environment—"

"He *is* in a stable environment."

"That's what the psychologist will determine. And better one we choose than the court."

"Fuck. Fine."

"I'm going to send you a copy of the petition and details on the psychologist visit and preparation."

"When is all this supposed to happen?"

"That's the thing. They must know somebody at the court-house. We're set to go before the judge next week."

My vision tunnels as black dots pop up.

"I'm sorry, Chris. I'll see what I can do on my end."

"Okay."

I drop my phone to the bed when what I want to do is hurl it against the wall.

"*Fuck!*" I clench my hands in my hair, barely stopping myself from ripping it from my head.

"Chris, what happened? Who was on the phone?" She's concerned, but another emotion joins the look on her face—fear.

Fear of me? My reaction? My normal chill is blown to shit after everything that's been tossed at me the last month. Gage's arrival. Noah's overdose. His leaving the band.

I can't fucking do this. The universe is trying to break me, and today, it's going to succeed. Burying my face in my hands, I take several deep breaths.

"Chris?" Jessie rubs my back in a soothing motion, and slowly, the fuzziness of my vision abates.

"They want to take my son away from me." My voice cracks and tears burn behind my eyes.

"What?" Jessie's shock mirrors my own. "Who?"

"The Sanderses." She's never met them, so she has no idea who I'm talking about. "Gage's grandparents."

Now I understand why we haven't heard from them since they dropped Gage off. I expected something, but nothing like this. They had their daughter taken from them. But they're so willing to take my son away from me?

"That's crazy."

Jessie's embrace is warm, and I lean into her touch.

"I can't—Jess—I can't lose him."

"You won't," she promises.

But we both know she doesn't control the decision.

"What else did the attorney say?" she asks.

About the time I'm done telling her about the court date next week and the psychologist that Gage will have to see, there's a small knock on the door.

"Daddy?" The handle rattles, but since it's locked, he can't open it.

Jessie looks down at her towel-covered body before glancing back at me, a panic-stricken expression on her face.

"It's fine." I pull her to me and press a kiss to her temple.

"I'm not usually in a towel," she hisses and tugs at the cloth, squeaking when it loosens around her chest.

"Daddy!" He wiggles the handle again. "I'm hungry. Where's Jessie?"

"Hi, buddy. We'll be out in just a minute."

"'Kay." Imitating a herd of elephants, he runs down the hall.

"What am I going to do?"

She shifts to her knees and cups my cheeks.

"We're going to go make your son breakfast," she tells me between kisses.

"Pancakes?" I have joined Gage in his love for the breakfast food.

She rolls her eyes with a laugh. "You and your son."

Me and my son. I'm not going to let anyone take him away.

We're almost done with breakfast when my phone rings again.

"Are you going to answer that?" Jessie asks while wiping Gage's mouth to remove the layer of syrup under his nose.

I give it a side-eye. "Maybe I shouldn't."

"It might be Frank."

Fuck, I didn't think of that. But it's not.

Marcus.

I've avoided him since Noah's announcement. Time to face the music. Heaving a sigh, I answer the call.

"Hi, Marcus."

"I want you and the other guys in our office in an hour."

I snort. "Traffic will take us longer than that."

"Fine. Two hours."

"Do the other guys—"

He hangs up, and for the second time this morning, I picture my phone shattering to a million pieces against a wall. Maybe not the wall. The garbage disposal? Mindful of little eyes that take in my every move, I grind my molars together and put the phone down with much less emotion than I want.

"Daddy, can we go swimming?"

Fuck.

"How about when I get home, buddy? I need to go to a meeting."

"Okay." He looks down at his plate.

I want to tell him to forget the meeting. I want to swim. I want to spend the day soaking up the love he and Jessie have for me.

"Gage, maybe we can work on our song today." Jessie distracts him.

His smile is back in place when he lifts his eyes. "I'm gonna go get dressed." He races from the table without another word.

"Dressed?" I ask.

She shrugs. "I told him we have to be dressed to work."

My hands snap out and tug her into my lap when she walks by me to grab Gage's plate.

"Chris!" Her squeal is full of laughter.

"I don't want to go." I pout, laying my cheek against her back.

She rubs a hand along my arm in comfort.

"I'm sorry. The label?"

"Yeah."

"About Noah?"

"Probably. I've avoided Marcus for a week. He didn't say anything other than he wanted us all there in two hours."

"You should probably get ready." She tries to stand up, but I tighten my arms and hold her in place.

"Do I have to?"

"No. But you'll drive yourself crazy if you don't."

"You know me so well." Pressing my lips to her shoulder, I allow myself a breath before I loosen my grip and let her stand.

She turns around and drops a quick kiss against my lips. "I'm here if you need me."

"Love you."

Fuck, those words are becoming an addiction I don't want to deny. The good news is, I don't have to.

"Love you." She blows me a kiss and sways her hips on the way to the sink. "Now text the guys and go get ready."

> We've been called to the principal's office. 2 hours.

EVAN

thumbs up emoji

> You want to ride together? I can pick you up.

His house is even farther up in the hills than mine, so it's not unusual for us to ride together.

> Sounds good.
>
> Thanks, man.
>
> Milo
>
> Finn
>
> Up and at 'em.

It's easy to ignore one text chime, but significantly harder when I spam both of their inboxes. Evan and I learned that trick after we tried multiple alarms on their phone that never woke them up.

EVAN

Milo

> If you don't answer, I'm going to share the picture of you from freshman year in high school.

> No, not that one.

> The coke-bottle glasses and buzz cut look nothing like him anymore.

EVAN

Exactly.

MILO

Fucker. I'm up. I'm going to burn every copy of the yearbook I can find.

FINN

Before you two can blackmail me, I'm up too.

> Two hours.

MILO

Yeah, yeah.

Surprisingly, Milo and Finn are already at the studio when Evan and I get there. I look around for Noah before it hits me again.

He won't be here.

Just One Yesterday is no longer comprised of five guys who've been together since high school.

"In here." Marcus opens the door to the conference room off the main lobby, and we file inside.

We all have our seats. The ones we sit in every time. But the separation between Evan and Finn is another awkward reminder.

"Any of you geniuses want to clue me the fuck in as to why I'm hearing about Noah's trip to rehab in Arizona through this?"

He slams a tabloid on the table, and my stomach curdles. The image is grainy, but clearly shows Noah walking from a car to a building. A building identified in another photo as Phoenix Lane, a rehab center that has hosted several other celebrities successfully.

"Fuck." Evan curses and slams a fist onto the table.

Marcus's face is a mottled red. "Let's try this question. How long is he going to be gone for?"

We all look at each other.

"Or how about this: how much farther off schedule will this little stint take us?"

"We don't know," I say, speaking for the band when no one else speaks up. Just like always.

I've never regretted my decision to be the spokesperson for the band. Until now.

"What the fuck do you mean you don't know?"

The mottled red turns a deeper shade. Is Marcus going to have a heart attack in front of us?

"Most rehab facilities are, what, a month?"

He zeroes in on me. I'm the person who speaks up. That's my job.

I shrug. "I guess. But this isn't a normal rehab place."

"What the fuck does that mean?" His pitch is so high, I'm surprised we can still hear him.

"It could be six months. It could be years."

That seems to take the wind from his sails.

"Years?" He collapses into a chair at the end of the table as the red fades to ghostly white.

"He...left the band. Permanently."

I hate that word. Permanent.

Unchanging.

Forever.

"So you're telling me we're overdue for the studio, have a tour coming right after that, and we have no keyboardist?"

The eerie calm is almost worse than the apoplectic ranting.

I nod.

Without saying another word, he leaves us alone in the conference room.

"Was that it?" Milo asks.

"Want to go grab a beer?" Finn chimes in.

"Guys. Seriously. Sit there and be quiet for a few minutes." Evan glowers, and they stay put. Thank Christ.

Marcus stalks back into the room, but this time he's not alone.

"As of right now, Cornerstone is taking complete control—music, image, PR, everything. Your freedom has done nothing but cause us headache after headache. We're done. This is Chloe. She's one of our new PR people."

Chloe looks all of about twenty-two. *What the hell does she know about PR?*

"What do we need PR for?" I ask.

"We need to get in front of the story of Noah's departure from the band to focus on his addiction." She pulls out a chair and sits. "And I need to know about any other skeletons in your closets, because shit is about to hit the fan."

Milo smirks and turns to face her. Fuck, I'm going to need to remind him that employees at Cornerstone are off limits. Still. After the last secretary he fucked leaked secrets to the paps, he was put on a short leash.

Obviously not short enough.

Marcus slams a stack of folders down on the conference table.

"What are those?" I turn my attention back to him and hope Evan will keep control over our drummer.

"Keyboardists. There are fifty in this stack. Before you leave here today, you'll narrow it down to ten for auditions."

What the fuck?

I want to say I get home in time to keep my promise to Gage. But it's well after midnight. Exhausted, I slide into bed and pull Jessie next to me, burying my nose in her hair, silently promising that I'll make it up to both of them when we wake up.

Déjà vu strikes again. My ringing phone pulls me from a

dreamless sleep. When I reach for Jessie, her side of the bed is cold. What the hell time is it?

"Hello?" My voice is hoarse from exhaustion.

"Chris, it's Frank. I need to see you right away."

Fuck.

I groan and ask him for an hour so I can shower and eat something. Spend a few minutes with Jessie and Gage. Only they're not home. Jessie took Gage to the beach with Jax and his family, according to the text waiting on my phone.

I'd give anything to head in that direction versus Frank's office.

"You needed to see me?" I ask, walking into his office an hour later.

"Sit down." Frank points to the chair in front of his desk.

Oh shit. The last time I heard that tone from him, I was a teenager and he was giving me guidance about record deals. So I sit.

"I got some insights into what the Sanderses are trying to stake their custody claim on."

He sets one printout after another on the desk. Tabloid images of me that are over ten years old. Me with a table of lines in front of me, Evan on one side and Noah on the other. Me with my tongue down the throat of some groupie whose name I never got.

"Fuck. Frank, you know this is all old bullshit." I gesture to the printouts.

"Oh really?"

Another image. Much more recently. The night at Aftershock when I saw Jessie. The woman who pulled away as she pressed her body against mine. It looks like I'm about to kiss her, even though I didn't. Even then, I'd been enamored with the brown-haired beauty on the first floor of the club.

"That was a label required appearance."

"Was she required too?" Frank asks, arching an eyebrow.

"I told her no."

"That's not how they're going to spin it."

"I've only been out once since Gage came to live with me."

"And their concern will be when you leave for extended tours. Will you be exposing Gage to this world or—"

"Fuck no. What kind of monster would do that? We don't pull shit like this anymore." I push off the chair and pace the width of his office. I yank on my hair to keep myself from screaming. "This is bullshit, Frank. They're making shit up so they can take my son away from me."

"I know, Chris. I've known you since you were a kid. You took a few years to learn, but you don't do this shit anymore. But it doesn't change the fact that you did and that there are images out there to prove it."

The glare he levels my direction makes me feel like a guilty teenager again.

"I did." I own all the mistakes of my past. Some of them fucking suck, but I wouldn't be the person I am today if I hadn't gone through it.

"The honesty is commendable, but it's not going to help you in court."

"What do I do?"

"That's what we're here to talk about."

CHAPTER 19

JESSIE

$\mathcal{T}$he weight of Chris's arm around my waist pulls me from sleep.

"You're home," I murmur and snuggle back against his warmth.

I hate going to bed alone, even though it's happening more and more lately. I hate leaving the bed when he's still there. But someone has to be there for Gage. And Chris can't be right now.

For the last three days, he's been gone until long past Gage's bedtime—hell, long past *my* bedtime. We see him for a few minutes in the morning, but then he's heading to meet with his attorney or the label. According to Chris, the label took full control over the band, and for the first time in years, they have no control over what's going on. Cornerstone says they need to find a new keyboardist by the end of the month or else. When I asked him what that meant, he didn't have a good answer.

When he's not stressing about the band, he's stressing about the custody case. The Sanderses are planning to use tabloid pictures of him. Ones he was embarrassed to tell me about, but images from his life before Gage. Before me. And since I've been around him enough to learn who he really is, I told him I didn't care.

Because I don't.

I love him. I care about him. And he's starting to worry me.

So is Gage. Day after day without his daddy is taking a toll on him. He's crawling back inside himself despite my best efforts.

"I am. I'm finally home. Fuck, I missed you." His lips find the sensitive spot behind my ear.

"Mmm. We missed you. Gage misses you."

I turn to face him, barely making out his features in the dark room.

"Fuck, I hate that I'm gone so much lately. I promised to go swimming with him."

"Three days ago."

"What?"

"You promised him three days ago."

"Three days? God, my days are blurring together."

"Gage needs you here. He thinks you're leaving him."

"What?" His head jerks back as if I slapped him.

"He's...regressing." I bite my lip after my confession, hating that I need to tell him this on top of everything else.

"Regressing? He's not speaking again?"

He sits up, and I lean over and turn on the light next to the bed, blinking to adjust to the brightness.

Dark circles ring his eyes, and the scruff I usually find so attractive is a few days beyond sexy rock star and is edging to backwoods lumberjack.

"No. He's still speaking, but...less. He was singing when we worked in the music room before, but now he's gone back to resting his hands on mine while I play."

He groans and buries his head in his hands.

"Fuck. I'm failing. I'm doing everything I can, and I'm still a fucking failure."

"You're not." I rush to reassure him. "You need help. What can I do?"

The despair on his face creates a physical pain in my chest. It's so acute that I lift my hand to rub it in hopes of easing the ache.

"I don't know. Every time I think I handle one thing, another pops up. Gage coming into my life, Noah leaving the band. Now this custody bullshit and the label with their goddamn demands. I can't find a balance with all these changes being thrown at me."

"Changes like me?" The question is out of my mouth before I can stop it.

"What? No."

"I'm another change in your life."

Am I a weight dragging him down? Another change he has no control over?

"That's not what I mean." He tugs at my arm and pulls me to him. "You're the best kind of change, love."

"I don't want to be another thing you regret. We always said this was casual—"

"It stopped being casual when I fell in love with you." His lips find the top of my head, and I snuggle against him. The gentle thud of his heart vibrates under my cheek while his fingers skate along my spine, tracing patterns on my shoulder and upper arm.

His hand stills and his breathing grows deeper and more even. When I glance up, his eyes are closed and his mouth is parted slightly as he sleeps. I press my lips against the cotton of his shirt where it covers his heart before I lay my head back down.

"Good night, baby."

♪♫ ♪♫ ♪♫

Bright sunlight streams through the windows, disorienting me. Did I forget to close the curtains last night?

"Chris?" Stretching my arm, I search for the heat of his body but only find cool sheets and an indentation on his pillow.

233

Damn. He's already gone. I wanted to talk more about Gage. Convince him to plan a day for the three of us. I don't realize how late it is until I grab my phone to text him.

9:14.

I never sleep this late. Neither does Gage, not anymore. Padding to his room, I peek in, ready to wake him up for breakfast. Only he's not there.

"Gage?"

Usually, if I'm not up when he wakes up, he bounces into the bedroom like a little kangaroo. I check his bathroom, the music room, and the gym before circling back to my room—my old room.

"Gage?"

No sign of him.

Downstairs? He knows not to try to make breakfast by himself, but he can reach the granola bars for a snack if he's hungry.

"Gage?" I rush down the stairs, nearly falling on my face when I miss the last one.

His giggle pulls me to the kitchen.

"Jessie!" He waves to me from his perch on the counter next to where Chris flips a pancake.

Chris glances over his shoulder and sends me a sexy smile. "Morning, sleepyhead."

"Morning." Moving behind him, I wrap my arms around his waist and press my lips to the center of his back. My heart rate slows as I let out a deep breath and just hold him. "I thought you were gone again."

"We're going to the zoo!" Gage's eyes are wide as he leans forward and nearly topples off the counter.

"Whoa, buddy." I steady him and look at Chris. "The zoo, huh?"

"I texted Frank and Evan this morning. I need to spend some

time with my family. So we're going to the zoo." He leans over and snags my lips with his.

"Daddy, don't burn it." Gage's warning breaks us apart, and Chris quickly flips the pancake.

"Thanks for the assist, little man."

Gage beams at his father's praise.

"Breakfast first?" I eye the lopsided stack of pancakes. They must have been up for a while.

"He wanted pancakes." Chris points to Gage, who is absorbed in watching the pancake cook.

"Of course." I laugh. "What else? I would have made them if you'd woken me up. I never sleep this late."

"You needed it. I kept telling myself that when I wanted to wake you up for an entirely different reason."

He growls the words against my neck, and I shiver. Electricity zips through my blood in a heated wave.

"I can be your sous chef. What do you need me to do?"

"What's that?" Gage asks, his little nose wrinkled as he tries to make out the word.

"What's what?"

"A soup chef."

"Sous chef? It's like an assistant."

"I'm Daddy's 'distant."

"Assistant," I correct gently.

"Assistant." Gage struggles with the word, but nods when he finally manages it.

"Good job, buddy." I extend my arm, knuckles out toward him, and he taps his against mine, making an exploding sound as he tilts his fingers up.

"All you need to do is grab yourself a cup of coffee and a seat. We're handling breakfast this morning." Chris nods in the direction of the coffeepot, and with nothing else to do, I follow his instructions and sit at the table with three place settings.

235

"Have you ever been to the zoo?" I ask and watch him flip another pancake.

He grew up with famous parents. Was it hard for him and his siblings to have a normal childhood?

Like yours was so normal.

The first time I remember going to the zoo in Austin was when I was in high school. There were pictures of me as a toddler, but I was too young to remember, and then I was too sick to go.

"A couple times. My parents would rent the zoo out for parties sometimes."

I nearly drop my coffee cup.

"Is that what you're doing today? Renting out the whole zoo?"

"No. I don't want to draw attention if we can help it."

"You think you can blend?"

"I've done it before." He drops off the plate of pancakes before going back and swooping the little boy off the counter.

His squeal brings an immediate smile to my lips, and my heart fills watching the two of them interact.

"How long has it been?"

"Since?"

"Since you last needed to blend?"

He shrugs. "It's like riding a bike."

"Uh-huh."

Our conversation stops as we listen to Gage list all the animals he hopes to see. By the time he's done with his list, his plate is clean, and he sprints out of the kitchen to get dressed.

I stand and take my plate and his to the sink.

"What about the old zoo? Have you ever been there? We played a concert there once."

"Nope." I've seen pictures, and Sydney told me about it, but I've never had the chance to go.

"We'll see if Abuelita can babysit. I'll take you."

"A date night?" When was the last time I went on a date?

His eyes round the longer he looks at me. "Shit."

"What? What's wrong?"

"We've never been on a date." He sounds surprised by that fact.

"No, we haven't." My heart races as he moves closer.

Something about the way he stalks toward me with a glint in his eye makes my core throb to life. I squeeze my thighs together as he stops in front of me, close enough that my breasts brush against his chest. The friction of the thin shirt I wore to bed is enough to have my nipples pebbling and my breasts aching for his touch.

"I'm going to fix that," he murmurs. I expect him to close the distance and pull me into his arms, but he keeps the small space between us.

"Chris," I whimper, caught in the spell of his gaze.

"New rule." He drags his index finger along my jaw, and the charged caress creates a shiver of awareness down my spine.

"What's that?"

"We won't have sex again—"

"What?" My eyes fly open, and a half smile curves his lips.

"Until I take you on this date." The expression on his face is a promise that I'm looking forward to. He lowers his finger so he can lean forward and seal the vow with a kiss.

"I'm ready!" Gage bursts back into the kitchen in a graphic t-shirt of an elephant and shorts that are inside out. His shoes are on the wrong feet and his hair crackles with static electricity, standing in all directions.

Chris and I burst out laughing as Gage bounces next to us.

"Bud, let's fix a few things first."

He holds still long enough for me to fix his shorts and shoes, and he lets Chris drag damp hands over his hair to calm the static.

"I guess we should get ready too," I say and take the hand Chris offers to help me off the floor.

Only he yanks me a little harder than necessary and I end up plastered against his body while he grinds his erection along my stomach.

"When are we going on our date?" he asks.

"Is tonight too soon?" My voice is breathy. No way can I wait days—or longer—for this date to happen.

"I'll text Mamá. Why don't you head up and get ready?"

"You're not coming?"

He steps closer, dropping his voice to avoid little ears.

"Angel, if I come upstairs with you while you're naked, I can guarantee we won't be going anywhere today."

Is spontaneous combustion a real thing? Because with the way he growled those words against my ear, it might be.

By the time Chris and I are also ready for the zoo, Dawn has agreed to keep Gage overnight for a grandkid sleepover with his cousins.

"Gage." Chris looks into the rearview mirror as we head to the zoo.

"Hmm?"

"Would you want to go to a sleepover at Abuelita's house tonight with your cousins?"

"Abuelita?"

"Yeah, buddy."

"Yes!" His little fist pumps into the air, and Chris and I share a smile at his excitement.

"She'll pick you up when we get back from the zoo." Chris lowers his voice so that only I can hear him. "And we're leaving the house for our date."

"We don't have to."

A night alone at home with Chris? Yes, please.

"We're going out."

His words stoke the anticipation that thrums through my body.

At the zoo, Chris disguises himself well enough that no one

comes up to him, even if they do a lot of double takes. The baseball cap is pulled low on his forehead, and with his dark sunglasses, I hardly recognize him as Gage rushes from exhibit to exhibit.

"Those girls keep looking at me," he murmurs as we follow Gage to the giraffes.

Glancing around, I see the group of "girls" he's talking about. They're in high school or college and send covert looks our way before giggling with each other.

"They don't recognize you."

"How do you know?"

"They think you're hot." I'd done the same thing with Sydney and other girlfriends when we went out in college.

"They do?"

"Uh-huh." I can't ignore the prick of jealousy at the four of them checking him out.

"You have nothing to worry about." He reaches over and weaves our fingers together.

"I know." Mostly.

"Oh really?"

"Yep. Because while they can only look at you, I can do this."

I stop in the middle of the path and reach up on tiptoes as I pull his head down. Our lips meet, and I tease his with my tongue until he opens and lets me deepen the kiss. One of my hands runs down the length of his chest and brushes against his piercing before I dip my hand into the deep pocket of his shorts and trace the outline of him through the material.

By the time I break the kiss, we're both breathing heavily, and the four girls are no longer in eyesight.

"Fuck, Jess." He inhales deeply, and we step apart.

"What?"

"I'm not sure if I should be promising to never make you jealous again or figuring out a way to do it sooner rather than later."

A laugh bubbles out of me at his words.

"You don't have to make me jealous to get me to kiss you."

"Good to know." He swings our joined hands as Gage waves at us to hurry up. "Think he wants to feed the giraffes?"

"I think that's a solid possibility." The five-year-old bounces next to the stand where we can buy food to feed the tall animals.

"Let's go get our boy."

My heart stutters in my chest.

Our boy.

♪♪ ♪♪ ♪♪

Our boy passes out in his car seat after running all over the zoo, only waking up when we pull him from the seat and remind him that Abuelita will be here soon to pick him up for his sleepover.

"Can you help him get ready while I change?" I motion to my shorts and t-shirt.

"We got this, don't we, dude?" Chris asks Gage, and the two of them race upstairs and into Gage's room to pack for his sleepover.

I can hear him directing his dad when I walk by the open door.

"No, Daddy. I want Stinky Face."

"Only this one?"

"Yes. And my dinosaurs."

Smiling at the two of them, I head into our bedroom to shower, piling my hair on top of my head since I don't want to take the time to wash and dry it. Chris has been secretive about what we're doing on our date, so I have no idea what to wear as I look at my clothes that hang in the closet next to his. He constantly sees me in jeans or shorts and t-shirts, and I want to do something different.

"This one." I grab the brown pinstripe dress and drop my

towel. I slide it up my legs and torso, then adjust the thin straps on my shoulders. Luckily, this one doesn't have a zipper, but it cinches around my chest before flowing to a skirt that ends right above my knees.

I avoid the one pair of heels I brought and slip on my brown flats before heading back into the bathroom to brush out my hair. My cheeks are flushed pink from our time at the zoo, so I only add a clear gloss and mascara.

"Jessie?" Gage's voice is close.

"In here."

He stops at the bathroom door and watches as I finish with my mascara.

"Did you need me for something?" I crouch down to his level and melt under the way he studies me.

"Abuelita's here."

"Oh. Okay. So you came to say bye?"

He nods.

"Well, give me a hug then."

I open my arms, and he rushes me, practically knocking me to the floor.

"Oof. Such a good hug."

He doesn't say anything but continues to hug me even after I stand and lift him into my arms.

"Are you okay, buddy?" I rub a hand up and down on his back.

He nods against my chest.

"Are you going to miss me?"

Another nod.

"I'm going to miss you too. But Daddy and I will pick you up tomorrow morning, okay?"

He leans back and looks at me. "Promise?"

It hits me then. Gage's mother's accident. Is our leaving a trigger for him?

"I promise. Would you rather stay home with Daddy and me?"

Chris will be as disappointed as I am, but if Gage needs us, we'd both willingly stay home.

"I wanna go play with my cousins."

"Are they fun?" I move from the bedroom to the stairs and walk down.

"Kyler and Toby are."

I try to place them at Gage's birthday party, but there were so many kids, it's hard to remember who's who.

"Is someone not fun?"

"'Rissa." He makes a face. "She wants to play with dolls."

I laugh and press my lips against his temple.

"You're a funny kiddo, Gage. I love you."

He circles my neck with his little arms and squeezes me tight. "Love you."

If both Rivera men didn't before, they now firmly own my heart. I blink back tears as we stop at the bottom of the stairs, where Chris and his mom are talking.

"Jessie. Hello." Dawn smiles warmly at me. "You look beautiful."

"Hi, Mrs. Rivera. Thank you."

"Dawn, please," she reminds me.

"Dawn."

"See that my son appreciates you. He was raised to behave like a gentleman."

"Mamá." He sounds so much like Gage now that I bite the inside of my cheek to hide a smile.

"Christopher, hijo. Take this young lady out and let her show off her pretty dress. Come, nieto, your cousins should be at my house by the time we get back."

Gage fidgets until I put him down so he can run to Dawn and grab her hand.

"Hey, bud, don't I get a goodbye?" Chris kneels and experiences the same energetic goodbye I did.

We wave to Dawn and Gage as they walk to Dawn's car until it's the two of us in the quiet.

"When did you change?" I ask. Chris is in a dark blue button-down and gray slacks.

"While you were in the shower." His eyes darken, and he moves closer until he can lift one of my arms to twirl me in a circle. "You look absolutely stunning."

"Thank you. I thought you said if you came upstairs when I was naked, we wouldn't be going anywhere."

"I survived. Barely. If Mamá hadn't been on her way, the outcome may have been different. Are you ready to go?"

"Go where?"

He smirks. "To show off your pretty dress."

I laugh at the use of his mother's words.

"We could always stay in," I offer again.

Instead of answering, he wraps his hand around mine and pulls me to the garage.

"You deserve more than that, love. And I'm going to show you."

CHAPTER 20

CHRIS

"*W*hat?" I ask.

Jessie's gaze hasn't wavered from me since we left the house.

"You're seriously not going to tell me?"

It must be the thousandth time she's asked. And for the thousandth time, I tell her no.

"What's the fun of surprises if you can't be surprised?"

"I bet I could make you tell me." The tone of her voice has my cock pushing against the fly of my pants.

"Oh yeah?" I spare a quick glance at her when we stop at a light close to our destination.

She drags her tongue along her lips, and I question my decision to leave the house. She looks good enough to eat, and my lips tingle with the urge to trace all the skin revealed along her shoulders and collarbone.

This is the right choice.

I can't believe I haven't taken her on a date yet. My mother would kill me if she knew. I was raised to respect a woman, not only use her for sex. And while Jessie and I do more than have sex—although that part is fan-fucking-tastic—we stay at home, we watch movies, we hang out with Gage. I've told her I love her, but my actions needed to back up my words.

I need her to know what she means to me.

She huffs and turns to look out her window.

I stare for another moment, then tear my focus away from the graceful lines of her neck.

"Are we going to the Hollywood Bowl?" She pivots back to me, her eyes bright with excitement.

I panic but try to compose myself. How the fuck did she figure it out?

"What—" My voice squeaks like I'm a pre-pubescent teenage boy, and I clear my throat. "Why do you say that?"

She thumbs behind us. "I just saw a sign for it."

Fuck. I didn't think about the street signs. I should have blindfolded her. Still an option. An image takes shape. Her naked and waiting for me, blindfolded, her lips parted as pleasure over-whelms her. My dick hardens in a painful rush.

Calm down, dude. Tonight isn't about that.

It's about showing Jessie that our relationship is more than physical attraction. So much more.

"If I ask you to close your eyes, would you?" I ask.

"Do you want me to?"

"I don't want to spoil the surprise."

With a sigh, she closes her eyes.

"Better?"

No. Because now I want to kiss her.

"Chris?" she asks when I don't respond right away.

"B-better." Fuck. Looks like twelve-year-old me is back, if my voice is any indication.

Dragging my attention back to the road, I follow the signs and wave to the guy who moves aside the gate marked "Private Access Only" so I can turn onto the other road. At the top, I park the car and take a deep breath.

Will she like what I planned?

"Are we here?" she asks, keeping her eyes closed.

Goddamn, she's beautiful. The sun sinks lower in the sky and rests against the hill behind the bowl, the pinks and corals washed with slashes of blue. Leaning over the console, I press a kiss against one eyelid and then the other.

"We're here," I whisper as I pull away.

Her eyes flutter open, and she gazes at me until I gesture out the windshield.

"Oh." Her breath catches, and she turns back to me. "The Hollywood Bowl?"

"Have you been here before?"

She nods. "But down there."

Pointing to the interior seating around the bowl, she looks around. "Where are we?"

"It's a picnic area."

"But we're the only ones here."

"I know someone." I shrug. "Asked if I could keep our date private. So they blocked the road until I got here and then blocked it again."

"No one else is coming up here?"

By the tone of her question, the idea excites her as much as it does me.

"Just us. Come on."

I open my door and rush around the hood to grab hers as well.

"Very chivalrous of you," she teases.

I smile. "Not many people see that side."

"I bet. But you let me see it."

When she looks up at me, I can't deny the need to graze her lips with mine, nibbling slightly before I pull away. I don't want to get carried away when our night is only beginning. Weaving my fingers with hers, I tug her from the car to the area where a picnic dinner is set up on a table. A gorgeous wooden basket with a bottle of wine poking out of it rests against the white linen tablecloth.

"A picnic? Someone else you know?"

"You too. Mamá."

"Your mom helped you set this up?"

I nod. "When I asked her if she could babysit, she asked me why. I told her how I feel about you and that I wanted tonight to be special."

"How do you feel about me?" She slinks her arms around my waist and rests her chin against my chest as she looks up at me.

"If you have to ask, I'm not doing a very good job of showing you." I tuck a strand of hair behind her ear. "I love you. Heart and soul. I have fallen so deep that I can't remember what it was like to not have you in my life. No…wait, that's a lie."

"A lie?" A frown carves lines between her eyebrows.

I rush to explain. "I remember…it was lonely. Until you. Only you."

"Chris." My name is a whisper on her lips as tears line her lashes.

"Don't cry."

"They aren't sad tears."

"No?" I ask as I capture two of them with my thumbs.

"I love you. I can't come up with words as beautiful as yours. But it's so much more than that." She lifts on tiptoes and brushes a kiss to my chin. "So much more."

The sound of tuning instruments fills the air, and I draw her into my arms, her back to my front. I can't help but touch my lips to the bare skin of her shoulder.

"Cold?" I ask when the hint of a shiver runs through her.

"No. Is this the Philharmonic?" She meets my gaze in the light blue of twilight, her eyes full of wonder.

I nod. "Have you ever heard them?"

"I came here for Christmas last year with Sydney. All Christmas carols."

The opening strains echo up the hill.

"*The Princess Bride?*" The smile on her face reinforces the choice I made.

"What? You don't like this movie, do you?"

She punches me lightly in the leg. "You remembered it's my favorite?"

I rub my thumb across her knuckles. "I remember everything about you."

When she turns around, her smile is shy, but so fucking perfect on her. I want to remember her like this. Forever.

"This is amazing. Thank you."

"Should we sit?" I gesture to the table and straddle the bench before I pull her between my legs. "Hungry?"

"Maybe in a bit."

We break into the picnic about halfway through the show.

"Having fun?" I take a sip of red wine. Mamá even remembered plastic wineglasses.

I owe her one for helping me set this up.

"This is…magical."

Have I ever seen her so happy? It fills me with a peace that I didn't think was possible after the last few weeks.

"Are you?" She looks up at me from the cocoon of my arms.

"Tonight is perfect," I murmur.

She turns back to the vista in front of us, and I lose myself in the weight of her pressed to my chest. We watch the rest of the show in silence as I relish the way she fits against me.

One by one, the lights go off until it's as if she and I are the only two people in this whole city of lights. She stands and stretches her arms over her head, her dress rising several inches against her thighs.

"Thank you for tonight," she says, smiling softly.

I pull her to me, pressing my lips against her stomach through the fabric of her dress.

"Thank you."

"For what?"

"Being you. I needed this tonight. Needed you."

"I'm right here."

"I want you." My words are blunt, but I can't think of any way to pretty them up right now. I need to touch her, to taste her, obliterating everything else as the urge takes over.

"Here?" she asks. I can't tell whether she's excited by that idea.

I surge off the bench and drag my lips along the column of her throat.

"I can't wait."

I need to lose myself in her goodness a little longer. I'm not ready to go back to the clusterfuck of my life right now.

"Yes."

She moans as I drag my lips along her jaw before closing the distance to her mouth. If she tells me to stop, I will. But I've wanted her since the moment she walked down the stairs in this dress and the light sheen of gloss that begged to be kissed off.

She shoves me back toward the bench, and I plop down against the wood, not sure what to expect. It definitely isn't Jessie gripping the hem of her skirt and pulling her dress up and off.

Fuck.

All the blood rushes to my already hard cock. Is it possible to come without touching her? Because I'm fucking close.

"You weren't wearing anything under that dress?" I watch her drop the dress to the dirt next to her.

Darkness surrounds us, but moonlight tips her breasts and luscious curves in silver. She's a fucking goddess. And she's mine.

She shakes her head and steps closer. Close enough for me to feel the heat that radiates from her skin.

"No."

"Why?" I reach out a hand to each hip and pray for control.

Why are you asking? Take.

"I wanted you to touch me."

"You planned this?"

An impish smile curls her lips. She lifts one shoulder and lets it drop, her breasts bouncing with the movement.

"You were the one who said no sex until our date. I like to think of it as being prepared for anything."

With a growl, I unfurl from the bench, still gripping her hips while I devour her lips. My tongue dives into her mouth as I slide my hands around to squeeze her ass. I bring her closer to me, driven insane by the fabric between us. But I know what happens the second I shed my clothes. And I refuse to rush this moment.

"Do you know what you look like right now?" I trail kisses along her jaw to her ear.

"Mmm. What?"

"Aphrodite."

"Wasn't Athena goddess of the moon?"

"No idea. But you're the goddess of my heart. Does that make you Jessie, goddess divine?"

I find the tip of one breast and swirl my tongue around her nipple while I cage her against me, forcing her back to arch, and push her farther into my mouth.

"Gah." She cries out, and the sound echoes around us. But there's no one to hear it but us.

She wraps a leg around my thigh and whimpers when the friction still doesn't hit. I lift her other leg and adjust my grip on her thighs, pulsing my hips against her center. Spinning, I set her on the edge of the linen-covered table. Her sharp nails prick into the back of my biceps while her tongue plays with mine. I lean over her until her back meets the table.

"I love you," I murmur against her lips.

She echoes the words while heat builds in my body and my clothes chafe against my skin. Her hands fly down the placket of buttons on my shirt, then she's pushing it away impatiently while her fingers toy with my piercing, sparking fireworks behind my eyes while another thread on my control snaps. I crush my lips against hers for a moment more, then I shift back and take several deep breaths to regain that hold.

"Chris." She lifts her hands, an invitation hard to ignore.

"Just a moment."

Dark hair spreads across the white tablecloth while her eyes fasten to mine, holding me captive for a heartbeat. The fire there calls to the lust that courses through my blood, and I take an involuntary step forward.

"Not yet." I clench my jaw and continue my appraisal.

Lips swollen from my kisses beg for more. Nipples puckered and equally hungry for my attention. Smooth skin along her stomach to the curve of her hip.

She doesn't wait for me to touch her. She lifts her hands to her breasts, thumbing the nipples before she travels down her stomach. Her thighs part, and her fingers glide through her folds until she finds the spot that makes her breath catch audibly.

I step between her spread legs and knock her hand to the side.

"Touch me," she begs.

"Do you know what you remind me of, spread on the table like this?" I drag my hands up her calves and along the inside of her thighs.

She lifts her hips, but I keep my touch barely out of reach from where she craves it.

"W-w-what?"

"A picnic."

"A picnic?" Her nose wrinkles at the comparison.

"One meant solely for me." I lift her hand and press a kiss against her palm before I move to her elbow and repeat the caress. Her shoulders, her neck, her collarbone. All on tonight's menu.

Swirling my tongue around one nipple, I suck the peak into my mouth, nibbling and sucking and soothing the bites. She arches her back to press herself more fully into my mouth.

252

"Ahh. *Chris.*" Her hands find my hair, holding me to her. As if there's any place I'd rather be.

My hand replaces my mouth as I switch to give equal attention to her other breast.

"*Chris.*" Sharp nails drag along my scalp, and I nip sharply at the beaded tip, rewarded by her surging against my mouth and her hips pressing up against my chest. The heat of her pussy against my bare skin makes me hungry for more.

I trail kisses lower, dipping my tongue into her navel while I spread her thighs wider.

"But if you're the picnic, love, then this is my dessert." Flattening my tongue, I lick her from back to front, loving her cries as she begs for more. As she calls my name when bliss takes a deeper hold on her.

I focus on the bundle of nerves at the top of the line, running circles around her clit before tapping my tongue against it.

"I'm going to come." She moans loudly, and the sound carries farther around us.

"I want to hear you." I growl against her, not letting up as I slide two fingers into her tight heat. Short, shallow thrusts as I circle her clit with my tongue and then longer, deeper thrusts as I tap against it. Curling my fingers, I suck her clit into my mouth.

"*Chris!*" Her pussy spasms around me, and her voice echoes against the rocks. She rides my fingers while I work her through her orgasm, only stopping when her hips collapse against the table.

But she doesn't stay still for long. She sits up and drags hot, open-mouthed kisses along the line of my jaw while she pushes my shirt completely off with fumbling hands. Once that task is accomplished, her fingers work my belt and the fly of my pants until she can push them down to pool at my ankles.

"You're not wearing underwear." She grips my cock, twisting her wrist and dragging the pressure downward.

"G-great minds think alike," I try to joke and groan as her thumb rubs against the piercing.

"I want you inside me," she pants.

"Now?"

"Now."

"Out here in the open like this?"

"Yes."

I notch my dick at her opening and press forward an inch. "Do you like that anyone could hear you as I make you scream my name?"

She moans when I pulse my hips and retreat.

"Answer me."

"*Yes.*"

"Is my angel an exhibitionist?" I hold back a groan when she tightens her pussy around my dick. "This turns you on. Me fucking you in the open like this. Where anyone could see."

Pushing her heels into my low back, she tries to pull me closer. When I don't give her what she wants, she whimpers.

"More," she begs.

I chuckle. "Tell me."

"Yes. Yes, it turns me on that people could hear us, that they could see us. That they could see you fuck me and make me come and scream your name."

With a growl, I thrust and retreat again, deeper than before. Over and over, until I'm seated inside her and a light sheen of sweat coats my skin.

"Let me hear you, angel. Let everyone hear you. Tell them all you're mine."

"I'm yours," she wails as I piston my hips.

"Fuck, you feel so good." I groan and sink my teeth into her neck. Her walls tighten around me, and I nearly come. "Did you do that on purpose?"

"Do what?"

The walls of her pussy tighten around me again, and I bite

harder into her neck. She moans and jolts, increasing the pressure, and any hope I had of control is gone. The orgasm builds along my spine, tightening my balls as I mark her neck, telling the world she's fucking mine.

I move a finger between us, finding and pressing against her clit as I continue to thrust. She screams her climax, and it echoes back to us, the loudest sound of the night. A moment later, I growl mine into her shoulder. White flashes fill my vision as the orgasm takes control.

Driving my hips over and over, I grind my pelvic bone against her clit, even as my piercing taps a place deep inside her. She grips my biceps as her orgasm persists, keeping time with mine in a race to the finish that neither of us will win.

"Fuck. I love you. I love you. I love you." The words are automatic as my release surges through me, stilling my hips as every muscle in me locks.

My chest brushes against hers as I catch my breath. The way her hands roam my back causes my hips to pulse against hers.

"Mmm." Her moan is going to set off round two if we don't leave soon. And I don't want to be caught with my pants down —literally.

"Time to go, love." I stand up and help her to her feet, holding her to me when she almost collapses in my arms.

"Wipe the smirk off your face, Christopher." Her attempts to scold me are amusing considering how little control she has over her naked body.

"I'm not smirking."

"Are to."

"Okay, I am," I admit. "But only because I like when you're at my mercy like this."

"I can walk."

She does, but she lacks her usual grace.

Buttoning my pants, I grab my shirt and her dress off the

ground and shake both out. It isn't until we're in the car that I speak again.

"So what you're saying is, I need to try harder."

Her moan is all the answer I need.

Much later, with Jessie sprawled next to me in bed, I turn my phone on for the first time since this morning. It was the only way I could guarantee the day was completely devoted to Gage and Jessie. When it finally settles in my hand, I open my text messages—the angry red notification builds a pit of dread in my stomach.

EVAN

We need to talk.

They've gone too far.

Who? Fuck. I keep reading to see if any of Evan's other messages will make sense.

They want us all in the studio tomorrow afternoon.

We have an audition with a keyboardist.

She isn't even one of our finalists.

Shit.

Sorry.

Turned off my phone.

Figured when I didn't hear from you.

Good for you.

What the fuck is Marcus thinking?

She wasn't even in our top five.

I don't know.

I'll see what I can find out tomorrow.

What's the worst that can happen? We waste an afternoon auditioning someone who won't fit?

This is OUR band.

I agree with you.

I don't think a woman will fit in with us.

Just...try to keep an open mind, okay?

Fuck.

Fine.

Mr. Open Mind. That's me.

I rub at the headache building between my eyes and lean my head back against the headboard.

Ev.

Please.

Do it for me.

It's a good thing you've been my best friend for 20 years.

I'll behave.

Thank fucking Christ for small miracles.

I'll see you tomorrow, okay?

thumbs up emoji

One headache down. I look at the other text thread with the red dot next to it.

FRANK

I need to speak with you.

About the hearing.

Chris.

I have some news.

Will be at your house at 8 AM to discuss.

I look at the time on my phone and groan.

Tugging Jessie back into my arms, I breathe in her scent and lose myself for a little longer until sleep claims me.

CHAPTER 21

JESSIE

I stretch across the bed and groan at the ache in my muscles. But instead of the warm-bodied male who occupied my dreams last night, the bed is empty and the sheets are cool to the touch.

"Chris?" I lift my head and call his name, then wince and press my fingers close to where my neck and shoulder meet.

Silence greets me. We didn't talk about what he had going on today. I assumed he and I would pick up Gage this morning. And he wouldn't leave without saying goodbye. Right? I glance at my phone and yelp before scrambling from the bed. We didn't set a time to pick up Gage, but since it's nearly ten, I need to get a move on.

I rush into the bathroom, my neck protesting at the quick movements. It isn't until I check it on my way out that I discover why.

"He gave me a hickey?" The light brown mark is easily visible with the natural light streaming through the windows. "God dammit. We're going to talk about this."

I don't have time to shower since I need to figure out a way to cover the mark. After some deliberation, I settle on a button-

259

down I find in Chris's closet, knotting it at my waist. It'll have to do.

I rush down the stairs, stopping when I hear Chris's voice. Maybe he'll go with me to pick up Gage. Maybe I can even persuade him into a beach day with us if I promise to wear my new red bikini. I'm approaching the door to the room he's in when I hear someone tell Chris to calm down. It isn't a voice I recognize.

"I don't want to fucking calm down. Anyone who knows me knows I'm not into that shit anymore."

"Anymore being the key word in that statement. You're telling me that after twenty years of that lifestyle—twenty years of hard parties, women, drugs—you changed? Just like that?"

"Tell me how you actually feel, Frank." Chris's voice drips with sarcasm.

"It's not me, Chris. It's what the Sanderses' attorney is going to say. He's not known for playing nice."

"I hate this. What gives people the right to judge me? To question me?"

"You're in the public eye. You should be used to being judged and questioned."

"That was before I ran the risk of losing my son." The anguish when he says those words creates a sympathetic ache in my heart. I want to step into the room and soothe him, but something Frank said holds me back.

Chris used to be into all those things. But he changed. Didn't he?

Of course he did. He hasn't given you a reason to question him. Don't start now.

"Be that as it may, what are you going to say when you're asked that question?"

A deep breath, like a sigh, echoes through the room before Chris speaks again.

"I always wanted a family—wife, kids, dog, all of that. Yes, I had a reputation. *Had*. But I curbed that lifestyle when it stopped being appealing. There wasn't much to change when Gage came into my life because I realized that life without a family was empty. And I didn't want to be the quintessential 'rock star' forever."

Is he actually okay with his "family" consisting only of Gage and me? He used the plural when he talked about kids. Anxiety curdles in my stomach, and I try to push it away by reminding myself of what Chris and I have become to each other. I'm about to walk away—no good comes from eavesdropping—when I hear my name.

"You've recently been spotted with Jessie Bryant. Several sources identified the two of you looking cozy at a hospital recently."

There's a long pause. Too long.

"I—we were there together, yes."

What does that mean?

"Why?"

"Why? I don't know. We were both there. She planned a birthday party for Gage and invited a bunch of her friends over. When one of them went into labor, I thought it would be the right thing to do to make sure everything went well."

What?

"When did you meet her?"

"I was attending a barbecue her brother was throwing—"

"Who is her brother?"

"Jax Bryant. He co-owns Arrhythmic Records."

"Why were you there?"

"He invited me over to discuss a potential collaboration. Using one of the songs Just One Yesterday wrote for one of their artists. The discussion ran long, so he invited me to stick around."

Collaboration? This is the first time I've heard about one. Why?

"And Jessie?"

"What about her?"

"Since the news story broke about Noah and his overdose, the Sanderses are going to call in to question anyone you associate with."

"This is bullshit." His voice is farther away. Is he pacing?

"Bullshit it may be, Chris, but I need to be prepared walking into that courtroom. Now tell me about Jessie."

Yes, tell him about Jessie.

"Fuck. What do you want to know?"

"What is your relationship to her?"

"What do you mean?"

The knot in my stomach cinches tighter. It's hard to breathe holding myself so still.

"Chris. Answer the question."

Yeah, Chris, answer the question.

"What is your relationship with Jessie Bryant?"

"There's…nothing there. She's the help. My son's nanny. Nothing more."

Air saws in and out of my lungs, but a suffocating sensation still wraps around my windpipe. I lean against the wall as his words sink in.

Nothing more.

There's nothing there.

Just the help.

Nothing.

It's a dark word that blocks out all the light in my universe, surrounding me inch by inch, discoloring all my memories with Chris. Our heart-to-heart in the hot tub. The kitchen afterward. The music room. Last night. I bite my lower lip to hold back either a sob or a scream of rage, and the metallic taste of blood fills my mouth as tears run unchecked down my cheeks and drip on the fist clenched against my heart.

I stumble upstairs to my room—*my* original room—and lock

the door behind me. Lying on the bed, I pull my knees to my chest and a pillow to my face as sobs rack my body. I'm an idiot. How was I so wrong? So blind?

No, not blind. Naïve.

I believed him when he said he loved me. He claimed to be different. Turns out he was like every other rock star—excluding my family.

He told you what you wanted to hear so he could use you.

I drown the pillow with a fresh wave of sobs, but these are tears of rage, not sadness. Here I was falling in love, and he was only interested in using my body. The echoes of his words swirl in my head.

I love you.

Goddess.

You are enough.

All pretty lies. I can't. I can't stay here right now. Can't be in this house without feeling like I'm going to either murder him or lose my mind or both. Shifting up, I toss the pillow onto the bed, grateful that I was in a rush to pick up Gage, so I'm already dressed.

In his shirt.

Hell, no.

I rip the thing off and toss it in the corner while I search for something in my dresser. I find a higher-necked t-shirt that will have to work. Wiping the tears from my face, I take a deep breath and then another. I refuse to let this break me.

I'm going to walk out the door. But first, I have something to say. Rushing down the stairs, I turn into the living room. A guy in a pair of chinos and glasses looks up, surprised by my entrance. Chris's face is full of concern, but there are traces of something else. Guilt.

"Jess? You okay?"

"No. But I will be. Fuck you, Topher."

He raises his eyebrows and has the *nerve* to look confused.

"Topher?"

"I'm sorry I ever met you. I'm sorry I ever fell for your lies. You're a liar and an asshole. You're worse than Bowie. Because unlike the 'wannabe,' you fucking knew better."

"Jessie." He moves closer, arms raised.

"Stay away from me. I'm done. I don't need you or your job. I don't need any of this."

"What about Gage?" he asks quietly, still trying to placate me.

"He's the only thing I don't regret about this whole fucked-up situation. But I pity him for having a lying asshole for a father."

He moves closer, and I hold up a hand. "I swear to god, if you move closer, I'm going to lay you out on your ass."

That gives him pause.

"Jess."

"Stay the fuck away from me. I'm done."

I spin on my heel and rush to the door, then slam out of the house before diving into my car. I crank the ignition and ignore Chris when he steps out onto the covered porch, waving frantically at me. I turn my head, tears forming again as my heart pulses around the broken edges. He takes a step closer, and I throw the car in gear and pull away. My phone rings as soon as he's no longer in sight.

Chris.

Today I hate that my phone auto connects to the Bluetooth in my car. Within seconds, his name flashes in my eyeline as my car's robotic voice tells me he's calling.

I decline the call. I'm not interested in listening to more lies. All I can do in the raw state I'm in is feel. And hurt and rage are still battling for the top spot.

"Message from Chris. Listen to message?"

"No," I tell my car. "I'm not listening to any messages from that asshole."

The car has barely shut up when my phone rings again.

Chris.

Again.

Nope. Decline.

It rings a third time, his name flashing on my screen. But instead of declining, I let it ring until it goes to voicemail. It no sooner stops than the ringing starts again.

"Please. I can't do this right now." I'm not sure who I'm talking to, but hopefully the universe hears me.

The phone rings again.

Apparently not.

Pulling over to the side of his driveway—because of course I'm still in his long-ass driveway—I decline the call, but this time I power down my phone and toss it in my bag. Then I sit up straight, wipe a hand across my upper lip, and drive.

I'm going home.

♪♫♪♫♪♫

"Nothing? He seriously said there was nothing between you?" Sydney's hands clench into fists, and she jumps up from the couch. "I'm going to kick his ass."

"Syd, don't." I tug her back down on the couch. "It's not worth it."

"You are."

A fresh round of tears forms at her words. They're so similar to what Chris told me a few weeks ago. Was that his first lie? Or has he ever told me the truth?

"What? What did I say?"

I wave her away and grab a tissue from the box in front of me.

"Nothing. It doesn't matter."

"It does matter. Want me to hack his phone and share information on the web?"

"No, don't. I don't want Gage to be caught in the crossfire."

He's completely innocent, and guilt eats at me that I'm not

keeping my promise today. I promised to pick him up this morning. And it's hours later.

"Okay, so maybe not share info. What if I hack him and change his search history to only reflect porn sites?"

"Can you do that?"

Her Cheshire Cat smile scares me a little.

"I can do that and more."

"Remind me never to end up on your bad side." I take a drink of water that Sydney forced in my hand when I declined the wine she offered first.

"Nope. Bestie status for life." She reaches over to hug me, relieving some of the pain.

"That's good." I try to smile, but it's a foreign sensation.

"So what are you going to do?"

"I'm going back."

"*What?*"

"I have to."

"Who says? You don't have to go back."

"Yes, I do. For one, what about all my clothes and stuff?"

Although I'll probably be burning every single bikini I own.

"We'll send him boxes."

"Syd."

"What? It's a realistic option."

"What about Gage?" I ask. He has no idea what's happened.

How badly the situation between his dad and me got fucked up.

But none of that is his fault.

"What about him?"

"I can't leave him." I'm as in love with him as I am—was—with his dad. Maybe more.

"You're not going back there."

"I'm not going to run away from my problems."

"It doesn't mean you need to let the asshat walk all over you."

I shake my head. "I'm not. I'm done with him. I'll stick around long enough for them to find a new nanny for Gage. That's it."

"You think he'll be okay with that?"

I shrug and feign nonchalance. "If not, then I won't stick around."

"You're sure?"

I stand, taking my water glass into the kitchen and dumping it slowly down the sink.

I finally learned my lesson once and for all—rock stars are bad news and need to be avoided at all costs.

"You're going now?" The shock is clearly written on her face when I step back into the living room and shoulder my bag.

"I promised Gage I would pick him up hours ago."

I'm sure by now Chris picked him up. But I made a promise. And even late, I need to fulfill it.

"If you need me, call me." She gives me a hug so big it squeezes the air from my lungs.

"I will," I gasp out.

I wait until I'm in my car to power on my phone and wait for all the messages to load.

CHRIS

Jess, what the hell just happened?

Where did you go?

Why aren't you answering your phone?

Jess, please answer me.

Jess?

I have to go to an audition. My mom still has Gage.

Call me.

Please.

The knots in my stomach grow tighter with every text from him. But I have the relevant information I need. The rest? Eventually it will fade. Pulling up Dawn's contact information in my phone, I hit the call button.

"Hello?"

"Dawn? It's Jessie."

"Jessie. Chris said you had something come up and asked me to hang on to Gage while he went to a meeting with his label. Is everything okay?"

No, everything is not okay. But she doesn't need the nitty-gritty details of the implosion of my relationship with her son.

"Um, it's fine. I'm so sorry to leave Gage there so long. I can come pick him up now."

"Of course. His cousins are all still here as well. I'll text you the address."

"Okay. Will you let Gage know I'm on the way, please? I feel awful. I promised him—"

"It's hard, right?"

"What?" I ask, confused by the bemusement in her voice.

"Balancing life with children."

"Oh, umm…" How do I answer that?

Gage isn't mine.

Despite what my heart says.

She chuckles. "We'll see you when you get here, okay?"

"Okay."

She hangs up, and a few minutes later, I have her address. She doesn't live too far from Jax. My phone pings once on the way from my apartment to Dawn's, and my Bluetooth reads the text over my car speakers.

CHRIS

Jess? I'm worried about you. I haven't heard from you all day. What's going on? Would you please call me? I love you.

The last three words have tears building in my eyes. After this morning, I'm surprised there are any left. Shouldn't I be numb to words I know aren't true?

Wrong on both counts.

I turn on some music, desperate for a distraction, and keep driving.

Focus on Gage. You promised.

Sniffling, I pull into Dawn and Tony's driveway and stare at their house. Mansion would be a better word. Is this the house Chris grew up in?

Who cares? It doesn't matter. He doesn't matter.

I'm here for Gage.

I flip the visor down and rub under my eyes to clear the shine of tears away, but nothing can hide the puffiness. The visor pings back against the roof of the car as I slam it up, disgusted with myself and my inability to see through bullshit.

I take several deep breaths on my walk to the front door and ring the doorbell once. It sounds like there's a herd of elephants in the foyer, and I step back should they decide to break down the door on their rampage.

"Basta! Enough, nietos." Dawn's voice is clear, even in the cacophony coming from behind the door. "Abuelita will answer the door."

Four kids surround Dawn when she opens the door, and all five stare at me. It takes Gage a moment, but as soon as recognition hits, he's wrapped around my legs with no intention of letting go.

"Hi, buddy." I reach down awkwardly for a hug. "Did you miss me?"

I look up at Dawn for confirmation, and she nods. The separation was not easy on him.

You and me both, buddy.

"Gage?" Dawn addresses her grandson. "Would you like to go pack up your toys and books?"

He looks from me to her and back again, and my heart thuds in my chest.

"It's okay. I'll go inside with you."

His little shoulders slump in relief, and he follows his cousins into the house while I trail behind Dawn.

"I'm sorry to be so late like this."

"I enjoy keeping them. All of them. But they have more energy than I can keep up with." Her smile turns to a wince when something crashes to the floor upstairs.

"It's okay!" floats down the stairs.

"I should have been here earlier to pick him up."

That's what a real nanny would do.

But you haven't been the nanny. You've been the live-in girlfriend.

No, girlfriend is the wrong word. And the only other terms I can think of are worse than I want to think about.

"Did you enjoy the concert?"

I tense at her question, then try to relax my muscles into a more natural pose.

"Er, yes. Thank you. And thank you for the picnic. It was very thoughtful."

"Of course. I was only happy to help. It was all Christopher's idea…" She narrows her eyes at me, studying me for several moments in a way that reminds me of her son. "Jessie, is everything all right? Forgive me for saying this, but you look as if you've been crying."

"No, I—"

"I recognize the signs from myself and my daughter. Plenty of teenage tears with that one."

"I…no, everything is fine."

No way am I going to tell Chris's mom that her son is a two-faced rock star who broke my heart. But the words push at my lips, waiting to be said.

"If there is ever something you need to talk about—"

"I appreciate the offer. I'm okay."

Gage skids into the hall, putting an end to the awkward conversation.

"Ready to go?" I ask him.

He nods.

"Do you want to go give your grandma a hug goodbye and say thank you?"

He nods again.

"Thank you for coming to spend time with me, nieto." Dawn scoops him up and peppers him with kisses. "I enjoyed our sleepover."

He giggles and pushes her face away.

"Thank you, Abuelita."

"I love you, little one."

"Love you too."

He looks at me, and I see the question in his eyes. *Are we done yet?* I bite back a smile and reach for his hand, loving the way it fits in mine. In another life, this could have been my little boy. I'm going to be doubly heartbroken when I have to leave him behind. Gage is quiet on the drive home and during our normal routine of dinner, bath, stories, and bed.

"Jessie?" he asks as I tuck the covers around him.

"What's up, buddy?"

"Are you sad?"

He sees more than most adults would give him credit for.

"Why do you ask?"

"You look sad. You look like me when I think about Mommy."

"You must miss her an awful lot."

He nods. "Yeah."

"You know you can talk to me about that, if you want."

"Okay," he says. I'm nearly to the door when he calls my name again. "Jessie?"

"Yeah, buddy?"

"I missed you."

Be still my melting heart.

"I missed you too." My smile is watery around the edges.

"Do you think next time we do a sleepover, you could come too?"

I have no idea how to answer that question.

"I'll think about it, okay?"

"'Kay. Good night."

"Night, buddy."

I leave his door open a crack and walk into Chris's room. I gather everything from the nightstand, the closet, the bathroom. I erase my presence from his room bit by bit until what's left is exactly what he said was between us.

Nothing.

With a sigh, I walk back to my room, grateful for the en suite bathroom so I can store my shampoo back in my shower. I've barely finished hanging up the last of my clothes when my phone buzzes in my pocket.

CHRIS

Mamá said you picked up Gage.

She said you looked like you were crying.

Jess?

I clear the notifications and tuck my phone back in my pocket. Without my thesis to keep me busy, I lie on the bed and pull up Netflix. I'm three more episodes into the second season of Bridgerton when someone knocks on my door. No, not someone.

Chris.

"Jessie?" He tries the knob, but I had the foresight to lock the door. He knocks again. "Can we talk?"

With a sigh, I drag myself out of bed and pad to the door.

Fake it 'til you make it.

I can do that. Probably.

When I finally open the door, he pushes inside the room and wraps his arms around me.

"Fuck, I was so worried about you."

I don't return the hug, and eventually his arms fall to his sides.

"Why are you in here?" he asks.

"This is my room. That's your room." I point in the direction of the master.

"What? No, it's ours." He steps toward me, and I retreat. "What's going on? Why'd you go off on me like that earlier?"

"I—" *Be strong, girl.* "I don't think this is going to work out between us."

He sucks in a breath.

"What? Why? Where is this coming from? I don't understand."

"I heard you earlier. Talking to Frank."

"I don't—"

"There's nothing between us, right? I was hired to be your son's nanny. Nothing more than an employee. *The help.*"

I watch all the color drain from his face as I repeat the words he used earlier.

"Love—" He steps forward again, and I retreat. "Fuck, stop walking away from me." He runs a hand through his hair. It isn't the first time today he's done that based on the chaos of his hair around his face.

"I just, I need to be careful right now. I can't simply shout to the world that we're in a relationship."

"Are you fucking kidding me? You were the one who kept saying you didn't want to keep us a secret. Now you act like you're ashamed of me."

"Angel, I'm not, but—"

I'm done listening to his bullshit. Maybe if he had agreed to keep us a secret in the first place, this wouldn't hurt as bad.

Fuck that. It would still hurt.

"Consider this my notice. I will stay on board until you find a new nanny for Gage or until my new job starts. Whichever comes first." I may be breaking apart on the inside, but I reveal nothing.

"Jess, would you at least let me explain? Obviously you over-heard what I said earlier."

"How can you explain the words you used, Topher? I'm nothing to you. Your son's nanny."

"Jess—"

"You know, here I was thinking we were falling in love—" My voice cracks, and I stop.

"I do love you," he says in the silence.

"I don't believe you. Either you lied when you said you loved me, or you lied to your attorney earlier. I can't do this. I can't be what you want and sacrifice myself—"

"I want you."

"I'm no longer an option. I will be your son's nanny. Only his nanny. That's all it should have ever been."

"You're saying you regret what happened between us?"

Do I regret how this whole thing played out? How I learned my lesson for a second—and final—time?

"No."

His shoulders slump with my whispered response. "We can—"

I keep going as if he didn't speak.

"I don't regret what happened between us because you reaf-firmed what I already knew. Something I'd started to forget. Rock stars and me? We don't mix. And I will never, *ever* test that theory again. So thank you for the reminder."

"Jess—"

"That's all I have to say. Unless you need to talk to me about Gage, we have nothing else to discuss, and you have no need to be here."

"Jess—"

"Get the fuck out of my room, Topher." I don't raise my voice, the strength of my words found in how calmly I can utter them.

"That's not my name. I'm Chris." He grits out the words, a muscle ticking in his jaw.

"No. Chris doesn't exist. He's a make-believe version that a rock star used to trick me."

"Jess—"

"Either get out of my room or I'll leave. Permanently." There's a power in the word I deliberately choose.

He blanches. "Is that really what you want?"

"Yes."

It's what I should want. What I mostly want. What I'll fully want once my heartbreak heals. Again. He nods once and makes his way slowly to the door, holding on to the jamb to wait. For what? Who cares?

You do.

I ignore the voice that sounds too much like my heart to listen to right now.

"Good night, Topher." I close the door and push him the rest of the way into the hallway before I twist the lock.

I get back in bed and curl around one of the pillows, only then letting the tears fall.

CHAPTER 22

CHRIS

I've slept alone—except for the occasional woman—for all thirty-six years of my life. Jessie shared my bed for a month. But now I can't fucking sleep without her. Throughout the night, I search for her, and I grow more and more restless by her lack of presence next to me. By the time the sun comes up, I'm lying on my back while I try to figure out why I lied to Frank.

I didn't need to lie. I have nothing to hide. I love Jessie and she loves me. Or she had. Until I was a massive dumbass. Jessie is a beautiful woman, inside and out. She loves my son as if he were her own.

She's still thirteen years younger than you.

Is that the reason I lied? Because I was worried about being judged? The age difference doesn't bother me. Our connection transcends the years stamped on our driver's licenses. But other people would judge. The Sanderses. The paparazzi. They'll all have something to say about it. And what about her brother? Her parents? Her entire extended family?

And when I panicked at Frank's questions, I let those questions dictate what I said. Like anyone else's opinion matters.

But no excuse justifies what I did. I hurt the woman I love. And I'll live with that fact for the rest of my life.

"Fuck." I scrub a hand down my face and toss the covers aside.

Our bedroom is lonely without her. She may have said it was mine only, but since the first night she was in my bed and in my arms, it's been ours. Regardless of what we said, our arrangement had never been casual. And I was an idiot to think that it could be.

The bathroom is worse. I'm haunted by the mental images that cycle through my mind. From the first time when I pictured her in the shower with me to actual memories of her in here.

How can I miss her so much when she's in the same house?

Unable to handle the onslaught, I leave the bathroom and head downstairs and into the kitchen.

"Daddy!" Gage wiggles out of his chair and rushes me, his arms locking around my legs as he squeezes me.

"Gage!" I lift him into my arms, and Jessie's whole body tenses.

Fuck.

"Jessie made pancakes," he tells me happily, unaware of the tension building in the room.

"I see that."

The pancakes are still mostly whole on Jessie's plate when she stands and scrapes the food into the disposal.

God dammit.

"Would you like some pancakes?" Her voice is monotone, her attention focused on the plate in her hands as she loads it into the dishwasher.

"I—"

"You love Jessie's pancakes, Daddy. Eat with me." He looks at me with those big hazel eyes.

I can't say no.

Someday I'll need to learn that parenting skill, but right now, I'm still too overwhelmed by everything that happened yesterday.

I ignored Frank and rushed after Jessie to…to what? Explain? Apologize? Anything that could make up for my massive mistake. Frank had left shortly after that, wearing a stern look, and I was left alone, not knowing how the hell to fix what I had done.

But time hadn't been on my side since I'd had to be at the audition for the keyboardist. When Mamá had called to ask what time we were picking up Gage, I got worried. I assumed Jessie had gone to pick him up. So where had she gone?

Distracted, I let Gage pull me to the table. Jessie sets a plate down in front of me and spins away, but I snag her wrist before she can walk away.

"Wait." I fucking hate the tension that radiates from her at my touch. "Aren't you going to eat?"

"I did." She keeps her eyes focused elsewhere, no emotion in her voice.

This is what hell is like. The woman I love at my fingertips, and I can't reach her.

She scraped her food into the disposal. But can I call her out in front of the little boy whose eyes bounce back and forth between the two of us like a ping-pong ball?

"Can you let go of my wrist, please?" Her voice is so low, I doubt Gage heard it.

"Jess." I try to catch her eye, hoping to connect with her on even the smallest level. But when she turns to face me, I wish I hadn't. She's not looking at me, she's looking through me.

"Let go." Her voice is a little louder, and she tugs to break free.

What the fuck did I do? Why had I done it? And more importantly, how can I fix it?

"Gage, finish your breakfast and come up to the music room, okay?"

"'Kay."

Without another word or glance in my direction, she walks away.

"Daddy?"

"Yeah, buddy?"

"Why is Jessie sad?"

My fork clatters to my plate at his question. He might as well have asked me to solve a Rubik's Cube blindly.

"Did you ask her?"

He nods.

"What did she say?"

"She said sometimes people are sad."

"That's true."

Especially when someone says horrible things.

"Did she say anything else?" This is a new low. I'm pumping my five-year-old for insights into Jessie's state of mind. Christ.

"No."

He's silent for a few moments as he slides a piece of pancake through the syrup coating his plate.

"Daddy?"

"Hmm?"

"Are you sad?"

"Yeah, buddy, I'm sad." No use trying to hide it.

"Because Jessie's sad?"

"Yeah."

"Oh." He finishes his pancake and takes his plate to the sink. Another piece of Jessie. She's taught him so much. Encouraged him to clean up after himself. Helped him find his voice again.

She's changed so much since that first day. Including my heart.

And I fucked it up.

"Bye, Daddy." Gage squeezes my neck, and the smell of maple syrup invades my senses.

He no longer asks me to do things with him. And I hate that he doesn't think he can anymore. He's supposed to be my number one priority. My actions are supposed to show Jessie how much I love her.

When did life get so fucked up?

Sighing, I pull my phone out of my pocket and bring up the text thread with Mamá. Maybe she can give me some advice.

> I screwed up.

MAMÁ
So I gathered.

Can you fix it?

> She gave me her notice last night.

> Said she'll stick around until we find a replacement.

I see.

Fuck. I hate that phrase. It reminds me of Mamá standing in front of me, hands perched on her hips as she purses her lips. When I was a teenager, it was the phrase that never failed to clue me in to how much trouble I was in. *I see* always came before shit hit the fan.

> What do I do?

If I tell you what to do, it won't be you doing it.

And fixing it must come from you.

Shit. I was afraid of that.

> I don't know what to do.

Think about it.

The right answer will come to you.

Great. Mom wisdom. Maybe Papá can help.

And don't think of asking your father for help.

He's been told that this is your mistake to fix.

Damnit. And he'll listen to her, so that's a dead end.

> Okay.

> What if I can't?

Then you're not trying hard enough.

And hijo?

> Yeah?

Even though you screwed up, I still love you.

> Love you too, Mamá.

"Chris, she's not a good fit for the band." Evan runs a hand through his hair before resting his elbows on his knees.

I left the house before the awkwardness got worse. I want to hide it from Gage, but the little man is more insightful than a five-year-old should be. No doubt Jessie would say something about kids and awareness that would make it all make sense, but I can't ask her. Not with the way things are between us right now.

It's about Gage. Maybe you could?

I roll my eyes and focus on Evan, who is now pacing his living room. I came here under the premise of talking about yesterday's audition when really the tension in my house has me ready to explode.

"She's good." She played through a couple of our songs and then a few other covers before playing a full song with all of us.

"Then how come no one else is clamoring to sign Lilah

Stevens to their band?" The way he sneers her name tells me exactly what he thinks of her. My only question is why.

"Don't you think it might have something to do with her background? Not many rock pianists train at Julliard." She's classically trained—unlike the rest of our top candidates—but it could move our sound to a different level.

"Exactly. She has no idea what it's like to be a rock and roller."

"Ev. Think back to us when we started the band. What the hell did we know about being rock and rollers? We had to learn lessons the hard way more than once."

"She doesn't fit." He crosses his arms and glares at me. I half expect him to stomp his foot with his tantrum.

"Tell me why. If you have a good reason, we'll listen. Milo and Finn thought she was a good fit."

He scoffs. "Yeah, for a ride."

"Fuck, Evan." I stand up from the couch and stop in front of him. "Give her a goddamn chance. She's good. Pull that stick out of your ass. This isn't you. I know you don't like change, bro. But Noah isn't coming back."

"So you're saying I'm outvoted?"

We operate the band as a democracy—majority rules. Unless Milo and Finn want something stupid, in which case Evan and I have full veto authority. But Lilah isn't a stupid decision.

"I want you on board with this. It won't work if you're not committed to it. Give it a month. If it's not working out, we'll tell Marcus to find someone else." I need one fucking thing in my life to not be a battle right now.

I need Evan on my side. He studies me for several moments before nodding. "Fine, a month."

I release my breath and drop my shoulders. "Thank you."

Flopping back down on the couch, I let out an exhausted breath

"Everything okay?" he asks. "You don't usually lose your shit over a difference of opinion."

"I'm fine." I'm always fine. My role in the band is Mr. Fine. Mr. Unshakable. Mr. Calm, Cool, and Collected.

Even when I'm anything but.

"Really?" He arches an eyebrow and maintains eye contact until I look away first.

"No. It's not fine. Not by a fucking long shot."

"All the custody shit with Gage?"

I shrug. "That's part of it."

"What's the other part?"

"I fucked up with Jessie."

"Jessie? Last I heard, everything was hearts and rainbows and shit. What happened?"

"Like I said, I fucked it up."

He chuckles. "Yeah, I caught that. What did you do?"

"Frank came over yesterday to talk about the custody hearing next week."

"Okay…" He waves his hand in front of him in a hurry up motion.

"For almost two hours, we talked about what I would say when questioned by the other attorney. Questions about the band, tour schedules, the time I could devote to Gage. All those old tabloid articles and pictures? I had to explain each one. Explain how we didn't do that anymore."

"We used to."

"Right? That's what I said."

"How did you fuck up? You were being honest."

His word choice makes me wince.

"Not exactly."

"What does that mean?"

"Frank started asking me about Jessie. Why I was seen at the hospital looking 'cozy' with her."

"Cozy? Jesus Christ. When did you become a Hallmark movie?" He rolls his eyes.

"Asshole." I flip him the bird, but the smile on my face is more natural than it has been since yesterday morning.

"What did you tell Frank?"

"That I was just there to help. That I wanted to make sure the woman who went into labor at my house was fine."

"Seriously?"

"That's not all," I continue.

"Dude." He raises both eyebrows in question.

"Frank straight out asked me about my relationship with Jessie."

"Oh, fuck. I think I can see where this is going."

"If you're thinking that I said there's nothing between us—that she's the hired help, just my son's nanny—you're right."

The lie curdles in my stomach. Her ex-boyfriend had used her as a means to Jax and a potential record contract. But he never denied her. I didn't plan for her to hear me, but it doesn't make it right.

"Why the fuck would you say something like that?"

"I don't know."

"Bullshit. Why?"

"Because I'm older than her by thirteen fucking years." I explode off the couch and pace his living room. "Because every fucking pap in the town is going to glom on to that little tidbit and drag us through the dirt. Because what if, by telling the truth, I lose my son?"

"Seriously? Chris, you're a smart guy. But you are all fucked up in the head right now."

"Thanks for being on my side," I grumble.

"I am. Which is why I'm going to tell you to pull your head out of your ass. You think you're the first guy to love a younger woman?"

"Are these guys fighting custody battles for children they just found out they have?"

"Is Jessie a bad person? A gold digger? Does she treat Gage badly?"

"What? No. She's the opposite of what you're describing."

"Why is being in a relationship with someone like her a bad thing?"

"It's not."

"So why lie about it?"

I hate how he can take the logical path and make sense right now.

"I told you I fucked up."

"With flying colors." He snorts. "How do you feel about her?"

"I love her. I told her that."

"Actions speak louder than words, man. How do you think it felt to overhear you say all that shit to Frank?"

The haunted look in her eyes last night was a clear indicator.

"Like shit. I can't lose her, Ev. I had no idea where she was most of yesterday and was practically crawling out of my skin with worry by the time I finally saw her last night."

"Yeah, I figured. We could all tell something was off with you yesterday."

"She hates me."

"I don't think she—"

"She told me to find a new nanny for Gage. Told me things were done between us."

"Do you blame her?"

Fuck his logic.

"No."

"Then what are you going to do to win her back?"

"Maybe it would be better to let her go—ow."

Before I finish the statement, Evan smacks the back of my head.

"What the hell?"

"One, stop feeling sorry for yourself. Two, fuck everyone else and what they think—"

"I had that thought too."

"Glad to see your brain is still somewhat functional. Three, figure how the hell to win her back."

"I don't know what to do. I asked my mom, and she told me to think about it."

He snickers. "You had to ask your mom? Dude, are you completely hopeless?"

"I don't know what to do!" I shout.

"How about a conversation with her? Apologize. That's at least a step in the right direction."

"I can do that."

Maybe. I can try, but Jessie's not giving me very much opportunity. If Gage is asleep, she's locked in her bedroom. If he's awake, she's with him. After three days of trying to get her alone, I'm standing outside her bedroom, staring at a door I want to rip off the fucking hinges.

Just knock.

Only this isn't neutral territory. She handed me my ass several days ago inside that room before she literally pushed me out the door. But otherwise, she makes sure she's never alone and uses Gage as a human shield. Gage has been asleep for an hour, and I've been staring at her bedroom door for almost that long.

The knob rattles and the door opens. When she sees me standing on the other side of the hall like a fucking creeper, she jumps.

"I-I-I didn't know you were out here." She starts to close the door, and I surge forward to keep it open.

If she'd known I was out here, she would still be locked in that bedroom. It's not hers. Hers is down the hall with me.

"I've been trying to work up the courage to knock on the door." I smile sheepishly.

"Oh."

Oh. Just one word. Two letters.

She opens the door wider and skirts me to head for the stairs.

"Are you going out?" I wince at the stupid question. She's wearing pajamas, so obviously not. The sleep shorts hug her curves in mouth-watering detail.

She glances over her shoulder and rolls her eyes. "No."

"Can you at least give me more than one-word answers?"

"Doubtful." She smirks.

I grind my teeth together and rush down the stairs after her.

"Can we talk?" I ask and watch as she opens the cabinet for a mug and a tea bag.

I'd rather have hot chocolate. But now is not the time to remember *that* night.

"About Gage?" She doesn't turn around. But her shoulders tense—she must feel at least something between us.

"No, about us."

She doesn't answer, just makes her tea in silence. When she heads out of the room, I try again.

"Jess, please."

"There's no us to talk about, Topher."

I hate that fucking name.

"That's not my name."

"Would you prefer Mr. Rivera?"

What. The. Fuck?

"Mr. Rivera?"

"Maybe the staff shouldn't refer to their boss so informally."

At the rate my molars are grinding together, I'm not going to have any teeth left at the end of the night.

"Jess."

"Good night, Mr. Rivera."

She leaves the kitchen, and I stare after her.

That went well.

Now what?

CHAPTER 23

JESSIE

The awkwardness between Chris and me over the last few days has put me on edge. If I thought my awareness of him before was distracting, it's even worse when I'm trying to avoid him.

"I can't keep doing this, Syd." The phone is tucked between my shoulder and ear as I fold Gage's laundry.

"Has he found a new nanny?" The clack of her keyboard almost drowns out her voice.

"To tell you the truth, I don't know if he's even started looking."

"Come home, Jess."

I sigh. "I can't."

"Gage?" she asks.

"I can't leave him."

"Do you think Chris told Dawn about your resignation?"

"Maybe?"

Something tells me he hasn't since he won't stop trying to talk to me about us.

Us. Like that exists. There's a me and a him and a fucked-up situation.

"Maybe you should give your resignation to her."

"Maybe."

But then it makes it real.

It's already real.

Chris needs to find a new nanny—my time with the Rivera men is ending. And I need it to happen before I lose my resolve and give Chris another chance to make me a fool. No, not Chris. Topher. The whole "fake-it-'til-you-make-it" is a lot harder than it looks. Especially when I feel the weight of his gaze on me any time we're in the same room. Or when I catch him playing with Gage, the sound of the little boy's laughter tugging on my heart-strings and reminding me I used to be a part of that.

The worst is when Topher says my name. It reminds me of when it was only the two of us and I believed his pretty lies.

"Jess, did you hear me?"

"Sorry, what?"

"Text Dawn. Give her your notice."

"I will."

"How long until you're home?"

"Soon, hopefully." But is it actually my home anymore?

"We're going out when you get back." Sydney doesn't ask. In her mind, it's a foregone conclusion.

I groan. "Syd, I appreciate the thought. But I don't want to go out."

"I'm not saying tonight."

"I'm not sure I want to go out for a while."

First, I need to glue the pieces of my heart back together. Then I can move on.

My phone beeps before she can respond.

University of California.

"Syd, I gotta go. School's on the other line."

"'Kay. Talk later. Bye."

I transfer to the other call and take a deep breath. This could be news about the outcome of my thesis. Time is running out.

"Hello?"

"Jessie?"

"This is she. Professor Habib?"

"Yes. Do you have a moment to discuss your thesis?"

"Yeah, um, yes, I do." With everything that's happened, my thesis has been the least of my worries. I sit on the edge of the bed, careful not to topple the pile of clothes.

How does a five-year-old go through so many clothes in a week?

"The evaluation committee and I met earlier today to discuss your final submission."

"You did?" I sound like an idiot who can't string more than a few words together, but so much is riding on their approval. I don't know how else to respond.

"You made a lot of changes."

"I did."

Were they good changes or bad changes?

"You must know that the balance between information and emotion is a hard one to strike."

This is it. This is where he tells me I didn't achieve that balance. I close my eyes and brace myself.

"And one you managed to do in a way that was page-turning."

Say what now?

"Page-turning?"

"Your examples of the young boy who recently lost his mother and stopped speaking and what you did to help him are quite impressive."

"Thank you?"

"You must care an awful lot about the little boy. It shines through the entire paper."

Care about him? No. I love him. But Dr. Habib doesn't need those details.

"He's a very special child." My throat is tight with tears. I love him and I hate to leave him.

But I can't stay.

"Indeed." Dr. Habib clears his throat. "Let me be the first to congratulate you on your accomplishments, Jessie. Once I forward our approval to the registrar's office, they'll be in touch with details regarding graduation."

I make sure the phone call is over before I squeal loudly enough to bring Gage running into my room.

"Jessie?"

He beelines for me, and I pick him up and twirl him around, excitement lighting me up from the inside.

"It's okay, bud. That was a happy scream."

He eyes me dubiously, and I can't blame him. I've been moping around here like the walking dead for the last several days.

"Happy?" he repeats.

I nod. "Very happy."

"'Kay." He fidgets until I put him back down. Without another word, he runs back to his room where he's been playing.

I open the email app on my phone and send a note to the managing director of Chords, Crayons, and Counseling to give her a status update. The swoosh of the email sounds, and I stand, ready to pocket my phone, when it chimes with a text.

SYDNEY

Have you texted Dawn yet?

> Not yet. Just got off the phone with Dr. Habib.

And????

> They approved my thesis. I'm going to graduate.

GIF of woman clapping

I knew you could do it.

Now text Dawn.

You're not going to let this go, are you?

Nope. Not until you text me that you did it.

You're mean.

It's tough love.

Just do it. Get it over with.

With a sigh, I click out of my texts with Sydney and pull up Dawn's phone number. I'm going to take the coward's way out and text her.

Hi, Dawn. I just wanted to see if Mr. Rivera told you about my resignation.

I'm starting my new job soon and wanted to give you as much time as possible to find my replacement.

It's a logical reason. And true now that I've heard from Dr. Habib.

DAWN

Resignation? Oh no.

He hasn't mentioned anything to me.

Exactly like I thought.

I'll speak to Christopher and make sure he has started the process.

Thank you for telling me, Jessie.

I'm sorry to see you go.

I'm sorry to go. But I don't tell her that.

Thank you. I appreciate that.

Would you like to sit in on the interviews?

Sitting in on the interviews would give me a say in who will take my place. Will Gage even remember me in a few years? Or will I only be a blurry memory?

♪♪ ♪♪ ♪♪

"Jessie…Jessie…Jessie." A little hand pushes at my chest.

Cracking one eye open, I find Gage next to the bed, wide eyes shining in the darkness.

"Hey, buddy, what's the matter?"

"I had a bad dream."

"Aww, poor guy. Come here." I snuggle with him under the covers.

"What was your dream about?" I smile when he twists a strand of my hair with his chubby little finger. It's his tell when he's tired.

"I couldn't find Daddy."

The tension between his dad and me intensifies as the days tick by. The custody hearing is later today. No wonder he had a nightmare.

"Daddy's in his room," I whisper in his ear.

He shakes his head. "I checked. Daddy's not there."

His lower lip quivers, and I pull him tighter into my arms, running my hands along his back.

"It's okay, buddy. I'm here. We'll find Daddy in the morning, okay?"

According to my phone, it's two a.m. Where the fuck is he? Why isn't he here to help Gage with his nightmares? To know he's out somewhere right now and not here with us—Gage— creates an ache where my heart is still healing. I may pretend it already has, but I can't lie to myself in the darkness.

Gage snuggles against me, and his finger relaxes in my hair—

he's asleep. Brushing a kiss against his temple, I close my eyes. But it's a long time before sleep finds me once again.

CHRIS

The judge wants to see Gage at 1 PM.

I wake up to the text from Chris, and worry settles in my stomach. This wasn't part of the original plan. Why does the judge want to see Gage?

The boy in question is still passed out next to me, his arms thrown over his head in total abandon.

"Gage. Hey, buddy. Time to wake up."

I rub a hand down his arm and watch him stretch and blink his eyes open.

"Pancakes?"

At least he's consistent. I double-check the time on my phone.

"Yeah, we've got some time. But then we need to get ready. I need to take you to where Daddy is."

His brow furrows. "Where is Daddy?"

I'm not sure where he was last night—and that fucking hurts —but he's at the courthouse now.

"He's talking to your grandma and grandpa about you."

"Abuelita?" he asks.

I shake my head.

"Grandma—" I don't remember what Chris said Mrs. Sanders's first name is. "Your mom's mom and dad."

He pouts. "I don't wanna go."

"You don't want to see them?"

"No. I make them cry."

Tears burn the back of my eyes at his words. Is that what he thinks?

"Oh, no, baby. You don't make them cry." I hug him to me and breathe in his little boy scent. "They're sad. Remember how we talked about you being sad about Mommy?"

He nods.

"They're sad too. Sad for themselves and sad for you."

"So I don't make them cry?"

"Oh no, buddy, they love you."

Otherwise they wouldn't be trying to get custody. Right?

"Come on. Let's heat up some pancakes and we'll eat. Okay?"

"Okay."

Gage is quiet through breakfast and doesn't bat an eye when I put him in a light blue polo shirt and beige shorts. He doesn't even fight me when I comb his hair—a task he usually hates.

"Buddy, are you okay?" I ask as I buckle him into his car seat.

"My tummy feels funny."

So does mine.

"Do you feel sick?" I place the back of my hand against his cheek and forehead, but he isn't warm.

He shakes his head.

"Or like the time you ate too many pancakes?"

Another shake.

"What does it feel like?"

"Like when I woke up last night."

"Scared?"

He nods.

"It's okay to be scared, buddy. But I'll be there with you the whole time, okay?"

"Promise?" Trust for me shines in his eyes.

"I promise."

When we arrive at the courthouse, Dawn is waiting outside the assigned courtroom.

"Come here, nieto."

He goes willingly into her arms and giggles the same way he did the other day when she kisses him.

"Abuelita, down." His little demand has several people turning in our direction and smiling.

God, he's cute.

She sets him on his feet and looks at me.

"How are you, mija?"

I shrug. "I'm fine."

"Fine?" She raises her eyebrows and studies me intently.

"Worried about Gage," I correct.

"Just Gage?"

"Have you had any luck finding a new nanny?" I change the subject, not willing to talk about Chris.

"We are reviewing candidates—"

She's interrupted when the door to the courtroom opens and Chris steps into the hallway. He's wearing a charcoal gray suit and a royal blue button-down shirt. His hair is combed back from his clean-shaven face. He's never looked like this. All the moisture in my mouth relocates somewhere south at how good he looks. Chris in anything is sexy. In nothing at all, he's three-alarm-fire level. In a suit?

There are no words.

Obviously, he packed clothes to take to wherever he was last night.

I ignore the prick of pain that accompanies that thought. Where he was or who he was with is none of my business. I'm only the nanny. And not even that for much longer.

At the same time I'm cataloging his appearance, he studies me. His gaze takes in my floral wrap dress and flats. When his eyes find mine, my breath catches at the heat banked in the depths.

"Are they ready for us, hijo?" Dawn steps between Chris and me, breaking the spell.

Chris nods and leans down to Gage's level. "You ready, little man?"

"Am I in trouble?" He turns back to look at me.

"No, buddy, you're not in trouble. Remember? I'm going with you."

I reach out my hand, and he latches on to it, squeezing tightly.

Chris straightens and leads the way back into the courtroom. An older couple sits on one side, next to a sharply dressed attorney, while an open chair next to Frank shows where Chris has been sitting. The judge is an older woman with silver hair who smiles warmly at us as we make our way to the front.

"Your honor, this is my son Gage, my mother Dawn Rivera, and Jessie Bryant."

I don't even warrant the title of nanny anymore. But it doesn't lessen Gage's grip any.

"Hello, everyone. My name is Judge Morales. We're here today to discuss the matter of custody for Gage Christopher Rivera."

"That's me." Gage's free hand shoots up, and we all chuckle.

"Hello, Gage. Do you want to sit right there while I talk to your daddy?"

Gage nods and climbs onto the bench. His hand is still connected to mine, so down I go as well, and Dawn sits on the other side of her grandson.

"Mr. Rivera, before I begin, I'm allowing Mr. Chen the opportunity to ask questions he and the Sanderses have. Would you mind taking a seat here?"

She motions to the seat next to her.

"Yes, ma'am."

As soon as he's seated, the Sanderses' attorney stands and begins. He asks about Chris's lifestyle, about pictures that were taken years ago, about Noah and Club Panic.

Throughout the questioning, my hands clench into fists until my knuckles are white. How dare they bring up all this crap? None of it proves that Chris isn't fit to maintain custody of Gage.

"I want to ask you about Jessica Bryant," the attorney says.

I'm ready to smack him. Jessica is what Mama calls me when I'm in trouble, and it's usually accompanied by my middle name. Otherwise, I'm Jessie.

But the anger doesn't override the need to hold my breath. I don't know if I can hear this all a second time.

Chris doesn't flinch. "Okay."

"What is your relationship with Jessica?"

I brace myself for the words.

Gage's nanny.

Nothing between us.

His gaze locks onto mine, and breathing becomes even more difficult while my heart thumps in my chest painfully.

"I could just say that Jessie is my son's nanny. It's what she was hired for. And Frank is probably going to have a stroke, but since I have the opportunity, I'm going to take it."

He sits a little straighter and focuses on Mr. Chen.

"She's so much more than that. She's the love of my life, and I never saw her coming. I was resigned to being a bachelor forever. To figure out, alone, how to raise my son the same way my parents raised me—to be a good person, to be the type of person Jessie is. She is a kind, genuine woman who stole my heart before I even realized it."

His focus is on me now, and I can't look away. I can't blink.

"She loves my son. Adores him. She helped him find his voice again after—" He falters, but he doesn't look away. Tears drip down my cheeks as, word by word, action by action—telling everyone how he feels about me—he puts my heart back together. "I cannot imagine my life, or the life of my son, without her in it."

"And she makes good pancakes too," Gage chimes in from next to me, and suddenly I'm laughing and crying at the same time.

"Does that answer your question?" Chris asks the attorney, but his attention never wavers from me. The half smile on his face speaks to the happiness filling me.

"Er, yes. Thank you. Your honor?"

"I don't have any questions for you, Mr. Rivera. It's obvious from your responses that you have done well to make adult decisions and set your life on its proper track. For you and your son."

Her attention shifts from Chris to Gage. "Gage, do you mind if I speak with you alone for a few minutes?"

He looks at me for reassurance, but frowns at my tears.

"It's okay. I bet she's nice," I whisper to him.

He nods solemnly. "She looks nice."

"Do you want to go talk to her?" I ask him.

"Will you come with me?"

I smile sadly. "She wants to talk to you by yourself, buddy. But how about this?" I pull off the hair tie around my wrist and place it around his. "Why don't you take this with you? Then it's like I'll be there too."

He smiles and nods once, hopping off the bench.

"Okay."

"Court is in recess for ten minutes." Judge Morales bangs her gavel.

"I'll be right back," I tell Dawn.

I rush out of the courtroom and push into the closest bathroom.

I groan at my reflection. "I'm a mess." I run an index finger under my eyes to wipe away streaks of mascara. Waterproof, my ass.

"A beautiful mess."

I gasp at the familiar voice, and my eyes find Chris's in the mirror as he moves closer.

"Jessie, I—"

"Christopher Antonio Rivera!"

"Fuck."

Dawn steps farther into the bathroom and quickly shuts the door.

"It's a good thing I left your Papá at home today. He would not approve of you using language like that in front of your Mamá."

"Mamá—"

"No. I don't want to hear it. This is the women's restroom, and you will exit right now, or I will help you do so."

His eyes find mine again, full of everything he wants to say, and my breath locks in my lungs. There's something else too. Everything he's already said.

"Christopher, ahora."

With one last look, he follows his mom back out of the bathroom. Alone again, I splash my wrists with cold water, using a paper towel to dab water on the back of my neck and cheeks.

"Don't," I tell my reflection. "Don't fall for it again."

I might as well be talking to the cinderblock wall for all my heart wants to listen.

"Jessie?" Dawn pokes her head back in the door. "It's time."

Chris is nowhere in sight when I step back into the hallway, and Dawn points to the courtroom.

"Gage's grandparents asked to speak privately with him."

They're still talking when we walk back in. Only now, both attorneys are also involved.

What the hell is going on?

The door to the judge's chambers opens, and Gage walks through with the judge.

"Jessie!" Gage races to me. "Judge Morales said the cafeteria has ice cream."

She nods. "I thought you could take him for one while I speak to Mr. Rivera and Mr. and Mrs. Sanders."

"Can we go?" Gage asks, tugging on my arm.

"Sure, buddy. Let's go."

My eyes find Chris's as Gage pulls me out of the courtroom. For the first time in a week, I'm torn between following Gage or staying for Chris.

CHAPTER 24

CHRIS

*T*he look Jessie gives me as she exits the room with Gage allows hope to take root. I meant every word I said when the attorney asked me about her. The way she wrinkled her nose when he called her Jessica was fucking adorable. But I kept that tidbit to myself.

"I had the most enjoyable chat with that little boy," Judge Morales starts. "He has a very keen sense of humor and talked a lot about Jessie and how much he loves her. I also now have an invitation to come over and try her pancakes."

I chuckle, and Mr. and Mrs. Sanders smile.

"Your honor." The Sanderses' attorney stands.

"Mr. Chen?"

"Before you continue, my clients wish to drop the petition for custody of their grandson."

Judge Morales turns to the older couple. "Is that right?"

Mrs. Sanders nods. "Yes."

"Mr. Sanders?"

"Your honor, we were mistaken. We assumed he was like every other rock star you read about. And we were wrong."

Relief courses through me at his words. Even though they had come to me during the recess to tell me their intention of dropping the petition, I wasn't 100 percent sure until right now.

Judge Morales shifts her attention to me.

"Yes. I do believe Mr. Rivera defies that description. In my conversation with Gage, he told me about pool days and a recent trip to the zoo. He loves you very much, Mr. Rivera, so I would consider yourself fortunate to be the recipient of that love."

I swallow around the ball of emotion in my throat. "Thank you, your honor. I consider myself very lucky. And I love him just as much. It was a little scary how much I loved him even before I met him."

Judge Morales smiles at me. "A sentiment echoed by most parents. If that is all?"

Everyone nods.

"Then I consider this court adjourned. Mr. Rivera, why don't you go join your son for an ice cream?"

"Yes, ma'am."

I wait until the judge leaves before I pull my phone out.

> Finished here. Can I join you?

The dots pop up as she types her response. I look up as Mr. and Mrs. Sanders make their way to the door.

"Mrs. Sanders?"

They both stop, and I join them as Mamá comes up behind me. God love overprotective mothers. Mine is the best.

"I really do want Gage to have a relationship with you. Both of you. Maybe you could come over for dinner one night this week?"

"Yes, I'd like that. Very much." Mrs. Sanders looks at her husband, who nods.

"Great. I'll give you a call to set everything up."

"Thank you, Chris."

The two of them leave, and Mamá brushes a kiss against my

cheek, wiping at the stain of her lipstick almost immediately afterward.

"Mamá." I duck out of her grasp and rub at the spot.

"Have I told you how very proud I am of you?"

"Not lately."

She laughs. "It was touch and go there for a bit, Christopher. I am very glad you redeemed yourself."

"There was only one way to go—up."

"Very true. By the way, Jessie resigned last week."

Fuck.

"When I called the agency, I did start the process, but I told them we were looking for someone who could help the two of you with Gage." She winks.

"Thank you, Mamá. You're my favorite." I smile and wrap her in a quick hug.

She laughs. "If you tell Jessie I told you that, I'll deny it and stop making your birthday cakes."

Her dulce de leche cake is my favorite, so it's a serious threat.

"That's okay. If you tell Papá you're my favorite, I'll deny it and invite him to go on tour with us."

She gasps. "You wouldn't dare."

It's no secret that she never wants to go on tour again.

I blow her a kiss. "Try me."

"Good boy. Now go have an ice cream with your son."

We say our goodbyes, and I check my phone for Jessie's response.

JESSIE

Took Gage to the park across the street to enjoy
our ice cream.

I make my way outside and find Gage and Jessie cuddled together on a bench with massive cones.

"Hi, Daddy!" Gage waves. Ice cream drips onto his shirt and creates a ring around his mouth.

"Hi, buddy. How's your ice cream?"

"It's melting."

"I can see that." I share a smile with Jessie as my heart rate picks up.

Please let her forgive me.

"Are you ready to go home?" I ask Gage, but my attention bounces between him and the woman next to him.

"Yeah. Can we watch a movie?"

"Whatever you want, buddy. Do you want to ride with me or with Jessie?"

No surprise. Jessie.

I'd choose her too if I could. Instead, I walk them both to her car and buckle Gage into his car seat.

"See you at home?" I rest my hand inches from hers on the car door, and the hope that started with her look grows a little stronger. She didn't pull away.

"Yeah."

It takes every ounce of my control to not lift my finger and trace it along her jaw. But I don't want to push my luck. I close her door, staring after her as she pulls into traffic before I double back to my car. I'm almost there when my phone rings.

Evan.

"Hey."

"What the hell happened? What's the verdict?"

"No verdicts. It was family court."

"Thanks for the legal lesson, Mr. Big Shot. What happened?"

"They dropped the custody case."

"What? Man, that's awesome. It was my lucky suit, right?"

"If it's your only suit, can it be your lucky suit?"

Thank god Evan and I are close to the same size. I fell asleep at his house and woke up with no time to go home and change.

"Yes. And I want it back."

"I'll get it back to you soon."

"Are you still wearing it?"

"Yeah. I'm outside the courthouse."

"Are you going home to talk to Jessie?"

"Yes."

"Then keep it on. I'll talk to you later."

The phone beeps in my ear, and I chuckle before sliding into the driver's seat. I'm anxious to get home. The lucky suit even works on traffic—I'm back home in thirty minutes, versus the hour it usually takes.

"Hello?"

"In here." Jessie's voice comes from the family room, and I find her and Gage on the couch watching *101 Dalmatians*. My boy is obsessed with dogs. And cats. Maybe he needs a pet.

Jessie is still in her dress, but Gage is in a clean pair of shorts and a t-shirt.

"Can we talk?" My heart pounds as I wait for her response, a flood of relief washing through me when she nods.

I motion toward the back door, and Jessie brushes a kiss against Gage's hair.

It's automatic. As is her love for my son.

"I'll be right back, buddy, okay?"

"'Kay."

She follows me outside and squints in the bright sunlight.

"Here." I move a little farther until we're standing in the shade of the trellis. "Better?"

It is for me—it offers a little more privacy and gives me the opportunity to see her expressive eyes.

"Yeah."

I open my mouth at least twice—to say what, I don't know—but close it with a sigh.

"What happened after I left with Gage?" she finally asks.

I'm distracted by the way her teeth sink into her lip, by the way her fingers fidget by her waist.

I let my face shift into a pout. "Well…"

"Well?"

The pout slowly morphs, replaced by a tentative smile. "The Sanderses dropped the petition."

"What? Really?" Her eyes glow before she squeals and throws her arms around me.

Fuck. This is what's been missing all week. Her in my arms.

"Chris, that's amazing."

Her lips brush my neck, and I shiver.

Chris. Not Topher. Or Mr. Rivera. Thank Christ.

I hold on, breathing her in as my heart thuds against hers. I can't keep her here forever. But I missed her, and the thought of letting her go has my arms tightening even more.

She tenses and my time is up. "Chris."

Reluctantly, I lower her so her feet are on solid ground and cool air fills the distance she puts between us.

"Can I ask you a question?" I ask.

You just did, dummy.

"Umm…" She nibbles at her lower lip.

I want to replace her teeth with my own, but I fight the urge and stuff my hands in my pockets while I wait for her response.

"Okay?"

"Did you…what did you think about what I said earlier?" It should have been terrifying to tell the entire room of people how much I loved her. But instead, the weight on my chest had lifted, and my only concern was how she felt about me after I screwed up.

Was it a good sign that she couldn't take her eyes off me? Were her tears happy or sad?

"About me?"

"Yeah."

An eternity passes in those few heartbeats before she speaks again.

"I—did you mean it?" Doubts swirl in her eyes, and my heart plummets to my stomach.

Fuck.

"Did I mean it?"

"Yeah. I guess I'm not sure since the other day you told Frank one thing, and then today—"

"Jess."

She leans against the trellis and looks at me with shadows in her eyes. Ones I would do everything in my power to have never put there to begin with. But hopefully I can fix it. If I'm not too late.

"Fuck yes, I meant it. I'm so goddamn sorry for what I said the other day. None of it was true. Nothing—"

I break off when she winces at that word. It's a word that means exactly that. Nothing. But it doesn't fit. Not us. Not when she and my son are my entire universe.

"Everything I said today was the truth. I wasn't looking for you, but I can't imagine my life without you. I love you. So fucking much."

She swipes a hand against her cheek and wipes away a tear.

"Please don't cry." I move closer and use my thumbs to sweep the moisture away.

Her broken breath as she inhales makes it hard for me to breathe.

"How do I know it's true? I want to believe you, but I'm not sure I can."

"And that's my fault. I made you doubt us, doubt me. And I can't wave a magic wand and make that disappear, but I can keep telling you, keep proving to you that every word I said in that courtroom is a promise I intend to keep for the rest of my life. I made a mistake. A huge one. I'm not asking you to forgive me or forget what I did. I'm only asking for another chance. Please."

"I can't be that person. The one you want."

"Why do you say that?"

"Even if everything you said today was true and we tried again, there's another problem." Her lip trembles, the anguish so clear on her face that all I want to do is pull her into my arms and make it go away.

"What's this problem?"

"If you and I are together, Gage is it. I can't have kids, remember? How soon before you resent me for that? Before I'm not enough?"

"Angel, that's never going to happen. You are my family. You and Gage. You two own my heart in equal measure. Just like I can't imagine the world without my son asking me a million questions a day, I can't even fathom a world that I don't share with you. Where I don't have the chance to tell you a thousand times each day how much I love you."

"But—"

"Nothing you can say or do. Nothing you don't say or can't do will ever diminish my need for you. I love you. And I'm up to a handful of my thousand for the day."

Her smile is tremulous, but I'll fucking take it.

"Only a thousand?"

With those three words and the beginnings of an impishness in her smile, tension ebbs from my body. Not completely, but I didn't plan on that, given how close I came to losing her.

"Give or take infinity," I say with a smile. "Please tell me I didn't destroy us permanently. I was an idiot. And I'll spend the rest of my life making it up to you if you'll let me. Please don't leave me."

I close the distance, lining up our lower bodies in a way that makes both of us sigh. She lifts her hands, the prick of her nails digging into my biceps ratcheting the need for her impossibly higher.

"With every breath in my body, every beat of my heart, all of it is for you. To tell you how much I love you. How much I need you." I drop my head and trail my nose along her jaw. "Believe me. Please."

I bring my lips to hers, sliding one way and then the other

before settling over them fully. Every emotion over the last week, over every day since I first met her, is infused in that connection between her mouth and mine. I cup her jaw as I deepen the kiss, and she trails a path along my arms until she grasps my wrists. I double my efforts, terrified that she's going to push me away.

"Chris."

"Not yet," I murmur against her mouth. "I need more."

"How much more?" Her lips curve against mine, and I bring our foreheads together.

"How about until the day after forever?"

She runs her fingers through my hair, and goosebumps drag along my neck at the light scratch of her nails.

"Won't we have to eat?"

"Food is overrated." I kiss her again, sipping at her lips until they part and our tongues find each other.

"What about everything else?" she asks, breaking the kiss. "Gage, you and the band, me and my job, graduation—"

"Graduation?" I ask.

Her smile stretches across her face and makes me want to kiss her again.

"My thesis got approved."

"What? Angel, that's incredible. As for everything else—" I press my lips against one side of her jaw before I move them to the other side. "We can figure it out."

"How are you so sure?" Her question comes out on a sigh as she leans her head back, inviting me to keep going.

"Because I love you. And that's all that matters."

"What about how I feel about you?"

"That's pretty important too." I smile and nip at her lips, relishing the sound of her laughter. "How do you feel about me?"

"Hmm." She pulls back and taps a finger against her lips while she studies me. "How do I feel about you?"

"That's what I want to know." And she better answer in a fucking hurry. I'm desperate to have my lips on her again.

"I know. I'm thinking about it."

"Thinking about it? Thinking about it?" I run my hands down her sides, tickling her as she squirms between me and the trellis. "Do I need to give you more to think about?"

"I could always use more data to make my decision."

"How's this?" Moving slowly, I slide my hands from her hips to her ass, squeezing gently as I thrust against her.

"That's good." Her answer ends in a squeak as my hands move lower and my fingers trace the line of her panties under her skirt.

"Do you have an answer for me yet?" I move my hands back to her hips—a Herculean effort—and flex my fingers.

"Chris." My name is more of a whimper than any other sound.

"Hmm?" My lips find the pulse point in her neck and feather against the staccato vibration.

"You're not playing fair."

"I never said I would," I murmur and move to the sensitive spot behind her earlobe. "I only said I love you. And I asked if you loved me."

"I-I never stopped. Even when I wanted to, I couldn't," she admits in a rush. "I love you so much. Even if I'm terrified that you found someone else."

"Found someone else?" Those words pull me up short. What the hell is she talking about? "You're it for me. Forever."

"But you didn't come home last night. And this morning, you showed up dressed in this." Her hands fist into the material of the suit jacket. "I thought…that…"

"You thought I could simply turn off how I feel about you and find someone else?"

She nods, and I press another kiss against her lips.

"I fell asleep at Evan's. This is his 'lucky suit.' But I don't think he's getting it back."

"Why?"

"Because now it's my lucky suit. You're here." I flex my fingers against her hips and savor the way she tries to press closer.

"Luck had nothing to do with us," she says.

"No, but I wouldn't put it past fate. How else could I explain you? Explain us?" My lips are millimeters from hers, close enough that they rub against them when I talk. "You said you love me?"

"I love you. Now kiss me."

"With pleasure." My lips devour hers while my hands reacquaint themselves with her curves. It's been forever, wrapped in a week. Too long.

Never again.

It should make touring an interesting battle to plan.

Her legs are wrapped around my waist with her back pressed against the wall, and I'm busy tracing her curves with my tongue when the door opens.

"Daddy? Jessie?"

I groan.

"Shh," she whispers, laying a finger against my lips. I drag my tongue across it and suck it into my mouth, watching her pupils dilate as I do.

"Daddy! Jessie!"

"Y-y-yeah, buddy?" She bites her cheek against a moan as I thrust my hips against her center.

"I'm hungry."

"Is the movie over?"

"Uh-huh."

"Okay, buddy, we'll be there in a minute."

"'Kay. Can I put on the next movie?"

I groan at what must be his two millionth question for today.

"Shh." She shushes me again. "Do you know how?"

"Yeah."

"Okay."

There are no other questions, and the door slides shut.

"How many minutes do you think that buys us?" Her lips find my jaw.

"Not long enough for what I have planned."

She shivers at my promise.

"Later?" I ask.

"Do we have a choice?"

"Not really. Let's go feed the little man and get him bathed and in bed."

"Then what?" Her voice is breathy.

"Don't plan on getting much sleep," I growl against her lips and tighten my arms around her. "Because you're mine."

"Always."

CHAPTER 25

JESSIE

1 MONTH LATER

age is dressed." Chris walks into the bathroom and gathers me against him, his lips tracing from my shoulder to my neck.

"Thank you. Is he watching a movie?"

"No."

"Reading?"

"No."

My graduation starts in two hours, and Chris was put in charge of getting Gage ready.

"It's probably not a good thing it's so quiet if he's not doing either of those things."

"No." I say, a smile curving my lips.

"Be right back."

I'm almost done curling my hair when he comes back. He's wearing dress slacks now instead of the basketball shorts he had on before, but no shirt.

"Planning on getting dressed anytime soon?" I tease, unplugging the curling iron and grabbing my mascara from my makeup bag.

"Are you?" His hands slide along my stomach, and heat builds between my legs.

Since I'm only in my bra and panties, I guess he has a point. Squirming against his fingers, I hold up my mascara wand. "I need to finish this."

He snags the mascara from my hand and tosses it back on the counter, spinning me around and backing me against it while his lips crush mine. His tongue joins the party, and I moan before boosting myself to sit and wrap my legs around his hips.

"I thought you said you had to get ready," he murmurs against my lips as his mouth curves into a smile.

"Someone distracted me. But I really do need to finish my makeup."

He cups me through my bra before he drags his thumb over my lace-covered nipple.

"You don't need makeup. You're beautiful without it."

"Thank you, baby." I tease kisses against his lips until he holds my head in place and plunges his tongue to tangle with mine.

He trails his free hand down my body and tugs my panties to the side to find my clit with his thumb.

"Chris." My head falls back against the mirror, and I push against him.

"Think of this as stress relief, angel."

His fingers replace his thumb and swirl faster. I pant as the orgasm shimmers in my toes.

"Hold these." He wraps my fingers in my panties, and I continue to hold them to the side.

"I'm not stressed." I moan as he presses a finger inside me, his thumb now tapping against my clit.

"So I should stop?" A second finger joins the first, and he curls them up to rub along the spot that burns stars behind my eyes.

"Don't you dare." I growl and ride his hand as the orgasm builds up my legs, closing in on the spot that is the center of my pleasure.

"This is going to be fast." His thumb speeds up as his fingers scissor and press against the walls of my pussy.

The first jolt of my orgasm is lightning, a flash of heat and power that stretches from one end of my body to the other in arcing waves of pleasure. He continues to work me through my orgasm, only slowing to a stop when I lean my head against his chest.

Smoothing my panties back in place, he hands me my mascara wand like he didn't just finger fuck me in our bathroom. His erection strains against his dress slacks, and I reach out and palm him through the material.

"Fuck, angel." One hand wraps around my wrist while he brings the other to his lips, sucking the taste of me off his fingers. "Mmm."

"Why is that so hot?" I ask and try to stand on wobbly legs.

"I'll tell you later." He winks and bruises a kiss against my lips. "Now get dressed or we're going to be late."

"Shit." I spin back to the mirror and run through the rest of what I need to do before sliding on the white sundress I'll be wearing under my graduation gown.

By the time I rush downstairs, Chris has Gage in his car seat, and I duck into the passenger seat so we can take off for the stadium. We barely make it in time for me to join the other graduates filtering in.

"Good luck," Chris and Gage yell after me, and I spin around and blow them both a kiss.

"Your son is so cute," the woman next to me says.

"Oh, he's—" I could say he's not mine, but in my heart, he is. "Thank you."

The ceremony passes in a blur until my name is called over the speakers.

"Jessica Elaine Bryant."

I walk across the stage, overwhelmed by the cheering group that is my family—for better or for worse. My parents are here, Jax and Charlie and their kids, Nick and Meredith with their girls, Dylan and Claire with their kids, Mia and Garrett have Wyatt, and Michaela and West with their brood. Even the other members of Just One Yesterday have joined the group. Part of me worries that Lilah and Evan are going to kill each other, public venue or not. But Chris and Gage are the loudest of them all.

"Yeah, Jessie!"

"Yay, Jessie!"

I smile and wave toward them before I find my seat again. I expect to be swarmed after the graduation, but only Chris and Gage find me on the field.

"Congratulations, angel." Chris kisses me before Gage pushes between the two of us.

"Graduations, Jessie."

"Thank you, buddy." I lean down and press a kiss to the top of his head. "Where's everyone else?"

"Heading to our house for the barbecue."

Jax and Chris got into a huge debate over who would be hosting the party. Chris won but wouldn't tell me how.

"We should probably get going then."

Chris laces his fingers with mine while Gage hops along the field next to us, finally holding Chris's other hand when we get to the parking lot.

"How did you guys manage to keep all this quiet?" I ask in awe. Not a paparazzi in sight. Rare, given the fame of most of our group.

"I don't know what everyone else did, but I promised an exclusive story to an outlet who behaved for today." We're almost to the car, and I wait until we're both inside and Gage is buckled to ask.

"What story?"

"You'll see."

"Cryptic."

"Love you." He leans over and brushes his lips against mine.

"Love you too."

♪♪♪♪♪♪

I've lost track of how many people mingle around the pool or inside the house. Chris and the rest of the guys powered through dozens of hamburgers and hot dogs while everyone else handled the sides.

Charlie and Mia are starting to show, but Charlie looks much further along than Mia. "Are you sure there's only one baby in there?" I ask and rest my hand against Charlie's belly.

"As far as we know. The doctor told me I'm showing much earlier, given my other three pregnancies."

"Ohh."

"Jess, can you take Lainey for a minute?" Meredith thrusts the baby at me before charging off after Everly.

"Everly really is a mini-Meredith, huh?"

Charlie laughs and nods. "Exactly."

Lainey looks up at me with her dark eyes, and I smile at her.

"You look beautiful," Chris says over my shoulder.

"She's precious," I say and rock the baby in my arms.

"She is. You want to start rounding up the troops? It's time to eat."

I nod and make my circuit through the house and the back-yard, passing Lainey off to Nick when I spot him.

"I'm so proud of you, baby." Mama comes up and squeezes me.

"Mama. Can't breathe. Mama."

She releases me with a sniffle, and Daddy takes her place.

"Congratulations, Jessie."

"Thanks, Daddy."

He gives me a look I can't decipher before Mom pulls him in the direction of the food line. We all load up plates for kids before loading our own and settling into the various chairs around the pool. We're almost finished when Gage runs up to Chris.

"Daddy, is it time yet?"

"Time for what, buddy?" I ask him as he looks at his dad.

"Not yet. Soon."

Before I can ask him anything more, Gage rushes off, calling Millie's name.

"What was that all about?" I turn to Chris, who shrugs.

"No idea. Do you need anything else?" He gestures to my plate.

I groan. "No, thanks. I'm so full I'm ready to burst. Good thing I'm wearing a dress today."

His eyes heat, and he leans closer. "I'm enjoying your dress. I think it would be more enjoyable off you."

"Later."

"I'm holding you to that, angel." He takes my plate and Jax steals his seat.

"Congratulations, squirt."

"Thank you."

"I'm proud of you."

"Thanks, Jax." I lean over and give him a hug. "I couldn't have done this without you."

"I'm pretty sure you would have. I only hope I made it a little easier."

"You did." My attention bounces to all the adults and the kids. My family by blood or friendship.

"Are you happy, Jess?"

"What?" I turn back and focus on my brother.

"You seem happy. Are you?"

I nod. "I couldn't imagine being any happier than I am right now."

Music notes catch my attention, and I look around. The song sounds familiar, but I can't quite place it until Chris steps out of the house with a guitar. He walks toward me with Gage at his side. The other members of JOY have instruments with them, and they join in. So do Dylan, Jax, Nick, and Michaela.

"What's going on?" I ask Jax.

He shrugs and points to Chris, who is kneeling at my feet. He plays through the entire song, his eyes trained on me until the last chord fades. I recognize the song now—one Chris has been working on, "Angel in the Light." He told me I inspired it.

"Hi." He smiles up at me.

"Hi. What's going on?"

He puts the guitar down and reaches into his pocket.

"People are probably going to think I'm crazy. That it's too soon." He smirks. "But when have I ever given a fuck what other people think? I figured I missed my soul mate a long time ago, two paths that never connected. Until the day I walked into a backyard, and there you were. I didn't believe in love at first sight until that moment. But every other look made me fall deeper, until there was nowhere else to go. Because I was irrevocably and irreversibly yours. I love you. And that's never going to change."

He shifts. He's kneeling on concrete, which can't be comfortable, but he doesn't wince, and he doesn't get up.

"And Gage. My son. Our boy. If I didn't love you for yourself, I would for the love you show him. You helped him find his voice. You helped us become a family. That's what we are. You, me, and our son. Now I want to know what you think. And if you tell me right now that this is too fast, that we need to take things slower, so be it. But that won't stop me from asking you when you're ready, from hoping for the answer I want when I tell you I can't picture a life without you. Will you marry me?"

He opens the box, and the princess cut solitaire catches the light around us. But not simply physical light. It's a light of love.

"You asked for my opinion. So here goes. Fate exists to bring two people together. In this case, it was three. I have to be honest. I think I fell in love with Gage first. Once I did, I fell head over heels for you too. Maybe that's love at second sight? I don't know and I don't care. Because I love you both. I love Gage so much that my heart isn't big enough to hold all that love. And my love for you knows no physical bounds. It is infinite. Forever. So what if people say it's too soon? Life is too short and too precious to waste time worrying about what other people think. Yes. Yes, I'll marry you."

I launch myself from my chair and tackle him to the ground for a kiss that only ends when we both need oxygen.

"Should I put this on you?" he teases and holds up the ring.

"You better."

He slides the ring until it rests along my knuckle. Bringing my hand to his lips, he presses a kiss there and another in the palm of my hand.

"I love you," he tells me, eyes bright as he meets mine.

I lean down and brush another kiss on his lips.

"I love you."

"Does this mean you're going to be my mommy?" Gage rushes forward and lands on top of us.

"If you want. You can still call me Jessie, too."

"'Kay."

"I love you, Gage." I wrap my arms around him and tug him down next to me.

"Love you." He wiggles from my grip and back over to his friends.

Chris stands first and reaches down to yank me to my feet. His lips find mine without warning, but my moan doesn't make it beyond the fusion of our lips.

"Gage, you want to have a sleepover with Millie?" Claire asks and sends a wink my way after Chris breaks the kiss.

Both Millie and Gage cheer.

"Do you think it would be rude if we left people here and took our celebration somewhere more private?" Chris growls into my ear, and I shiver as my core throbs in response to his voice.

"Can we be inconspicuous about it?"

"I'll say I'm putting the guitar away."

"And I'll use the bathroom."

"Meet me in our room?"

I nod, the desire building to aching levels. I need him. Right now.

I start to leave first but am quickly caught by Meredith.

"Jess, where are you going?"

"Bathroom. I'll be right back."

Chris's look says something else. *The hell you will.*

I nearly trip over the step into the house with the heat of his look.

"I'm going to go put this away." Chris's voice carries into the kitchen from the backyard, and I rush up the stairs, barely crossing the threshold when his hands find my hips.

He closes the door and twists the lock.

"I love you." His mouth is moving along my shoulder and neck as his hands trace my body and look for a way to undress me. "How the fuck does this dress work?"

"Like this." Too impatient to pull it off correctly, I yank the skirt up to my hips and kick off my panties, watching desire darken his eyes until the only light in them is the fire that burns for me. "Touch me."

"This is going to be fast, angel."

"I'm okay with fast."

Turns out, it wasn't. One orgasm turned into two, and two turned into me losing count. Later, we find a note stuck to the fridge congratulating us on our engagement and stamina. We burst out laughing until he lifts me to the counter, popping the button-down shirt I'm wearing—his—down the middle with one yank.

"I'm in the mood for hot chocolate," he says, and my thighs quake with anticipation. "What about you?"

"With you? I'm up for anything."

EPILOGUE

3 MONTHS LATER

CHRIS

"*D*addy?"

I look at Gage in the mirror as we finish getting ready.

"How long do I have to wear this?" He tugs at the light blue button-down that matches mine.

I can't help but smile at the look of disgust on his face. "Just until the ceremony is over, okay, buddy? Then Abuelita has your shorts and t-shirt."

Jessie wanted a small wedding with our loved ones, some-where on a beach, and she had no interest in waiting. Just as quickly as we fell in love, she planned a wedding, and here we are.

Gage and I are getting ready in one cabana, while Jessie gets ready in another. Evan, Milo, and Finn have wandered in and out, and while the day is a happy occasion with plenty of smiles, we all recognize a part of us is missing—Noah. Lilah is an amazing addition to the band, and Milo, Finn, and I all get along well with her. But if Evan doesn't learn to quit bickering with her, I'm going to lock them both in a closet.

"Knock, knock." Jax steps through the tent flap wearing shorts and a button-down. By the end of tonight, this man will be my brother-in-law.

"Is it time?" It's not nerves that swirl in my stomach, but excitement.

In a little while, I'm going to marry the woman I've waited for all my life. And even though we've lived together since she first became Gage's nanny, there's a marked difference to today that I didn't expect.

"Last I heard from Charlotte, they were almost ready. Are you?"

"I've never been more ready for anything in my life."

If I had it my way, Jessie and I would have hit up the JOP the day after I proposed. But she wanted the wedding, and for her, I could be patient and wait to make her my wife. But in every other way, since the moment I met her, she's been mine. Making it official? I could be a little more patient. Whatever she wanted. If it's in my power, I'll do whatever I can to make her happy.

"I felt the same way about Charlotte." A half smile kicks up one side of his mouth. "I still do."

"Five years, right?"

"Edging closer to six, and almost four kids later. I'm really fucking glad she took a chance on me."

"I'm just thankful Jessie gave me another chance after I fucked up." That was one of the darkest weeks of my life, and I never want to go through something like that again.

"She can be pretty stubborn."

I snort, having experienced that side of her many times in our short relationship.

"You can say that again."

Jax smiles. "But I don't know anyone else who loves as much as she does."

It's true. The way she is with Gage, with her family, with all her patients. Every single one of them gets all of Jessie's heart. Including me.

"I don't know if it's what she went through when she was little or if it was always there, but she's special." His eyes meet mine, and the warning is clear. *Don't fuck up again.* "She loves you. Despite you being a rock star."

I bark out a laugh at the expression on his face. He looks just like her when she says the same thing.

"I count myself lucky that she broke her rule for me. Seriously, Jax. I can't imagine my life without her in it. I love her. I'm going to do everything in my power to make sure she knows that every day. To be there for her. Always."

He claps a hand on my shoulder. "Save the wedding vows for the ceremony, man."

His phone chimes with a text.

"Looks like they're ready. I'll see you out there."

He nods and makes his way back out of the tent.

"Gage, you ready?"

He looks up from the mountain of sand he's been building. When he stands, a waterfall of small granules pours down.

I brush him off until he's squirming and laughing in my arms. "You remember what we talked about?"

Jessie and I planned the ceremony, but I have a little surprise for her that I cooked up with my coconspirator.

"Uh-huh."

"Let's go, bud." He and I make our way to the makeshift altar.

The sun dips behind the Santa Monica Pier, and I shake my head at Jessie's idea for a venue. She wanted a party, one that kids could enjoy too, so we rented it out for the night, although I don't plan on staying long enough to enjoy it. I have plans for my wife that involve a suite at a hotel I can see from the pier. Tomorrow, I'll sweep her away for a honeymoon in the Maldives.

My parents will keep Gage for the weekend, and then he'll

spend two weeks with Tom and Bethany. Since they've been coming over for weekly dinners since the custody hearing that wasn't, they're no longer Mr. and Mrs. Sanders.

I take my place—with Evan next to me and Gage in front of me—and fidget while I wait for Jessie. Sydney comes first, in a flowy dress that flirts with the wind. The coral, blue, and cream blending with the beach and sunset clouds that dot the horizon. The music changes, and I hold my breath, waiting.

My heart stops when I spy her at the end of the aisle with her dad. Her dark hair is long and wavy, blowing lightly in the breeze from under the circlet of a braid at the crown of her head—a crown for my queen. While most of her makeup is barely visible, her red lips beckon to me like a siren. I want to kiss the color off to find the natural pink underneath.

The dress itself makes her look like she's floating across the sand. The lace top with a v-neckline flows into a cloud of tulle. Our eyes meet and hold, smiles mirroring each other's as she moves closer and closer until she and her dad finally stop in front of us. The pulse that flutters visibly in her throat is a magnet for my lips, and I barely resist the urge. This is my wedding, after all.

"Who gives this woman to this man?"

"Her mother and I do." Timothy Bryant kisses his daughter's cheek and shakes my hand before stepping back to sit with his wife.

Jessie's hand is light on mine as she takes the few steps to bring us next to one another. Leaning down, I can't resist brushing my lips against her jaw.

"You are absolutely stunning. More beautiful than my dreams." My whisper is for her ears only. "And you're about to be mine."

The last part is a growl in her ear, and it has its desired effect. She shivers, then lifts her eyes to meet mine. When she does, it's like that first moment all over again.

"I already am." Her words are quiet, but the rest of the world fades in their wake.

It's her and me.

We say our vows, and I slide her wedding band on her finger, a puzzle piece finally clicking into place. She does the same, and it's almost over. Even though it's our beginning.

"Mr. Rivera?" The officiant turns to me with a nod.

"Right. Gage, buddy, you ready?"

He's been sitting with Mamá and Papá in the front row, and bounds up to us.

"What's going on?" Jessie's attention pings from Gage to me.

I gesture toward the officiant, who begins.

"Today is a day of celebration as Jessie and Chris join their lives together. Their sacred vows are not just between them, because not only will they be a new couple, but they will also be a new family. Gage joins us at the altar so that we may join all. Jessie, do you promise to help guide Gage through his life, devoting yourself to creating a life of happiness and accomplishments, nursing his creativity, encouraging his independence, and making sure he always knows that love and family are with him?"

There are several sniffles from the front row. No one else knew what we were doing—only Gage and me. But my gaze is locked on the teary woman who looks at me before kneeling in the sand to meet the eyes of our little boy.

"I do."

"And, Gage, do you promise to always try your hardest in all things great and small, to give the best hugs as often as you can, and to listen to your dad and Jessie?"

"Yep." He smiles, and the sniffles turn to chuckles before he throws his arms around Jessie's shoulders. "I love you, Jessie."

"I love you too, buddy."

"Can I put my shorts on now?"

She laughs and ruffles his hair as she stands up. I wipe the errant tears from her face with my thumbs, holding her jaw as the officiant finishes.

"Since, then you have pledged your mutual vows, I by virtue of the authority vested in me by the State of California, pronounce you husband and wife. Chris, you may now kiss your bride."

Words I have been waiting for.

My mouth fuses to hers, and I take advantage of her slightly parted lips to slip my tongue in to taste her. Her moan is quiet, just between the two of us, and I deepen the kiss and lean her back until her hands grip the back of my shirt for purchase.

"Happy wedding day, Mrs. Rivera," I murmur against her lips.

"Happy wedding day, Mr. Rivera." A smile stretches across her face, and her fingers find my scalp.

I close my eyes as the light scratches create goosebumps along my neck.

"Ladies and gentlemen, for the first time ever, let me introduce you to the Rivera family—Chris, Jessie, and Gage."

We straighten to the sound of applause, my fingers tangled with hers.

"Who's ready to ride the Ferris wheel?" she asks, and all the kids squeal with excitement and rush for the pier.

"I love you." Her lips find my jaw while my hand rests on her hip to hold her close to me.

"I love you."

"Ready for our party?" she asks.

"How long do we need to stay?"

"Just a little while."

"I'm holding you to that."

I follow her to the pier with her laughter echoing in my ears.

JESSIE

The sound of the ocean greets me as I step onto the balcony, my eyes finding the lights of the pier, where we left our reception in full swing as we walked to our hotel. Our luggage for our two-week honeymoon is already in the car, and Chris only had to grab the overnight bag from the front desk when we checked in. The sliding door opens and closes before Chris wraps an arm around my waist.

"Did I tell you how beautiful you look?" His lips tickle as they trace the skin of my shoulder.

"Several times." With a smile, I lean my head back against his chest.

"What about right now? With the lights from the pier barely outlining you? Mmm, you smell like the ocean." His nose presses against my neck.

"I don't think I've heard that one before."

The sound of a zipper enters the stillness, and my dress loosens around my chest.

"I've waited all day to do that."

"I only put this dress on a few hours ago."

"A few hours is too long." He slides the shoulders of the dress down, his fingers skimming along the sensitive skin of my arms.

My nipples tighten as the cool air washes over my bare chest before the heat of his hands engulfs me.

"I guess I could change now. It was a beautiful dress." My words end on a gasp as he tugs and twists at my nipples with his talented fingers.

My arms thrown over his shoulders, I work my hands through his hair, pushing myself farther into his hands as lightning arcs from my breasts to my pussy.

"You know what's more beautiful than that dress?" His words are pressed against the skin of my throat as his lips settle against the pulse point at the base of my neck.

"What?" I mewl as his fingers tug, the lightning intensifying.

"You. Naked in the moonlight."

His words take me back to the night of the concert at the Hollywood Bowl. Lifting my hands to the dress gathered at my waist, I push it to the deck under our feet. The growl that echoes from his throat is worth the awkwardness of going commando at my own wedding.

"Fuck, were you naked under that dress the whole time?"

I nod, doing my best to look coy.

He sinks his teeth into my shoulder before pulling back and studying me. "Had I known that, we would have come here immediately after the ceremony."

I laugh. "But then we would have had to stay inside. It was still light out then."

"You like this better?" He presses his hips against my naked backside, his erection prominent through the lightweight cotton of his slacks.

I lick my lips and push back against him, needing more. "Mmhmm."

"Should we stay right here?" He smooths a hand down my stomach until his fingers slide through my folds to flick my clit. "Where anyone could see me filling up that sweet pussy? Where someone might hear you when I make you scream my name?"

Our room is dark. The only lights are the ones visible from the pier. The illicit sensation of being outside where anyone could see us, but no one will, has my thighs clenching together, trapping his hand between my legs.

"Please," I murmur.

"My little exhibitionist. I don't share. Good thing no one will see." He nudges me forward and bends me at the waist. "Hands on the railing, angel."

I do as he says and push my hips back to search for him, only encountering cool air.

"Chris?"

I crane my neck over my shoulder as he rips the shirt over his head, then rushes to unbuckle his belt. Stepping out of his pants, he stalks toward me, and my pussy clenches as desire coats my thighs.

I smile at the sight of his thick cock jutting toward me. "Looks like I wasn't the only one who was commando today."

"I wanted to be prepared." His smirk is all heat as he slides a hand down my spine, tracing a finger along each vertebra until he reaches my ass. Squeezing with one hand, he dips another back between my legs.

"Fuck." He sinks to his knees and cages my hips, flexing his fingers at the same time his tongue finds my clit.

He circles it until my knees buckle and taps it as my hips create a rhythm I'm powerless to stop.

"Chris. Oh god." The orgasm is arching me to my tiptoes even as I try to grind against his tongue.

He sucks my clit into his mouth and rubs the bundle of nerves harder, laving it with flat strokes.

"I...want you...inside me," I pant as I try to hold off my orgasm.

With one last flick of his tongue, he straightens from the floor and lines himself up at my entrance. My hands still grip the balcony railing, and his land on top of them, holding them in place as he thrusts into me with one hard stroke.

"*Yes.*" I keen at the fullness, his piercing brushing against my g-spot.

His hips retreat until only the tip remains, and I whimper. His hips snap forward again, and the whine turns into a moan. On his next retreat, I push my hips back, and stars dance in my vision.

"Let me hear you, angel."

He shifts my hands to one of his and drags the other back along my arm until he can cup my breast to toy with the nipple. His hips pulse in small, shallow strokes, the piercing tapping and rubbing at the sensitive spot.

"*Chris.*" I wail as pleasure pulls me under, drowning me.

He moves his hand from my breast to my clit, flicking it faster and faster to match the shallow strokes, forcing another whimper from my throat.

He increases the speed again. "I want to hear you. I want to hear how much you love this. Your pussy is tightening around my dick. Fluttering right here." He pushes further, and I moan and press my hips harder against him.

"Please," I beg loudly. "Please."

He pinches his forefinger and thumb around my clit, adding pressure as he pistons his hips against mine. The darkness around us shatters into a million prisms of multicolored light, pleasure driving me higher and higher while my orgasm crashes through me with every thrust and retreat of his hips. I struggle against his grip on my hands. The pleasure continues to build, moving beyond sensitive to pure ecstasy as a second orgasm crests. At the same time, he grows impossibly thicker, and he roars his release, not attempting to muffle the sound.

I'm still coming back to earth when he sweeps me into his arms and carries me into our suite. I lift my hand to his face, and he stops, pressing against me, chest to chest, and pushing me against the wall between the living room and bedroom.

"I don't think we're making it to the bedroom," he growls as he slides into me. My walls flutter around him as he moves, and another orgasm builds with the shift of his hips and the way he traces my collarbone with his tongue.

"Who needs a bed anyway?" I tease his lips with mine and tighten my pussy around him until he falls forward with a groan. "I need you."

"I'm right here." He moans his promise. "Hold on to me."

So I do.

THE END

Thank you so much for reading!

BEFORE YOU GO! Want a glimpse of life for Jessie and Chris one year later? What happens when Gage starts Kindergarten? How is Jessie's new job going? Turn the page and see what life for them is like.

BONUS EPILOGUE

1 YEAR LATER

JESSIE

"*A*re you excited, bud?" I squeeze the little hand in mine and try to fight the tears that clog my throat.

This is a happy occasion. And these are happy tears.

Gage wiggles like a puppy as he skips next to me, his little space-themed backpack shifting with every bounce. Dinosaurs are no longer his favorite. Now he's all about outer-space and aliens. It's amazing how quickly he's growing up, and I'm not talking about how he's celebrated another birthday since I first met him.

His features are changing, his face losing the toddler appearance. Every day, he looks more like the little boy he's becoming.

"Yep!" Another big bounce.

I share a smile with Chris over Gage's head.

In all truth, he probably was ready for kindergarten last year. But we decided to give him one more year to adjust to all the changes in his life. The nanny Chris and I hired was trained in elementary education and has already taught him some of the basics.

Other kids mill around the small playground in front of the kindergarten classrooms. The teachers are gathered in one group, and parents border the fence, watching their kids interact with one another. More than one parent holds a tissue. Taking in the moment brings the burn of tears back behind my eyes. At the gate to the playground, he stops suddenly and turns back to me.

"I want to go home."

Both Chris and I kneel to his level.

"What do you mean?" Chris asks, lifting his sunglasses to his head.

His eyes are filled with concern and love for our son. The way he parents Gage is one of the sexiest things about him. It's also one of the things I love most. How much he loves our kids. I spy the downy hair of our daughter, Cadence, in the carrier strapped to Chris's chest. We brought her home from the hospital just days after she was born, but only finalized the adoption two weeks ago. She's ours. And she already has Daddy and all her uncles wrapped around her petite little finger.

"What if I don't like it?" Gage scuffs the toe of his sneaker against the concrete.

"What makes you think you won't like it?" I ask.

He looks at me, his wide eyes reminding me of the little boy I first met.

He shrugs. "I dunno. I don't have any of my toys."

"You'll have so much to do, you won't even think about your toys," I tell him. "Remember how excited you were to show your teacher all the words you can write? Daddy and Gage—"

"And Cady." His nickname for his baby sister.

"And Cady," I agree.

"And Mommy."

My throat constricts, and I have a hard time forcing the word out. "And Mommy."

Mommy. Because that's who I am to Gage. We still talk about Melanie, and he sees pictures from his grandma and grandpa, but when he first called me Mommy, we all agreed to follow his lead.

"And look at the fun playground. Do you think I could use the swings?" Chris starts to rise.

Gage giggles. "No, Daddy, you're too big."

"I am? Well do you want to show me how it's done then?"

"Okay!" Nerves forgotten, he races into the play area while Chris and I observe from the wall. Another little boy comes to the gate and holds a construction truck out to Gage. Just like that, we're forgotten as he races to the sandbox to play with his new friend.

Chris tugs me to his side.

"You okay?" His whisper creates goosebumps along my neck and shoulder.

I sniffle. "He's getting too big."

The warmth of my husband's lips brushes my temple, and he squeezes me closer.

"He's going to love this. And have so much fun telling us all about it."

I lean my head against his shoulder and cradle the sleeping baby strapped to his chest with my hand.

"Promise she won't get so big so fast."

He chuckles. "Good luck with that. She already has a mind of her own, and she's not even six months old."

He's right. Everyone knows who runs our house, and her name is Cadence Faith Rivera.

The bell rings, and the teachers direct the kids to line up at their classroom doors. Gage fidgets in line and waves excitedly at us. Chris waves back, and I blow a kiss, happy when he returns it before following his classmates inside. When the last kid finally steps into a classroom, all the parents disperse, some in silence, some on their phones, and some in murmured conversation like Chris and me.

"Are you sure you need to go to work today?" He slides his hand from my back to my ass and gives it an inconspicuous squeeze.

"Yes. And so do you," I remind him, standing at the driver's door of my car. "I thought you said the guys and Lilah were coming over to talk through songs for the new album."

"They are." He sighs. "But I'd rather spend the day with my two favorite girls."

I lean against my car when my knees buckle at his swoony words.

"I'm only seeing two clients this morning. If you can persuade the band to agree on the songs early enough, we'll have the entire afternoon before we need to come back for Gage."

He leans closer, his lips tracing my jaw before moving to my ear.

"Sounds like you have something in mind, Mrs. Rivera."

What is it about his growl that has the power to wipe out every thought but him?

"I do."

"I love those words on your lips." His brush mine but are gone far too soon.

I whimper at the loss, but shake off the disappointment, knowing I get to come home to him after work. "I love you."

"Love you too." He soothes Cadence since she's growing fussy now that she's awake. "Only the two clients? So I should get the band out before lunch?"

"Don't forget I have an appointment too."

"Are you sure you don't want me to go with you?"

"It's only a checkup. But thank you for the offer." Another quick kiss, and I get into my car and watch my husband load our daughter into her car seat.

He waves from his car, and the two of us head in opposite directions—him for home and me to the clinic. My two clients are back-to-back and ones I've been working with since last year.

Once my appointments are done, I file a few notes from our sessions and grab my bag, then head to the doctor's office for my physical.

"Everything looks great. But you didn't need a physical for another few months. Is there a reason you wanted to see me today?" Dr. Stewart studies me over the top of her glasses.

I bite my lip, afraid to put a voice to my biggest fear.

"The last time I had a scan I was eighteen—" Something I was happy with at the time.

"That's correct. Your records indicate that everything looked normal before, and nothing indicated that the cancer had come back."

"I've just…I'm super run down lately. Tired. All the time."

"Well, you do have a baby at home."

"But Cadence is sleeping for four to six hours at a stretch. If— if the cancer has come back, then I need to find out. I need to prepare my family…"

Prepare them for the worst. Because it's a possibility. One I don't remember facing before but am absolutely terrified of now. I don't want to leave Chris alone with our kids.

"What makes you think your symptoms are caused by cancer?" Dr. Stewart's expression tells me she already knows the answer before I say it.

"Well, I googled—"

"Ah, yes. Dr. Google. Symptoms that could be attributed to anything from allergies to sore muscles list 'cancer' as a potential illness," she says wryly.

"But—"

"Jessie, let's run a few tests first. It could be a hormone imbalance or something as simple as a vitamin deficiency. I don't want to move to the doomsday scenario until everything else has been ruled out."

"Hormones?"

"It happens to all of us as we get older."

I bristle slightly. I only just turned twenty-five.

She has the nurse come in and draw blood. I hate needles. Probably from all my time spent as a human pin cushion as a child. The urine sample she asks for is less painful, but still awkward. After providing that, I'm back in the room, waiting on instructions from Dr. Stewart or her nurse.

When the door opens, the expression on Dr. Stewart's face creates a lump of fear in my stomach.

"What? What is it?"

"Jessie, are you still taking your birth control prescription?"

"No, to be honest, when we first brought Cadence home, I kept forgetting, and it messed with my cycles."

"Jessie, one of the standard tests we run is a pregnancy test."

"But why? I can't—"

"Jessie, you're pregnant."

Pregnant. No, it can't be right.

"But the doctors said…"

I'd been told for years that because of my cancer treatments, I couldn't have children.

"But we already have a baby." Without thought, I rest a hand against my flat stomach.

"Looks like you'll be having another in less than a year." Dr. Stewart smiles at her own joke. "And as for what the doctors told you, Jessie, I don't know what to say about that. Infertility is only guaranteed if you had your reproductive organs removed, and you didn't."

Disbelief still rests like a weight in my stomach, but joy fizzes through my blood, clearing the shock and anxiety.

"You're sure?"

"We can run a blood test to confirm."

I need that. I need to find out for sure. I don't want to get my hopes up until then.

"Yes, let's be sure."

CHRIS

"Where's Mommy, Cadence?"

The baby looks at me from her bouncy seat while we wait in the kitchen for Jessie to come home. It's past lunch time and edging closer to the time we need to leave to pick up Gage. I managed to get everyone to agree on the order the songs on the album should be in. It helped when Evan and Lilah supported me.

Jessie texted me a little while ago, but I'm still anxious about her appointment.

JESSIE

Appointment ran long. On my way home.

Why had her appointment run long?

Ice cold fear fills my veins. I caught her googling cancer symptoms the other day. Is that where she is? She said it was only her physical, but maybe she didn't want me to worry. Well, too fucking late. I'm scared as shit now.

I grab my phone from the counter, no longer content to simply wait for her to come home.

Fuck, what if she's sick?

I press the call button as Jessie walks through the door from the garage. I drop my phone to the counter and cross the kitchen in two strides, pulling her into my arms. My heart only slows once she's wrapped securely there and I can breathe in the scent of her shampoo.

"Miss me?"

I ignore her attempt at a joke, and when she looks up, I claim her mouth with mine. My tongue drags along the seam of her lips until she opens, her hands moving to grip my t-shirt. The prick of her fingernails against the back of my biceps builds the heat, and I shift my hands to her hips, squeezing tightly before shifting to her ass.

With a boost, she settles on the counter, and I step between her spread legs, not breaking the kiss. Every ounce of worry, of fear, is poured into the connection, until breaking the kiss is required to breathe. She rests her forehead against my chest, and I brush a kiss to her hair.

"I always miss you," I murmur. "What took so long?"

This time, her fingers tighten in the t-shirt at my waist, and I struggle not to crush my lips to hers again, doing my best to ignore the pit of fear in my stomach.

"Is it—is it—" I struggle to say the word. Cancer. "What you were googling the other day?"

"Where's Cadence?" Her change of subject has the pit growing bigger.

I lean to the side so she can see the now-sleeping baby in her bouncy seat. Jessie's face softens, and she takes a deep breath.

"What time do we need to pick up Gage?"

I glance at the time on the stove.

"We need to leave in about an hour. Jess, what's going on? You're freaking me out."

She leans forward, pressing a kiss against my heart through my shirt. It's pounding as she continues to avoid my question.

"Jess?" I grip her shoulders.

"I had my physical today."

"I know, angel. What happened? Is something wrong?"

"I mentioned to the doctor that I was feeling run down, and we talked about another scan to see if the cancer had come back. The last one I had was when I was eighteen."

No. No. No. No. No.

The universe wouldn't do this to me. To us.

I hold my breath and try to be strong enough for what comes next.

"The doctor wanted to run some tests before we did the scan. She said it might not be cancer."

"She's right. I know you were checking the other day, but maybe she's right."

"I, um, I got one of the test results already."

She bites her bottom lip while tears fill her eyes.

"Oh, fuck, angel. It's okay. I'm here. Whatever you need. However long it takes."

I tug her back into my arms as emotion clogs my throat. We haven't had enough time, but I'll be damned if I'm not going to fight for her.

"How about seven months?" Her voice is muffled by my shirt.

I shift back and look at her. "What?"

"How about seven months? That's how long I'm going to need."

"I don't…I'm not…what are you saying?"

She reaches for my hand and lays it flat against her stomach and covering my hand with hers.

"Chris, you're going to be a daddy. Again." Her eyes shine with unshed tears, and her smile is breathtaking.

Daddy? I'm going to be a daddy?

"Jess, you're pregnant?" I whisper the last word, afraid to say it too loudly in case I'm wrong.

Her enthusiastic nod reminds me of Gage.

"I am."

I curl my fingers slightly, cupping her stomach as wonder fills me.

"But the doctors said you couldn't have kids—"

"According to this doctor, they were wrong."

"But Cadence…" I glance at the baby over my shoulder. She's still snoozing away in her chair.

"Will make an amazing big sister. Are you okay with all of this? I mean, we didn't talk about more kids since we barely finalized the adoption with Cadence, but—"

I spin back around and claim her lips with mine, stopping the question. She moans as my tongue finds hers, and she wraps her legs around my waist to pull me closer. My cock pulses against the fly of my jeans as my erection rubs against the center of her pants.

"Fuck." I break this kiss, air sawing in and out of my lungs.

"The reason it took longer was because my doctor got me an appointment with an OB friend of hers. We needed an ultrasound to see how far along I am. Eight weeks." She answers my next question.

"I want to come to your next appointment."

"Which one?"

"All of them. Every step of the way." I cup her jaw. "I'm so fucking happy right now."

She holds on to my wrists, her slender fingers squeezing gently.

"I never in a million years thought this was a possibility."

"Guess we defied those odds."

"I guess so." She giggles.

"We need to leave soon," I say.

"I know. To pick up Gage."

"You think forty-five minutes is enough time?"

Confusion furrows her brows. "For what?"

"To worship you."

Her breath catches, and she drags her fingers back up my arms to tangle in the ends of my hair.

"I think we can make it work," she murmurs, tugging my head down until her lips graze mine. "I love you."

"I love you too. So fucking much."

I fuse my lips to hers, my heart so full it threatens to burst.

"Maybe we should take this upstairs." She breaks the kiss, her eyes luminous when they meet mine.

I shrug. "I don't know, angel. I'm partial to this kitchen."

I capture her smile as my lips find hers again. She's still got her legs wrapped around my waist, and I pulse my hips, rubbing them against her center. Leaning her head back, she moans quietly.

"Shh," I remind her of the sleeping baby in her seat across the room. "On second thought…"

I grab her thighs, loving the way her fingers tighten against my neck as I move through the back door and lower to one of the loungers outside.

"Let me hear you," I growl, nipping at her earlobe.

Her moan is louder this time, her fingers tugging at my shirt until I shrug out of it.

"I need you." She whimpers as my hands find her breasts through her top and bra.

"I'm right here." I brush her lips with mine. "Always."

Always. Not long enough, but it's a really good fucking start.

PLAYLIST

Chris and Jessie's playlist is so much different than the rest of the Heart Beats series. Chris's rock nature is found in songs like "When Legends Rise" by Godsmack and "Unbreakable" by Kingdom Collapse. Next to that Jessie shines with songs like "How to Fly" by Fireflight and Lauren Spencer Smith's "Fingers Crossed." My absolute favorite two songs are "A Thousand Years" by both The Piano Guys and Christina Perri. These songs absolutely made the scene where Jessie plays on piano and Chris joins her on guitar. SWOON!

Want to listen to the music that inspired *Falling the Beat*? Check out the playlist on Spotify by searching for the "Embracing the Beat" playlist or scan the QR code below.

You can find all the Heart Beats playlists on my website:

https://www.breannalynnauthor.com

BONUS TRACKS

Most of the time, my playlists for each book end up with over a hundred songs. While I can cull them down a bit—and I do—some songs still resonate so much with the story. There were six for Chris and Jessie's story. "Way Down We Go" by KALEO and the "I Feel Pretty/Unpretty" mash-up from the TV show *Glee* are just two of those tracks.

Want to listen to the rest? You can search Spotify for "Falling for the Beat: Bonus Tracks" or scan the QR code below.

ACKNOWLEDGEMENTS & AUTHOR'S NOTE

Writing *THE END* on this story is bittersweet. Falling for the Beat is currently the last of the Heart Beats series (but you'll still see the characters pop up in other worlds). This final chapter in this series is a surreal moment. And I'm in awe of everything that's happened in the last year and change since Written in the Beat first came out. Maybe it won't be the end, but I have other characters clamoring for their HEA next.

To you. Yes, you, you lovely reader. Thank you for being with me on this journey. For falling in love with Jax and Charlie, Meredith and Nick, Claire and Dylan, Garrett and Mia, Michaela and West, and finally Jessie and Chris. Thank you for taking the chance on them and on me. I hope you enjoyed these stories as much as I have enjoyed writing them.

For my family—thank you for supporting me in this dream. Whether it was asking for signed paperbacks, sharing posts, sending videos, or watching the Twinx, you always came through. I couldn't have done this without you! I love you!!

Claire and Alina—Thank you for your feedback as Chris and Jessie took shape. Thank you for telling me you had to change names or that you needed a cigarette after the kitchen scene. For making me laugh and for helping me reach the end of this series. I love you both and can't imagine what my world would be like without you.

Mae—thank you for letting me pick you brain and send you snippets to make sure I captured everything correctly!

Editor Jess & Kimberly—thank you for helping me craft this latest book. For comments sprinkled throughout the early stages of this manuscript that made me smile. And, Kimberly, I really do think it's a kid thing!

Beth—For sanity checking me with plural last names and when it gets possessive. For loving the early scenes I sent you and for loving every aspect of Chris. 😊 I'm so grateful to call you my friend and can't wait for our concert next month and Makinac the month after that!

Kate Farlow—Thank you for another beautiful cover! For talking me off the creative ledges I put myself on (and try to drag you along with me)!

Stevie—the acknowledgement is only the tip of the iceberg. I could probably write a whole book on why I'm grateful that you are not only my friend but a KICKASS PA. I couldn't do ANY OF THIS without you!!!

Lori—thank you for becoming another cheerleader for me. For sending me messages of encouragement and pride and helping Stevie and me navigate this crazy world. For reading an early version of Chris and Jessie and helping me get it where it is today! 🩶

To my ARC team—I could not imagine having a better team to help me in this journey! Thank you for taking a chance, for sticking around, and for keeping me going!

I can't imagine this journey without any of you! XOXO

ALSO BY BREANNA LYNN

Lead singer for Just One Yesterday Evan Andrews has a problem. A big one. A blonde haired, hazel-eyed one—the new keyboardist for the band, Lilah Stevens. His biggest problem? How attracted he is to her given that their record contract has a no-fraternization clause. But when has he ever let the record label tell him what to do? And when he finds out that Lilah is just as attracted to him, he's done denying the one thing he wants this year for Christmas. The feisty new keyboardist he can't stop thinking about.

TURN THE PAGE for a sneak peek at this enemies to lovers, rock star romance with a hint of Christmas magic.

ROCKIN' AROUND THE CHRISTMAS TREE

LILAH

"*C*all from *Mother*. Answer?" The robotic voice is about as excited as I am about my mother's call.

I roll my eyes. I would think after the third unanswered call, my mother would take the hint. But I can predict what happens if I decline it again.

Another call.

This one probably during the band meeting I'm running late for.

"Yes," I grit out.

"Am I finally important enough to earn a moment of your time?" Her tone tells me exactly how this conversation will go, and I grind my molars together so I can make it through as unscathed as possible.

"Hi, Mom."

"I keep getting your voice mail."

"I'm driving." My response is more of a sigh than words. What is it about her that makes me revert back to a sixteen-year-old?

"If you lived at home, you wouldn't need to drive. Our drivers can take you anywhere in San Francisco."

Which is exactly why I don't *live* in San Francisco.

But I keep that comment to myself.

"I live in LA," I remind her. "And I have a job, remember?"

I was over the moon when I was selected to join Just One Yesterday, and I foolishly thought my family would be excited too.

Wrong.

They told me it was time to give up my little music "hobby" and come back to San Francisco and settle down, a.k.a., marry a junior executive from my parents' company and become a lady who lunches. Like my mother. And my sisters.

Pass. I have zero interest in becoming the fourth—not counting my extended family—Stepford wife in my family. My Aunt Sarah, who is an archaeologist currently living at a site in Montana, is the only other woman to buck the status quo.

"Of course I remember. I'm your mother. I remember all of your hobbies."

"It's not a hobby, it's a job. One I'm good at."

"I sometimes feel like your father and I made a mistake entertaining your interest in music."

Because, according to her, Juilliard is nothing but a hobby. A waste of time and effort.

Do not lose your shit, do not lose your shit. It's not worth it.

Thank god I'm almost to Chris's house. Then I have an excuse to end the call.

Or I could feign terrible cell service. It *is* sketchy a little farther back in the hills. But I'm not going to avoid my problems. I simply try to keep them from getting bigger.

Hence why I pretend to be the daughter my mother wants.

"Was there something you needed, Mother?"

"I'm calling about the holiday."

I avoided Thanksgiving this year. I doubt my luck will hold to escape Christmas.

"Christmas?"

She sighs. "Yes, Lilah. It's not like we celebrate anything else in December."

Fucking ouch. My birthday was last week. Must have slipped her mind.

"What about it?"

"Your father and I are expecting you for our annual party on Christmas Day. I'll have your room readied, and you can spend the week with us. There's someone I'd love—"

"I can't, Mother."

"Can't?"

I swear her slow blink is audible through the phone. Like she doesn't understand why I don't immediately drop everything to do as she says.

"I have plans," I hedge.

I don't. But she doesn't know that.

"What plans? It's Christmas, and we're your family."

"The band is recording all month." Lie number two. "And then we're meeting with the label to discuss the tour that starts this spring."

"Lilah—"

Chris's gate is in sight, and I wave to the guard who lets me through.

"I gotta go, Mom. Bye."

I hang up on her sputtering and pull my car to the side of the road so I can lean my head against the steering wheel.

That won't be the last time Christmas and my "invitation" to come home for the holidays will come up. But I'll take my small reprieve.

Maybe I'll head to Montana to see Aunt Sarah.

The blast of a car horn jars me into an upright position. Evan's Jeep is behind me, and he flashes his lights like I don't see him.

"Asshole," I mutter to the rearview mirror.

It may be childish, but I keep my foot on the brake. If he can act like a four-year-old, then I will too.

Six months. One hundred and eighty days I've spent dealing with his not-so-veiled hostility. Since the day Chris called to tell me I had the job. No, before that. He barely looked at me during the *audition*. Why he hates me so much is a mystery. I tried getting to know him. Tried being his friend. When that failed, I gave it back as good as I got. No matter what I do, his behavior hasn't changed.

In response to another blast of his horn, I throw my car in reverse, the white lights illuminating the surprised expression on his face.

"Take that."

He shakes his head, peeling out and around my car, then speeding around the first curve and out of sight.

As soon as his taillights fade, my triumph does too. What good did that do? No doubt made him more pissed at me than he was before.

I shift my car into drive and follow Evan, albeit at a much slower speed. He's waiting in the driveway when I pull behind him, but I don't see Finn's motorcycle or Milo's car. At least I'm not the last one here. Had Evan not shot past me at the gate, I would have gotten here first.

"Glad to see you finally made it, princess," he sneers as soon as I open my door.

My fingers itch to flip him off, but instead, I take a deep breath and ignore his taunt.

"Not all of us are speed demons. Is it fun?"

His sneer morphs to confusion. "Is what fun?"

"Paying all that money for speeding tickets."

He barks out a laugh, appreciation softening the hard angles of his face.

Pissed-off Evan is enough to inspire all sorts of fantasies—hell, he still makes the Top 10 Sexy List for Rock Stars after twenty years. But this Evan? Smiling, laughing Evan?

This one makes my knees weak. It opens the door on all sorts of thoughts I shouldn't have since he's an ass 99 percent of the time. I smile, taking a step closer, and his smirk immediately fades into his resting dick face.

With a sigh, I shift back and almost pretend I didn't move closer. Instead, I reach into the back of my car for the large bag I use as a purse.

"You could house a family of seven in your bag, princess."

I shrug but otherwise ignore the comment.

"You could probably feed them for ten years with the money you spent on it." His taunt pulls me up short.

"How do you know how much my bag cost?"

"I don't. But that shiny little emblem on the front of your brand-new Mercedes tells me you have money, princess. And lots of it. Daddy's? Seems unlikely that a *struggling musician* could afford it."

My parents come from money, but I don't touch it—most of it will sit in a trust until I get married. Instead, my Aunt Sarah set up a different trust for me. One I gained access to when I turned twenty-five. And I used her financial manager after I got access. The hyper blue metallic Mercedes is a reminder that in a world of black and silver, I'm bright blue and proud of it.

"Eat a bag of dicks, Andrews. I don't answer to anyone, including your self-righteous ass."

The roar of a motorcycle echoes down the driveway in the silence after my outburst, and I use that as my excuse to slam my car doors and head for Chris's house, giving the dick in the driveway as much space as I can.

Screw Evan Andrews.

And not in the fun sense of the word either.

~

Can Lilah and Evan learn to get along? Want to find out?

Grab Rockin' Around the Christmas Tree now!

ABOUT THE AUTHOR

Breanna Lynn lives in Colorado with her two sets of twins (affectionately referred to as the Twinx), their two dogs, and two cats. A classy connoisseur of all things coffee, Breanna spends her time keeping the Twinx from taking over the world. When not coordinating chaos, Breanna can be found binge reading, listening to music, or watching rom-coms with a giant bowl of popcorn.

To stay up to date on the ramblings of her (often over-caffeinated) mind, Twinx Tasmania, or the latest news on her latest happily ever after, sign-up for her newsletter at breannalynnauthor.com/subscribe. Subscribers receive exclusive news, content, specials, and giveaways!

Want to follow Breanna? Scan the QR code for all the ways to stay caught up!

Made in the USA
Monee, IL
15 January 2024

51803813R00207